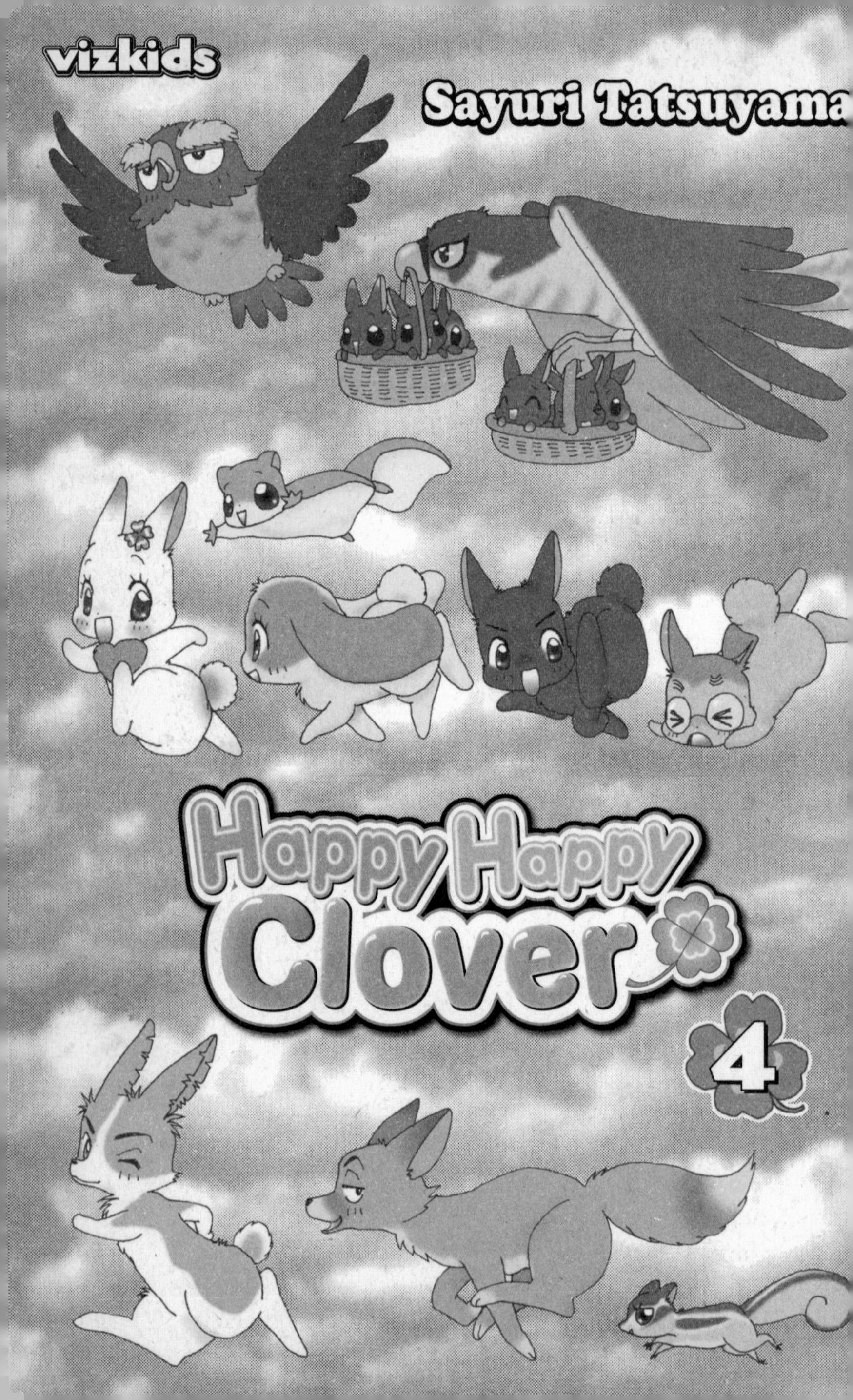
vizkids
Sayuri Tatsuyama
Happy Happy Clover
4

Happy Happy Clover

FOREST FRIENDS

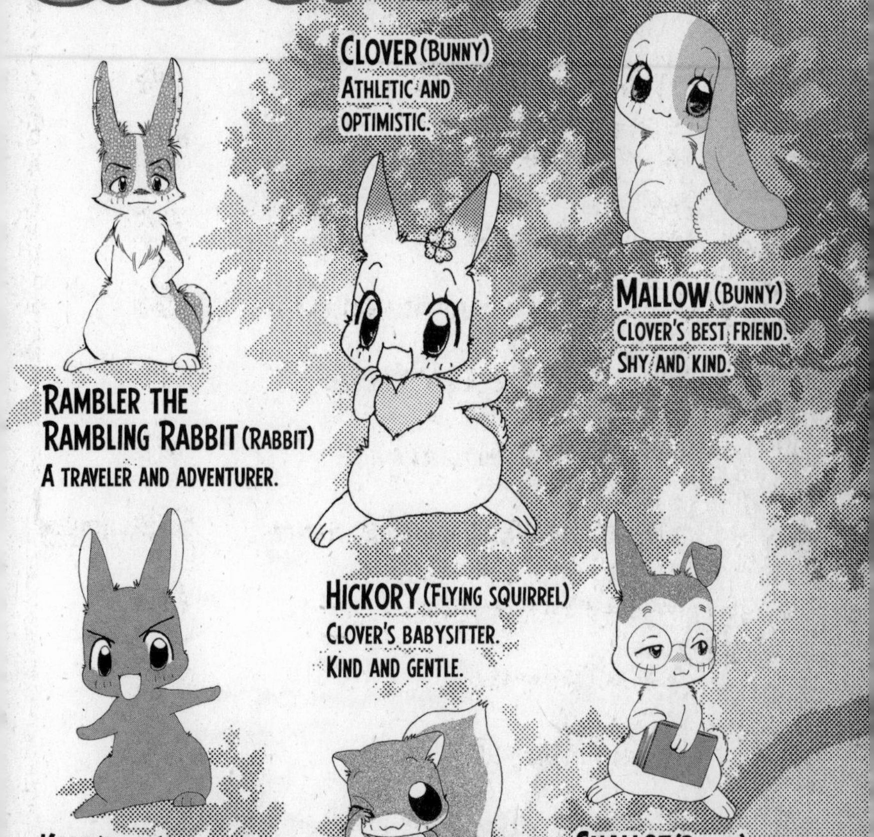

CLOVER (BUNNY)
ATHLETIC AND OPTIMISTIC.
MALLOW (BUNNY)
CLOVER'S BEST FRIEND. SHY AND KIND.
RAMBLER THE RAMBLING RABBIT (RABBIT)
A TRAVELER AND ADVENTURER.
HICKORY (FLYING SQUIRREL)
CLOVER'S BABYSITTER. KIND AND GENTLE.
SHALLOT (BUNNY)
CLOVER'S FRIEND. A BOOK LOVING PHILOSOPHER.
KALE (BUNNY)
CLOVER'S FRIEND. ALWAYS THERE FOR HIS FRIENDS AND FAMILY.

Clover here! I'm a bunny who lives in Crescent Forest!! I love my life in the forest surrounded by the bounty of nature and lots of friends. You can find me playing my heart out with my friends Mallow, Kale, and Shallot.

Happy Happy Clover

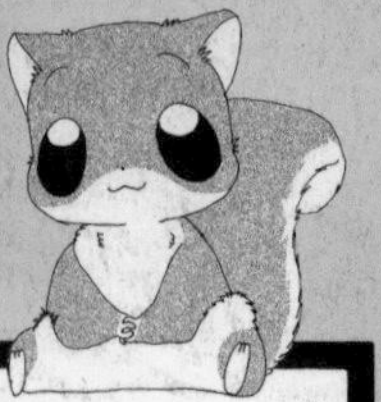

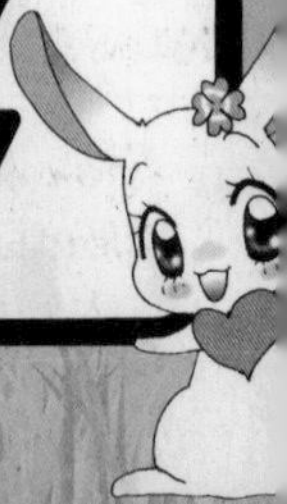

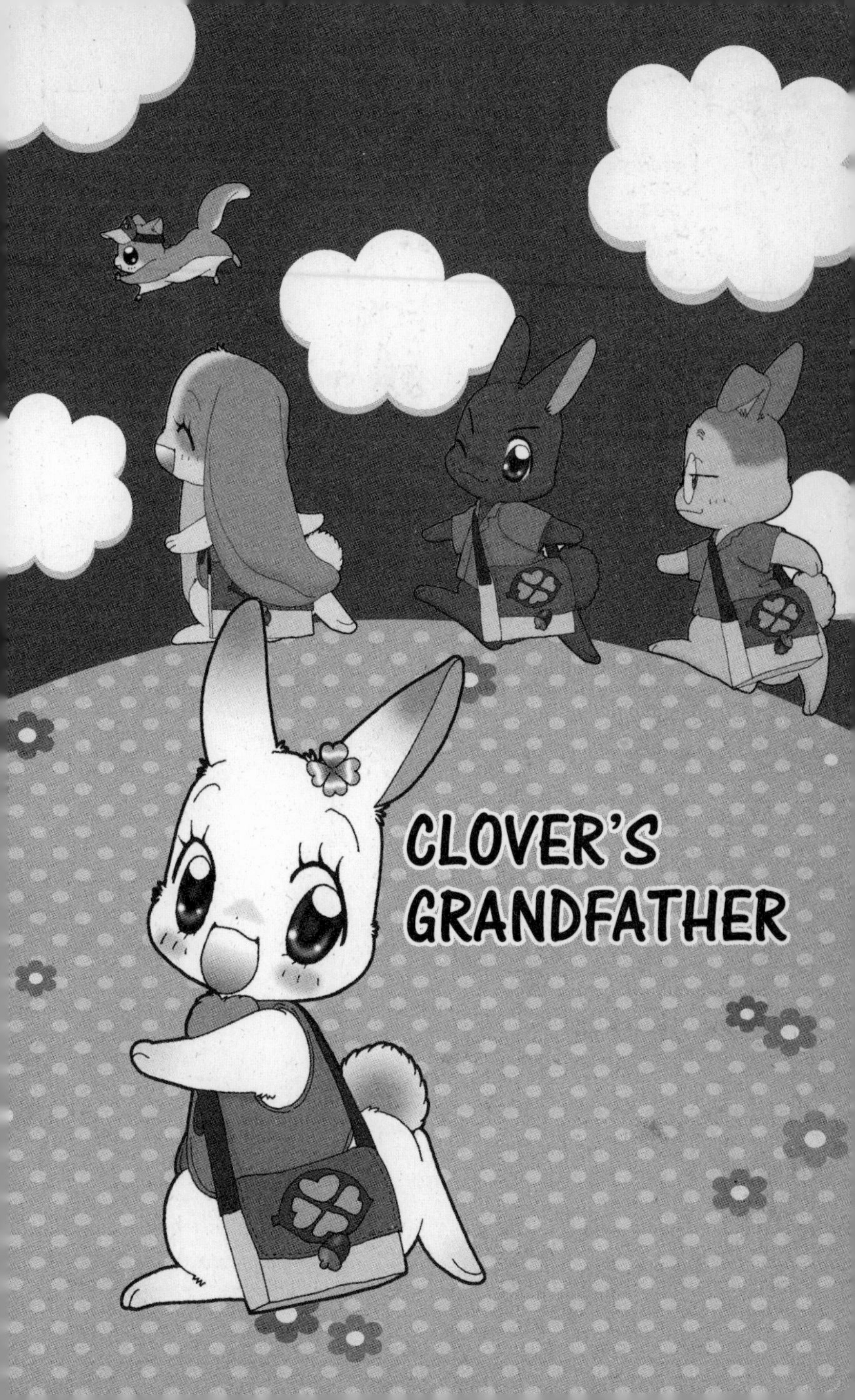
CLOVER'S
GRANDFATHER

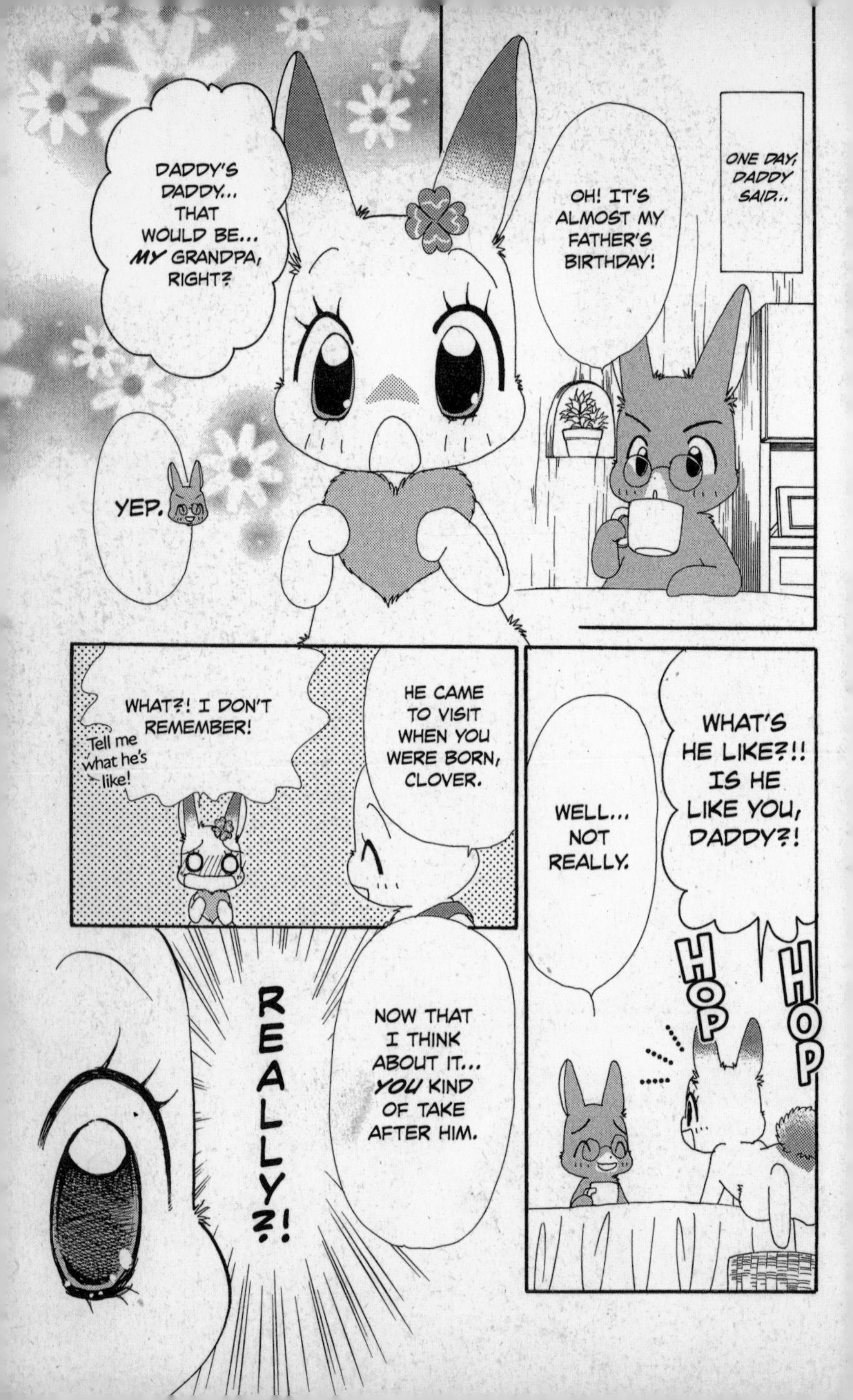
ONE DAY, DADDY SAID...
OH! IT'S ALMOST MY FATHER'S BIRTHDAY!
DADDY'S DADDY... THAT WOULD BE... *MY* GRANDPA, RIGHT?
YEP.
WHAT'S HE LIKE?!! IS HE LIKE YOU, DADDY?!
HOP
HOP
WELL... NOT REALLY.
HE CAME TO VISIT WHEN YOU WERE BORN, CLOVER.
WHAT?! I DON'T REMEMBER!
Tell me what he's like!
NOW THAT I THINK ABOUT IT... *YOU* KIND OF TAKE AFTER HIM.
REALLY?!

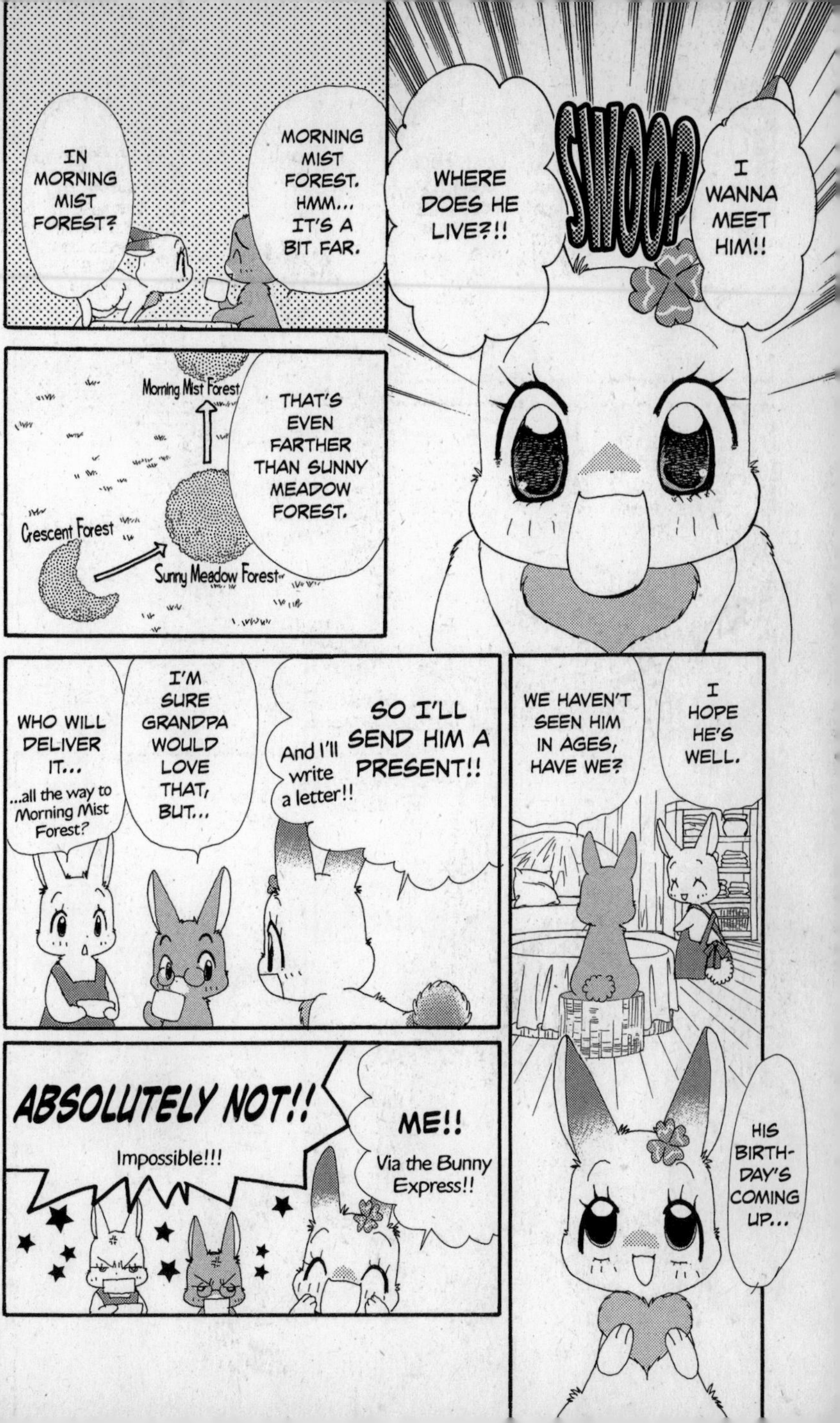
I WANNA MEET HIM!!
SWOOP
WHERE DOES HE LIVE?!!
MORNING MIST FOREST. HMM... IT'S A BIT FAR.
IN MORNING MIST FOREST?
THAT'S EVEN FARTHER THAN SUNNY MEADOW FOREST.
Morning Mist Forest
Crescent Forest
Sunny Meadow Forest
I HOPE HE'S WELL.
WE HAVEN'T SEEN HIM IN AGES, HAVE WE?
HIS BIRTH-DAY'S COMING UP...
SO I'LL SEND HIM A PRESENT!!
And I'll write a letter!!
I'M SURE GRANDPA WOULD LOVE THAT, BUT...
WHO WILL DELIVER IT...
...all the way to Morning Mist Forest?
ME!!
Via the Bunny Express!!
ABSOLUTELY NOT!!
Impossible!!!

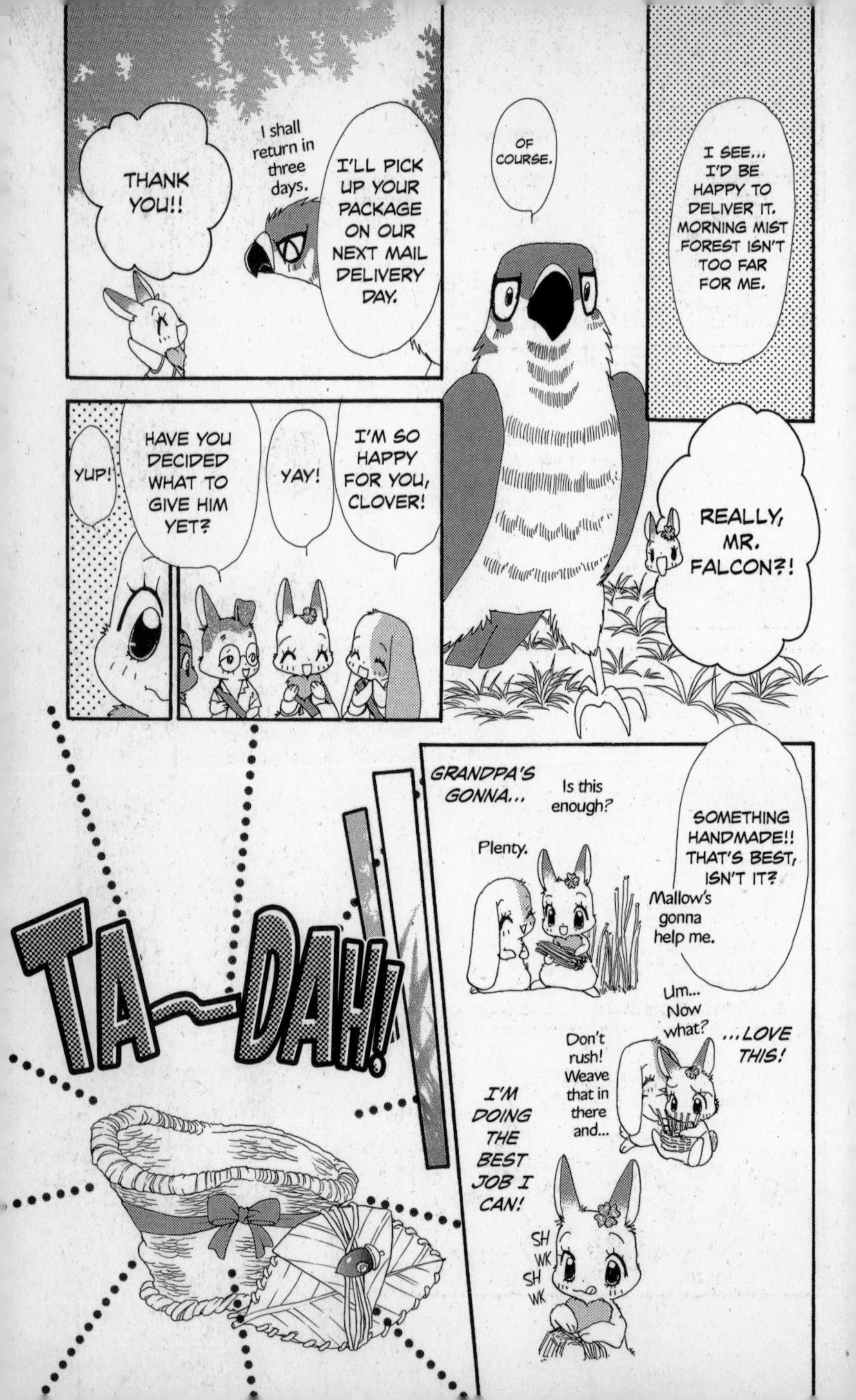
I SEE... I'D BE HAPPY TO DELIVER IT. MORNING MIST FOREST ISN'T TOO FAR FOR ME.
REALLY, MR. FALCON?!
OF COURSE.
I'LL PICK UP YOUR PACKAGE ON OUR NEXT MAIL DELIVERY DAY.
I shall return in three days.
THANK YOU!!
I'M SO HAPPY FOR YOU, CLOVER!
YAY!
HAVE YOU DECIDED WHAT TO GIVE HIM YET?
YUP!
SOMETHING HANDMADE!! THAT'S BEST, ISN'T IT?
GRANDPA'S GONNA...
Is this enough?
Plenty.
Mallow's gonna help me.
...LOVE THIS!
Um... Now what?
Don't rush! Weave that in there and...
I'M DOING THE BEST JOB I CAN!
SH WK SH WK
TA~DAH!

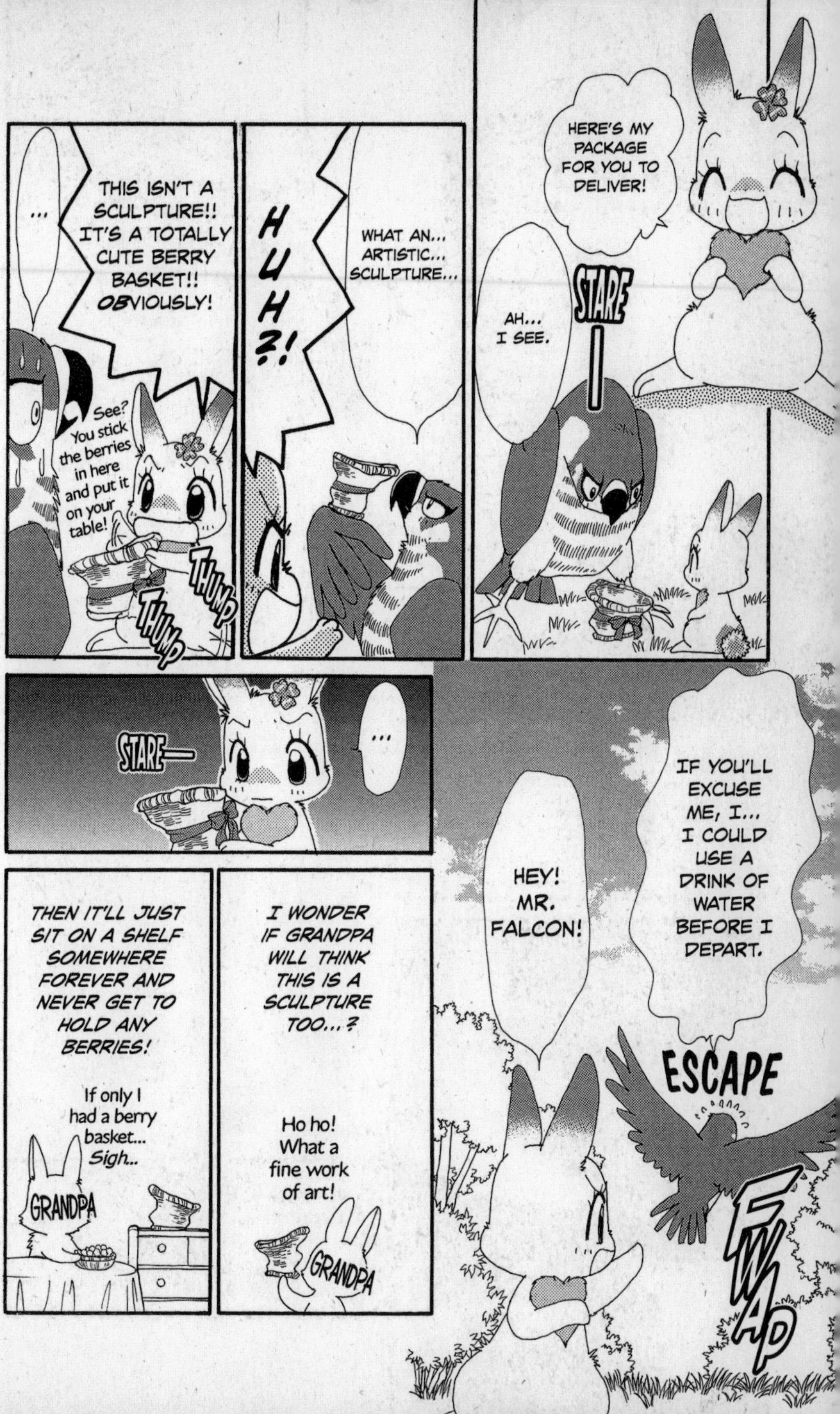
HERE'S MY PACKAGE FOR YOU TO DELIVER!
STARE
AH... I SEE.
WHAT AN... ARTISTIC... SCULPTURE...
HUH?!
THIS ISN'T A SCULPTURE!! IT'S A TOTALLY CUTE BERRY BASKET!! OBVIOUSLY!
...
See? You stick the berries in here and put it on your table!
THUMP
THUMP
IF YOU'LL EXCUSE ME, I... I COULD USE A DRINK OF WATER BEFORE I DEPART.
HEY! MR. FALCON!
ESCAPE
FWAP
...
STARE—
I WONDER IF GRANDPA WILL THINK THIS IS A SCULPTURE TOO...?
Ho ho! What a fine work of art!
GRANDPA
THEN IT'LL JUST SIT ON A SHELF SOMEWHERE FOREVER AND NEVER GET TO HOLD ANY BERRIES!
If only I had a berry basket... Sigh...
GRANDPA

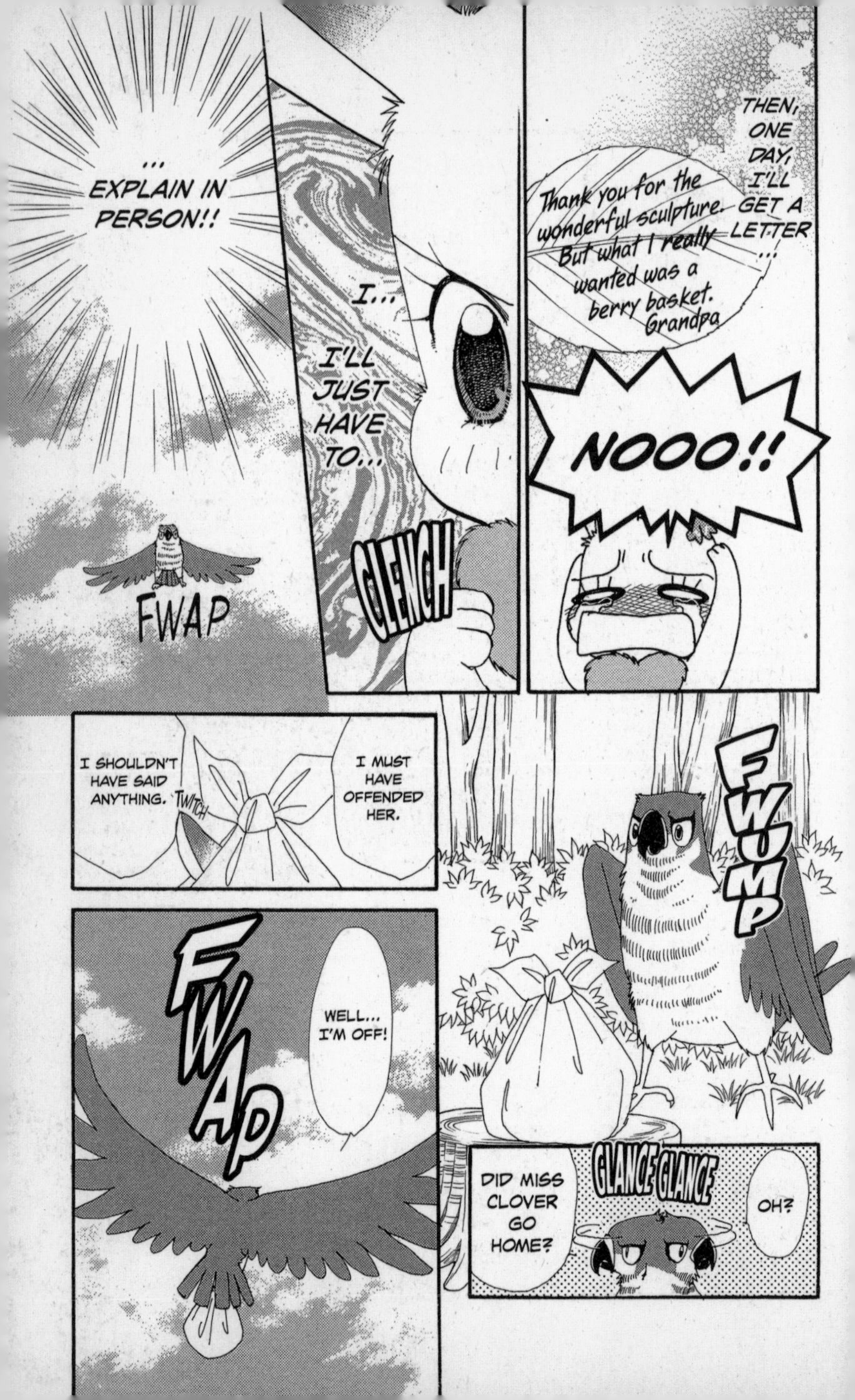
THEN, ONE DAY, I'LL GET A LETTER...
Thank you for the wonderful sculpture. But what I really wanted was a berry basket. Grandpa
NOOO!!
I...
I'LL JUST HAVE TO...
CLENCH
... EXPLAIN IN PERSON!!
FWAP
FWUMP
I MUST HAVE OFFENDED HER.
I SHOULDN'T HAVE SAID ANYTHING.
TWITCH
OH?
GLANCE GLANCE
DID MISS CLOVER GO HOME?
WELL... I'M OFF!
FWAP

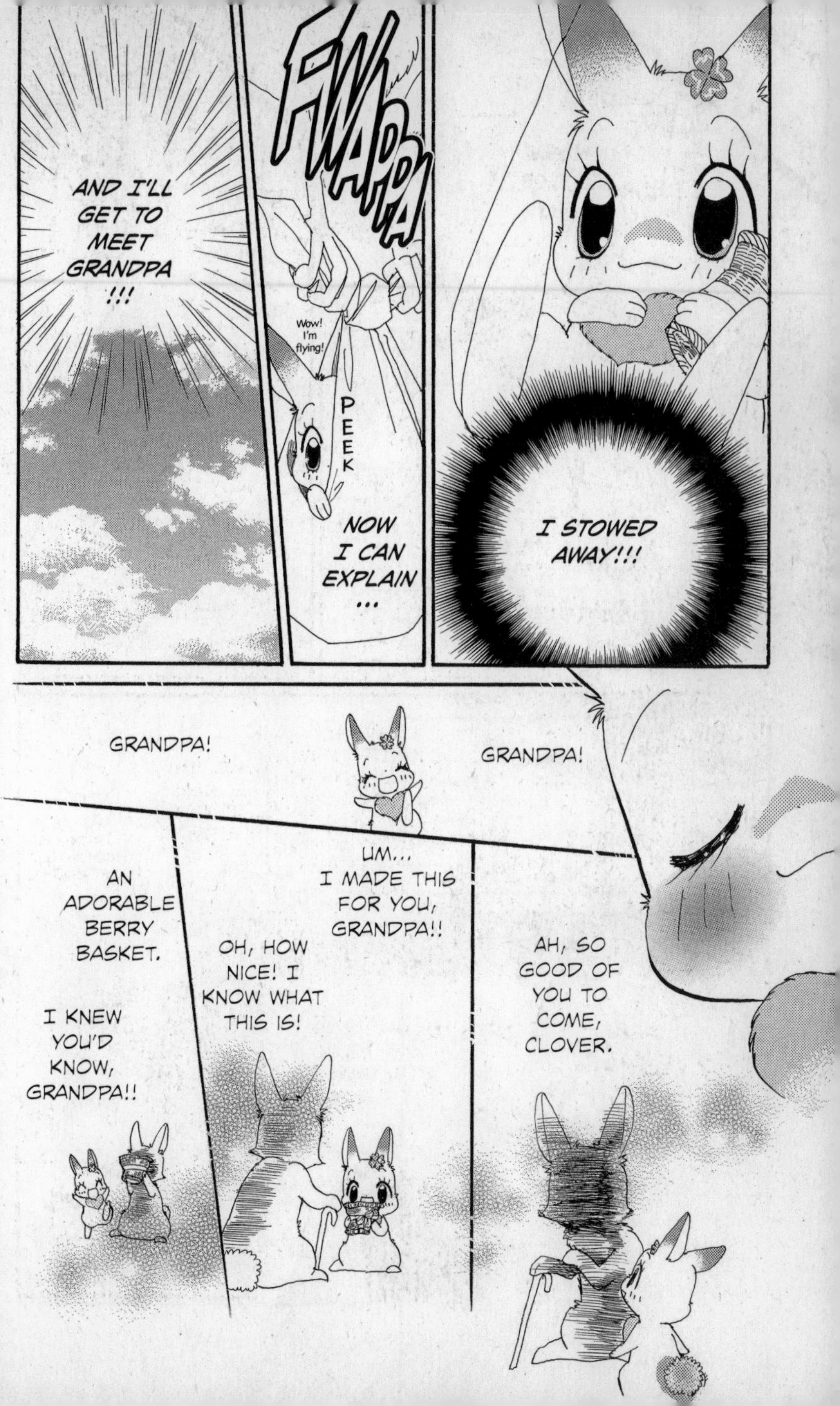
I STOWED AWAY!!!
FWAPPA
Wow! I'm flying!
PEEK
NOW I CAN EXPLAIN ...
AND I'LL GET TO MEET GRANDPA !!!
GRANDPA!
GRANDPA!
AH, SO GOOD OF YOU TO COME, CLOVER.
UM... I MADE THIS FOR YOU, GRANDPA!!
OH, HOW NICE! I KNOW WHAT THIS IS!
AN ADORABLE BERRY BASKET.
I KNEW YOU'D KNOW, GRANDPA!!

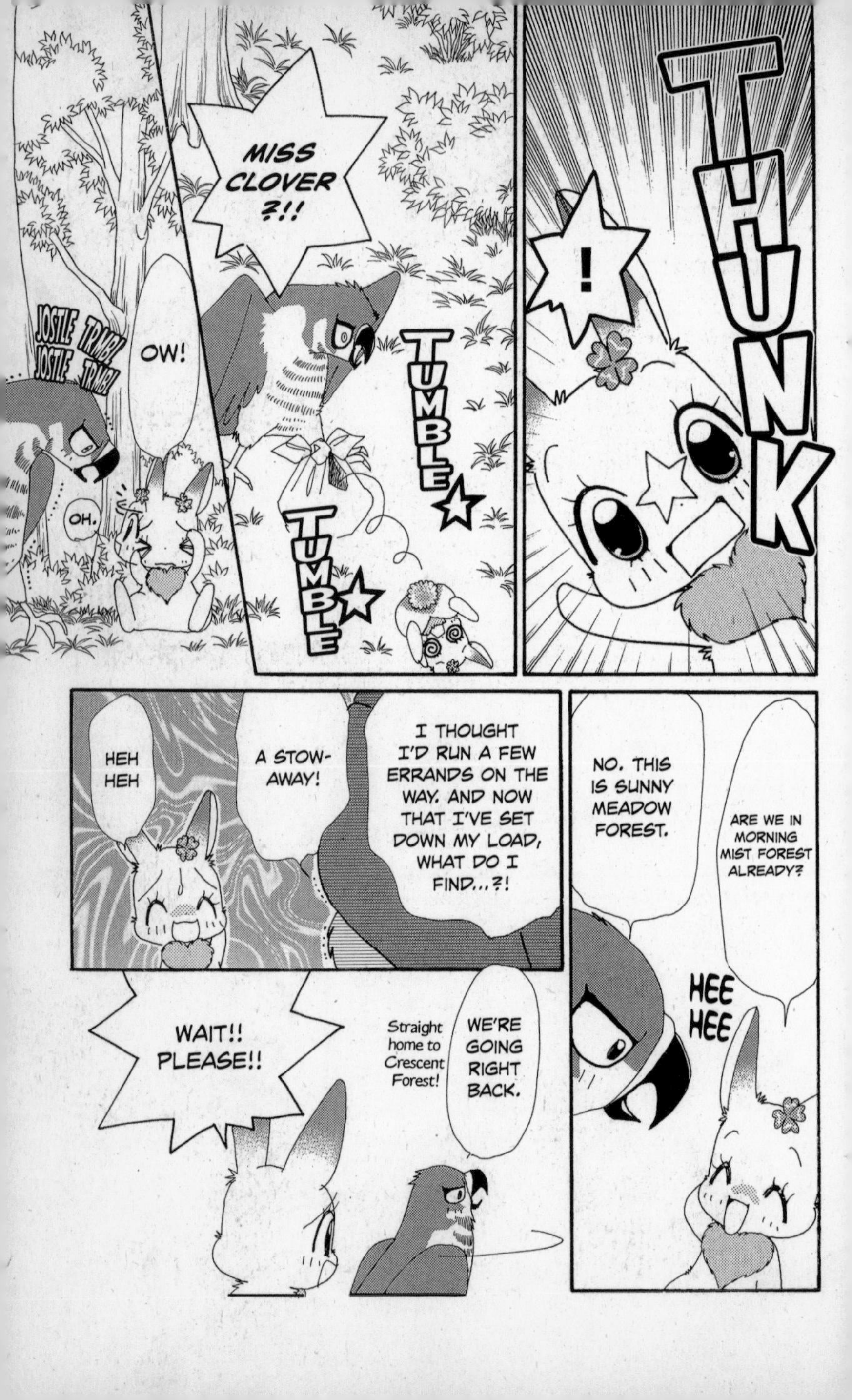
THUNK
!
MISS CLOVER ?!!
TUMBLE☆
TUMBLE☆
JOSTLE JOSTLE
TRMBL TRMBL
OW!
OH.
ARE WE IN MORNING MIST FOREST ALREADY?
NO. THIS IS SUNNY MEADOW FOREST.
HEE HEE
I THOUGHT I'D RUN A FEW ERRANDS ON THE WAY. AND NOW THAT I'VE SET DOWN MY LOAD, WHAT DO I FIND...?!
A STOW-AWAY!
HEH HEH
WE'RE GOING RIGHT BACK.
Straight home to Crescent Forest!
WAIT!! PLEASE!!

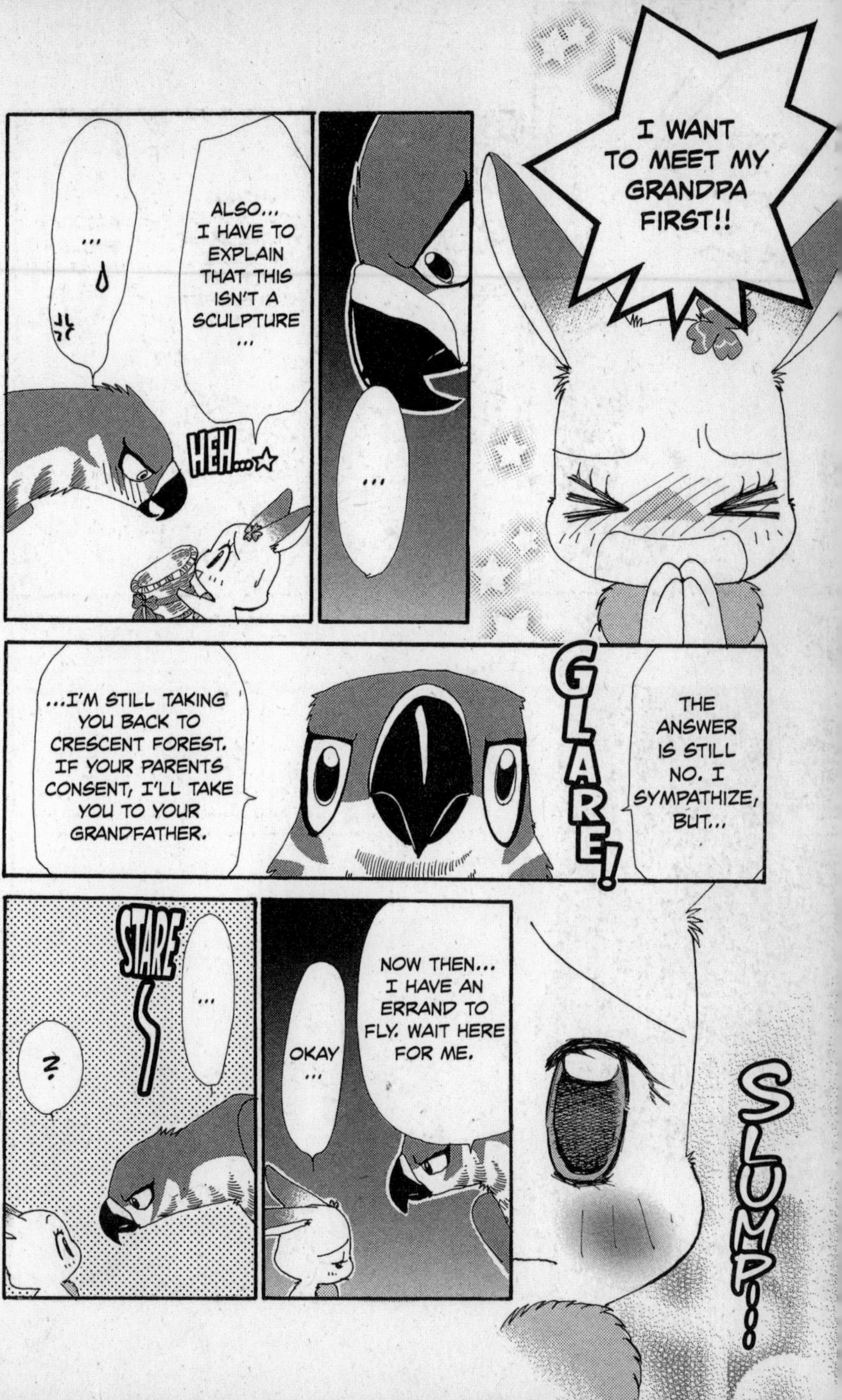
I WANT TO MEET MY GRANDPA FIRST!!
...
ALSO... I HAVE TO EXPLAIN THAT THIS ISN'T A SCULPTURE ...
...
HEH...☆
THE ANSWER IS STILL NO. I SYMPATHIZE, BUT...
GLARE!
...I'M STILL TAKING YOU BACK TO CRESCENT FOREST. IF YOUR PARENTS CONSENT, I'LL TAKE YOU TO YOUR GRANDFATHER.
SLUMP...
NOW THEN... I HAVE AN ERRAND TO FLY. WAIT HERE FOR ME.
OKAY ...
STARE
...
?

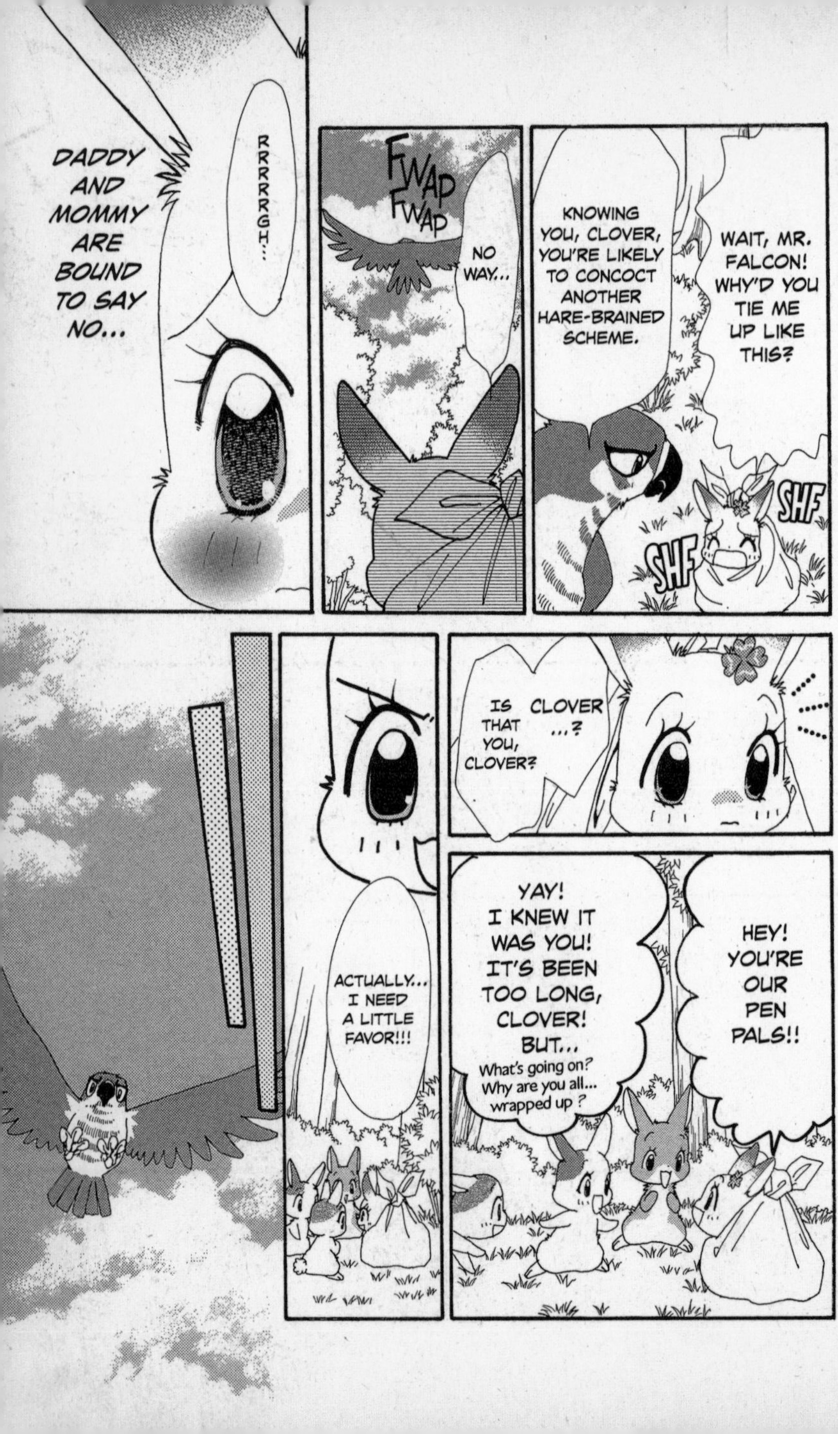
WAIT, MR. FALCON! WHY'D YOU TIE ME UP LIKE THIS?
KNOWING YOU, CLOVER, YOU'RE LIKELY TO CONCOCT ANOTHER HARE-BRAINED SCHEME.
SHF
SHF
FWAP FWAP
NO WAY...
RRRRRGH...
DADDY AND MOMMY ARE BOUND TO SAY NO...
CLOVER ...?
IS THAT YOU, CLOVER?
HEY! YOU'RE OUR PEN PALS!!
YAY! I KNEW IT WAS YOU! IT'S BEEN TOO LONG, CLOVER! BUT...
What's going on? Why are you all... wrapped up?
ACTUALLY... I NEED A LITTLE FAVOR!!!

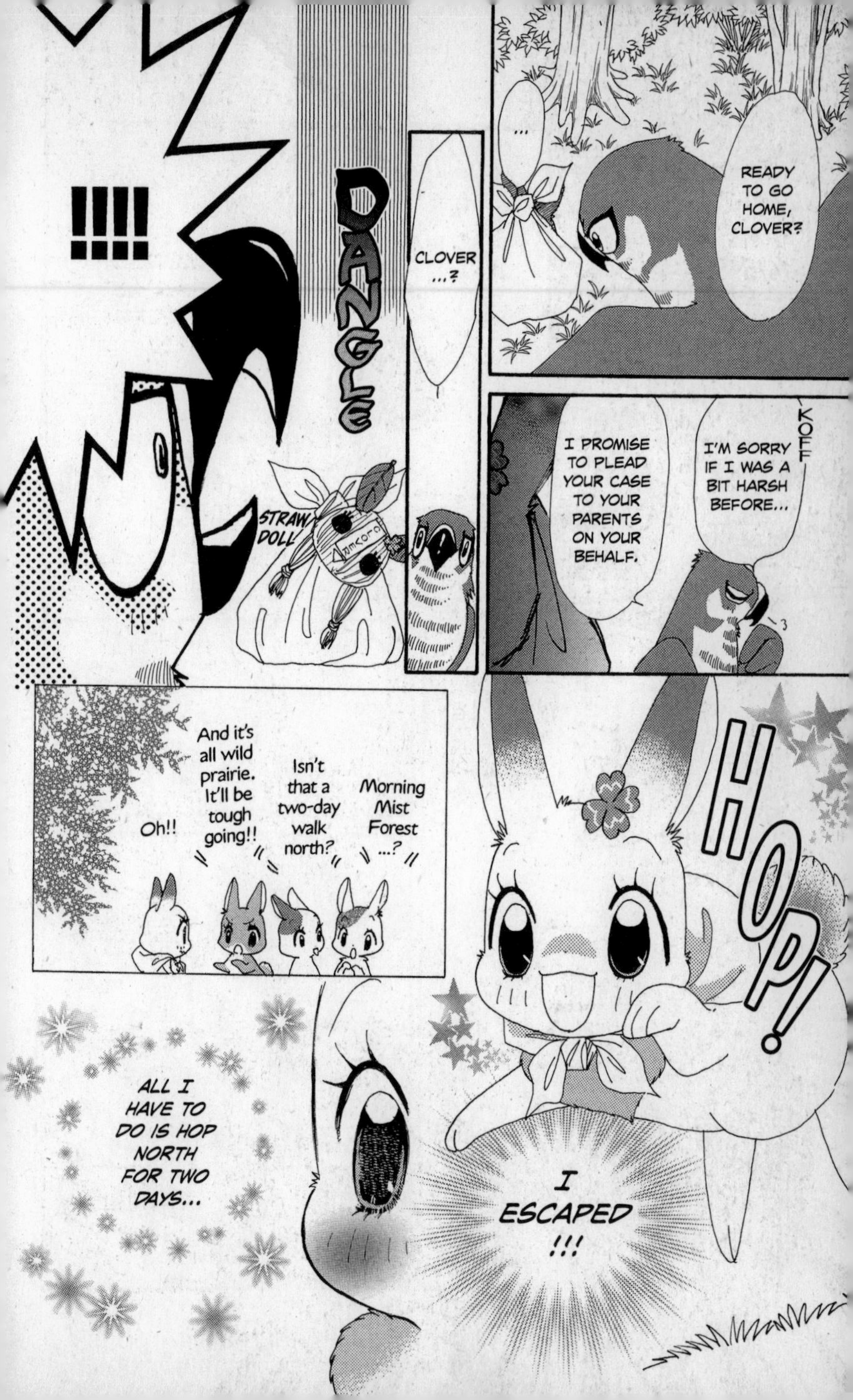
READY TO GO HOME, CLOVER?
...
I'M SORRY IF I WAS A BIT HARSH BEFORE...
KOFF
I PROMISE TO PLEAD YOUR CASE TO YOUR PARENTS ON YOUR BEHALF.
CLOVER ...?
DANGLE
STRAW DOLL
!!!!
HOP!
Morning Mist Forest ...?
Isn't that a two-day walk north?
And it's all wild prairie. It'll be tough going!!
Oh!!
I ESCAPED !!!
ALL I HAVE TO DO IS HOP NORTH FOR TWO DAYS...

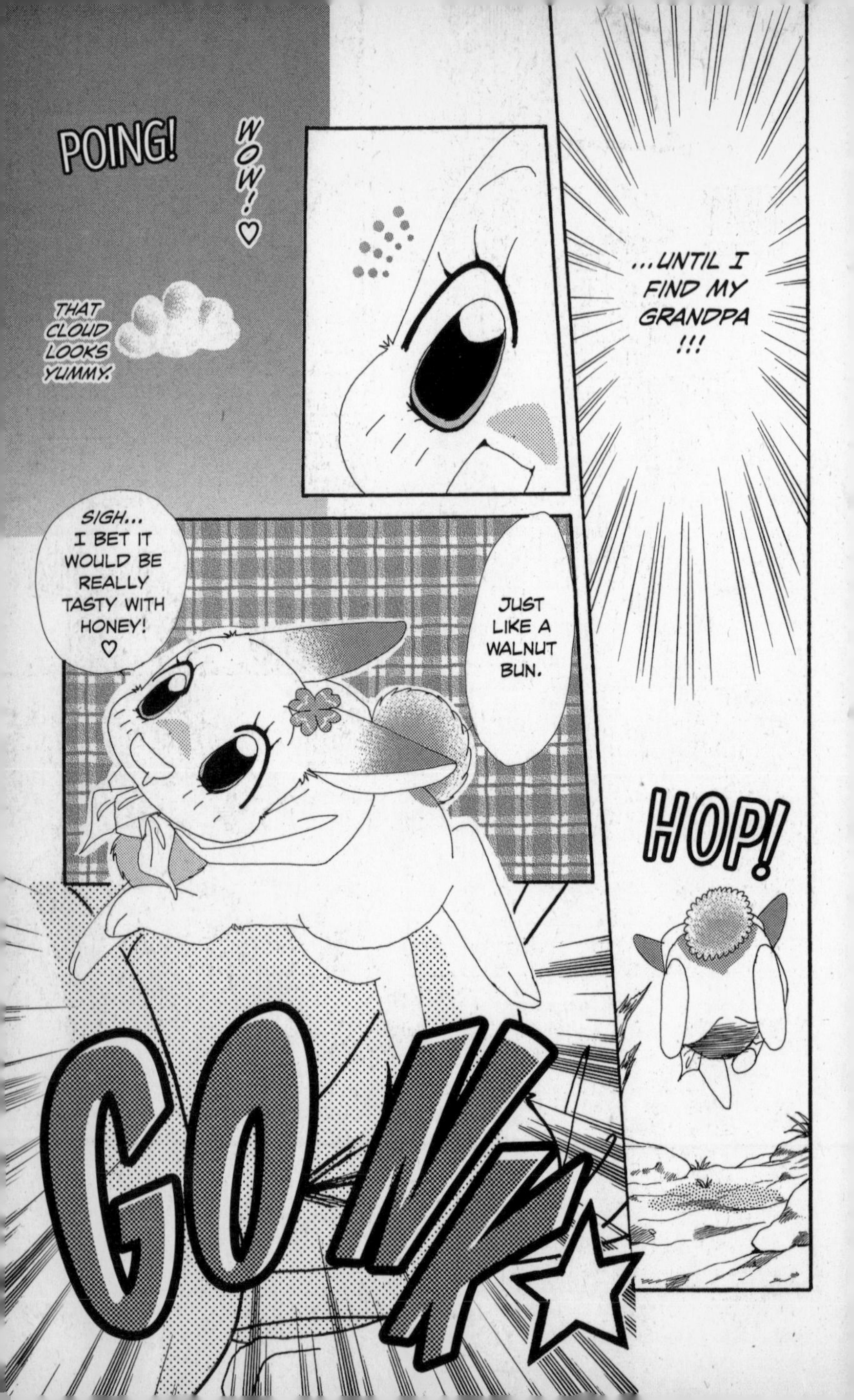
...UNTIL I FIND MY GRANDPA !!!
HOP!
WOW! ♡
POING!
THAT CLOUD LOOKS YUMMY.
JUST LIKE A WALNUT BUN.
SIGH... I BET IT WOULD BE REALLY TASTY WITH HONEY! ♡
GONK

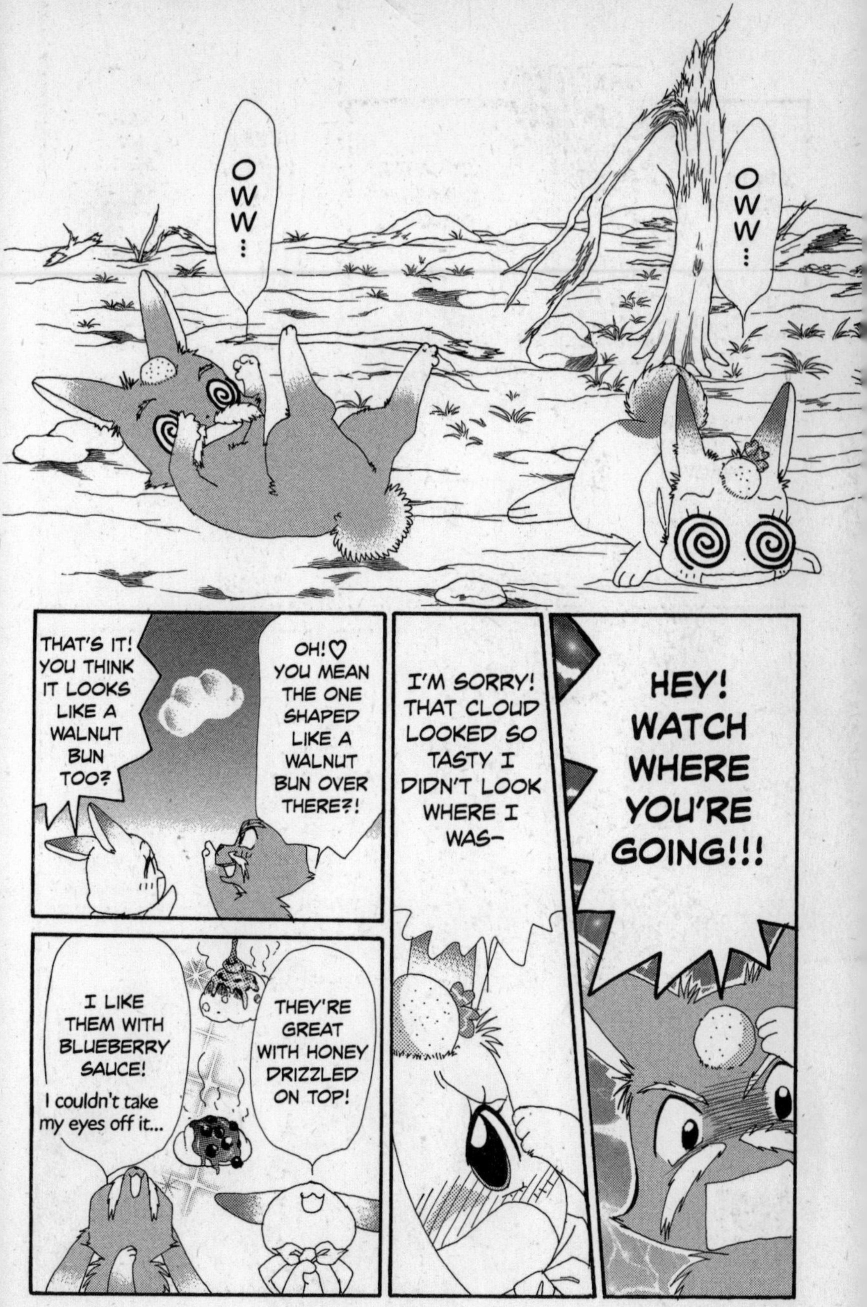
OWW...
OWW...
HEY! WATCH WHERE YOU'RE GOING!!!
I'M SORRY! THAT CLOUD LOOKED SO TASTY I DIDN'T LOOK WHERE I WAS–
OH!♡ YOU MEAN THE ONE SHAPED LIKE A WALNUT BUN OVER THERE?!
THAT'S IT! YOU THINK IT LOOKS LIKE A WALNUT BUN TOO?
THEY'RE GREAT WITH HONEY DRIZZLED ON TOP!
I LIKE THEM WITH BLUEBERRY SAUCE!
I couldn't take my eyes off it...

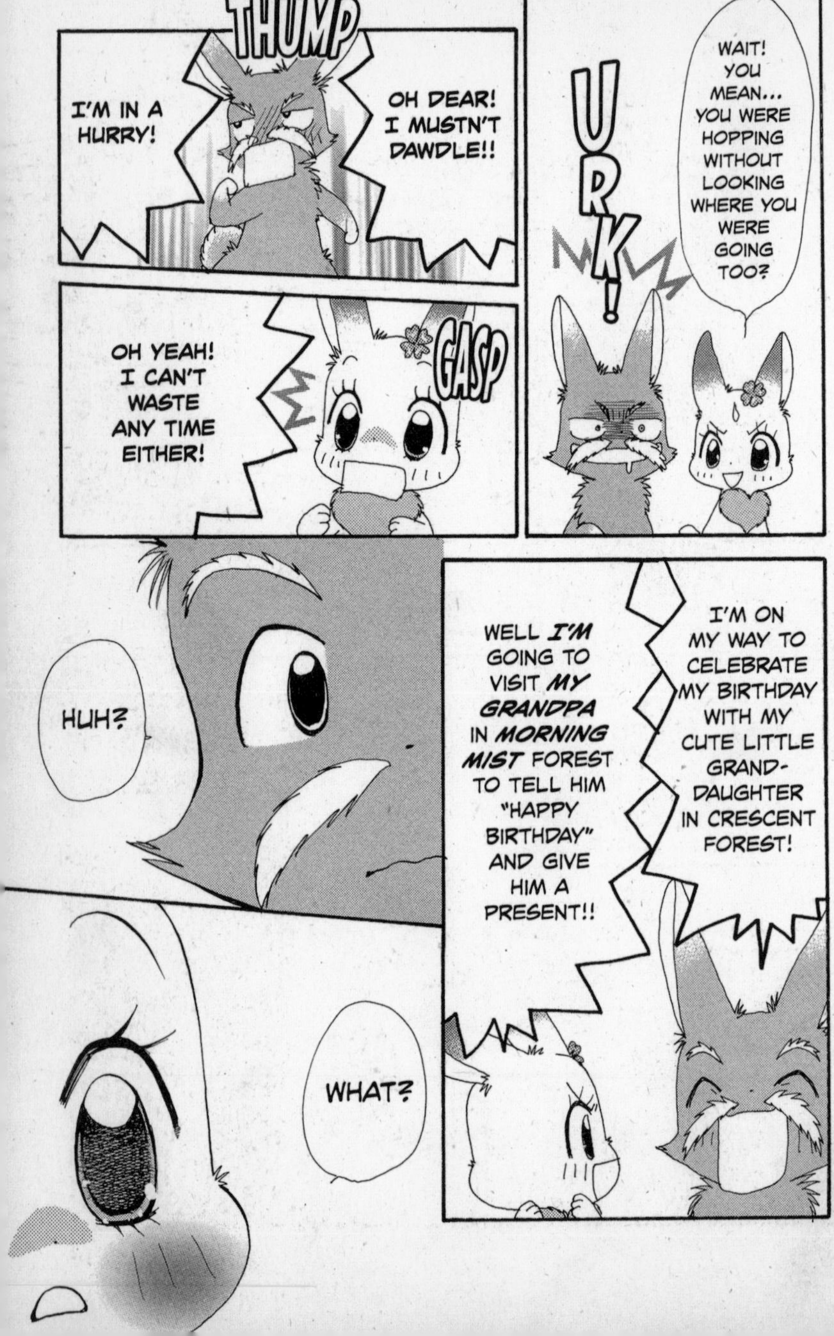
WAIT! YOU MEAN... YOU WERE HOPPING WITHOUT LOOKING WHERE YOU WERE GOING TOO?
URK!
THUMP
OH DEAR! I MUSTN'T DAWDLE!!
I'M IN A HURRY!
GASP
OH YEAH! I CAN'T WASTE ANY TIME EITHER!
I'M ON MY WAY TO CELEBRATE MY BIRTHDAY WITH MY CUTE LITTLE GRAND-DAUGHTER IN CRESCENT FOREST!
WELL *I'M* GOING TO VISIT *MY GRANDPA* IN *MORNING MIST* FOREST TO TELL HIM "HAPPY BIRTHDAY" AND GIVE HIM A PRESENT!!
HUH?
WHAT?

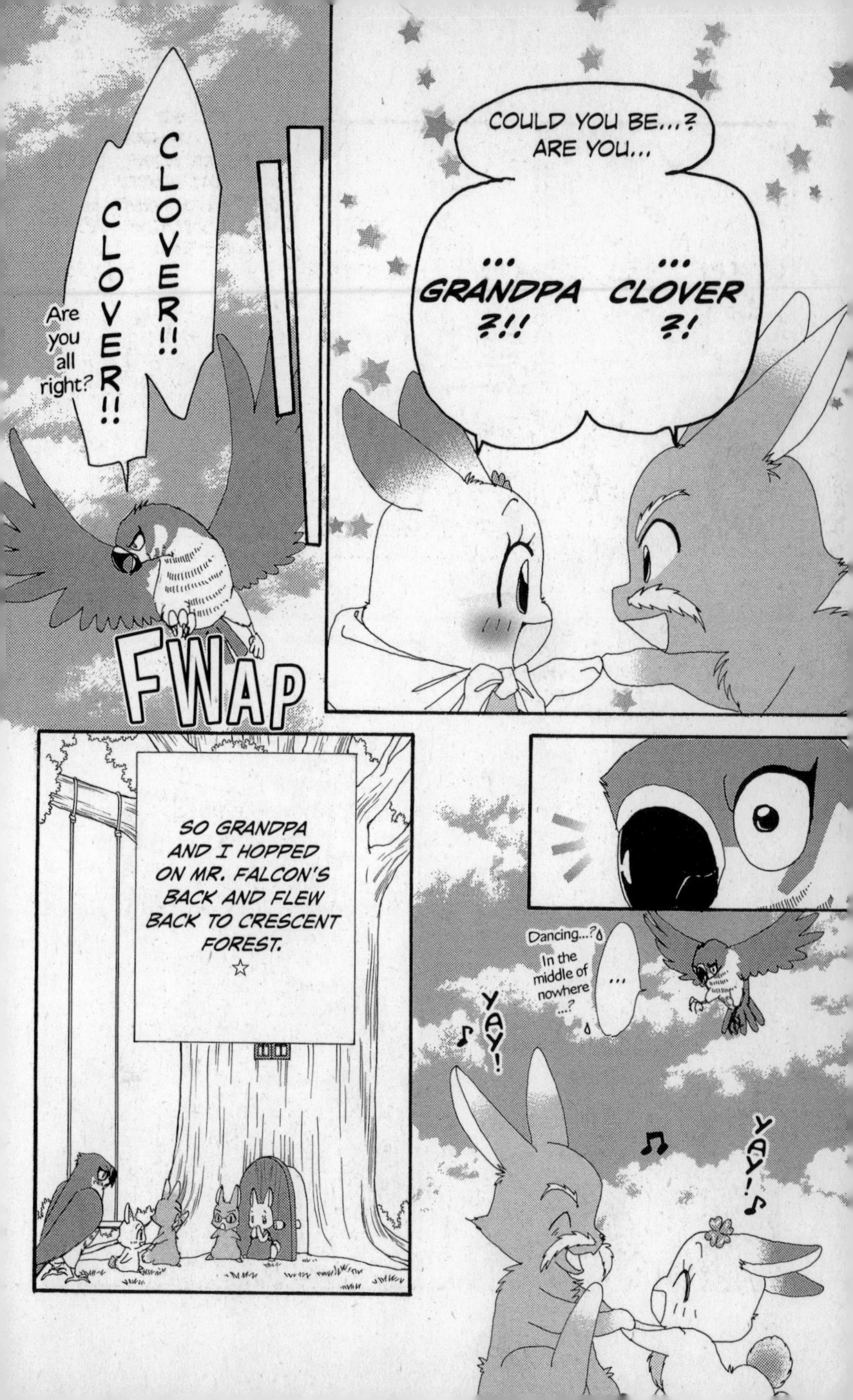
COULD YOU BE...? ARE YOU...
...CLOVER ?!
...GRANDPA ?!!
CLOVER!!
CLOVER!!
Are you all right?
FWAP
...
Dancing...? In the middle of nowhere...?
YAY!
YAY!
SO GRANDPA AND I HOPPED ON MR. FALCON'S BACK AND FLEW BACK TO CRESCENT FOREST. ☆

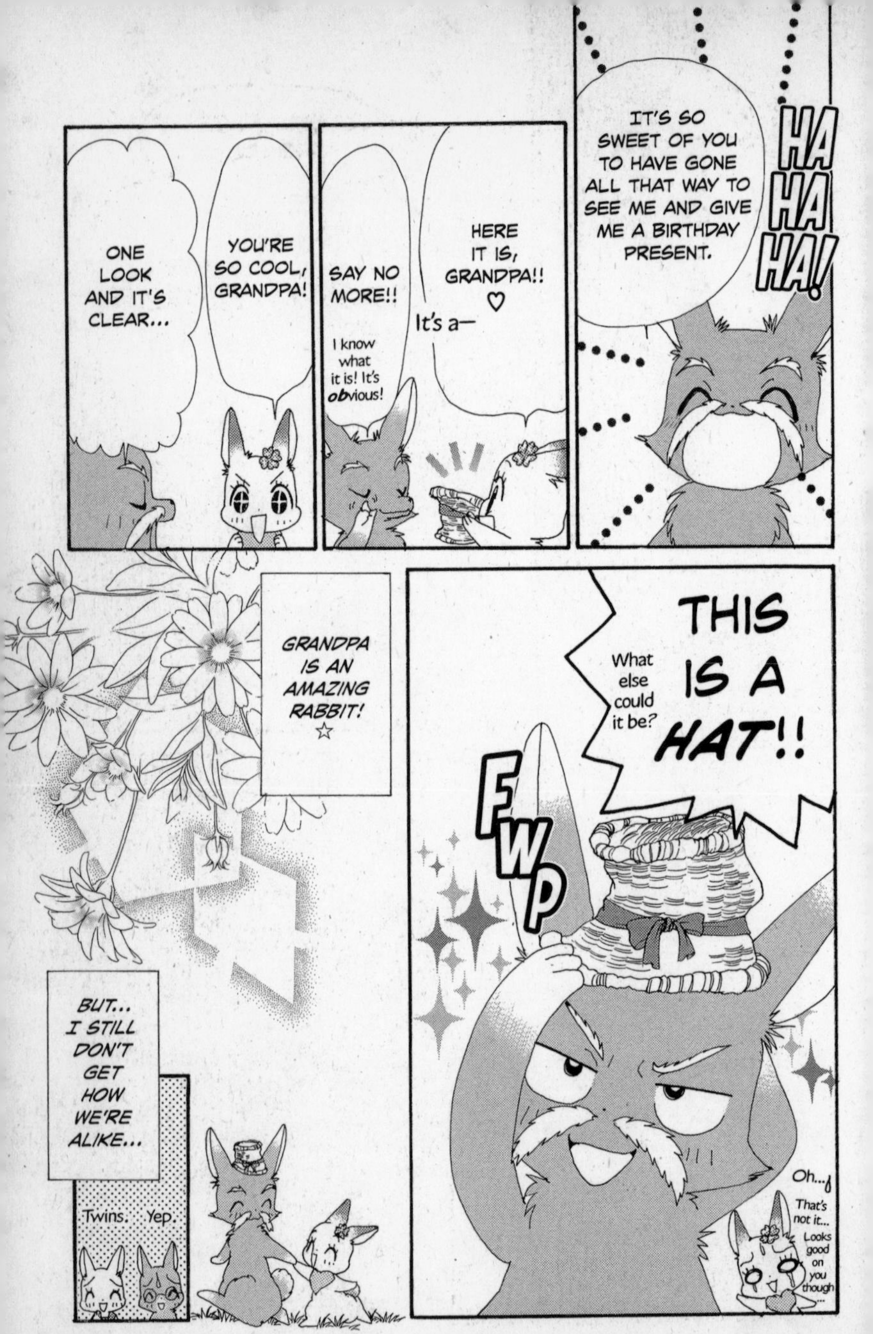

IT'S SO SWEET OF YOU TO HAVE GONE ALL THAT WAY TO SEE ME AND GIVE ME A BIRTHDAY PRESENT.
HA HA HA!
HERE IT IS, GRANDPA!! ♡
It's a—
SAY NO MORE!!
I know what it is! It's *ob*vious!
YOU'RE SO COOL, GRANDPA!
ONE LOOK AND IT'S CLEAR...
THIS IS A *HAT*!!
What else could it be?
FWP
Oh...
That's not it... Looks good on you though...
GRANDPA IS AN AMAZING RABBIT! ☆
BUT... I STILL DON'T GET HOW WE'RE ALIKE...
Twins.
Yep.

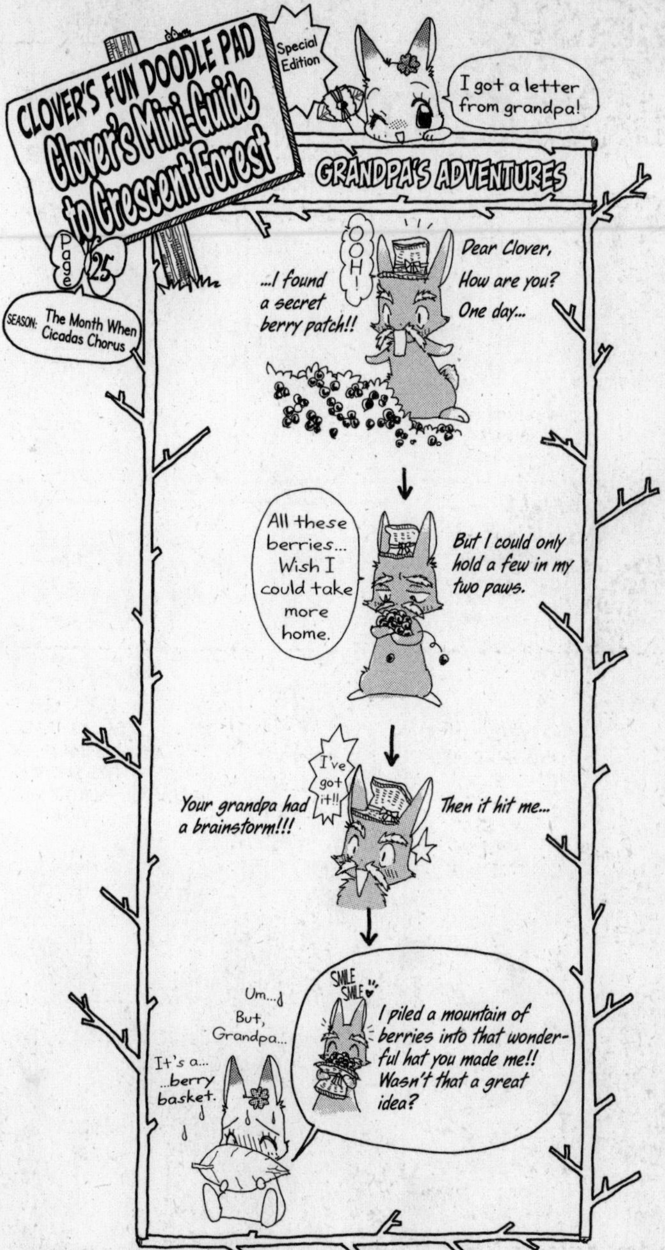
CLOVER'S FUN DOODLE PAD
Clover's Mini-Guide to Crescent Forest
Special Edition
Page 25
SEASON: The Month When Cicadas Chorus
I got a letter from grandpa!
GRANDPA'S ADVENTURES
Dear Clover, How are you? One day...
OOH!
...I found a secret berry patch!!
But I could only hold a few in my two paws.
All these berries... Wish I could take more home.
Then it hit me...
I've got it!!
Your grandpa had a brainstorm!!!
SMILE SMILE
I piled a mountain of berries into that wonderful hat you made me!! Wasn't that a great idea?
Um... But, Grandpa...
It's a... ...berry basket.

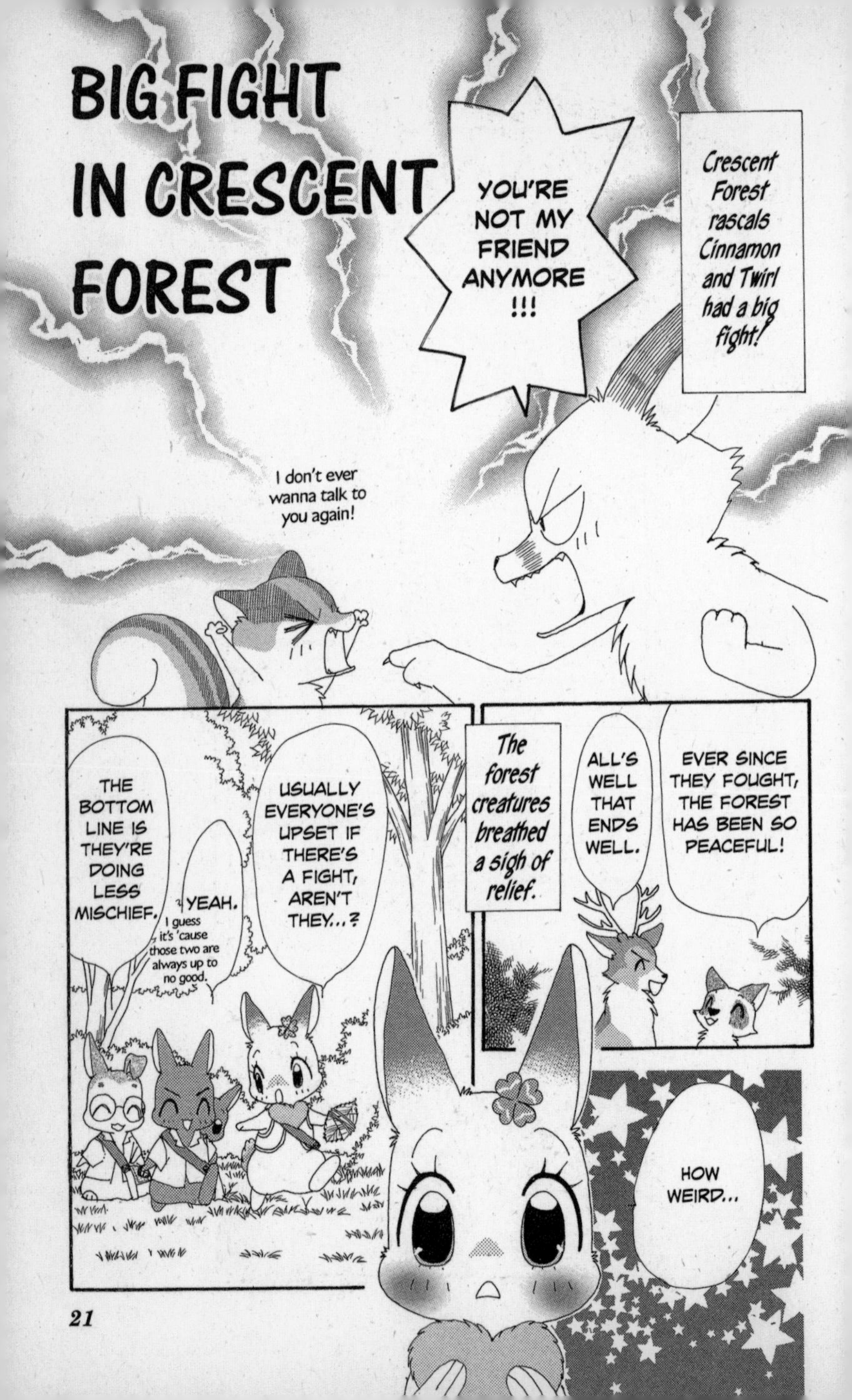
BIG FIGHT IN CRESCENT FOREST
Crescent Forest rascals Cinnamon and Twirl had a big fight!
YOU'RE NOT MY FRIEND ANYMORE!!!
I don't ever wanna talk to you again!
EVER SINCE THEY FOUGHT, THE FOREST HAS BEEN SO PEACEFUL!
ALL'S WELL THAT ENDS WELL.
The forest creatures breathed a sigh of relief.
USUALLY EVERYONE'S UPSET IF THERE'S A FIGHT, AREN'T THEY...?
YEAH.
I guess it's 'cause those two are always up to no good.
THE BOTTOM LINE IS THEY'RE DOING LESS MISCHIEF.
HOW WEIRD...

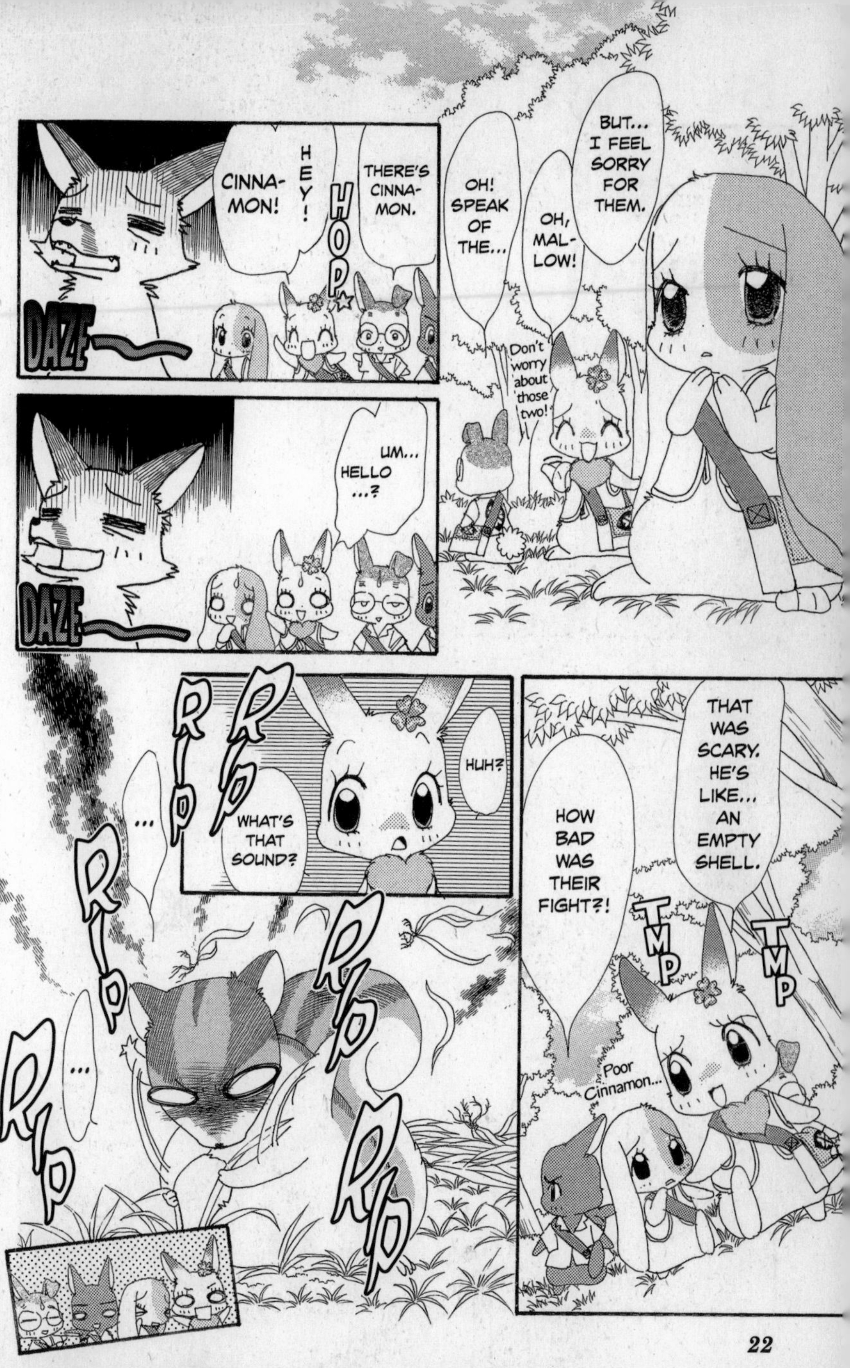
BUT... I FEEL SORRY FOR THEM.
OH, MALLOW!
OH! SPEAK OF THE...
Don't worry about those two!
THERE'S CINNAMON.
HOP
HEY!
CINNAMON!
DAZE
UM... HELLO...?
DAZE
THAT WAS SCARY. HE'S LIKE... AN EMPTY SHELL.
HOW BAD WAS THEIR FIGHT?!
TMP
TMP
Poor Cinnamon...
HUH?
WHAT'S THAT SOUND?
RIP
RIP
...
RIP
RIP
RIP
...
RIP

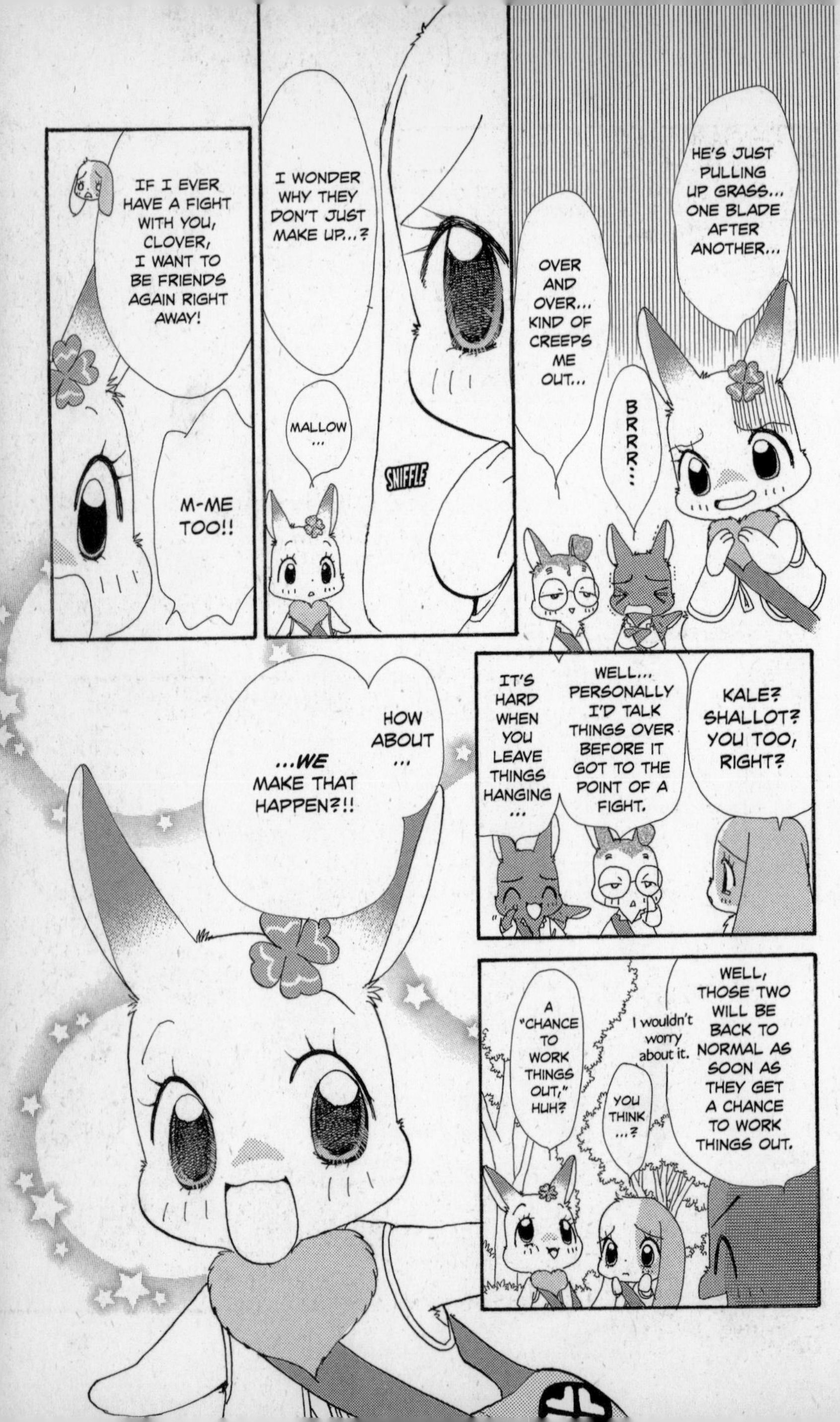
HE'S JUST PULLING UP GRASS... ONE BLADE AFTER ANOTHER...
OVER AND OVER... KIND OF CREEPS ME OUT...
BRRR...
I WONDER WHY THEY DON'T JUST MAKE UP...?
MALLOW...
SNIFFLE
IF I EVER HAVE A FIGHT WITH YOU, CLOVER, I WANT TO BE FRIENDS AGAIN RIGHT AWAY!
M-ME TOO!!
KALE? SHALLOT? YOU TOO, RIGHT?
WELL... PERSONALLY I'D TALK THINGS OVER BEFORE IT GOT TO THE POINT OF A FIGHT.
IT'S HARD WHEN YOU LEAVE THINGS HANGING...
WELL, THOSE TWO WILL BE BACK TO NORMAL AS SOON AS THEY GET A CHANCE TO WORK THINGS OUT.
I wouldn't worry about it.
YOU THINK...?
A "CHANCE TO WORK THINGS OUT," HUH?
HOW ABOUT...
...WE MAKE THAT HAPPEN?!!

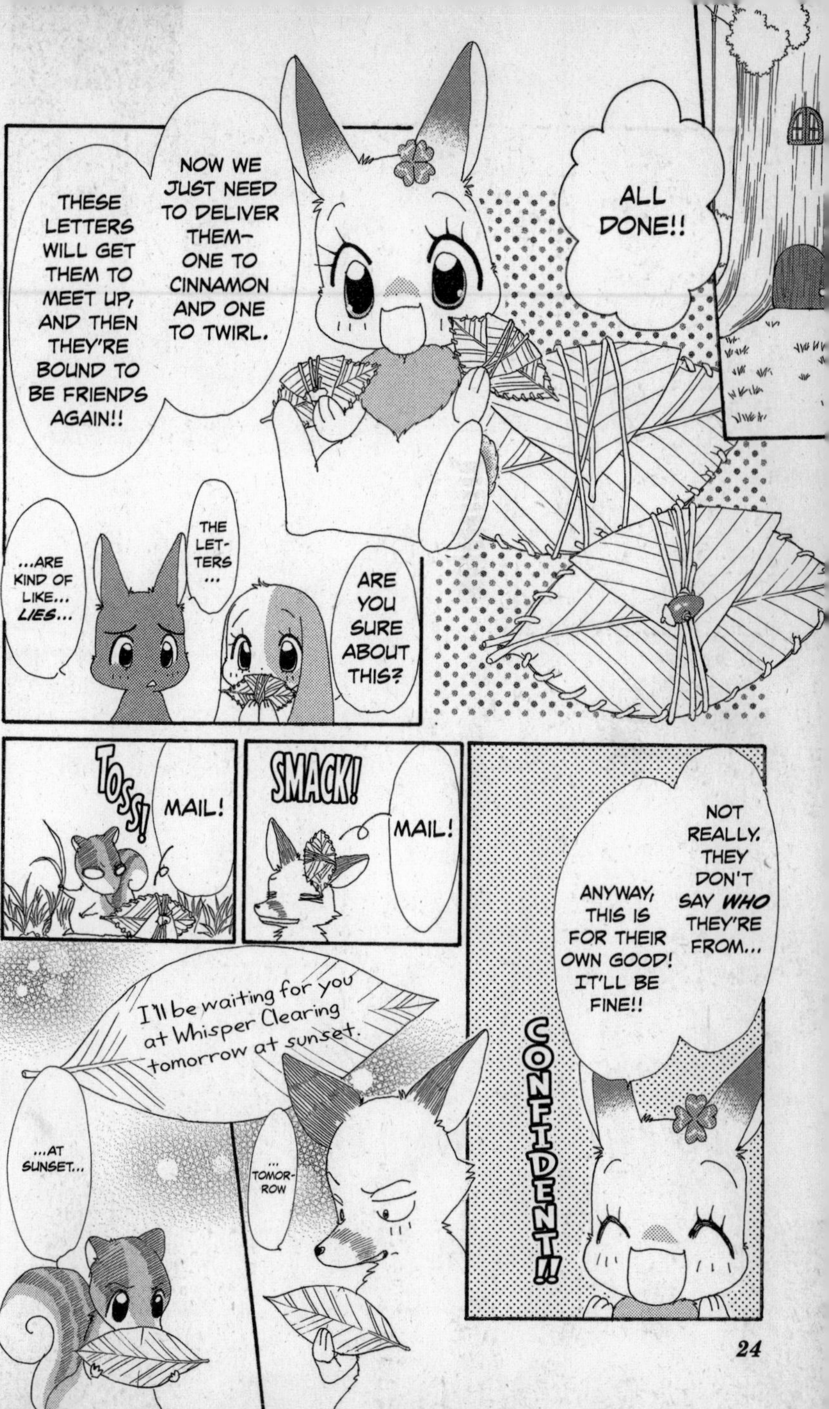
ALL DONE!!
NOW WE JUST NEED TO DELIVER THEM— ONE TO CINNAMON AND ONE TO TWIRL.
THESE LETTERS WILL GET THEM TO MEET UP, AND THEN THEY'RE BOUND TO BE FRIENDS AGAIN!!
ARE YOU SURE ABOUT THIS?
THE LET-TERS...
...ARE KIND OF LIKE... *LIES*...
NOT REALLY. THEY DON'T SAY *WHO* THEY'RE FROM...
ANYWAY, THIS IS FOR THEIR OWN GOOD! IT'LL BE FINE!!
CONFIDENT!!
SMACK!
MAIL!
TOSS!
MAIL!
I'll be waiting for you at Whisper Clearing tomorrow at sunset.
...TOMOR-ROW
...AT SUNSET...

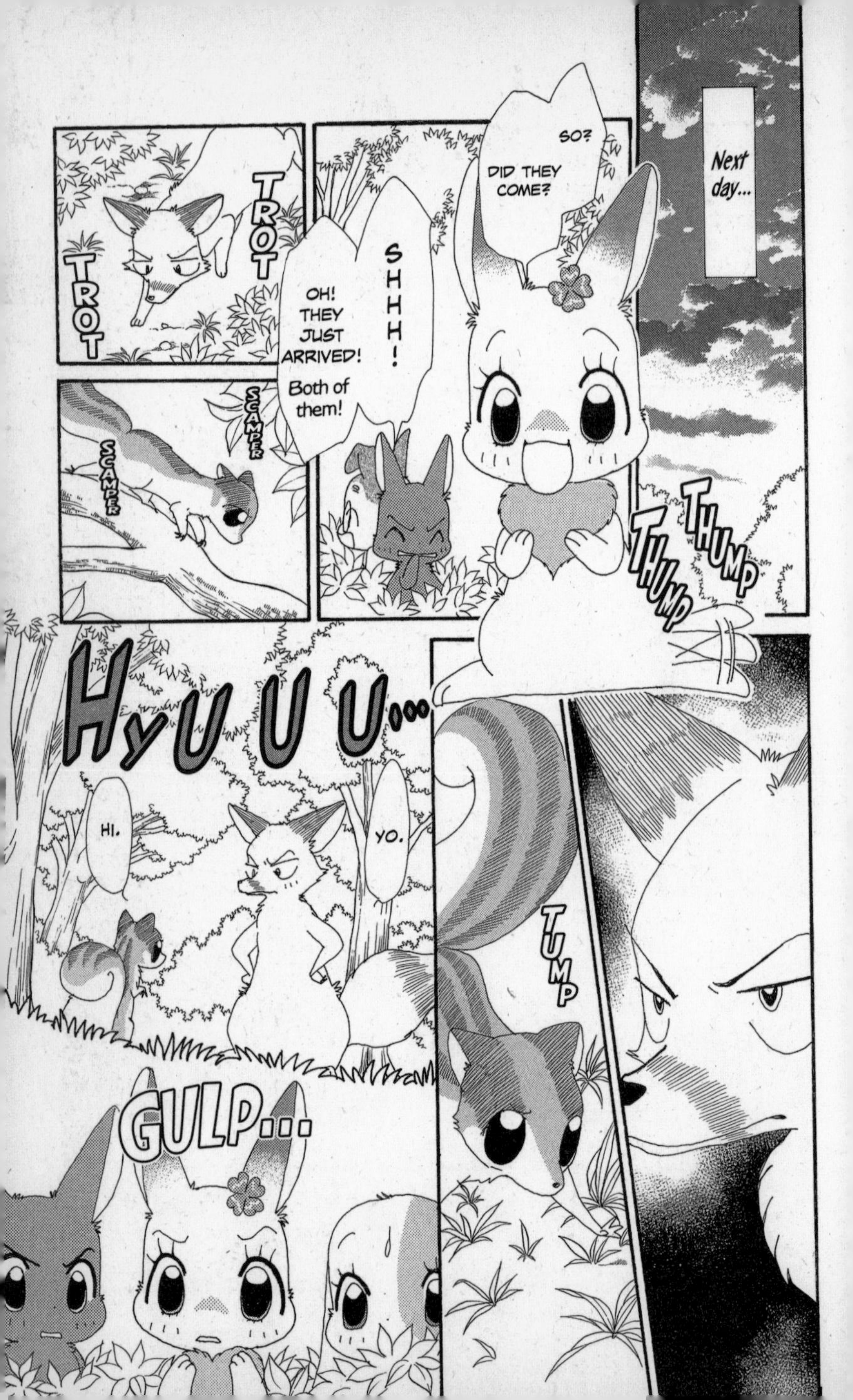
Next day...
THUMP
THUMP
SO? DID THEY COME?
SHHH!
OH! THEY JUST ARRIVED!
Both of them!
TROT
TROT
SCAMPER
SCAMPER
TUMP
HYUUU...
YO.
HI.
GULP...

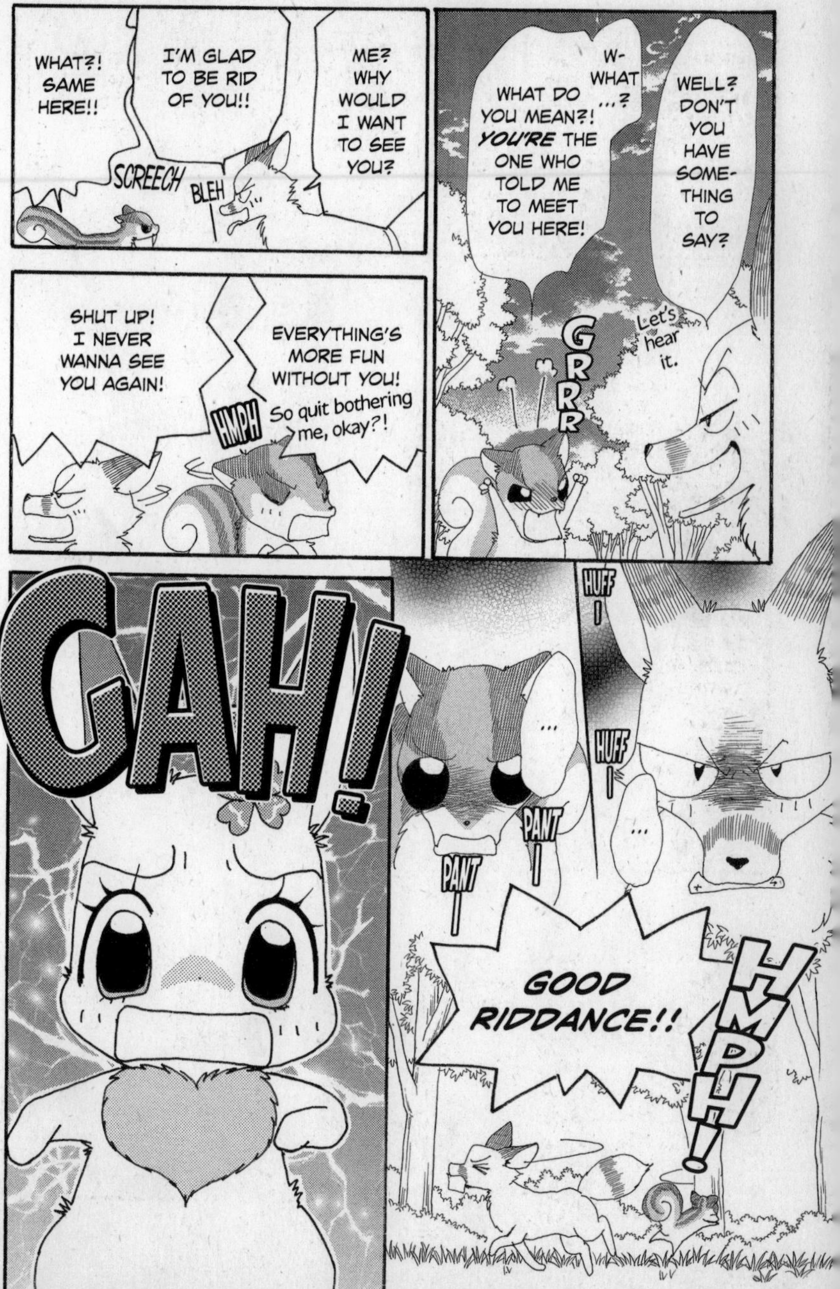

WELL? DON'T YOU HAVE SOME-THING TO SAY?
Let's hear it.
W-WHAT ...?
WHAT DO YOU MEAN?! *YOU'RE* THE ONE WHO TOLD ME TO MEET YOU HERE!
GRRR
ME? WHY WOULD I WANT TO SEE YOU?
I'M GLAD TO BE RID OF YOU!!
BLEH
WHAT?! SAME HERE!!
SCREECH
EVERYTHING'S MORE FUN WITHOUT YOU!
So quit bothering me, okay?!
HMPH
SHUT UP! I NEVER WANNA SEE YOU AGAIN!
HUFF
HUFF
...
...
PANT
PANT
HMPH!
GOOD RIDDANCE!!
GAH!!

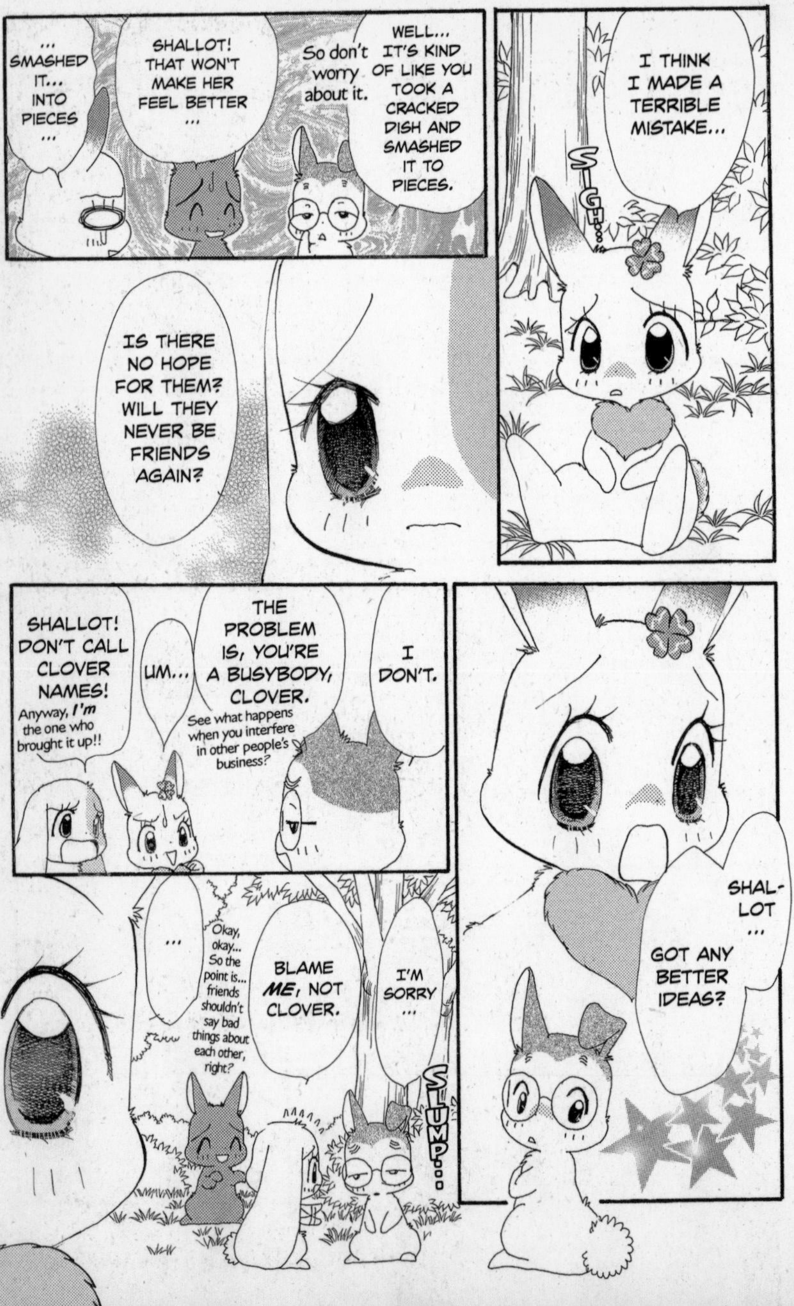
I THINK I MADE A TERRIBLE MISTAKE...
SIGH...
WELL... IT'S KIND OF LIKE YOU TOOK A CRACKED DISH AND SMASHED IT TO PIECES.
So don't worry about it.
SHALLOT! THAT WON'T MAKE HER FEEL BETTER ...
... SMASHED IT... INTO PIECES ...
IS THERE NO HOPE FOR THEM? WILL THEY NEVER BE FRIENDS AGAIN?
SHAL-LOT ... GOT ANY BETTER IDEAS?
I DON'T.
THE PROBLEM IS, YOU'RE A BUSYBODY, CLOVER.
See what happens when you interfere in other people's business?
UM...
SHALLOT! DON'T CALL CLOVER NAMES!
Anyway, *I'm* the one who brought it up!!
SLUMP...
I'M SORRY ...
BLAME *ME*, NOT CLOVER.
Okay, okay... So the point is... friends shouldn't say bad things about each other, right?
...

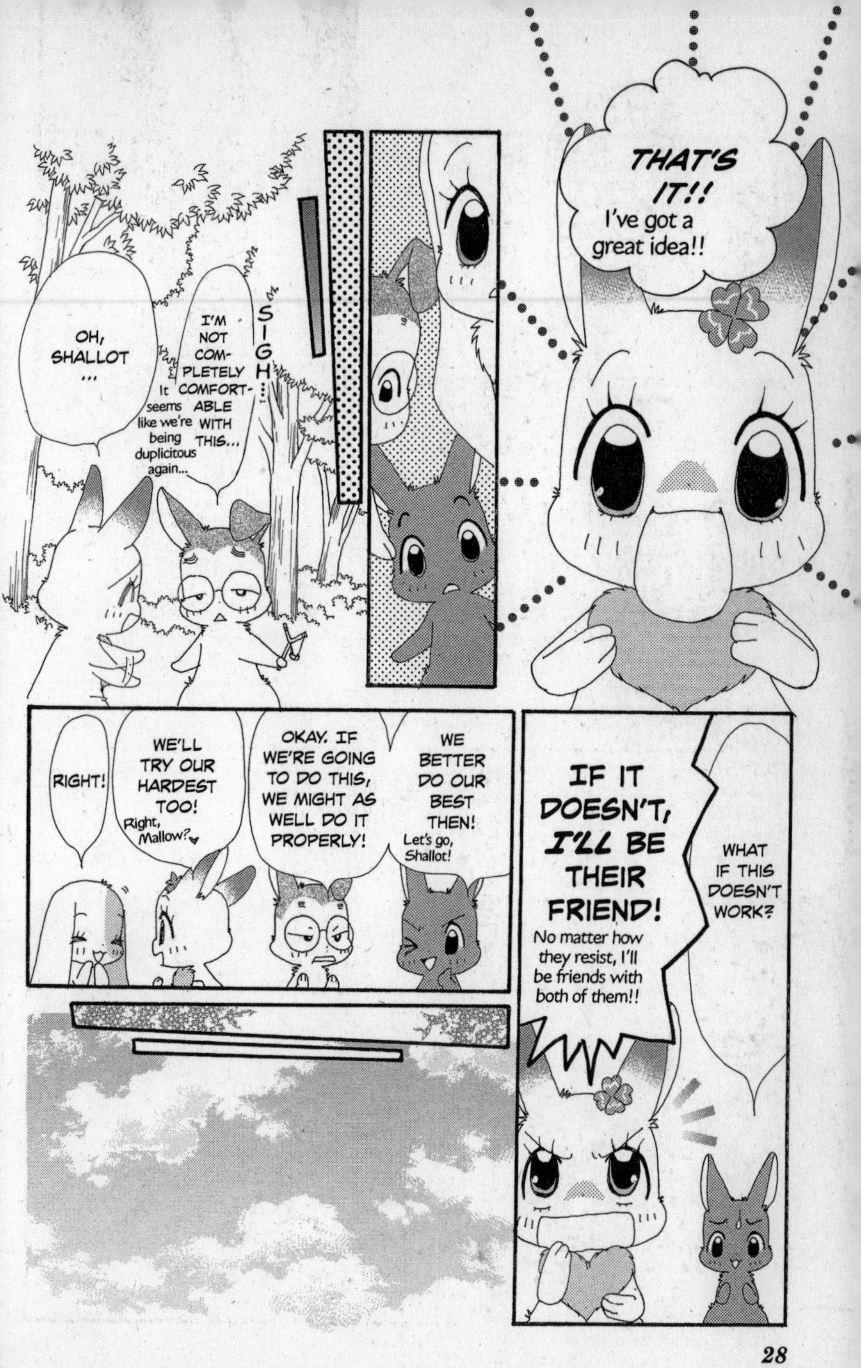
THAT'S IT!!
I've got a great idea!!
SIGH...
I'M NOT COMPLETELY COMFORTABLE WITH THIS...
It seems like we're being duplicitous again...
OH, SHALLOT...
WHAT IF THIS DOESN'T WORK?
IF IT DOESN'T, I'LL BE THEIR FRIEND!
No matter how they resist, I'll be friends with both of them!!
WE BETTER DO OUR BEST THEN!
Let's go, Shallot!
OKAY. IF WE'RE GOING TO DO THIS, WE MIGHT AS WELL DO IT PROPERLY!
WE'LL TRY OUR HARDEST TOO!
Right, Mallow?
RIGHT!

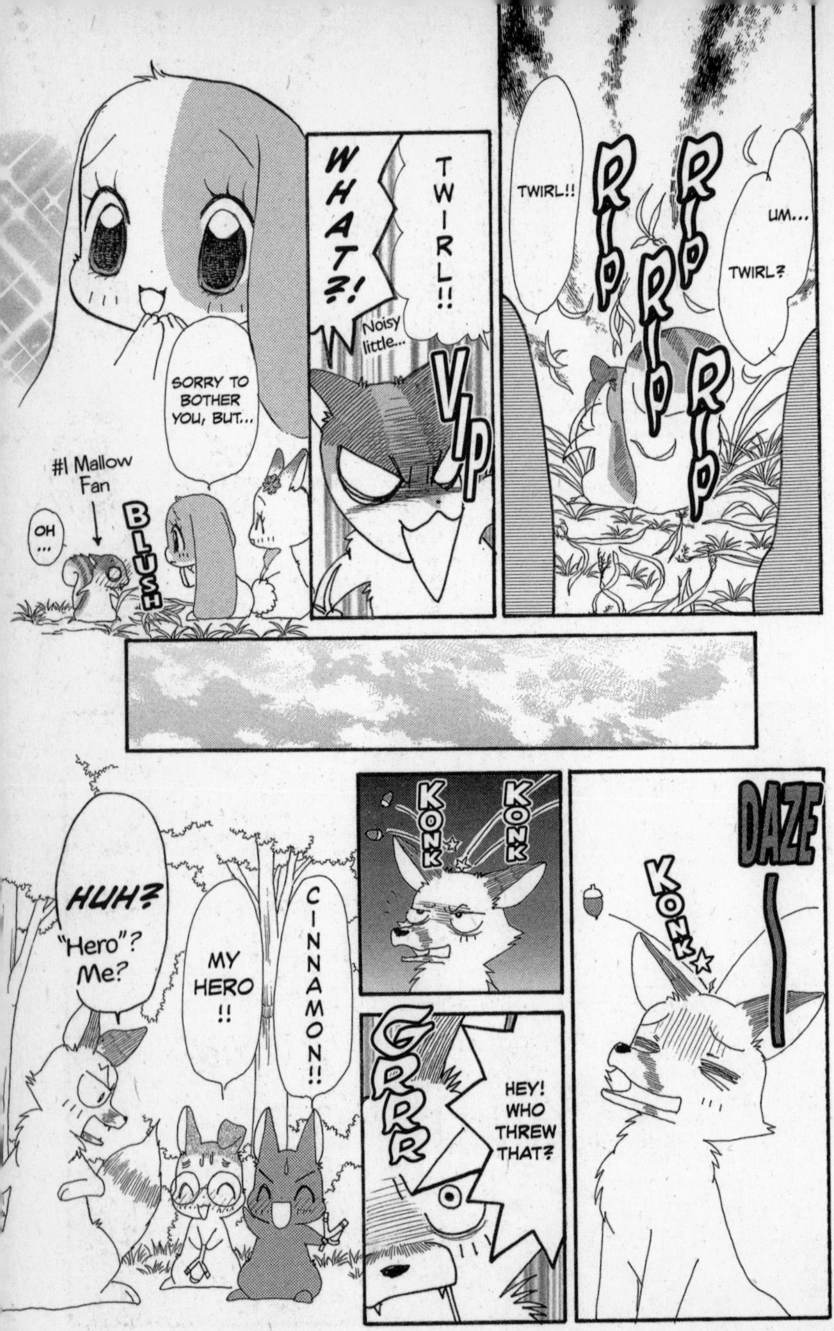
UM... TWIRL?
RIP RIP RIP RIP
TWIRL!!
TWIRL!!
WHAT?!
Noisy little...
VIP
SORRY TO BOTHER YOU, BUT...
#1 Mallow Fan
BLUSH
OH ...
DAZE
KONK
KONK KONK
HEY! WHO THREW THAT?
GRRR
CINNAMON!!
MY HERO!!
HUH?
"Hero"? Me?

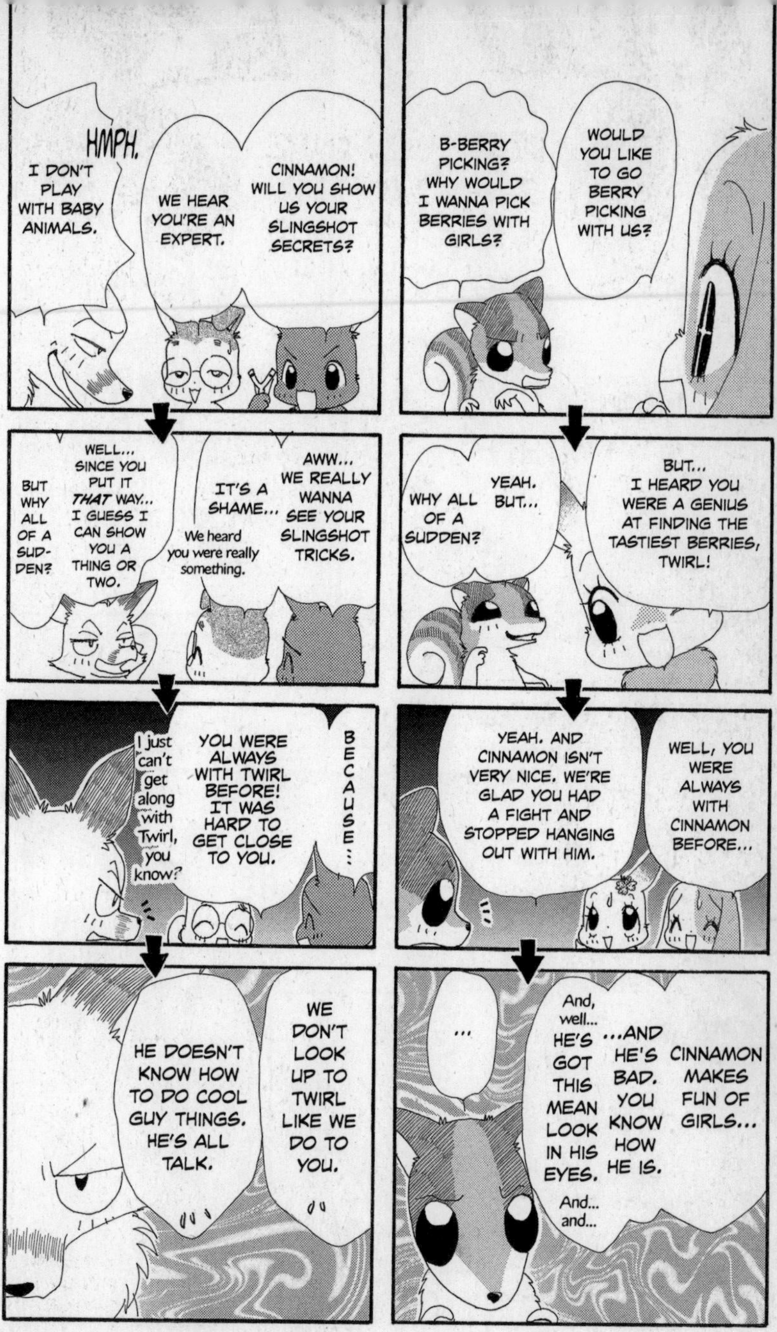
WOULD YOU LIKE TO GO BERRY PICKING WITH US?
B-BERRY PICKING? WHY WOULD I WANNA PICK BERRIES WITH GIRLS?
BUT... I HEARD YOU WERE A GENIUS AT FINDING THE TASTIEST BERRIES, TWIRL!
YEAH. BUT...
WHY ALL OF A SUDDEN?
WELL, YOU WERE ALWAYS WITH CINNAMON BEFORE...
YEAH. AND CINNAMON ISN'T VERY NICE. WE'RE GLAD YOU HAD A FIGHT AND STOPPED HANGING OUT WITH HIM.
CINNAMON MAKES FUN OF GIRLS...
...AND HE'S BAD. YOU KNOW HOW HE IS.
And, well...
HE'S GOT THIS MEAN LOOK IN HIS EYES.
And... and...
...
CINNAMON! WILL YOU SHOW US YOUR SLINGSHOT SECRETS?
WE HEAR YOU'RE AN EXPERT.
HMPH.
I DON'T PLAY WITH BABY ANIMALS.
AWW... WE REALLY WANNA SEE YOUR SLINGSHOT TRICKS.
IT'S A SHAME...
We heard you were really something.
WELL... SINCE YOU PUT IT *THAT* WAY... I GUESS I CAN SHOW YOU A THING OR TWO.
BUT WHY ALL OF A SUDDEN?
BECAUSE...
YOU WERE ALWAYS WITH TWIRL BEFORE! IT WAS HARD TO GET CLOSE TO YOU.
I just can't get along with Twirl, you know?
WE DON'T LOOK UP TO TWIRL LIKE WE DO TO YOU.
HE DOESN'T KNOW HOW TO DO COOL GUY THINGS. HE'S ALL TALK.

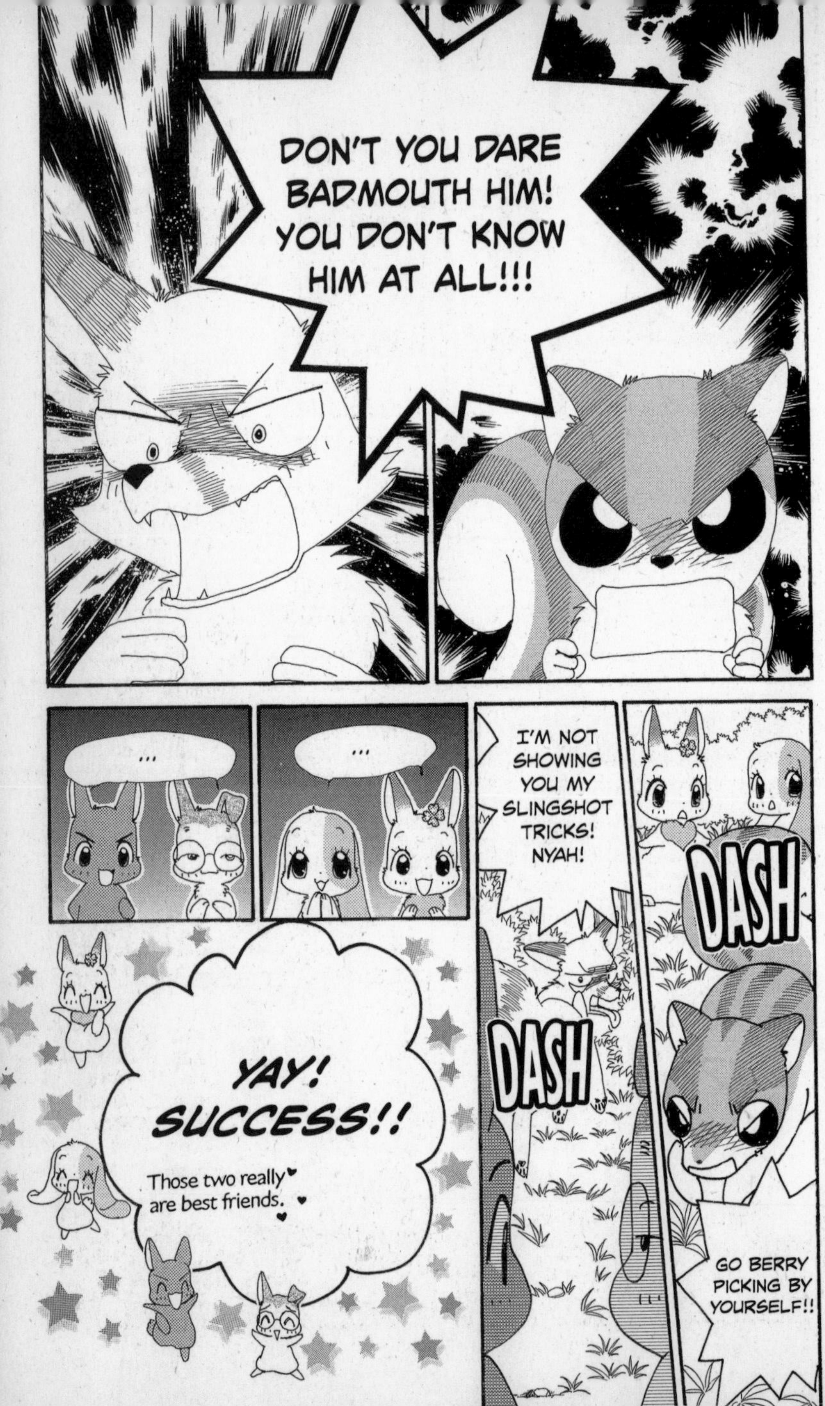
DON'T YOU DARE BADMOUTH HIM! YOU DON'T KNOW HIM AT ALL!!!
DASH
GO BERRY PICKING BY YOURSELF!!
I'M NOT SHOWING YOU MY SLINGSHOT TRICKS! NYAH!
DASH
...
...
YAY! SUCCESS!!
Those two really are best friends.

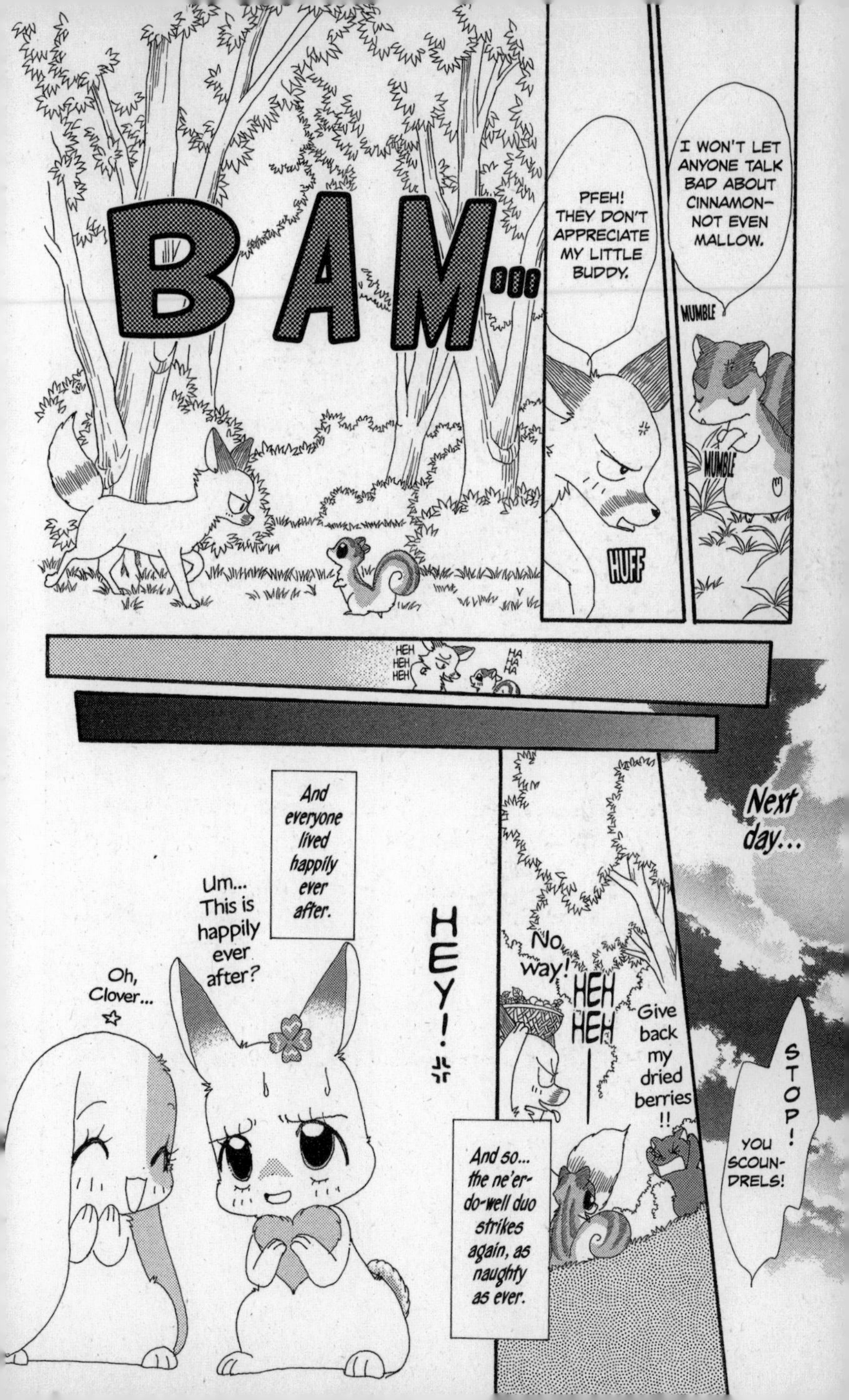
I WON'T LET ANYONE TALK BAD ABOUT CINNAMON—NOT EVEN MALLOW.
MUMBLE
MUMBLE
PFEH! THEY DON'T APPRECIATE MY LITTLE BUDDY.
HUFF
BAM...
HEH HEH HEH
HA HA HA
Next day...
STOP! YOU SCOUN-DRELS!
Give back my dried berries!!
HEH HEH
No way!
And so... the ne'er-do-well duo strikes again, as naughty as ever.
HEY!!
And everyone lived happily ever after.
Um... This is happily ever after?
Oh, Clover...

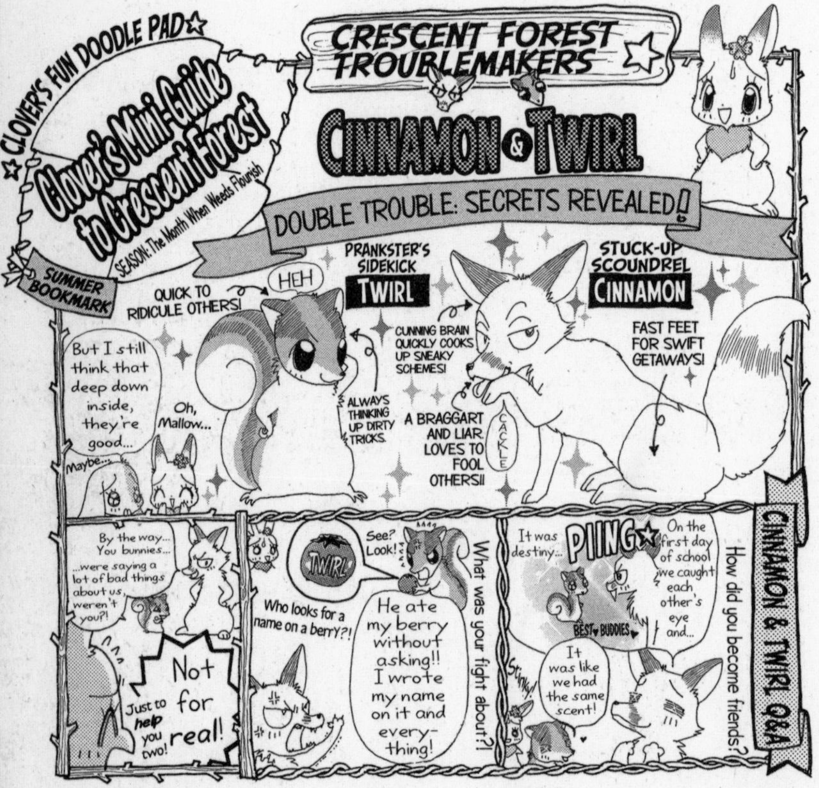

☆CLOVER'S FUN DOODLE PAD☆
Clover's Mini-Guide to Crescent Forest
SEASON: The Month When Weeds Flourish
SUMMER BOOKMARK
CRESCENT FOREST TROUBLEMAKERS
CINNAMON & TWIRL
DOUBLE TROUBLE: SECRETS REVEALED!
STUCK-UP SCOUNDREL CINNAMON
FAST FEET FOR SWIFT GETAWAYS!
CUNNING BRAIN QUICKLY COOKS UP SNEAKY SCHEMES!
A BRAGGART AND LIAR. LOVES TO FOOL OTHERS!!
CACKLE
PRANKSTER'S SIDEKICK TWIRL
HEH
QUICK TO RIDICULE OTHERS!
ALWAYS THINKING UP DIRTY TRICKS.
Oh, Mallow...
But I still think that deep down inside, they're good...
Maybe...
CINNAMON & TWIRL Q&A
How did you become friends?
On the first day of school we caught each other's eye and...
PIING☆
It was destiny...
BEST♥BUDDIES♥
It was like we had the same scent!
Stinky!
What was your fight about?!
See? Look!
TWIRL
He ate my berry without asking!! I wrote my name on it and every-thing!
Who looks for a name on a berry?!
By the way... You bunnies...
...were saying a lot of bad things about us, weren't you?!
Not for real!
Just to help you two!

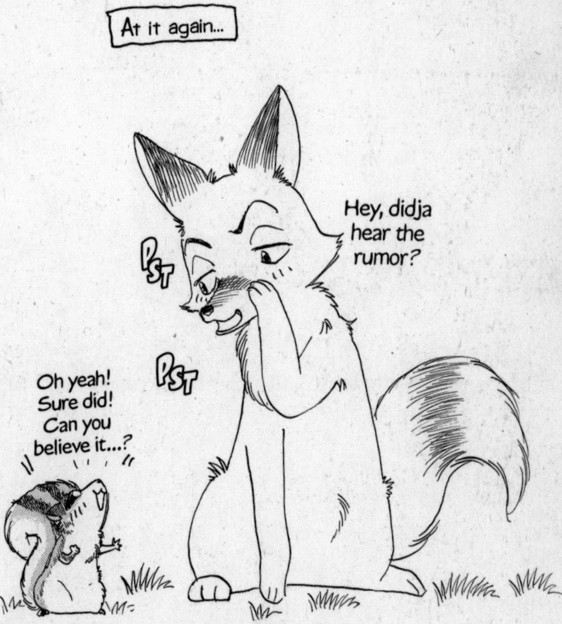
At it again...
Hey, didja hear the rumor?
PST
PST
Oh yeah! Sure did! Can you believe it...?

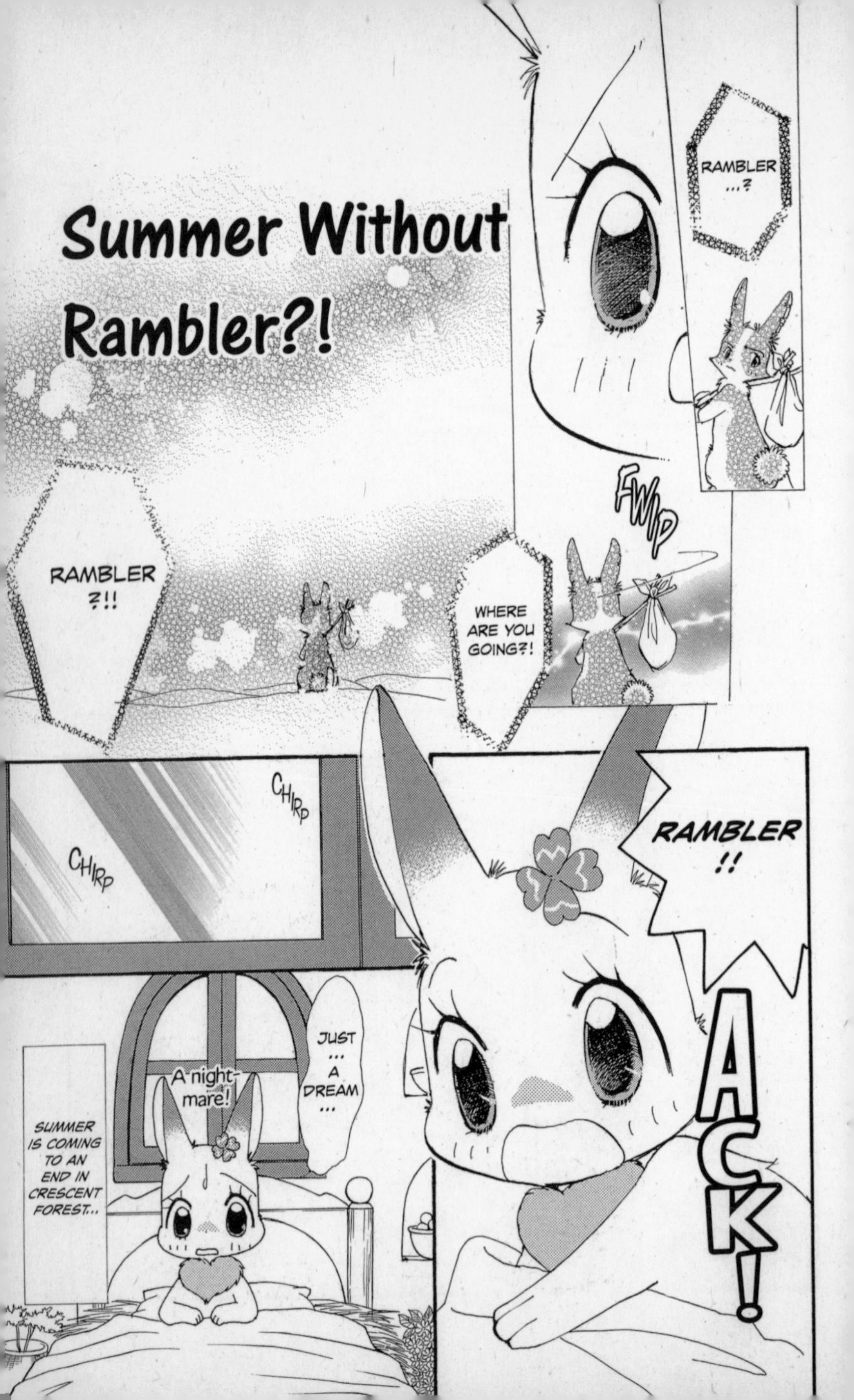
Summer Without Rambler?!
RAMBLER ...?
FWIP
WHERE ARE YOU GOING?!
RAMBLER ?!!
RAMBLER !!
ACK!
CHIRP
CHIRP
JUST ... A DREAM ...
A night-mare!
SUMMER IS COMING TO AN END IN CRESCENT FOREST...

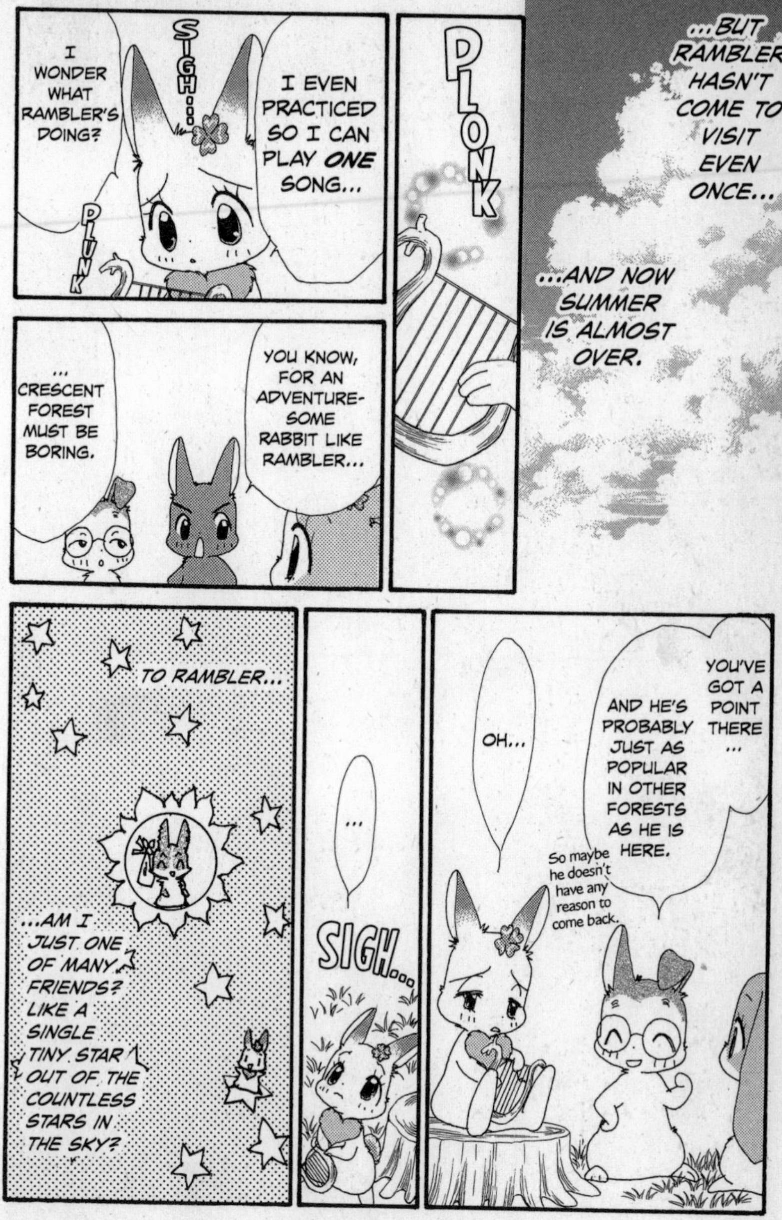
...BUT RAMBLER HASN'T COME TO VISIT EVEN ONCE...
...AND NOW SUMMER IS ALMOST OVER.
PLONK
I EVEN PRACTICED SO I CAN PLAY *ONE* SONG...
SIGH...
I WONDER WHAT RAMBLER'S DOING?
PLUNK
YOU KNOW, FOR AN ADVENTURE-SOME RABBIT LIKE RAMBLER...
...CRESCENT FOREST MUST BE BORING.
YOU'VE GOT A POINT THERE...
AND HE'S PROBABLY JUST AS POPULAR IN OTHER FORESTS AS HE IS HERE.
So maybe he doesn't have any reason to come back.
OH...
...
SIGH...
TO RAMBLER...
...AM I JUST ONE OF MANY FRIENDS? LIKE A SINGLE TINY STAR OUT OF THE COUNTLESS STARS IN THE SKY?

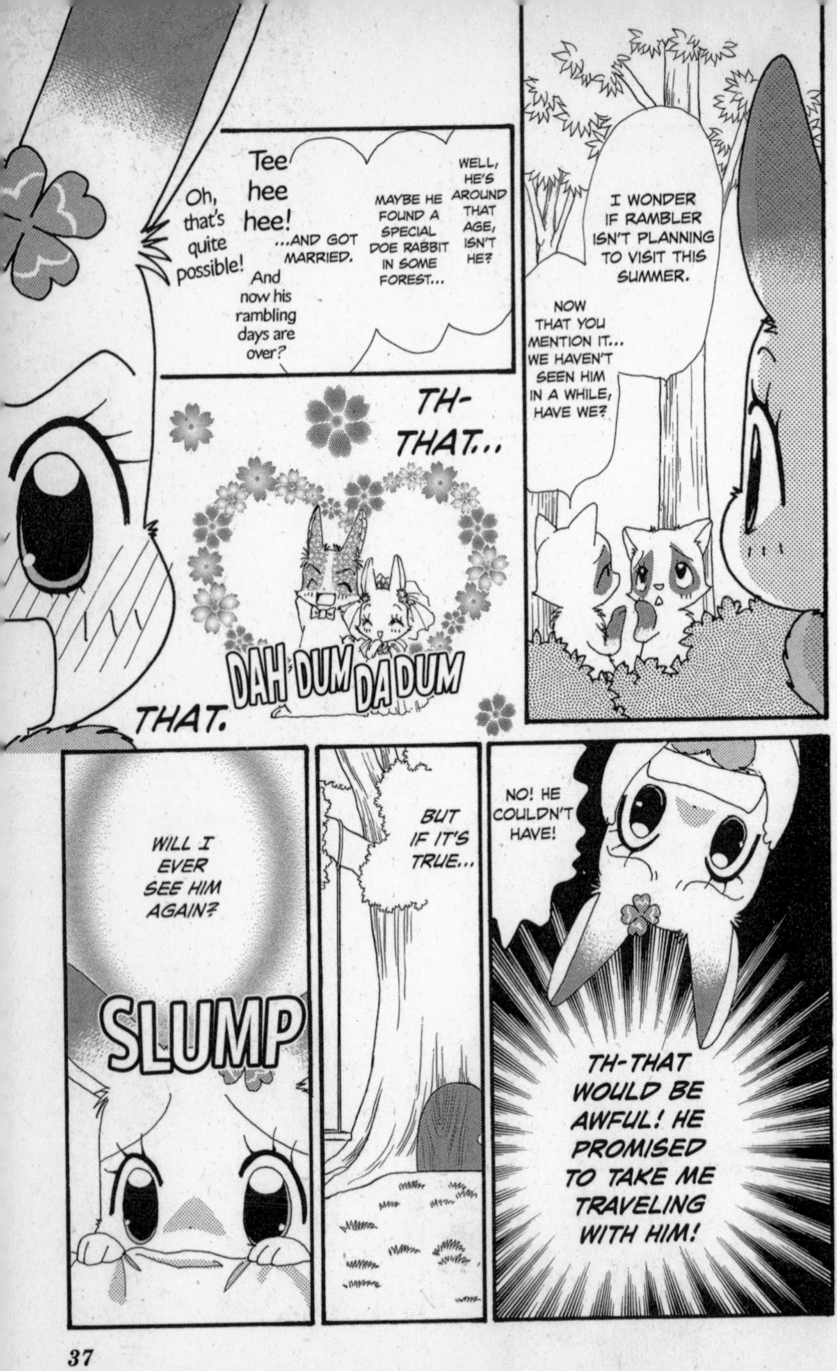
I WONDER IF RAMBLER ISN'T PLANNING TO VISIT THIS SUMMER.
NOW THAT YOU MENTION IT... WE HAVEN'T SEEN HIM IN A WHILE, HAVE WE?
WELL, HE'S AROUND THAT AGE, ISN'T HE?
MAYBE HE FOUND A SPECIAL DOE RABBIT IN SOME FOREST...
...AND GOT MARRIED.
Tee hee hee!
And now his rambling days are over?
Oh, that's quite possible!
TH-THAT...
DAH DUM DA DUM
THAT.
NO! HE COULDN'T HAVE!
TH-THAT WOULD BE AWFUL! HE PROMISED TO TAKE ME TRAVELING WITH HIM!
BUT IF IT'S TRUE...
WILL I EVER SEE HIM AGAIN?
SLUMP

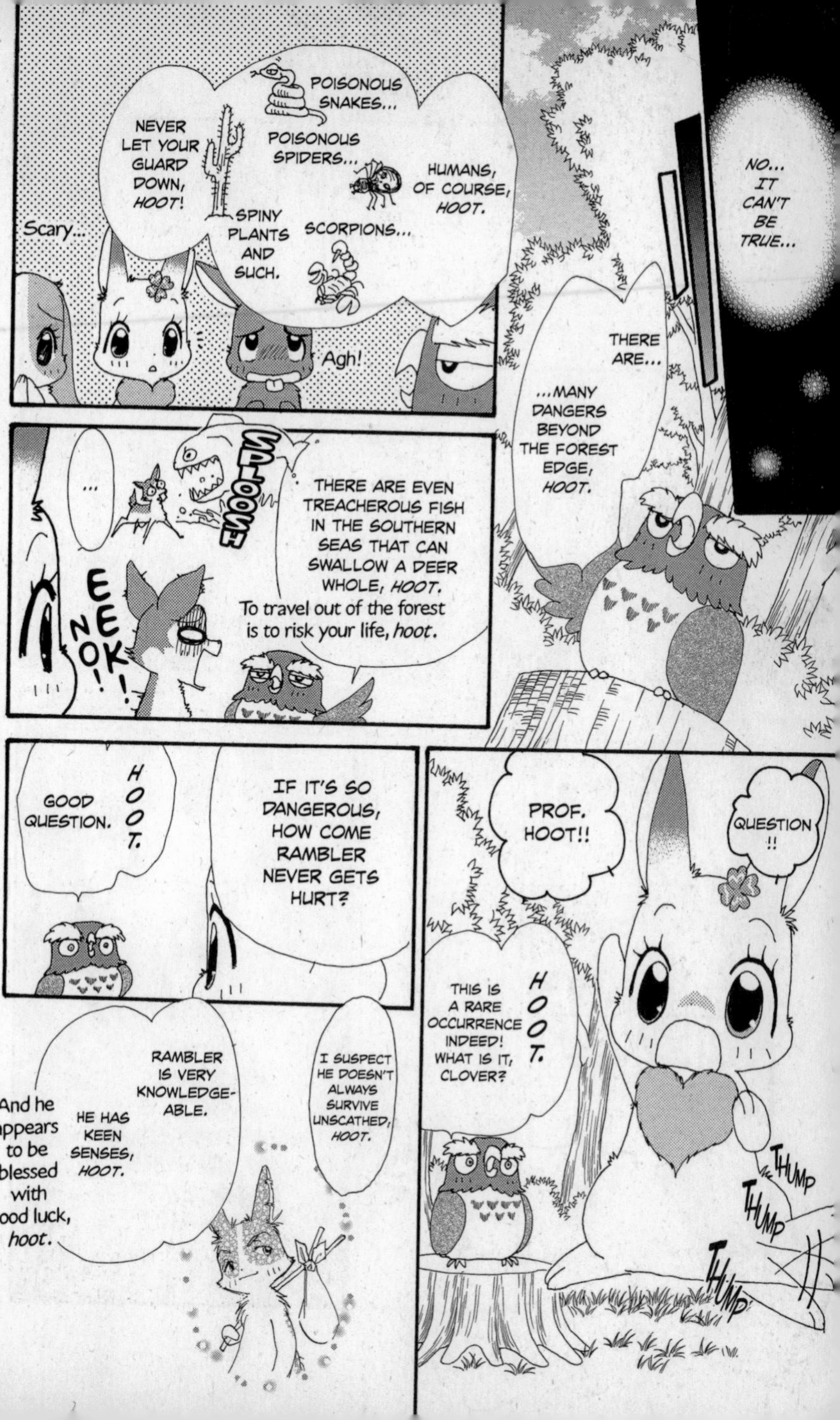
NO... IT CAN'T BE TRUE...
THERE ARE... ...MANY DANGERS BEYOND THE FOREST EDGE, HOOT.
NEVER LET YOUR GUARD DOWN, HOOT!
POISONOUS SNAKES...
POISONOUS SPIDERS...
SPINY PLANTS AND SUCH.
SCORPIONS...
HUMANS, OF COURSE, HOOT.
Agh!
Scary...
THERE ARE EVEN TREACHEROUS FISH IN THE SOUTHERN SEAS THAT CAN SWALLOW A DEER WHOLE, HOOT.
To travel out of the forest is to risk your life, hoot.
SPLOOSH
...
EEK NO!!
QUESTION!!
PROF. HOOT!!
THIS IS A RARE OCCURRENCE INDEED! WHAT IS IT, CLOVER?
HOOT.
THUMP
THUMP
THUMP
IF IT'S SO DANGEROUS, HOW COME RAMBLER NEVER GETS HURT?
GOOD QUESTION.
HOOT.
I SUSPECT HE DOESN'T ALWAYS SURVIVE UNSCATHED, HOOT.
RAMBLER IS VERY KNOWLEDGE-ABLE.
HE HAS KEEN SENSES, HOOT.
And he appears to be blessed with good luck, hoot.

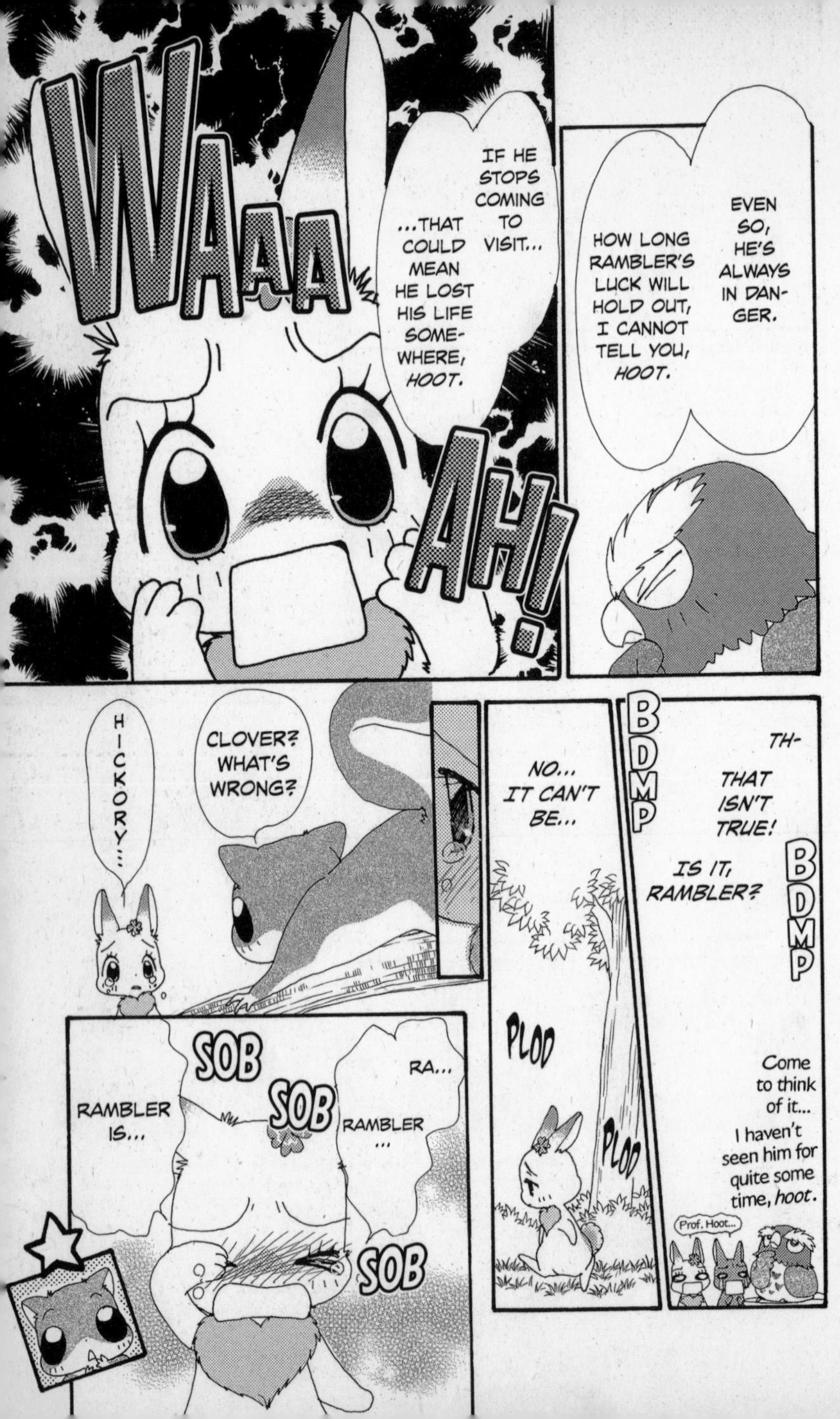
EVEN SO, HE'S ALWAYS IN DANGER.
HOW LONG RAMBLER'S LUCK WILL HOLD OUT, I CANNOT TELL YOU, *HOOT*.
IF HE STOPS COMING TO VISIT...
...THAT COULD MEAN HE LOST HIS LIFE SOMEWHERE, *HOOT*.
WAAAAH!
TH- THAT ISN'T TRUE!
BDMP
IS IT, RAMBLER?
BDMP
Come to think of it... I haven't seen him for quite some time, *hoot*.
Prof. Hoot...
NO... IT CAN'T BE...
PLOD
PLOD
CLOVER? WHAT'S WRONG?
HICKORY...
RA...
RAMBLER ...
SOB
SOB
RAMBLER IS...
SOB

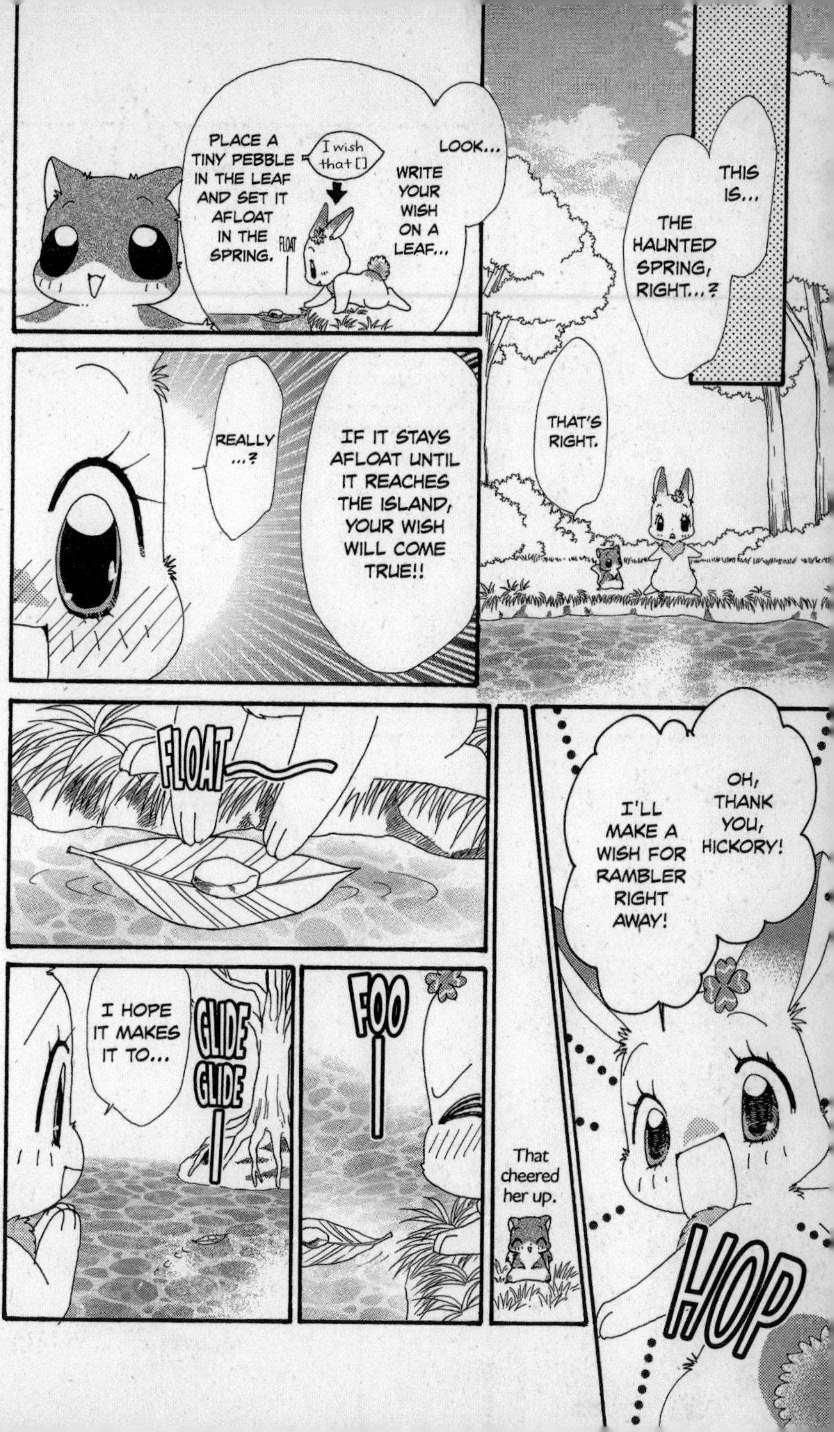
THIS IS...
THE HAUNTED SPRING, RIGHT...?
THAT'S RIGHT.
LOOK...
WRITE YOUR WISH ON A LEAF...
I wish that []
FLOAT
PLACE A TINY PEBBLE IN THE LEAF AND SET IT AFLOAT IN THE SPRING.
IF IT STAYS AFLOAT UNTIL IT REACHES THE ISLAND, YOUR WISH WILL COME TRUE!!
REALLY ...?
OH, THANK YOU, HICKORY!
I'LL MAKE A WISH FOR RAMBLER RIGHT AWAY!
HOP
That cheered her up.
FLOAT
FOO I
GLIDE GLIDE I
I HOPE IT MAKES IT TO...

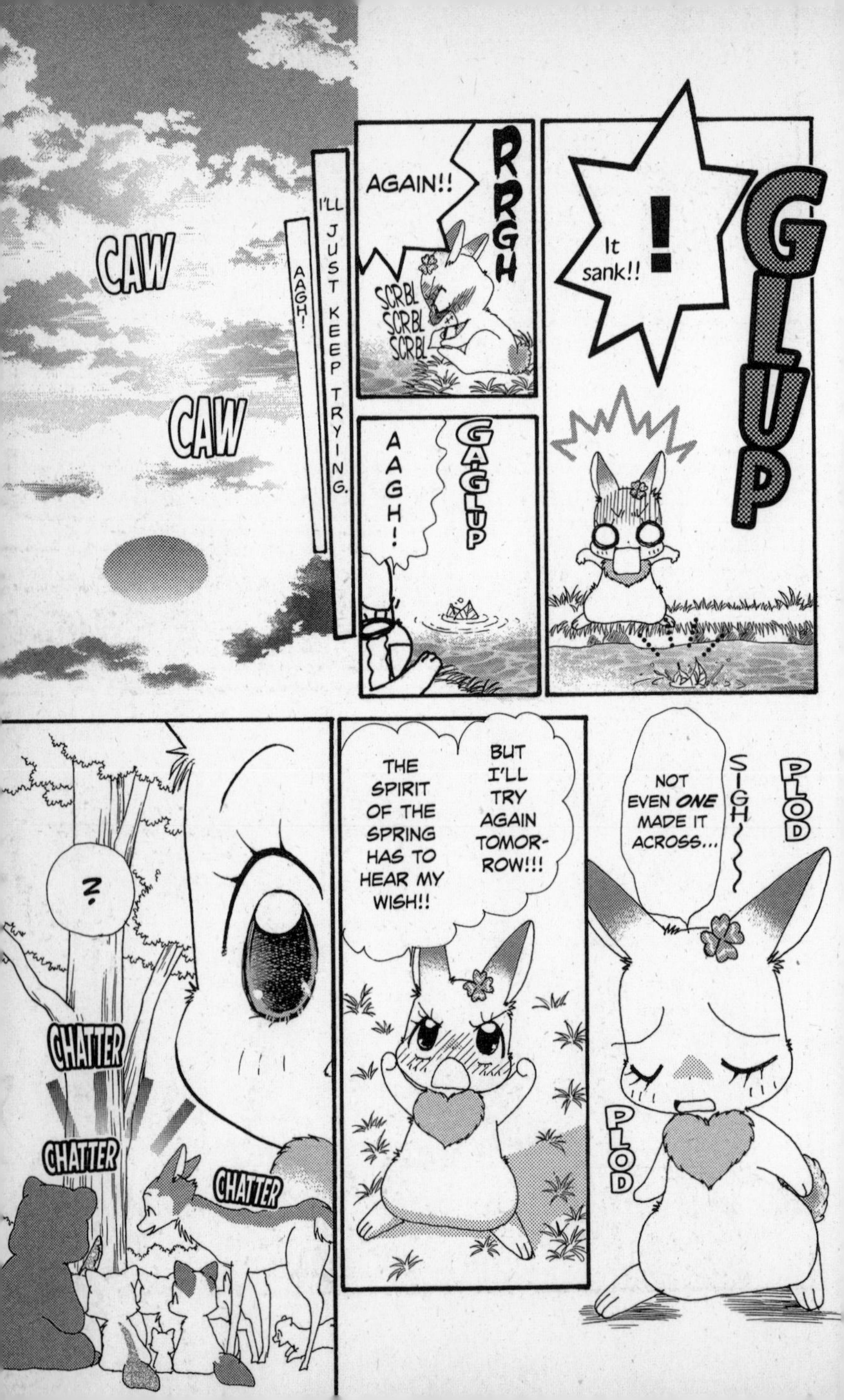
GLUP
!
It sank!!
RRGH
AGAIN!!
SCRBL SCRBL SCRBL
GAGLUP
AAGH!
I'LL JUST KEEP TRYING.
AAGH!
CAW
CAW
PLOD
SIGH
NOT EVEN ONE MADE IT ACROSS...
PLOD
BUT I'LL TRY AGAIN TOMORROW!!!
THE SPIRIT OF THE SPRING HAS TO HEAR MY WISH!!
?
CHATTER
CHATTER
CHATTER

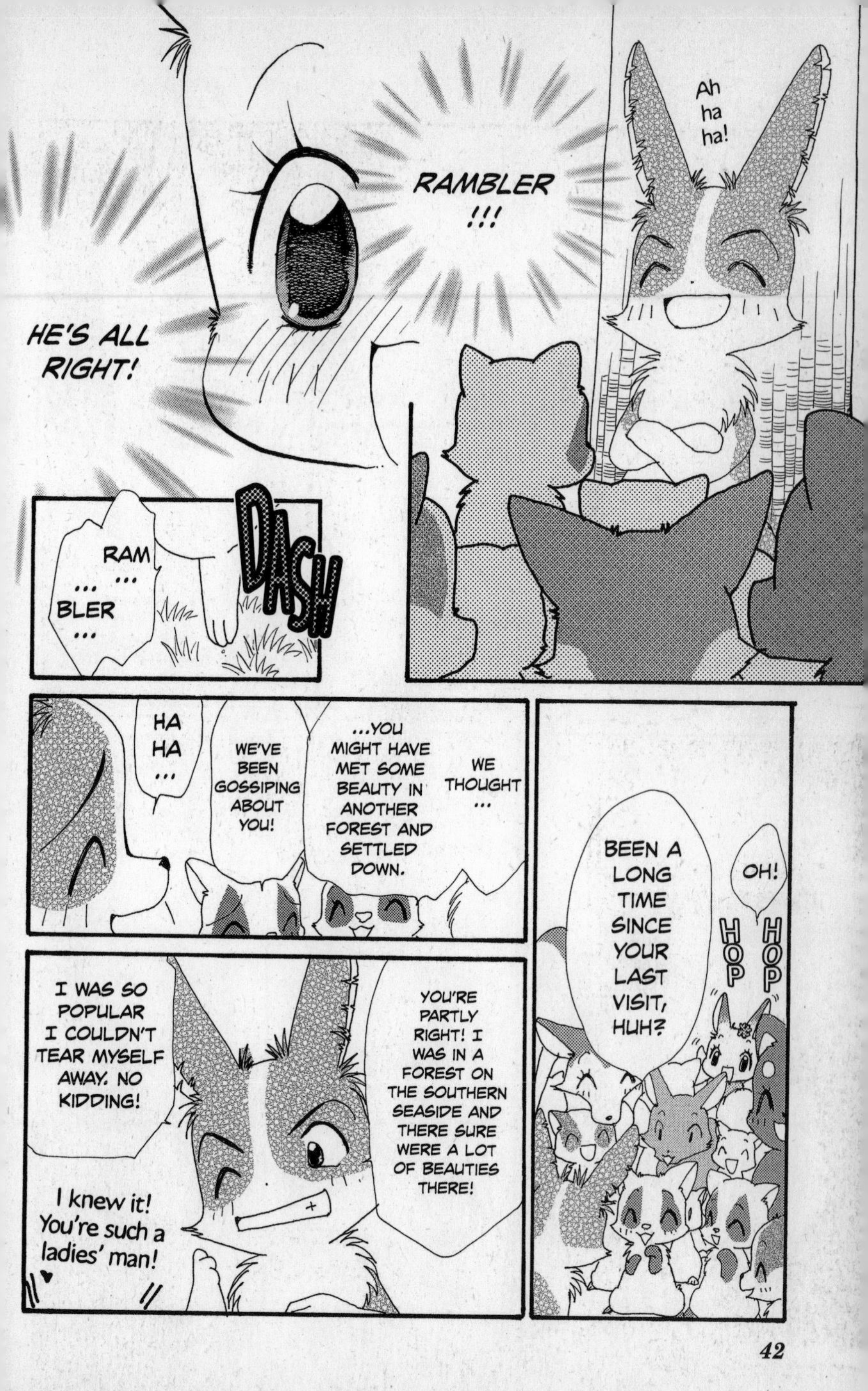
Ah ha ha!
RAMBLER !!!
HE'S ALL RIGHT!
RAM ... ... BLER ...
DASH
OH!
BEEN A LONG TIME SINCE YOUR LAST VISIT, HUH?
HOP HOP
WE THOUGHT ...
...YOU MIGHT HAVE MET SOME BEAUTY IN ANOTHER FOREST AND SETTLED DOWN.
WE'VE BEEN GOSSIPING ABOUT YOU!
HA HA ...
YOU'RE PARTLY RIGHT! I WAS IN A FOREST ON THE SOUTHERN SEASIDE AND THERE SURE WERE A LOT OF BEAUTIES THERE!
I WAS SO POPULAR I COULDN'T TEAR MYSELF AWAY. NO KIDDING!
I knew it! You're such a ladies' man!

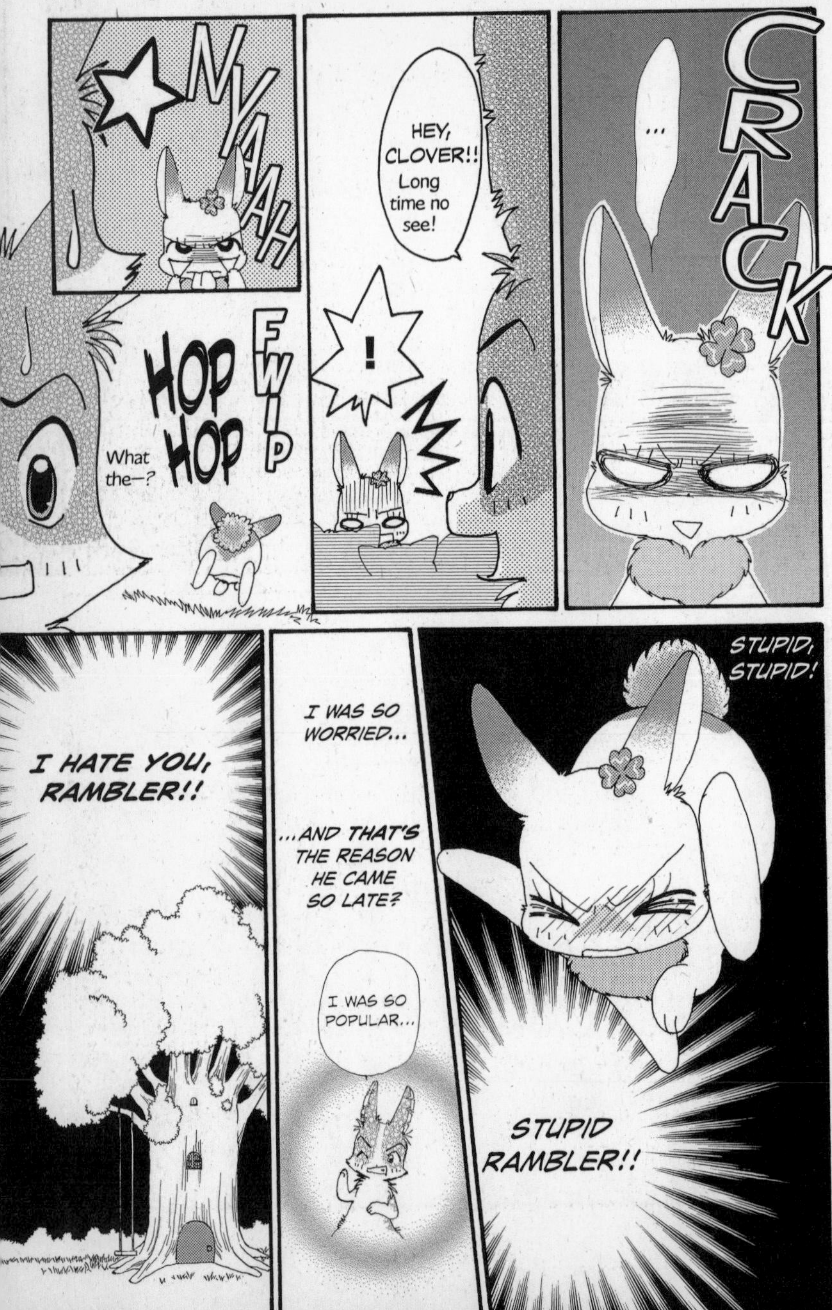
...
CRACK
HEY, CLOVER!! Long time no see!
!
NYAAH
FWIP
HOP HOP
What the—?
STUPID, STUPID!
STUPID RAMBLER!!
I WAS SO WORRIED...
...AND THAT'S THE REASON HE CAME SO LATE?
I WAS SO POPULAR...
I HATE YOU, RAMBLER!!

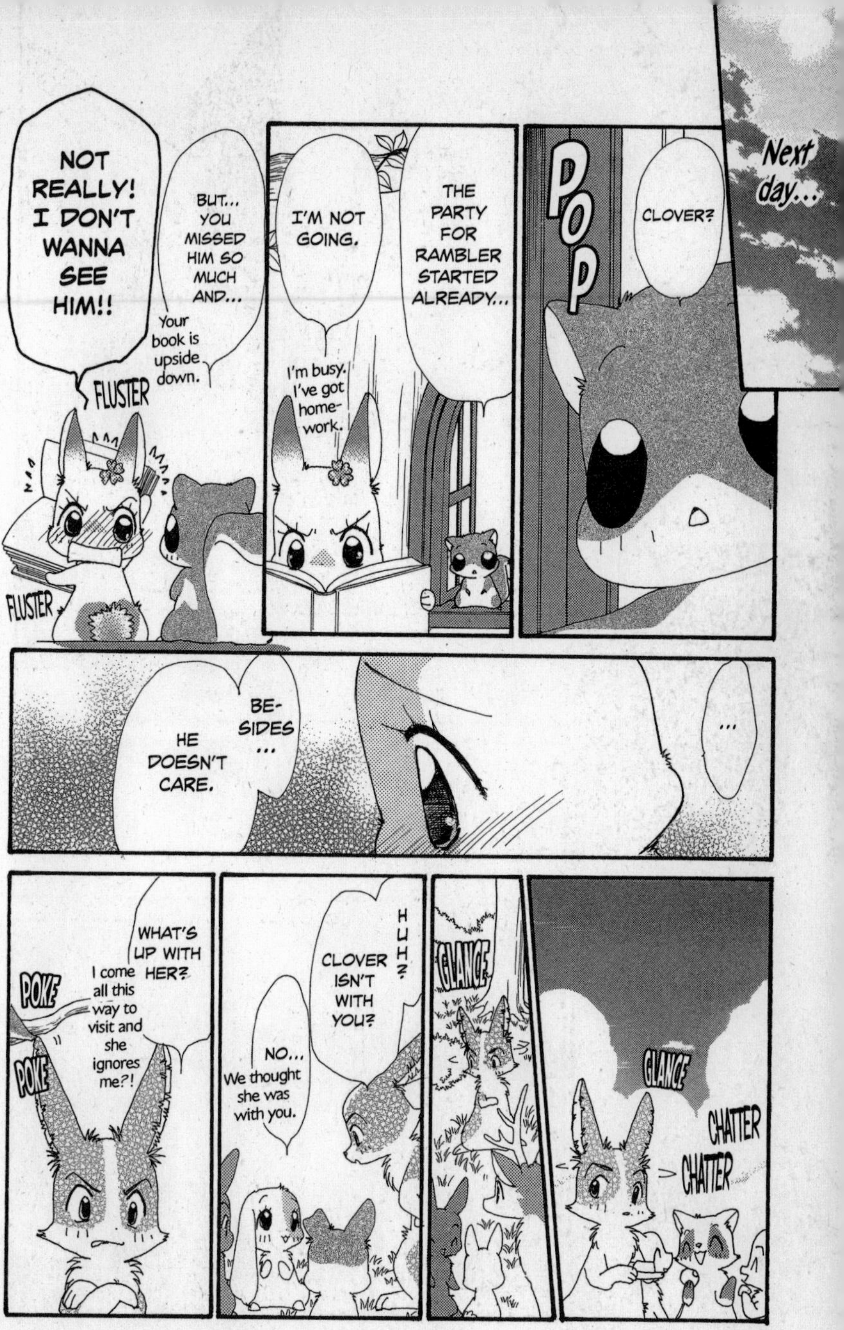
Next day...
POP
POP
CLOVER?
THE PARTY FOR RAMBLER STARTED ALREADY...
I'M NOT GOING.
I'm busy. I've got home-work.
BUT... YOU MISSED HIM SO MUCH AND...
Your book is upside down.
NOT REALLY! I DON'T WANNA SEE HIM!!
FLUSTER
FLUSTER
...
BE-SIDES...
HE DOESN'T CARE.
CHATTER
CHATTER
GLANCE
GLANCE
HUH?
CLOVER ISN'T WITH YOU?
NO...
We thought she was with you.
WHAT'S UP WITH HER?
I come all this way to visit and she ignores me?!
POKE
POKE

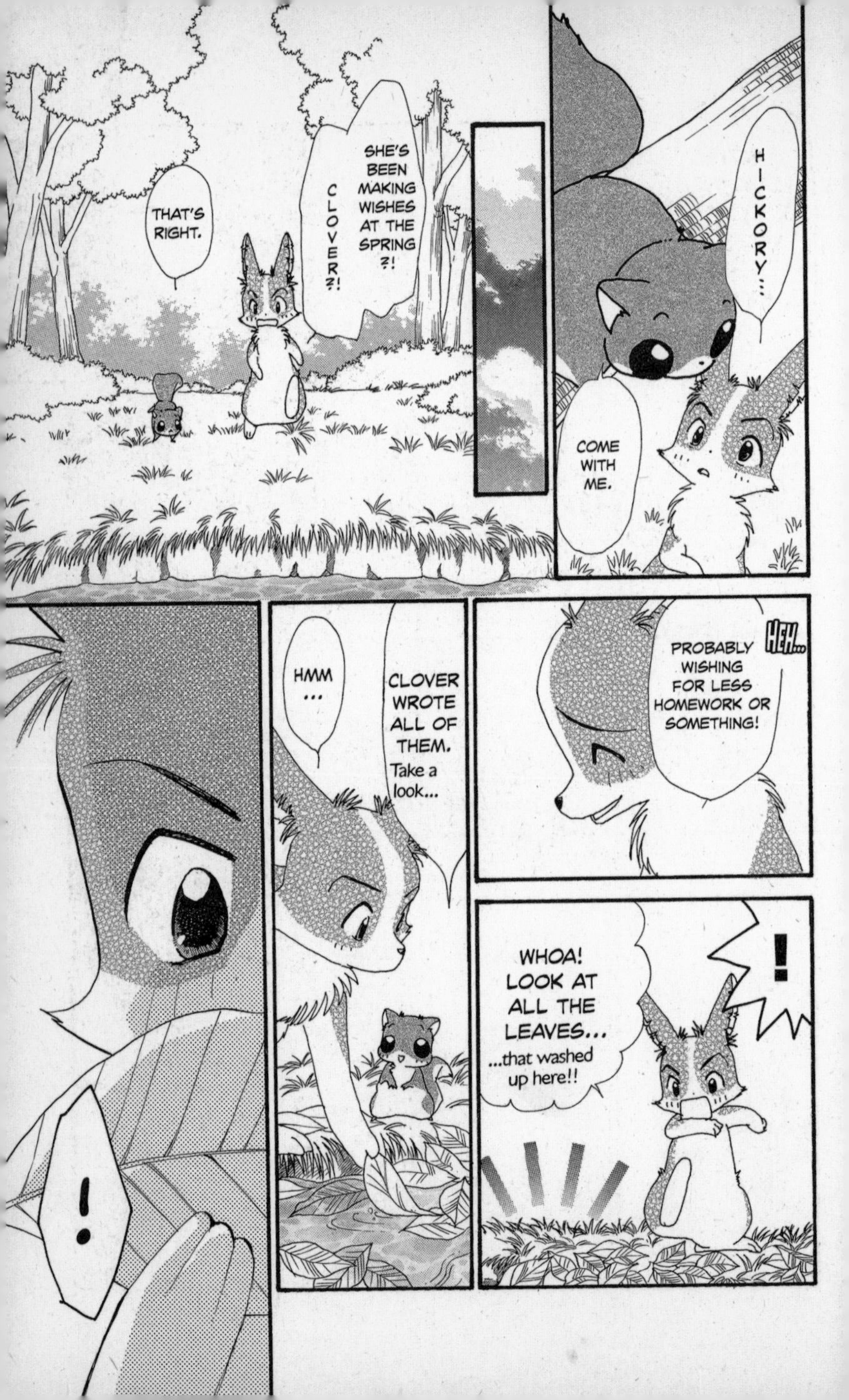
HICKORY...
COME WITH ME.
SHE'S BEEN MAKING WISHES AT THE SPRING?!
CLOVER?!
THAT'S RIGHT.
HEH...
PROBABLY WISHING FOR LESS HOMEWORK OR SOMETHING!
!
WHOA! LOOK AT ALL THE LEAVES...
...that washed up here!!
CLOVER WROTE ALL OF THEM.
Take a look...
HMM ...
!

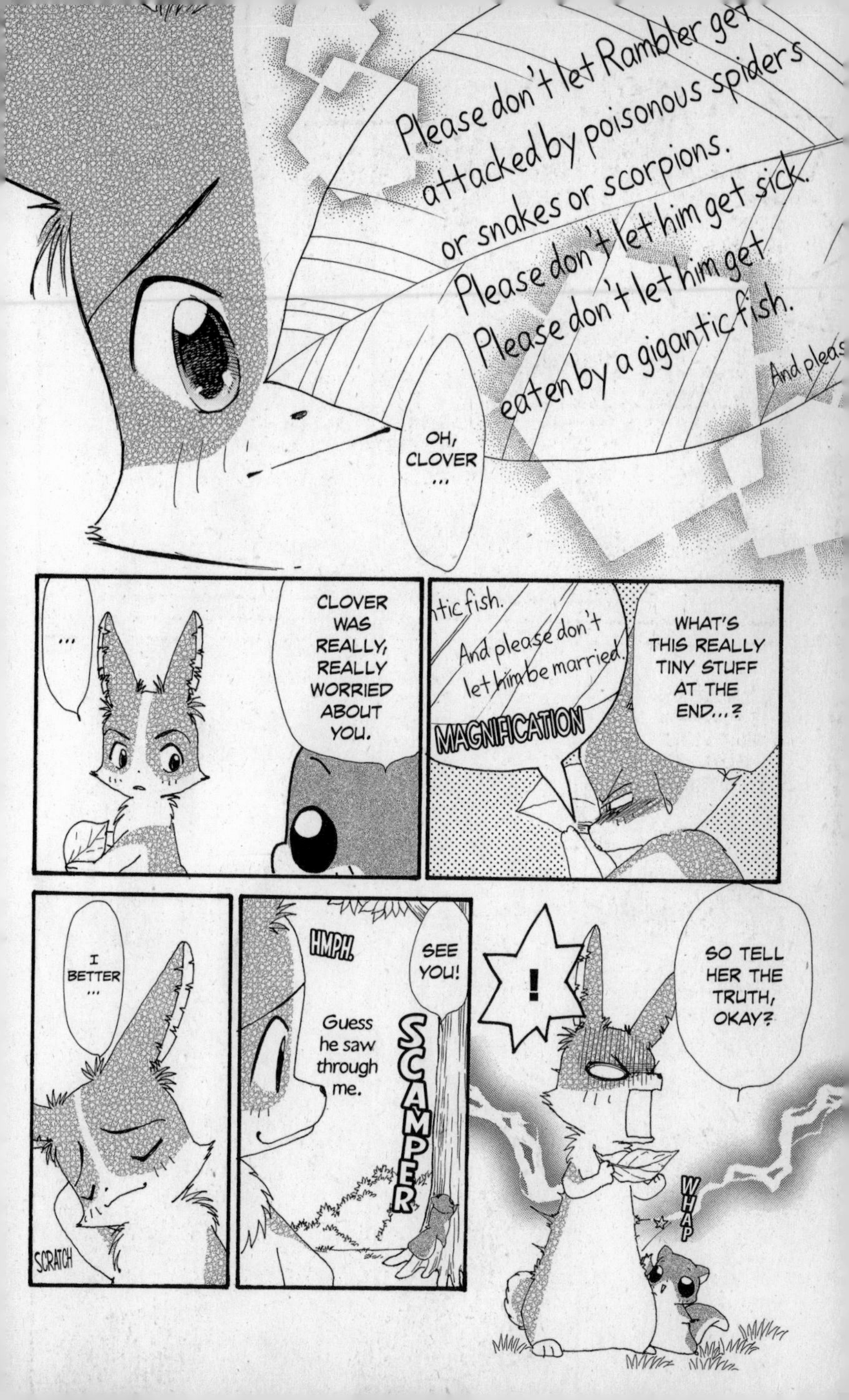
Please don't let Rambler get attacked by poisonous spiders or snakes or scorpions.
Please don't let him get sick.
Please don't let him get eaten by a gigantic fish.
And pleas
OH, CLOVER ...
ntic fish.
And please don't let him be married.
WHAT'S THIS REALLY TINY STUFF AT THE END...?
MAGNIFICATION
CLOVER WAS REALLY, REALLY WORRIED ABOUT YOU.
...
SO TELL HER THE TRUTH, OKAY?
!
WHAP
SEE YOU!
HMPH.
Guess he saw through me.
SCAMPER
I BETTER ...
SCRATCH

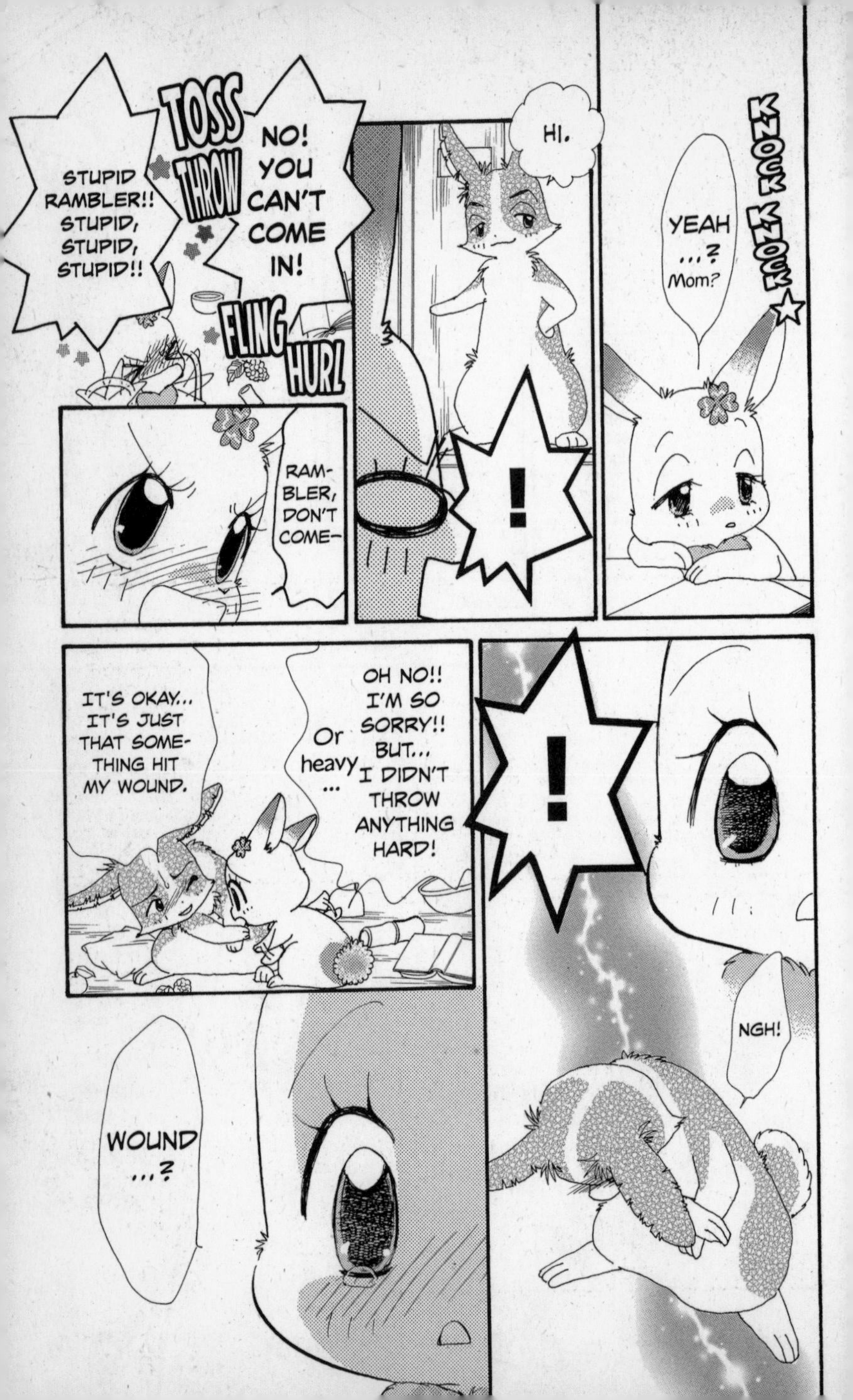
KNOCK KNOCK☆
YEAH ...? Mom?
HI.
!
NO! YOU CAN'T COME IN!
TOSS
THROW
STUPID RAMBLER!! STUPID, STUPID, STUPID!!
FLING
HURL
RAM-BLER, DON'T COME-
!
NGH!
OH NO!! I'M SO SORRY!! BUT... I DIDN'T THROW ANYTHING HARD!
Or heavy ...
IT'S OKAY... IT'S JUST THAT SOME-THING HIT MY WOUND.
WOUND ...?

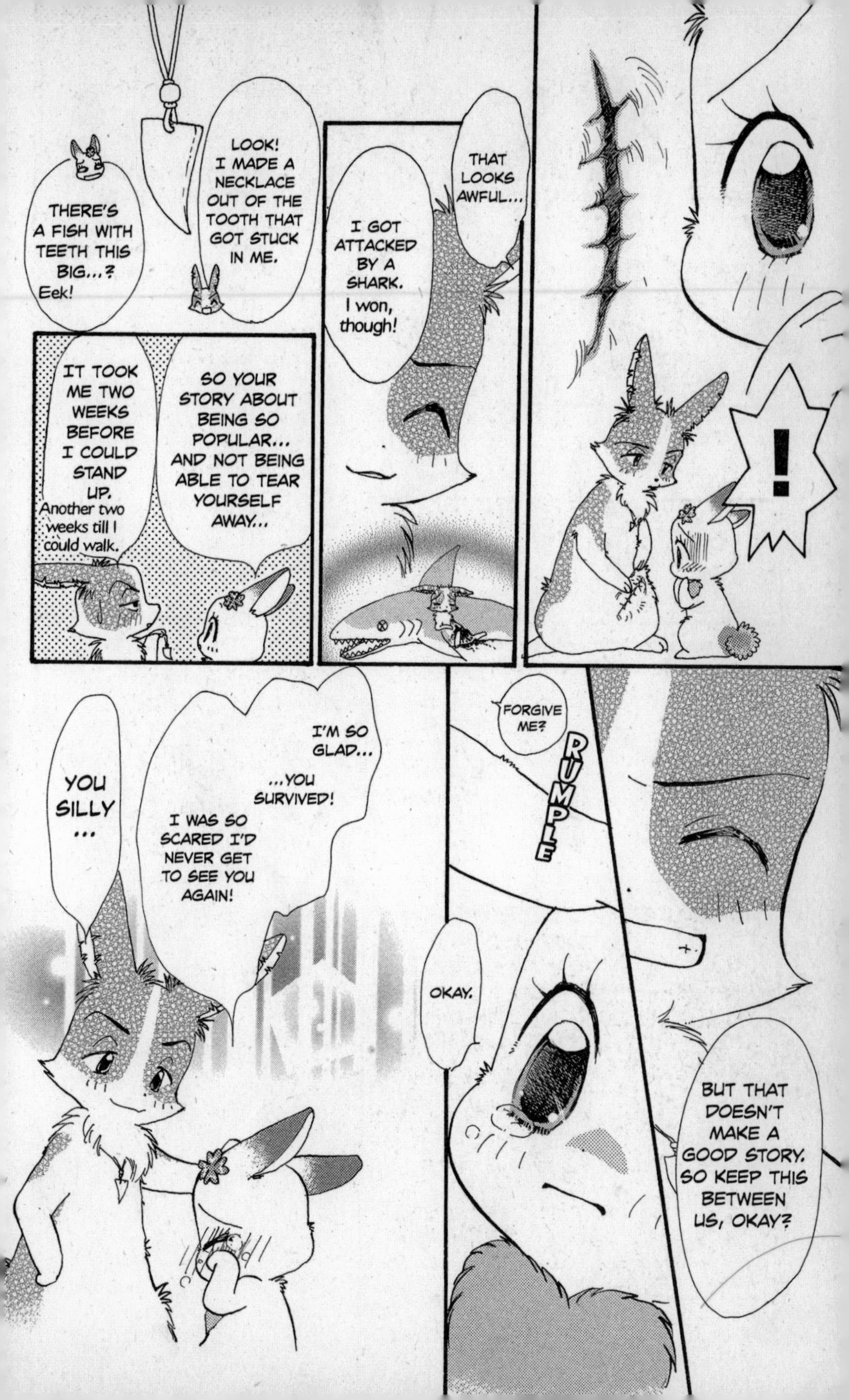
!
THAT LOOKS AWFUL...
I GOT ATTACKED BY A SHARK. I won, though!
LOOK! I MADE A NECKLACE OUT OF THE TOOTH THAT GOT STUCK IN ME.
THERE'S A FISH WITH TEETH THIS BIG...? Eek!
SO YOUR STORY ABOUT BEING SO POPULAR... AND NOT BEING ABLE TO TEAR YOURSELF AWAY...
IT TOOK ME TWO WEEKS BEFORE I COULD STAND UP. Another two weeks till I could walk.
FORGIVE ME?
RUMPLE
BUT THAT DOESN'T MAKE A GOOD STORY. SO KEEP THIS BETWEEN US, OKAY?
OKAY.
I'M SO GLAD... ...YOU SURVIVED! I WAS SO SCARED I'D NEVER GET TO SEE YOU AGAIN!
YOU SILLY...

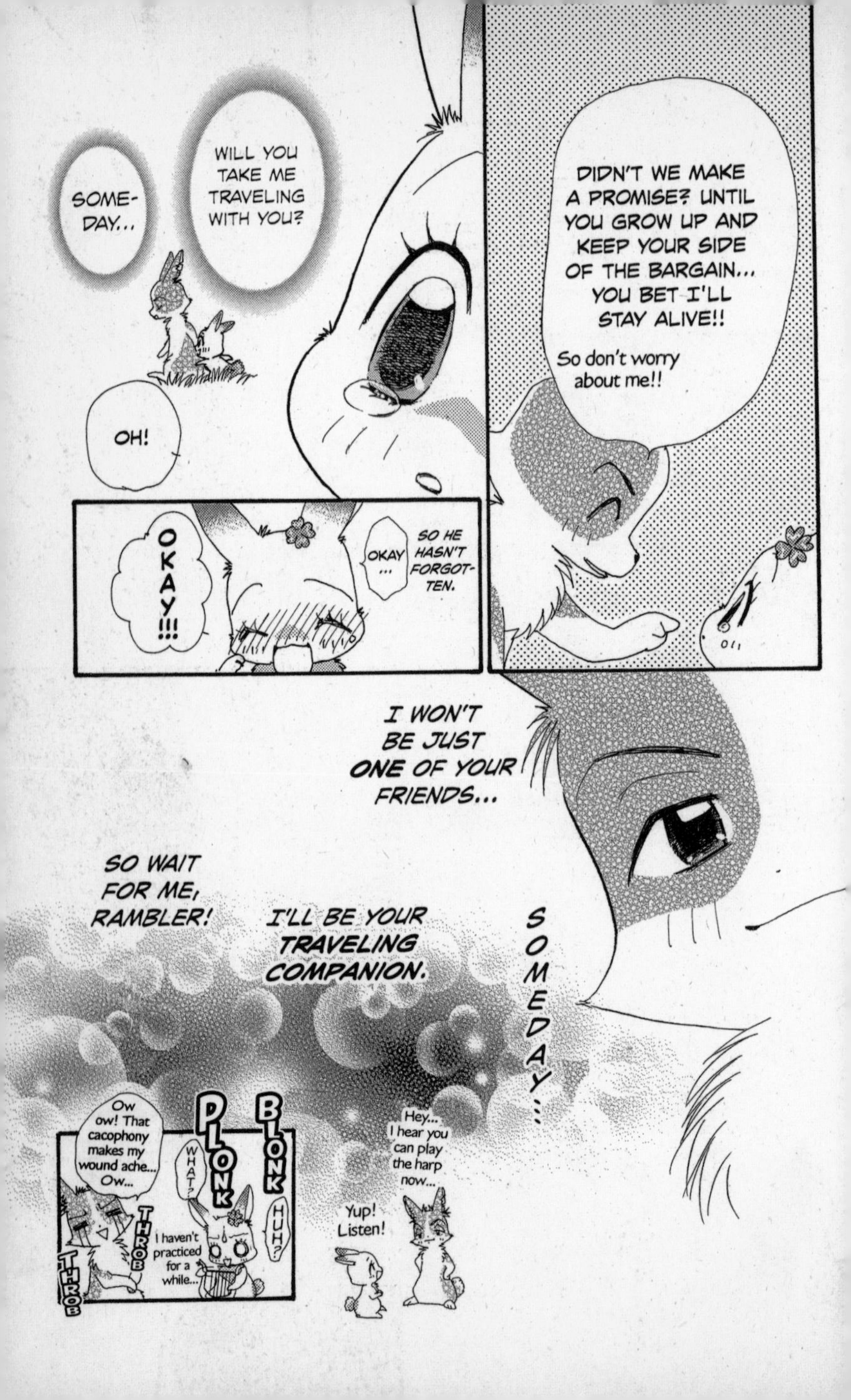
DIDN'T WE MAKE A PROMISE? UNTIL YOU GROW UP AND KEEP YOUR SIDE OF THE BARGAIN... YOU BET I'LL STAY ALIVE!!
So don't worry about me!!
WILL YOU TAKE ME TRAVELING WITH YOU?
SOME-DAY...
OH!
SO HE HASN'T FORGOT-TEN.
OKAY...
OKAY!!!
I WON'T BE JUST ONE OF YOUR FRIENDS...
SOMEDAY...
I'LL BE YOUR TRAVELING COMPANION.
SO WAIT FOR ME, RAMBLER!
Hey... I hear you can play the harp now...
Yup! Listen!
BLONK
HUH?
PLONK
WHAT?
I haven't practiced for a while...
Ow ow! That cacophony makes my wound ache... Ow...
THROB
THROB

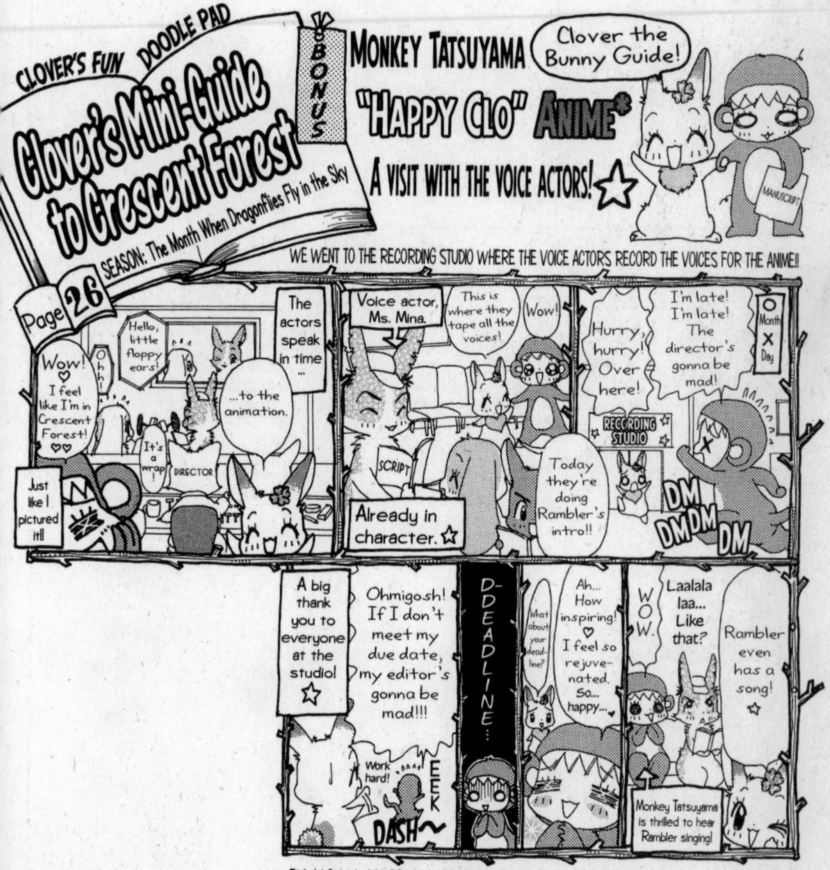
CLOVER'S FUN DOODLE PAD
Clover's Mini-Guide to Crescent Forest
SEASON: The Month When Dragonflies Fly in the Sky
Page 26
BONUS
MONKEY TATSUYAMA
"HAPPY CLO" ANIME*
A VISIT WITH THE VOICE ACTORS!
Clover the Bunny Guide!
MANUSCRIPT
WE WENT TO THE RECORDING STUDIO WHERE THE VOICE ACTORS RECORD THE VOICES FOR THE ANIME!!
O Month X Day
I'm late! I'm late! The director's gonna be mad!
Hurry, hurry! Over here!
RECORDING STUDIO
Today they're doing Rambler's intro!!
DM DM DM DM
Wow!
This is where they tape all the voices!
Voice actor, Ms. Mina.
SCRIPT
Already in character.
The actors speak in time ...
...to the animation.
Hello, little floppy ears!
Ohh!
Wow! I feel like I'm in Crescent Forest!
It's a wrap!
DIRECTOR
Just like I pictured it!!
Rambler even has a song!
Laalala laa... Like that?
WOW.
Monkey Tatsuyama is thrilled to hear Rambler singing!
Ah... How inspiring! I feel so rejuvenated. So... happy...
What about your dead-line?
D-DEADLINE...
Ohmigosh! If I don't meet my due date, my editor's gonna be mad!!!
Work hard!
EEK
DASH~
A big thank you to everyone at the studio!

• IN JAPAN, *HAPPY HAPPY CLOVER* HAS BEEN TURNED INTO AN ANIME!

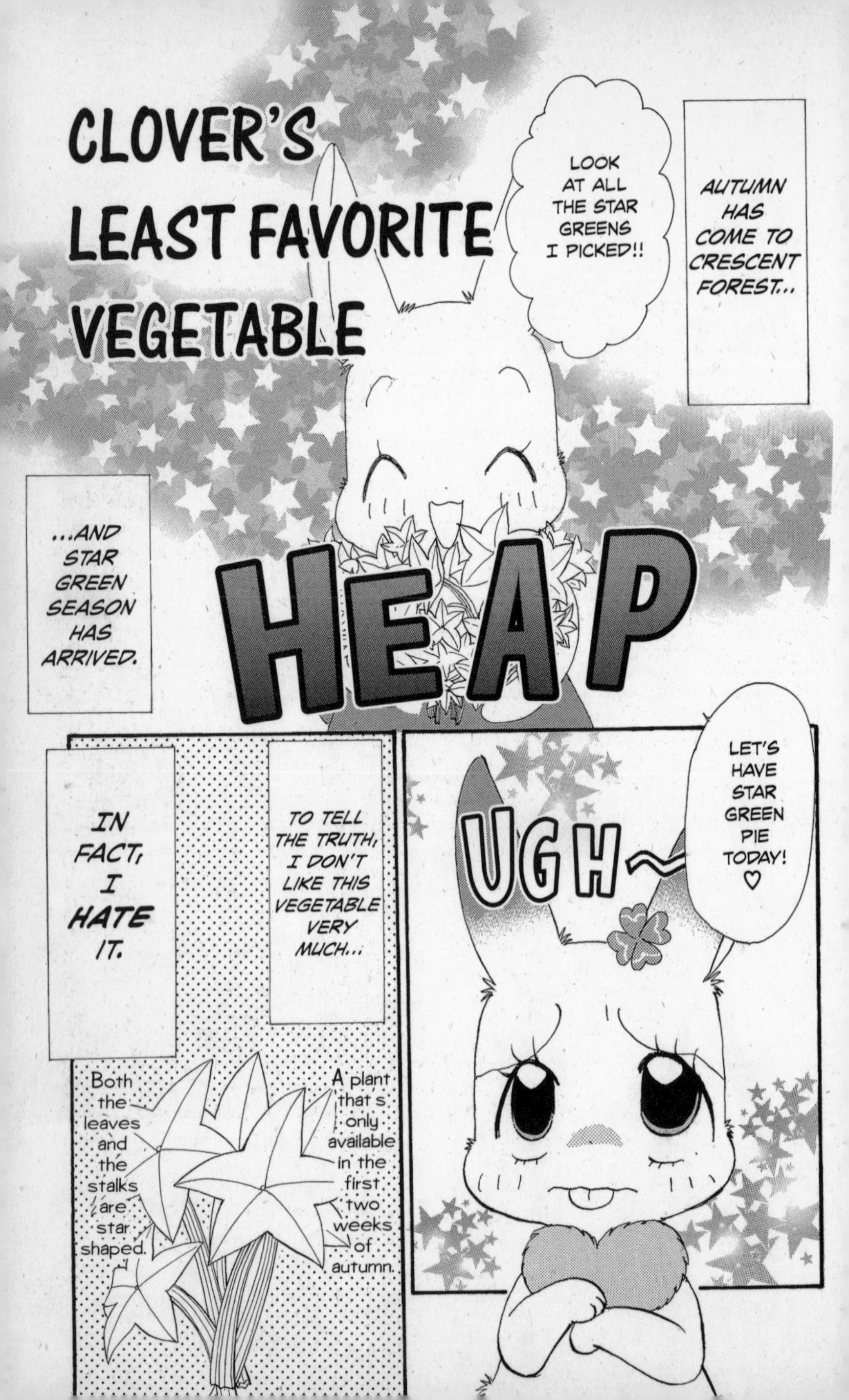
CLOVER'S LEAST FAVORITE VEGETABLE
AUTUMN HAS COME TO CRESCENT FOREST...
LOOK AT ALL THE STAR GREENS I PICKED!!
...AND STAR GREEN SEASON HAS ARRIVED.
HEAP
LET'S HAVE STAR GREEN PIE TODAY! ♡
UGH~
TO TELL THE TRUTH, I DON'T LIKE THIS VEGETABLE VERY MUCH...
IN FACT, I HATE IT.
A plant that s only available in the first two weeks of autumn.
Both the leaves and the stalks are star shaped.

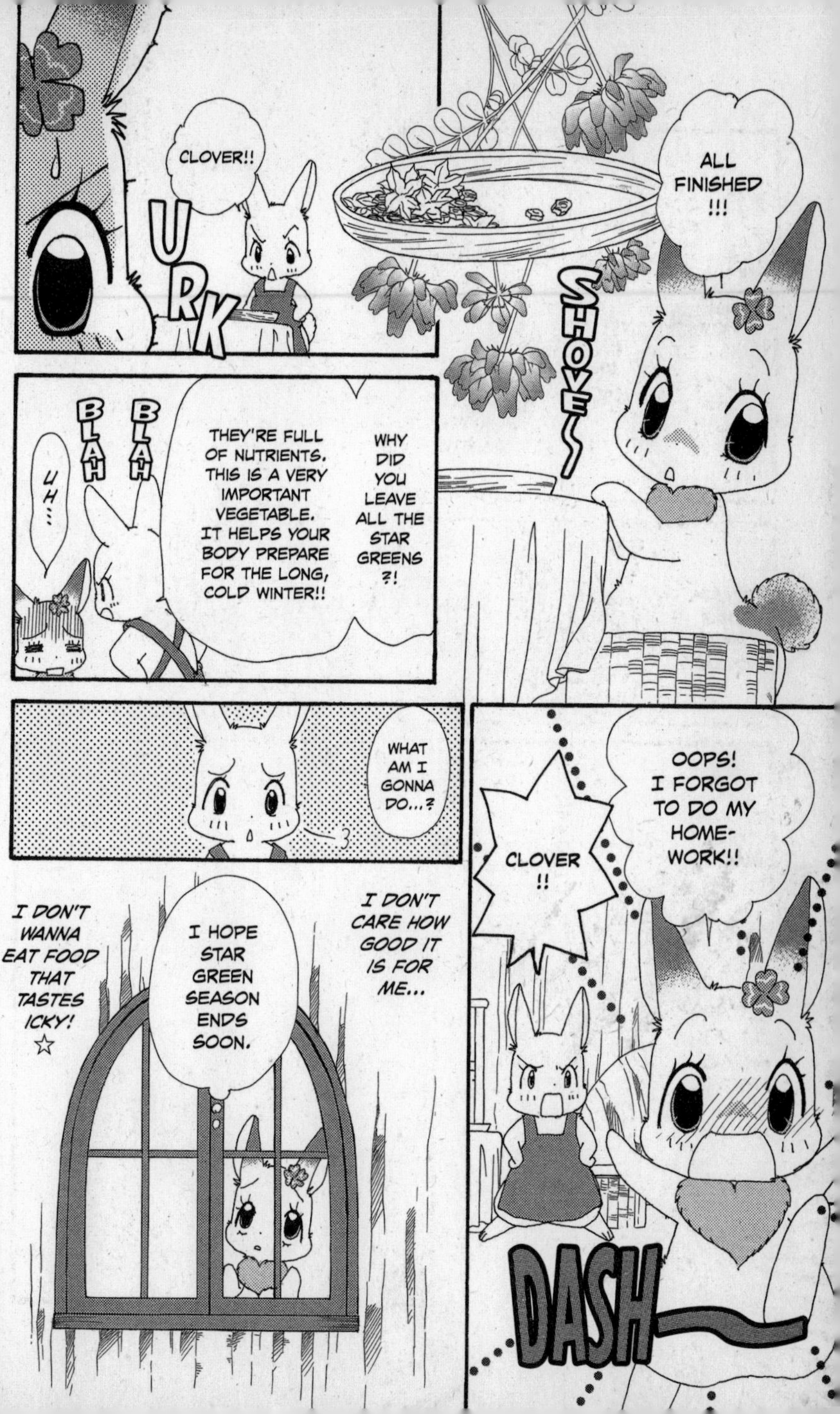
ALL FINISHED!!!
SHOVE
CLOVER!!
URK
WHY DID YOU LEAVE ALL THE STAR GREENS?!
THEY'RE FULL OF NUTRIENTS. THIS IS A VERY IMPORTANT VEGETABLE. IT HELPS YOUR BODY PREPARE FOR THE LONG, COLD WINTER!!
BLAH
BLAH
UH...
OOPS! I FORGOT TO DO MY HOME-WORK!!
CLOVER!!
DASH
WHAT AM I GONNA DO...?
I DON'T CARE HOW GOOD IT IS FOR ME...
I HOPE STAR GREEN SEASON ENDS SOON.
I DON'T WANNA EAT FOOD THAT TASTES ICKY! ☆

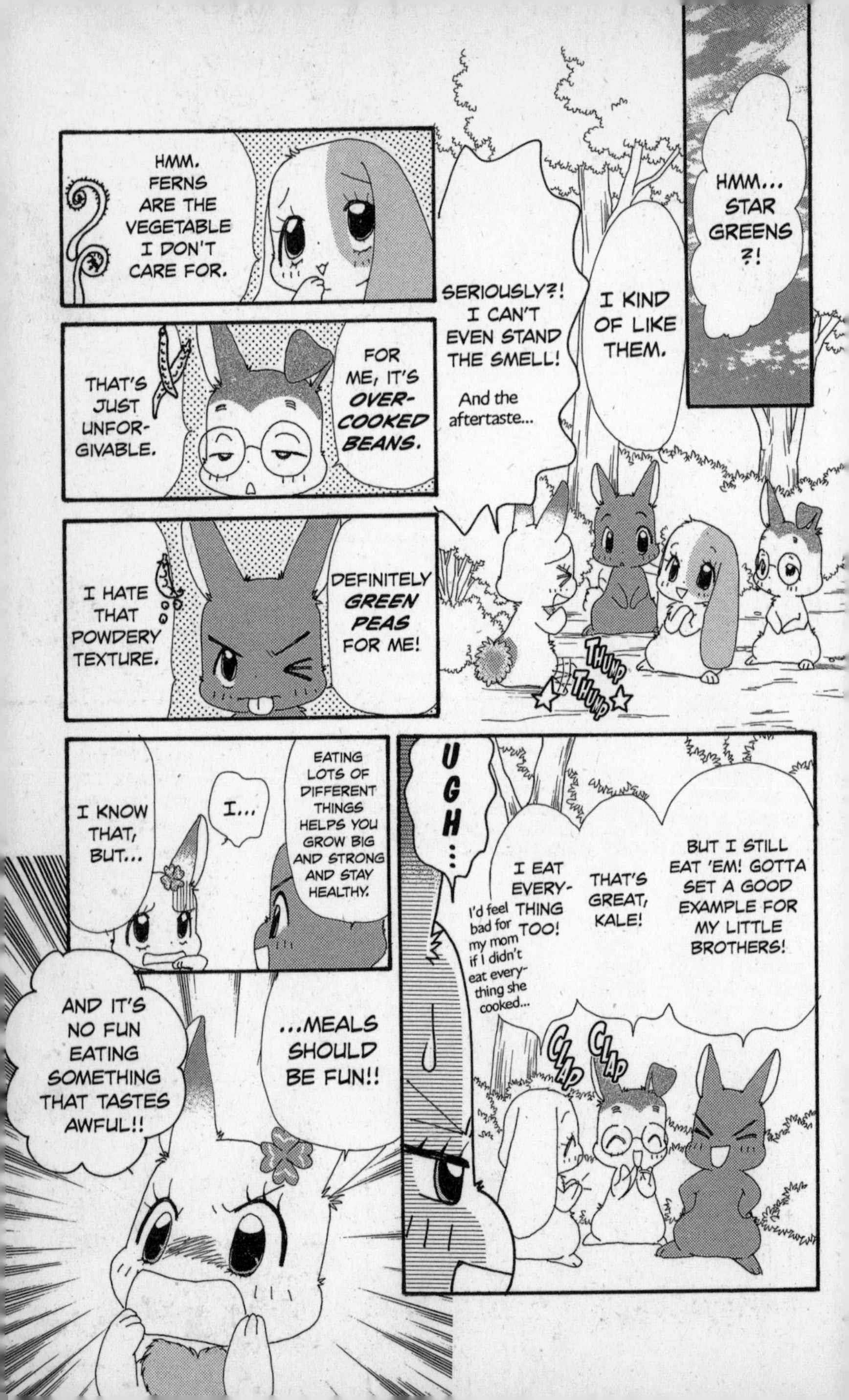
HMM... STAR GREENS?!
I KIND OF LIKE THEM.
SERIOUSLY?! I CAN'T EVEN STAND THE SMELL!
And the aftertaste...
THUMP THUMP
HMM. FERNS ARE THE VEGETABLE I DON'T CARE FOR.
FOR ME, IT'S *OVERCOOKED BEANS.*
THAT'S JUST UNFORGIVABLE.
DEFINITELY *GREEN PEAS* FOR ME!
I HATE THAT POWDERY TEXTURE.
BUT I STILL EAT 'EM! GOTTA SET A GOOD EXAMPLE FOR MY LITTLE BROTHERS!
THAT'S GREAT, KALE!
I EAT EVERYTHING TOO!
I'd feel bad for my mom if I didn't eat everything she cooked...
UGH...
CLAP CLAP
EATING LOTS OF DIFFERENT THINGS HELPS YOU GROW BIG AND STRONG AND STAY HEALTHY.
I...
I KNOW THAT, BUT...
...MEALS SHOULD BE FUN!!
AND IT'S NO FUN EATING SOMETHING THAT TASTES AWFUL!!

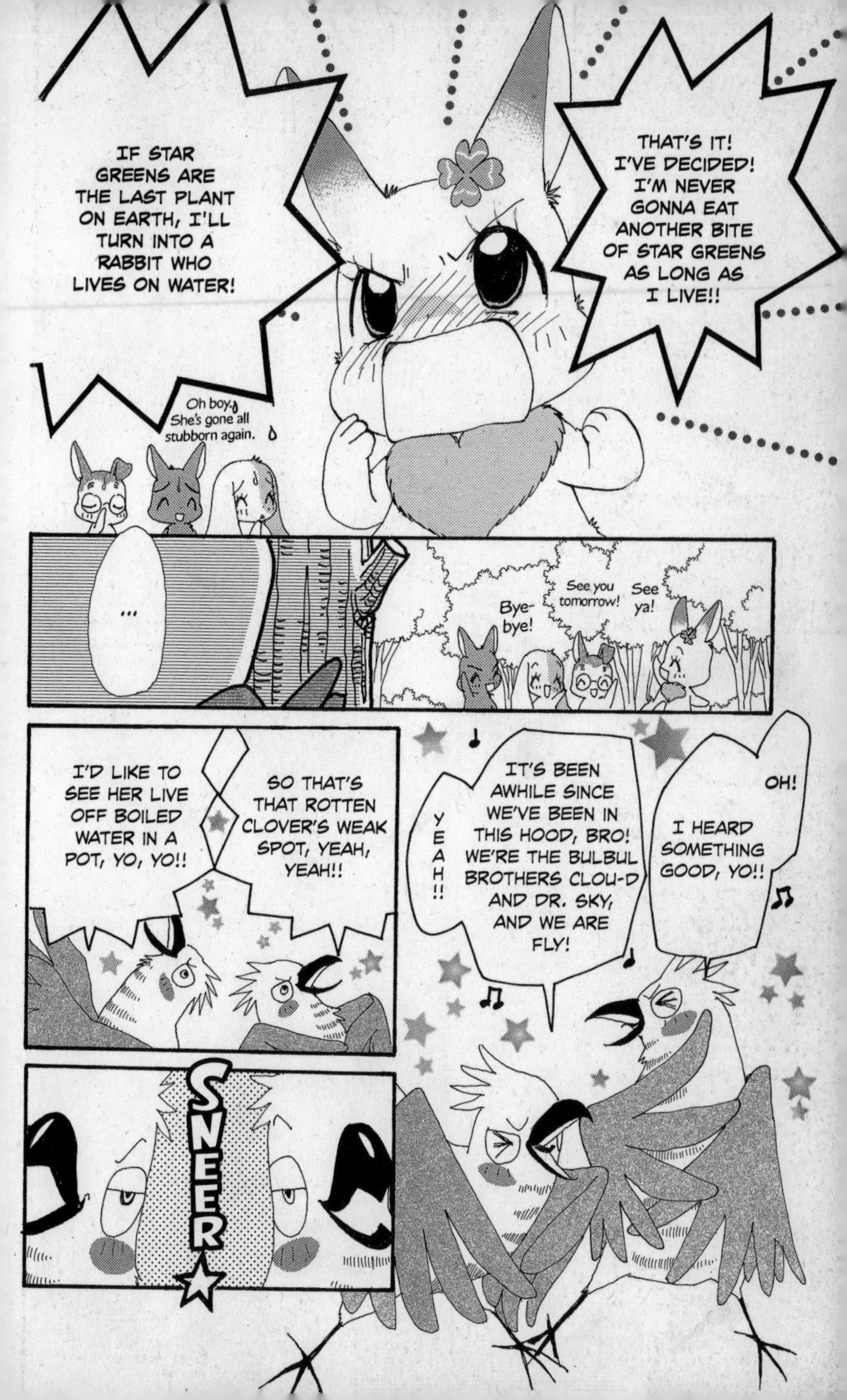
THAT'S IT! I'VE DECIDED! I'M NEVER GONNA EAT ANOTHER BITE OF STAR GREENS AS LONG AS I LIVE!!
IF STAR GREENS ARE THE LAST PLANT ON EARTH, I'LL TURN INTO A RABBIT WHO LIVES ON WATER!
Oh boy. She's gone all stubborn again.
See ya!
See you tomorrow!
Bye-bye!
...
OH!
I HEARD SOMETHING GOOD, YO!!
IT'S BEEN AWHILE SINCE WE'VE BEEN IN THIS HOOD, BRO! WE'RE THE BULBUL BROTHERS CLOU-D AND DR. SKY, AND WE ARE FLY!
YEAH!!
SO THAT'S THAT ROTTEN CLOVER'S WEAK SPOT, YEAH, YEAH!!
I'D LIKE TO SEE HER LIVE OFF BOILED WATER IN A POT, YO, YO!!
SNEER

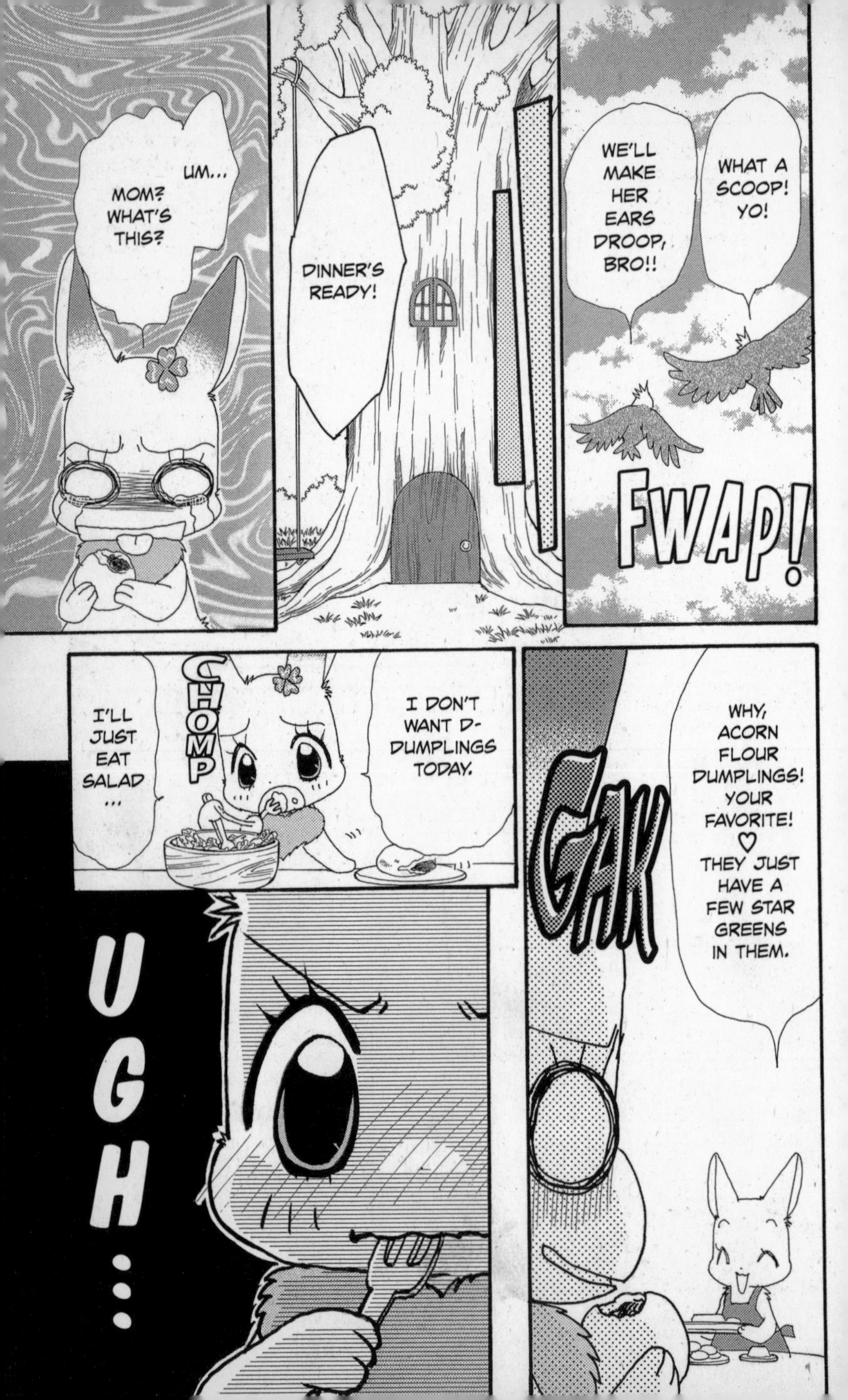
WHAT A SCOOP! YO!
WE'LL MAKE HER EARS DROOP, BRO!!
FWAP!
DINNER'S READY!
UM...
MOM? WHAT'S THIS?
WHY, ACORN FLOUR DUMPLINGS! YOUR FAVORITE! ♡ THEY JUST HAVE A FEW STAR GREENS IN THEM.
GAK
I DON'T WANT D-DUMPLINGS TODAY.
CHOMP
I'LL JUST EAT SALAD ...
UGH...

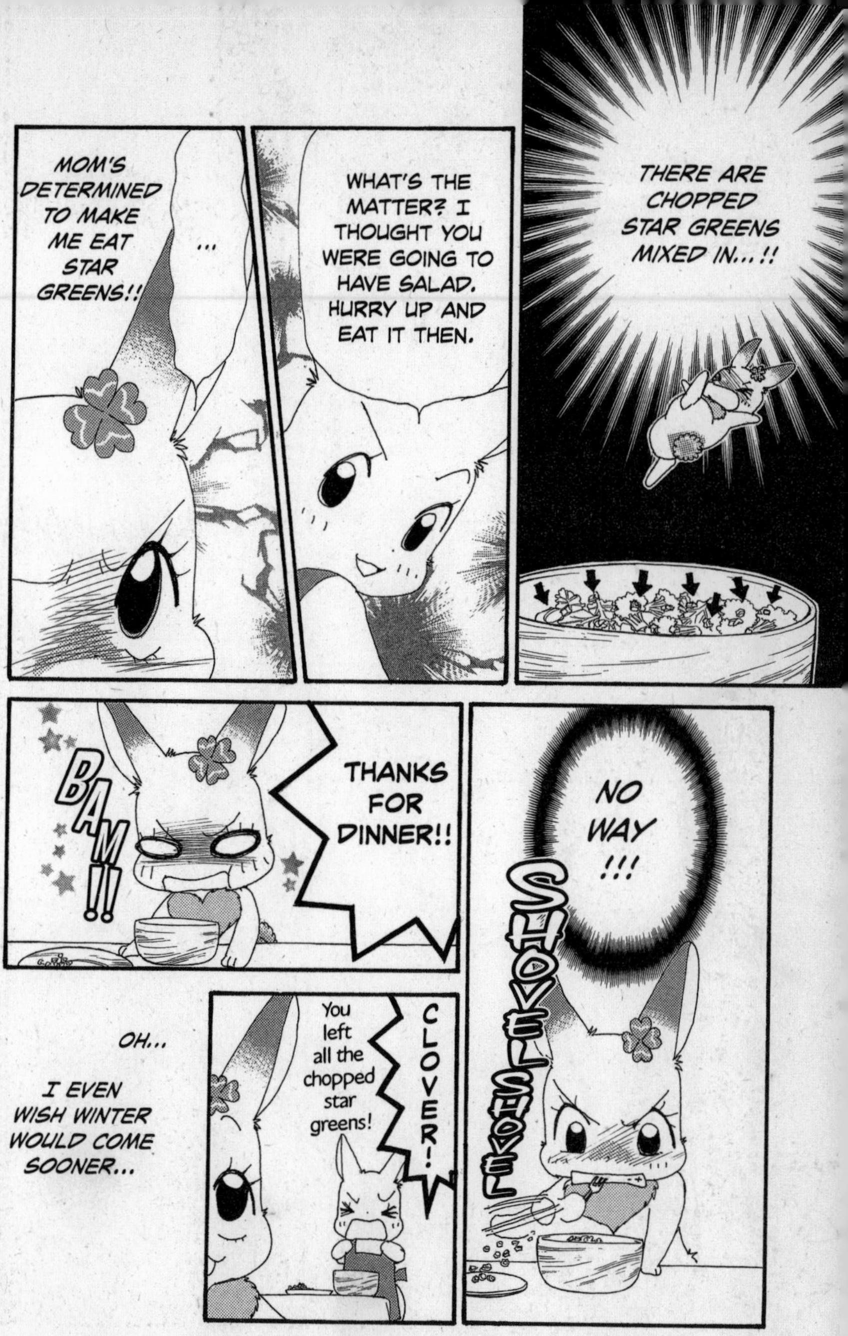
THERE ARE CHOPPED STAR GREENS MIXED IN...!!
WHAT'S THE MATTER? I THOUGHT YOU WERE GOING TO HAVE SALAD. HURRY UP AND EAT IT THEN.
...
MOM'S DETERMINED TO MAKE ME EAT STAR GREENS!!
NO WAY!!!
SHOVEL SHOVEL
THANKS FOR DINNER!!
BAM!!
CLOVER!
You left all the chopped star greens!
OH...
I EVEN WISH WINTER WOULD COME SOONER...

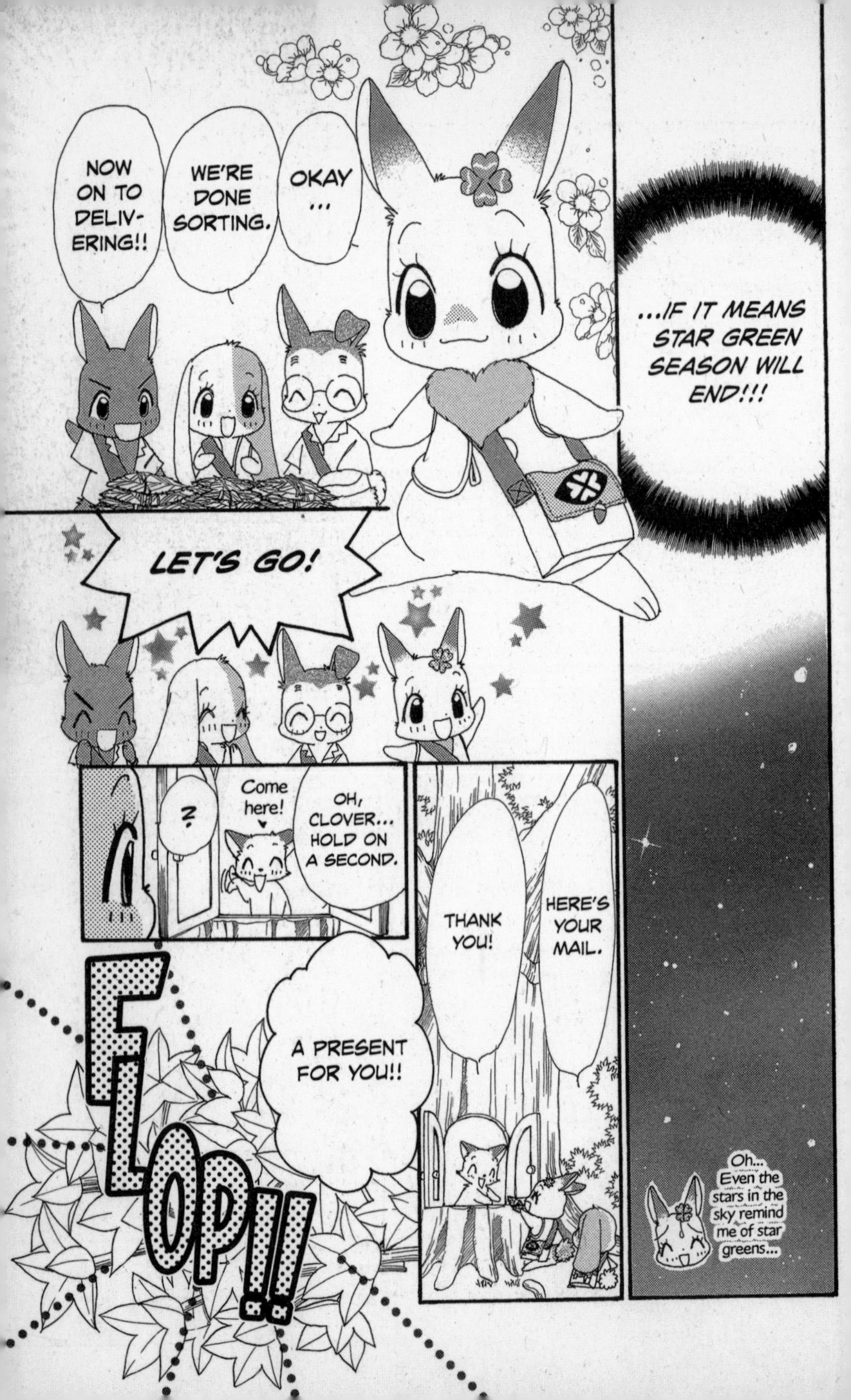

...IF IT MEANS STAR GREEN SEASON WILL END!!!
Oh... Even the stars in the sky remind me of star greens...
OKAY ...
WE'RE DONE SORTING.
NOW ON TO DELIV-ERING!!
LET'S GO!
HERE'S YOUR MAIL.
THANK YOU!
OH, CLOVER... HOLD ON A SECOND.
Come here!
?
A PRESENT FOR YOU!!
FLOP!!

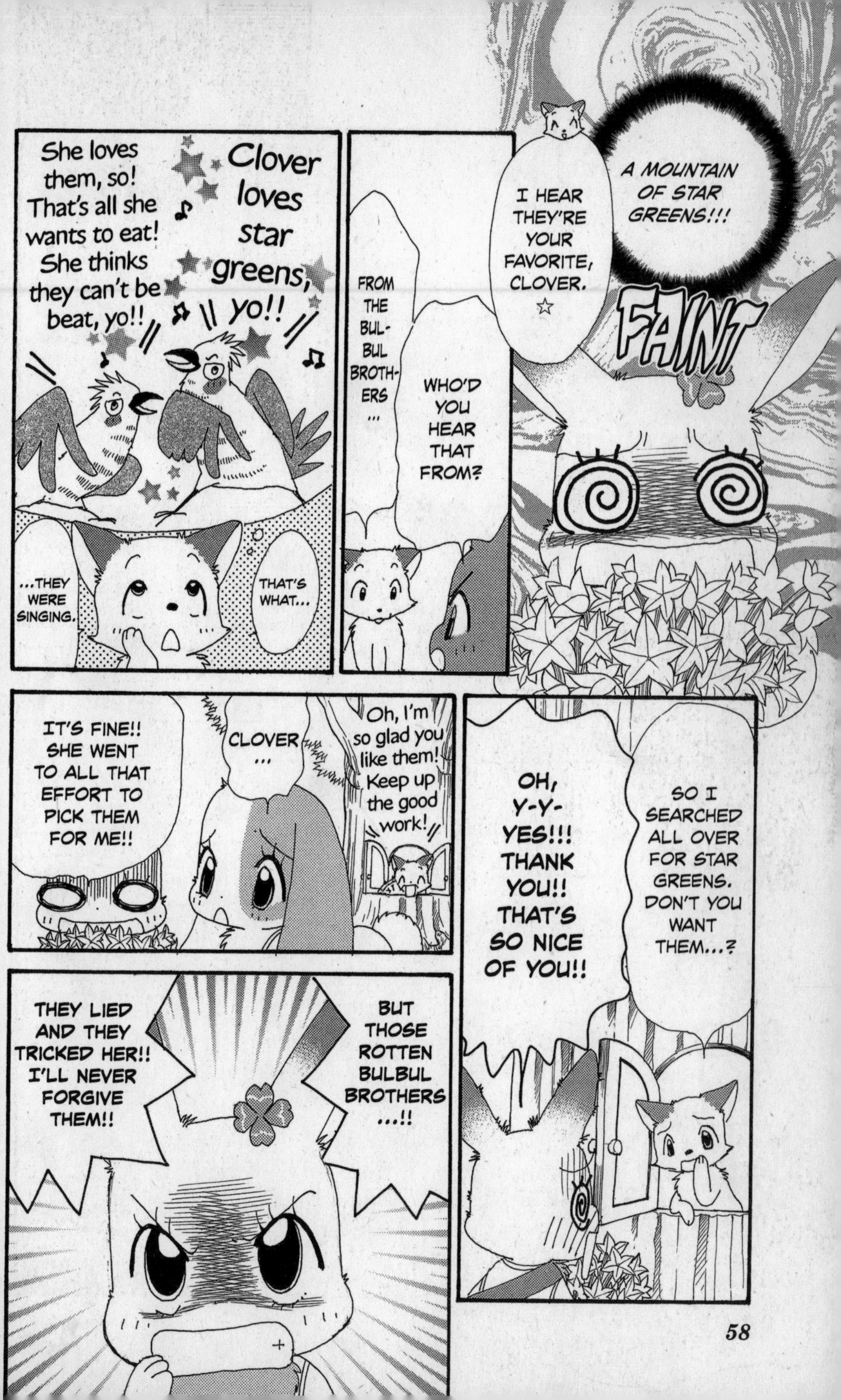
A MOUNTAIN OF STAR GREENS!!!
I HEAR THEY'RE YOUR FAVORITE, CLOVER. ☆
FAINT
WHO'D YOU HEAR THAT FROM?
FROM THE BUL-BUL BROTH-ERS ...
Clover loves star greens, yo!!
She loves them, so! That's all she wants to eat! She thinks they can't be beat, yo!!
THAT'S WHAT...
...THEY WERE SINGING.
SO I SEARCHED ALL OVER FOR STAR GREENS. DON'T YOU WANT THEM...?
OH, Y-Y-YES!!! THANK YOU!! THAT'S SO NICE OF YOU!!
Oh, I'm so glad you like them! Keep up the good work!
CLOVER ...
IT'S FINE!! SHE WENT TO ALL THAT EFFORT TO PICK THEM FOR ME!!
BUT THOSE ROTTEN BULBUL BROTHERS ...!!
THEY LIED AND THEY TRICKED HER!! I'LL NEVER FORGIVE THEM!!

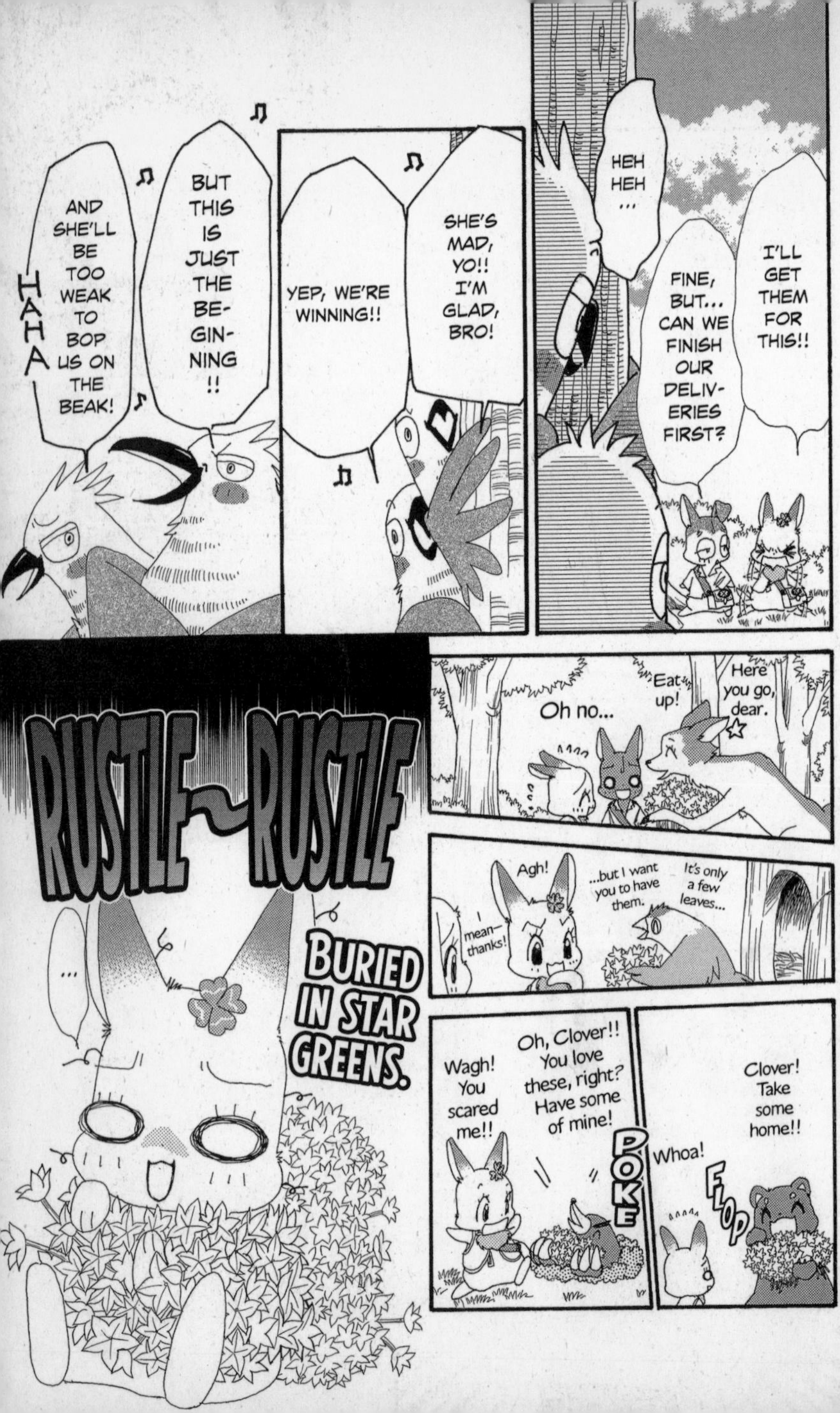
HEH HEH ...
I'LL GET THEM FOR THIS!!
FINE, BUT... CAN WE FINISH OUR DELIVERIES FIRST?
SHE'S MAD, YO!! I'M GLAD, BRO!
YEP, WE'RE WINNING!!
BUT THIS IS JUST THE BEGINNING!!
AND SHE'LL BE TOO WEAK TO BOP US ON THE BEAK!
HAHA
Here you go, dear.
Eat up!
Oh no...
It's only a few leaves...
...but I want you to have them.
Agh!
I mean—thanks!
Clover! Take some home!!
FLOP
Whoa!
POKE
Oh, Clover!! You love these, right? Have some of mine!
Wagh! You scared me!!
RUSTLE~RUSTLE
BURIED IN STAR GREENS.
...

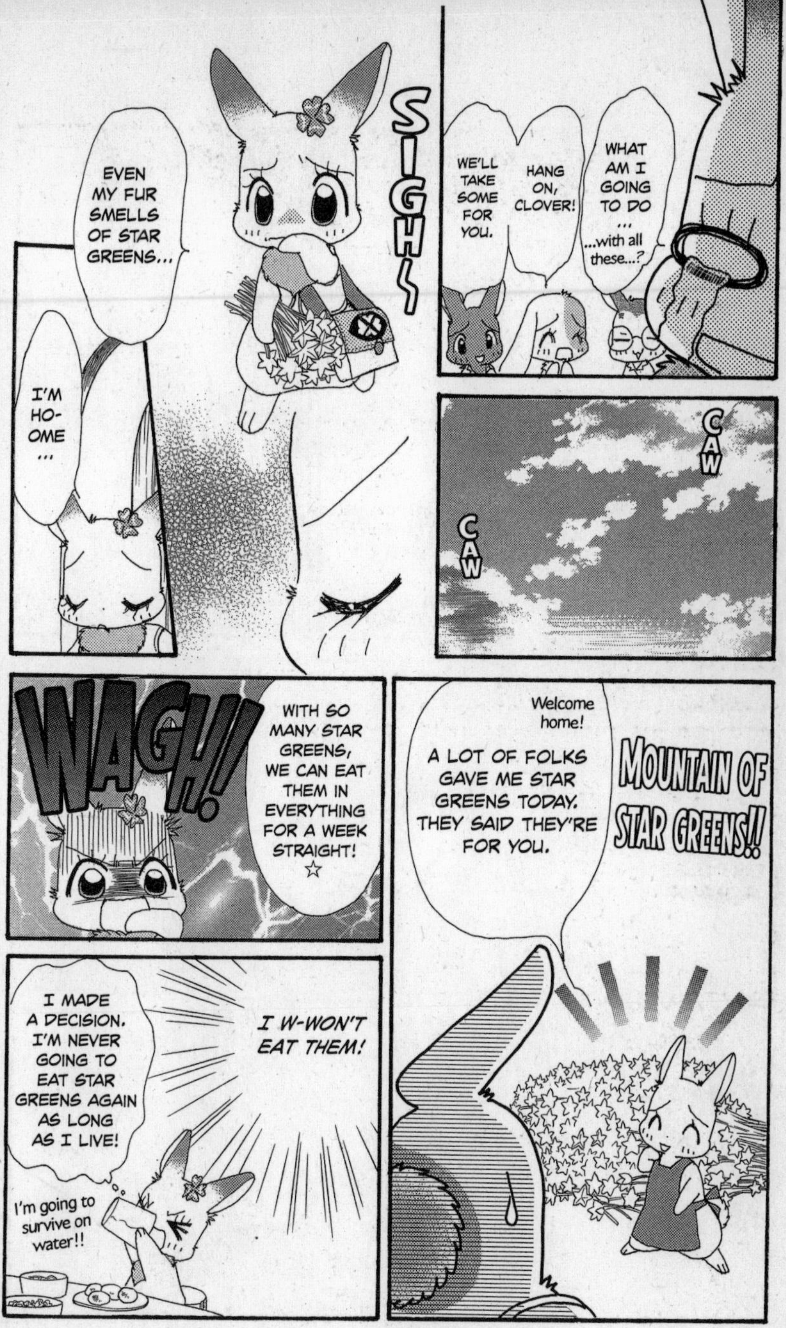
WHAT AM I GOING TO DO ... ...with all these...?
HANG ON, CLOVER!
WE'LL TAKE SOME FOR YOU.
CAW
CAW
SIGH
EVEN MY FUR SMELLS OF STAR GREENS...
I'M HO-OME ...
Welcome home!
A LOT OF FOLKS GAVE ME STAR GREENS TODAY. THEY SAID THEY'RE FOR YOU.
MOUNTAIN OF STAR GREENS!!
WITH SO MANY STAR GREENS, WE CAN EAT THEM IN EVERYTHING FOR A WEEK STRAIGHT! ☆
WAGH!
I W-WON'T EAT THEM!
I MADE A DECISION. I'M NEVER GOING TO EAT STAR GREENS AGAIN AS LONG AS I LIVE!
I'm going to survive on water!!

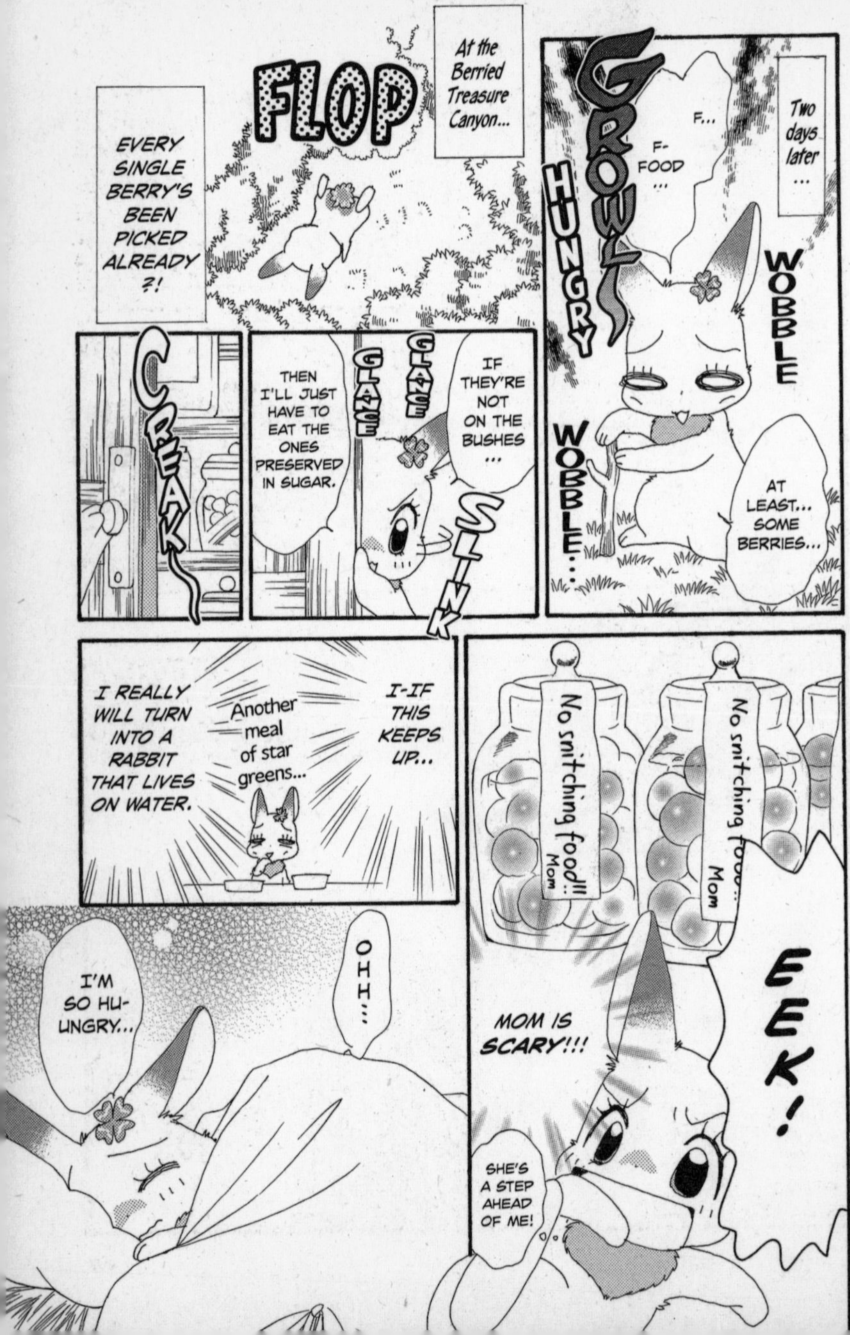
Two days later...
GROWL
HUNGRY
F...
F-FOOD...
WOBBLE
WOBBLE...
AT LEAST... SOME BERRIES...
At the Berried Treasure Canyon...
FLOP
EVERY SINGLE BERRY'S BEEN PICKED ALREADY?!
IF THEY'RE NOT ON THE BUSHES...
GLANCE
GLANCE
THEN I'LL JUST HAVE TO EAT THE ONES PRESERVED IN SUGAR.
SLINK
CREAK
No snitching food!! Mom
No snitching food... Mom
EEK!
MOM IS SCARY!!!
SHE'S A STEP AHEAD OF ME!
I-IF THIS KEEPS UP...
Another meal of star greens...
I REALLY WILL TURN INTO A RABBIT THAT LIVES ON WATER.
OHH...
I'M SO HU-UNGRY...

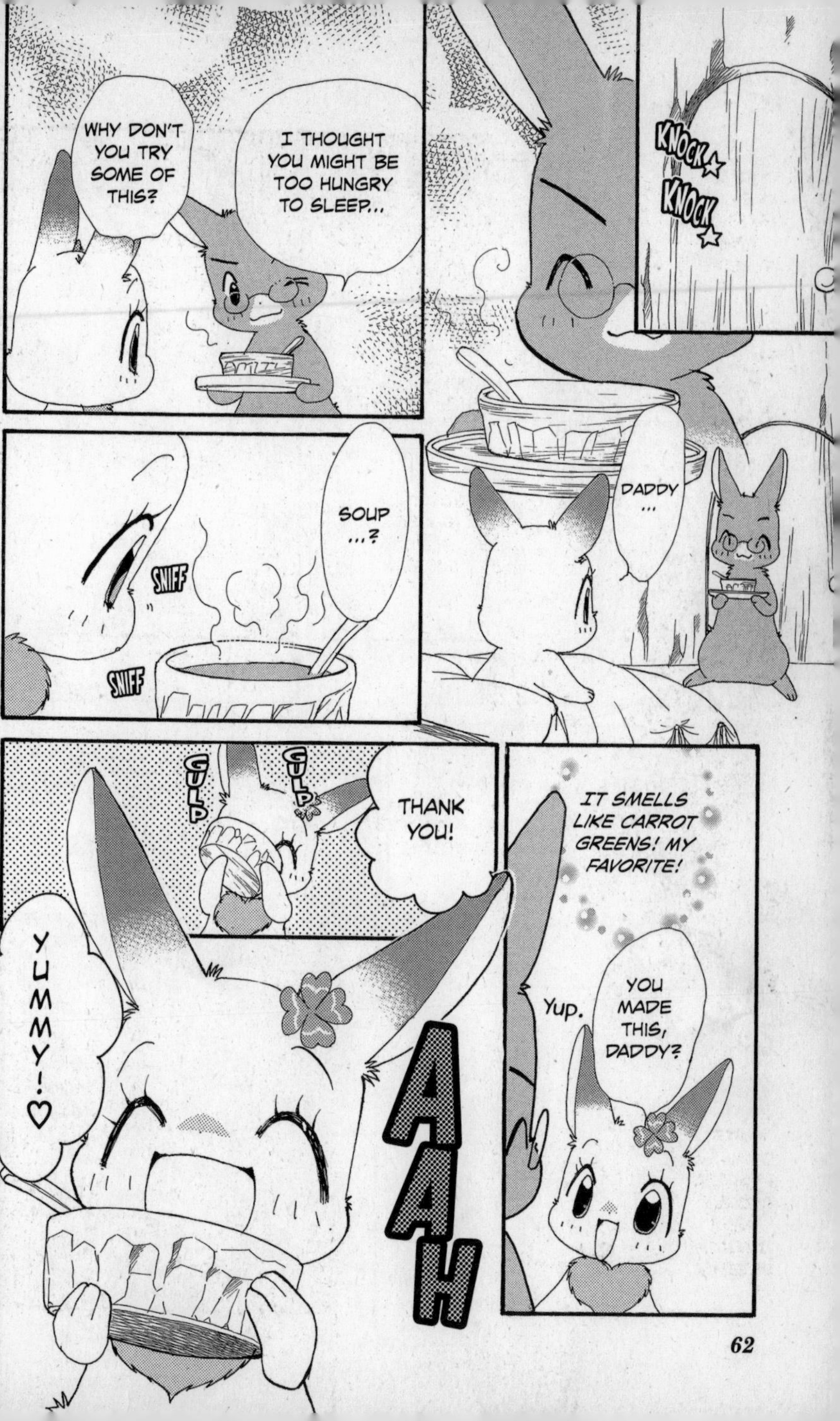
KNOCK☆
KNOCK☆
DADDY...
I THOUGHT YOU MIGHT BE TOO HUNGRY TO SLEEP...
WHY DON'T YOU TRY SOME OF THIS?
SOUP...?
SNIFF
SNIFF
IT SMELLS LIKE CARROT GREENS! MY FAVORITE!
YOU MADE THIS, DADDY?
Yup.
THANK YOU!
GULP
GULP
YUMMY!♡
AAH

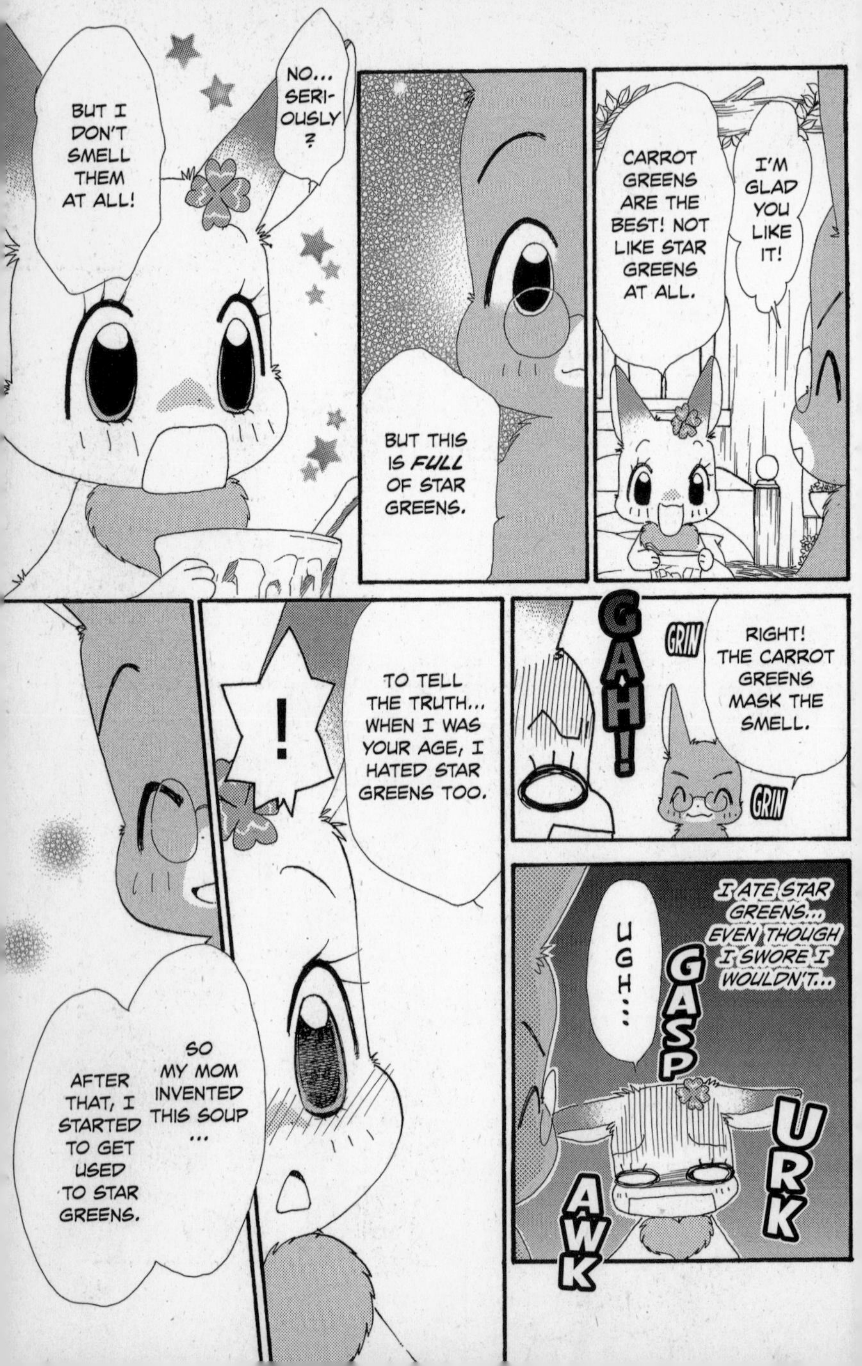
CARROT GREENS ARE THE BEST! NOT LIKE STAR GREENS AT ALL.
I'M GLAD YOU LIKE IT!
BUT THIS IS *FULL* OF STAR GREENS.
NO... SERIOUSLY?
BUT I DON'T SMELL THEM AT ALL!
GRIN
RIGHT! THE CARROT GREENS MASK THE SMELL.
GRIN
GAH!
I ATE STAR GREENS... EVEN THOUGH I SWORE I WOULDN'T...
UGH...
GASP
URK
AWK
!
TO TELL THE TRUTH... WHEN I WAS YOUR AGE, I HATED STAR GREENS TOO.
SO MY MOM INVENTED THIS SOUP...
AFTER THAT, I STARTED TO GET USED TO STAR GREENS.

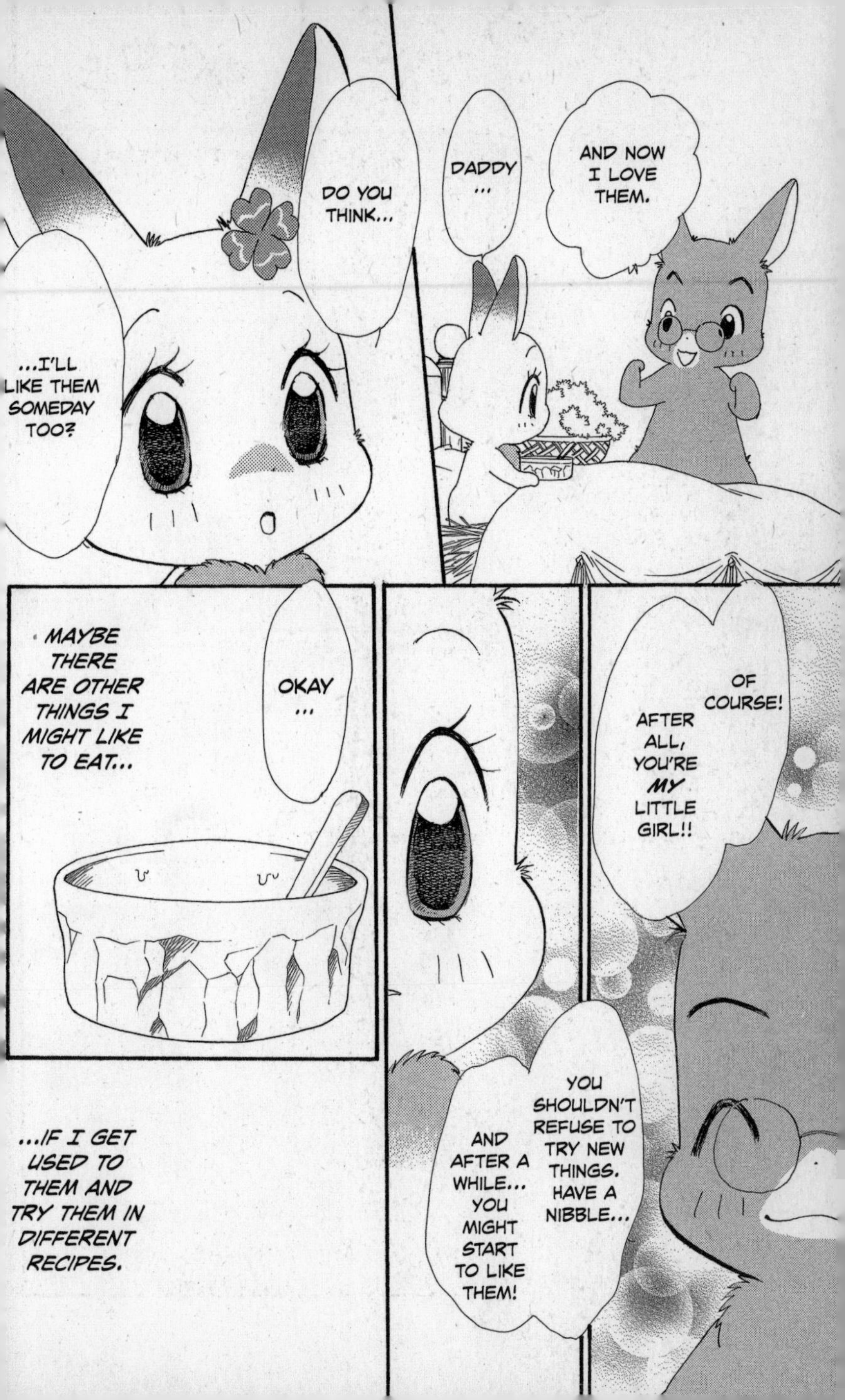
AND NOW I LOVE THEM.
DADDY ...
DO YOU THINK...
...I'LL LIKE THEM SOMEDAY TOO?
OF COURSE!
AFTER ALL, YOU'RE MY LITTLE GIRL!!
YOU SHOULDN'T REFUSE TO TRY NEW THINGS. HAVE A NIBBLE...
AND AFTER A WHILE... YOU MIGHT START TO LIKE THEM!
OKAY ...
MAYBE THERE ARE OTHER THINGS I MIGHT LIKE TO EAT...
...IF I GET USED TO THEM AND TRY THEM IN DIFFERENT RECIPES.

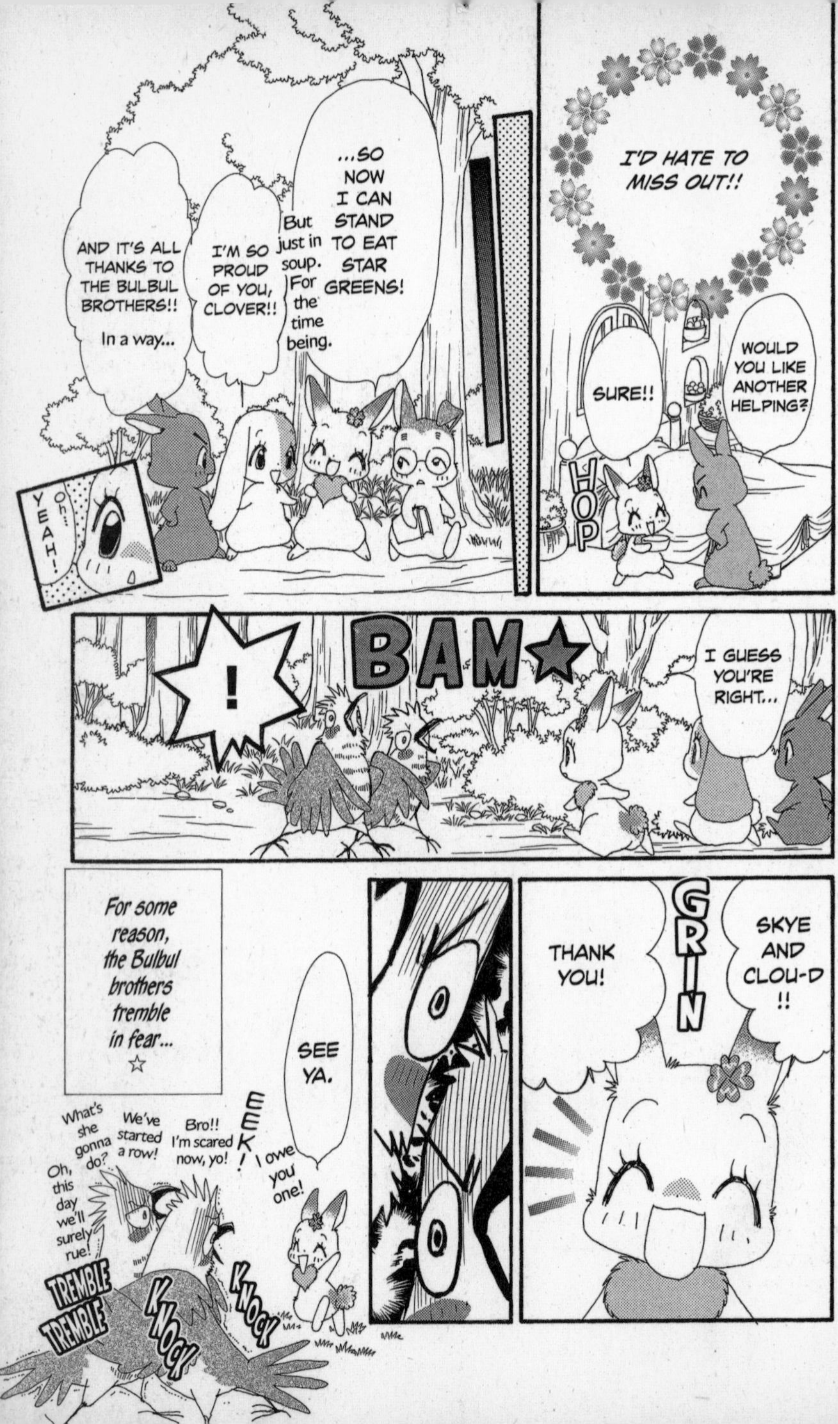

WOULD YOU LIKE ANOTHER HELPING?
SURE!!
HOP
I'D HATE TO MISS OUT!!
...SO NOW I CAN STAND TO EAT STAR GREENS!
But just in soup. For the time being.
I'M SO PROUD OF YOU, CLOVER!!
AND IT'S ALL THANKS TO THE BULBUL BROTHERS!!
In a way...
Oh...
YEAH!
I GUESS YOU'RE RIGHT...
BAM★
!
SKYE AND CLOU-D !!
GRIN
THANK YOU!
For some reason, the Bulbul brothers tremble in fear... ☆
SEE YA.
I owe you one!
EEK!
Bro!! I'm scared now, yo!
We've started a row!
What's she gonna do?
Oh, this day we'll surely rue!
KNOCK
KNOCK
TREMBLE
TREMBLE

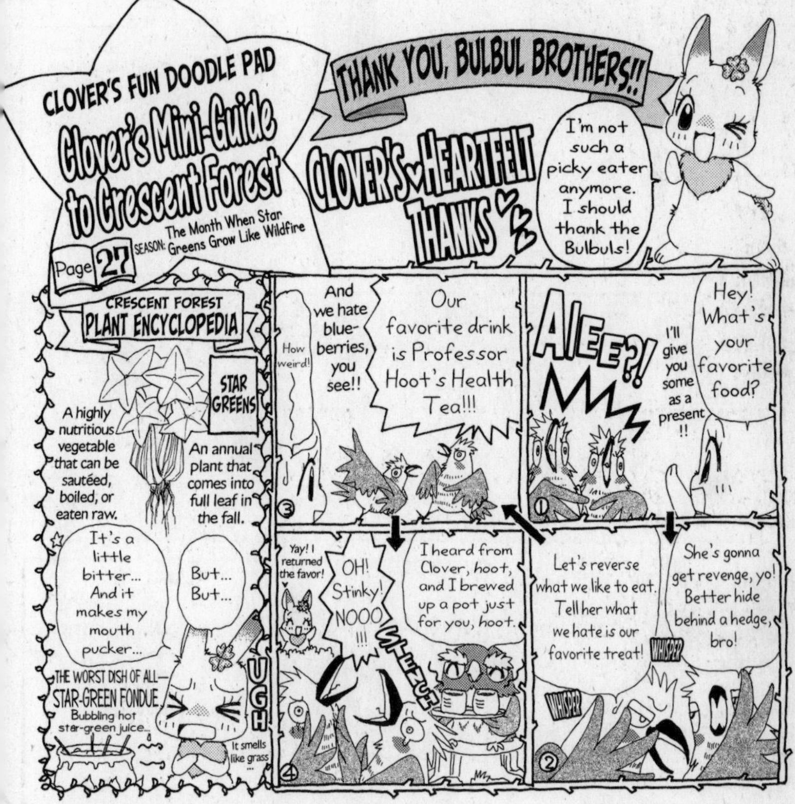
CLOVER'S FUN DOODLE PAD
Clover's Mini-Guide to Crescent Forest
Page 27
SEASON: The Month When Star Greens Grow Like Wildfire
THANK YOU, BULBUL BROTHERS!!
CLOVER'S ♥ HEARTFELT THANKS
I'm not such a picky eater anymore. I should thank the Bulbuls!
Hey! What's your favorite food?
I'll give you some as a present!!
AIEE?!
She's gonna get revenge, yo! Better hide behind a hedge, bro!
Let's reverse what we like to eat. Tell her what we hate is our favorite treat!
WHISPER
WHISPER
Our favorite drink is Professor Hoot's Health Tea!!!
And we hate blue-berries, you see!!
How weird!
I heard from Clover, hoot, and I brewed up a pot just for you, hoot.
OH! Stinky! NOOO!!!
STENCH
Yay! I returned the favor!
CRESCENT FOREST PLANT ENCYCLOPEDIA
STAR GREENS
An annual plant that comes into full leaf in the fall.
A highly nutritious vegetable that can be sautéed, boiled, or eaten raw.
But... But...
It's a little bitter... And it makes my mouth pucker...
UGH
It smells like grass...
THE WORST DISH OF ALL—STAR-GREEN FONDUE
Bubbling hot star-green juice...

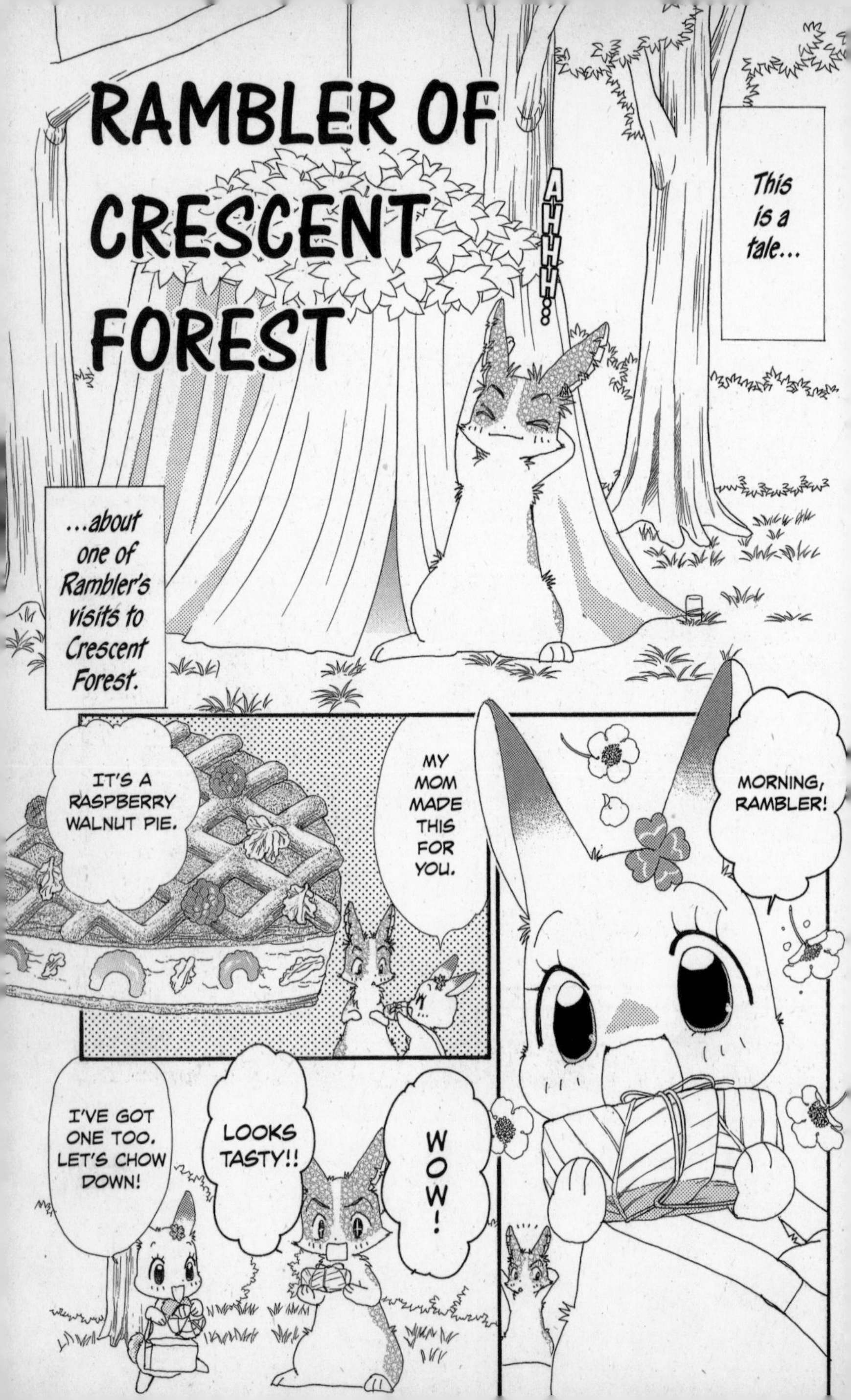
This is a tale...
AHHHH...
RAMBLER OF CRESCENT FOREST
...about one of Rambler's visits to Crescent Forest.
MORNING, RAMBLER!
MY MOM MADE THIS FOR YOU.
IT'S A RASPBERRY WALNUT PIE.
WOW!
LOOKS TASTY!!
I'VE GOT ONE TOO. LET'S CHOW DOWN!

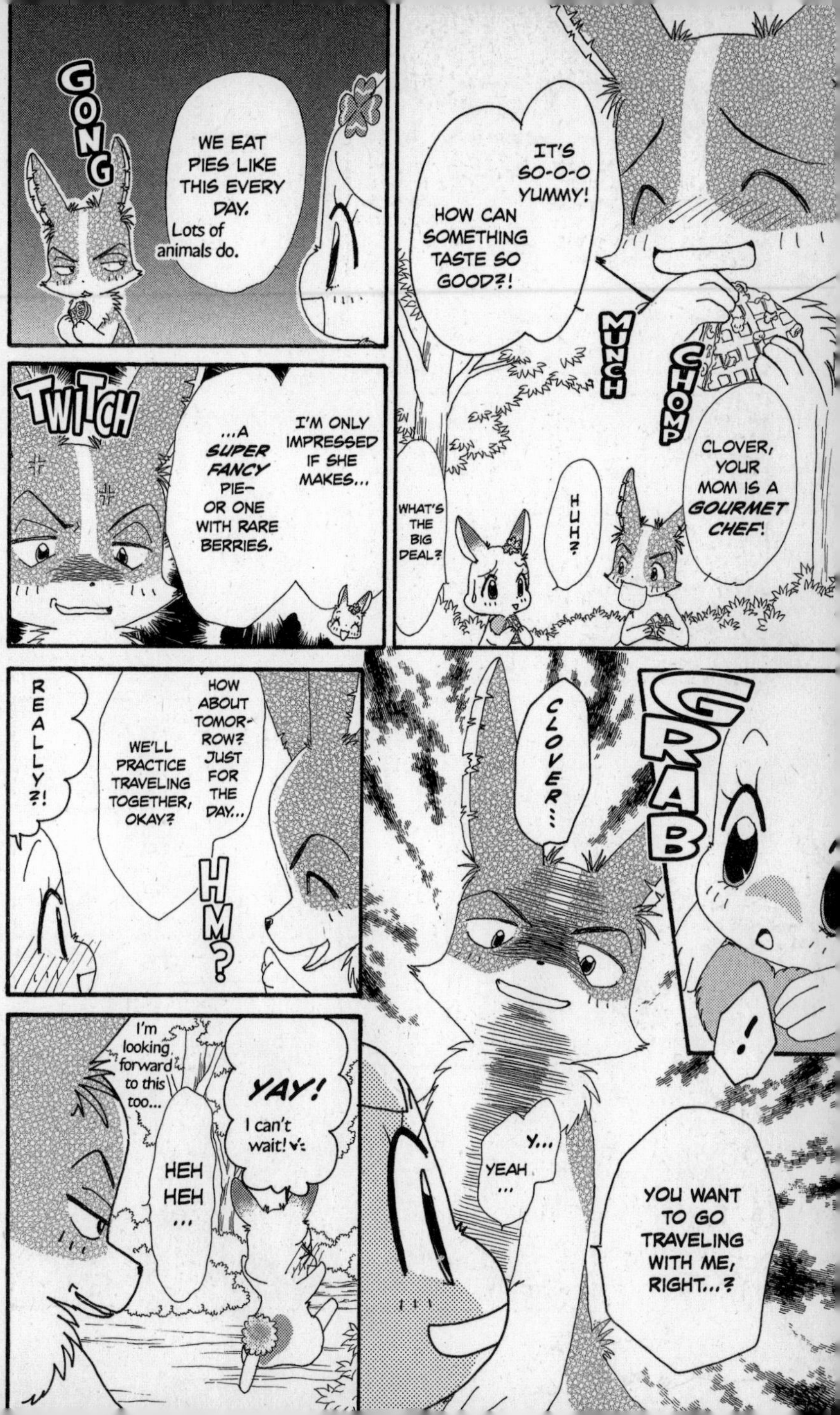
IT'S SO-O-O YUMMY!
HOW CAN SOMETHING TASTE SO GOOD?!
MUNCH
CHOMP
CLOVER, YOUR MOM IS A *GOURMET CHEF*!
HUH?
WHAT'S THE BIG DEAL?
GONG
WE EAT PIES LIKE THIS EVERY DAY.
Lots of animals do.
TWITCH
I'M ONLY IMPRESSED IF SHE MAKES...
...A *SUPER FANCY* PIE— OR ONE WITH RARE BERRIES.
GRAB
CLOVER...
!
YOU WANT TO GO TRAVELING WITH ME, RIGHT...?
Y... YEAH...
HOW ABOUT TOMORROW? JUST FOR THE DAY...
WE'LL PRACTICE TRAVELING TOGETHER, OKAY?
REALLY?!
HM?
YAY! I can't wait!
I'm looking forward to this too...
HEH HEH...

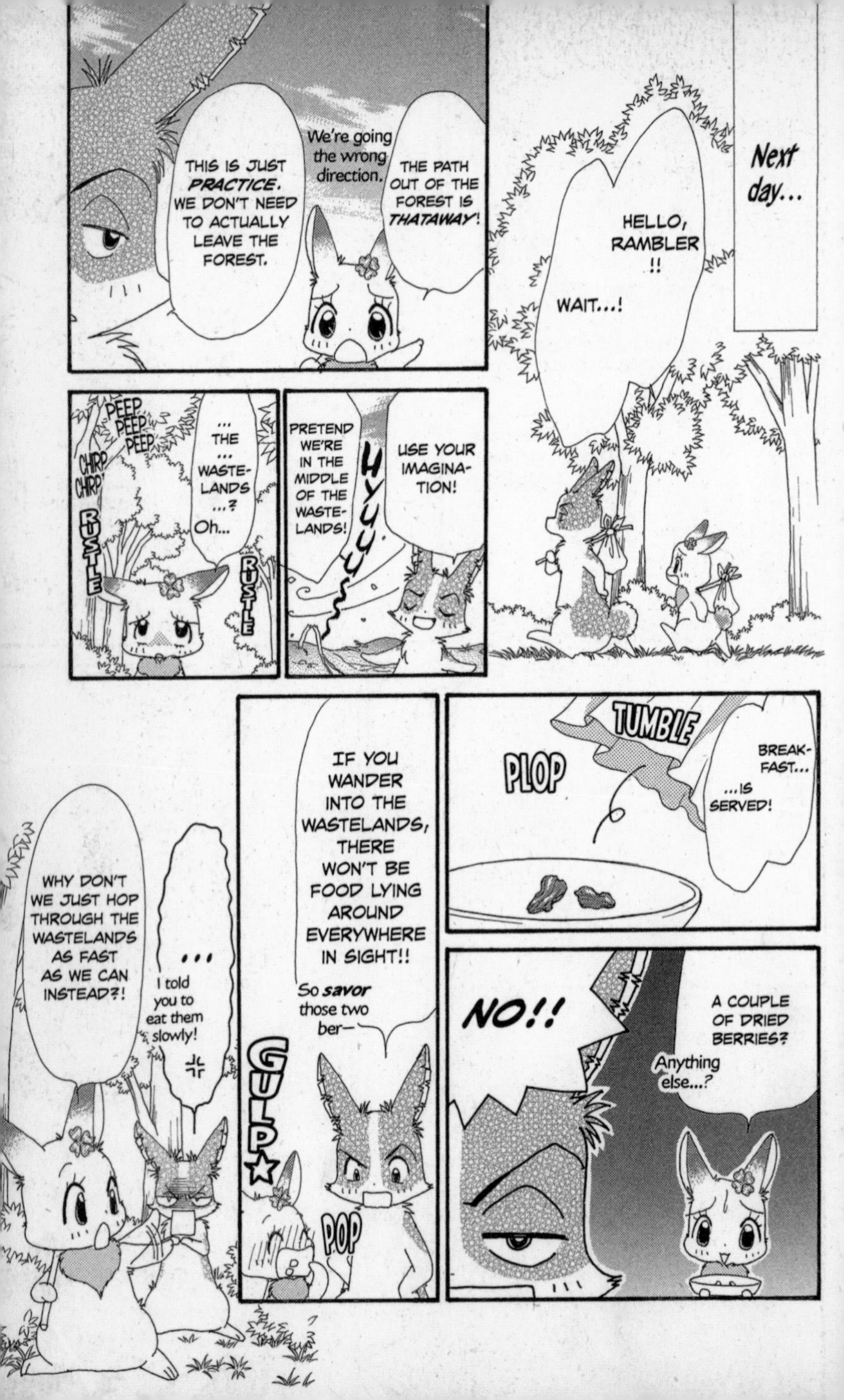

Next day...
HELLO, RAMBLER!!
WAIT...!
THE PATH OUT OF THE FOREST IS *THATAWAY*!
We're going the wrong direction.
THIS IS JUST *PRACTICE*. WE DON'T NEED TO ACTUALLY LEAVE THE FOREST.
USE YOUR IMAGINATION!
PRETEND WE'RE IN THE MIDDLE OF THE WASTE-LANDS!
HYUUUU
... THE ... WASTE-LANDS ...?
Oh...
PEEP PEEP PEEP
CHIRP CHIRP
RUSTLE
RUSTLE
BREAK-FAST...
...IS SERVED!
TUMBLE
PLOP
A COUPLE OF DRIED BERRIES?
Anything else...?
NO!!
IF YOU WANDER INTO THE WASTELANDS, THERE WON'T BE FOOD LYING AROUND EVERYWHERE IN SIGHT!!
So *savor* those two ber—
GULP☆
POP
WHY DON'T WE JUST HOP THROUGH THE WASTELANDS AS FAST AS WE CAN INSTEAD?!
...
I told you to eat them slowly!

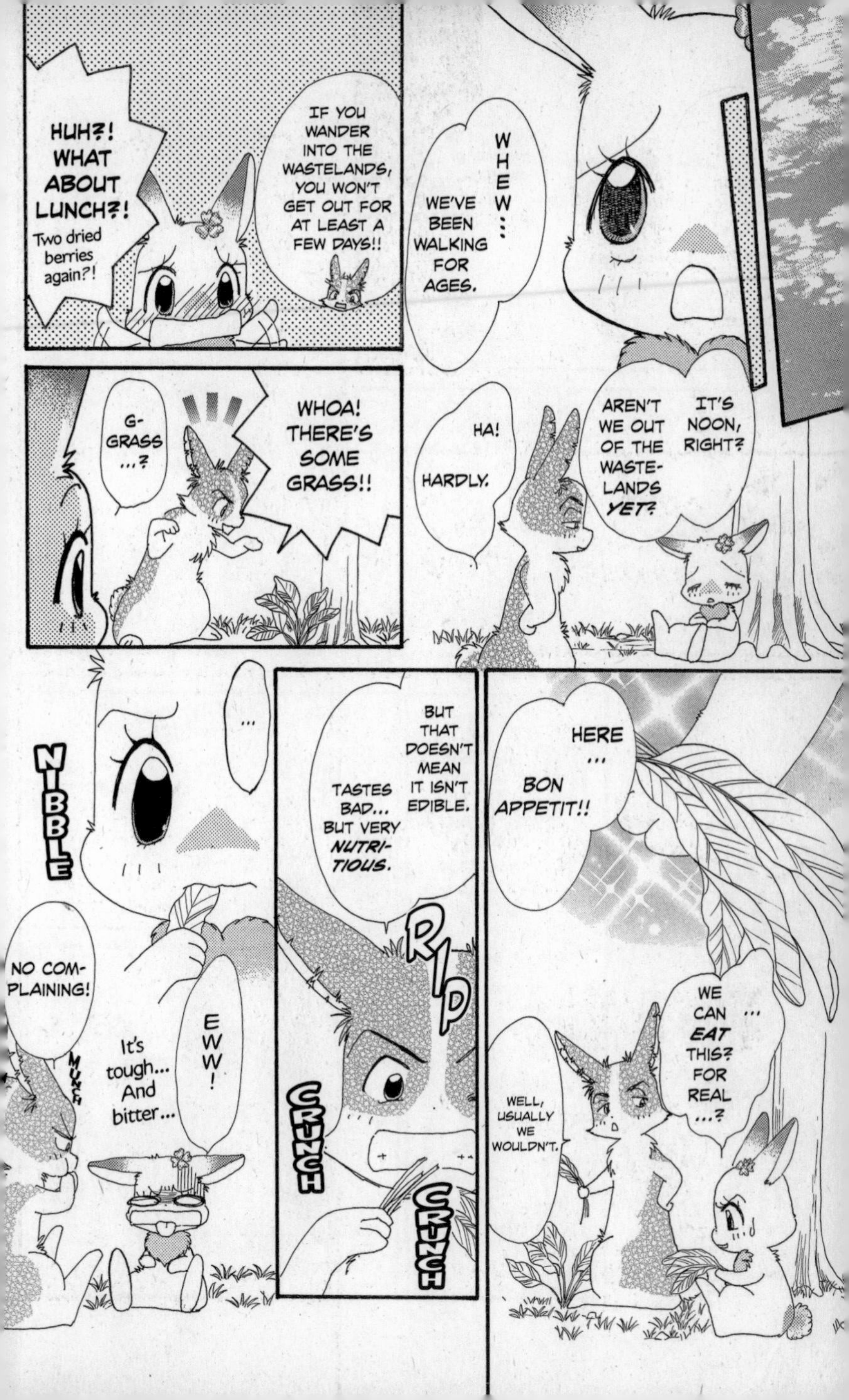
WHEW...
WE'VE BEEN WALKING FOR AGES.
IT'S NOON, RIGHT? AREN'T WE OUT OF THE WASTELANDS YET?
HA! HARDLY.
IF YOU WANDER INTO THE WASTELANDS, YOU WON'T GET OUT FOR AT LEAST A FEW DAYS!!
HUH?! WHAT ABOUT LUNCH?!
Two dried berries again?!
WHOA! THERE'S SOME GRASS!!
G-GRASS...?
HERE... BON APPETIT!!
WE CAN... EAT THIS? FOR REAL...?
WELL, USUALLY WE WOULDN'T.
BUT THAT DOESN'T MEAN IT ISN'T EDIBLE.
TASTES BAD... BUT VERY NUTRITIOUS.
RIP
CRUNCH
CRUNCH
...
NIBBLE
EWW!
It's tough... And bitter...
NO COMPLAINING!
MUNCH

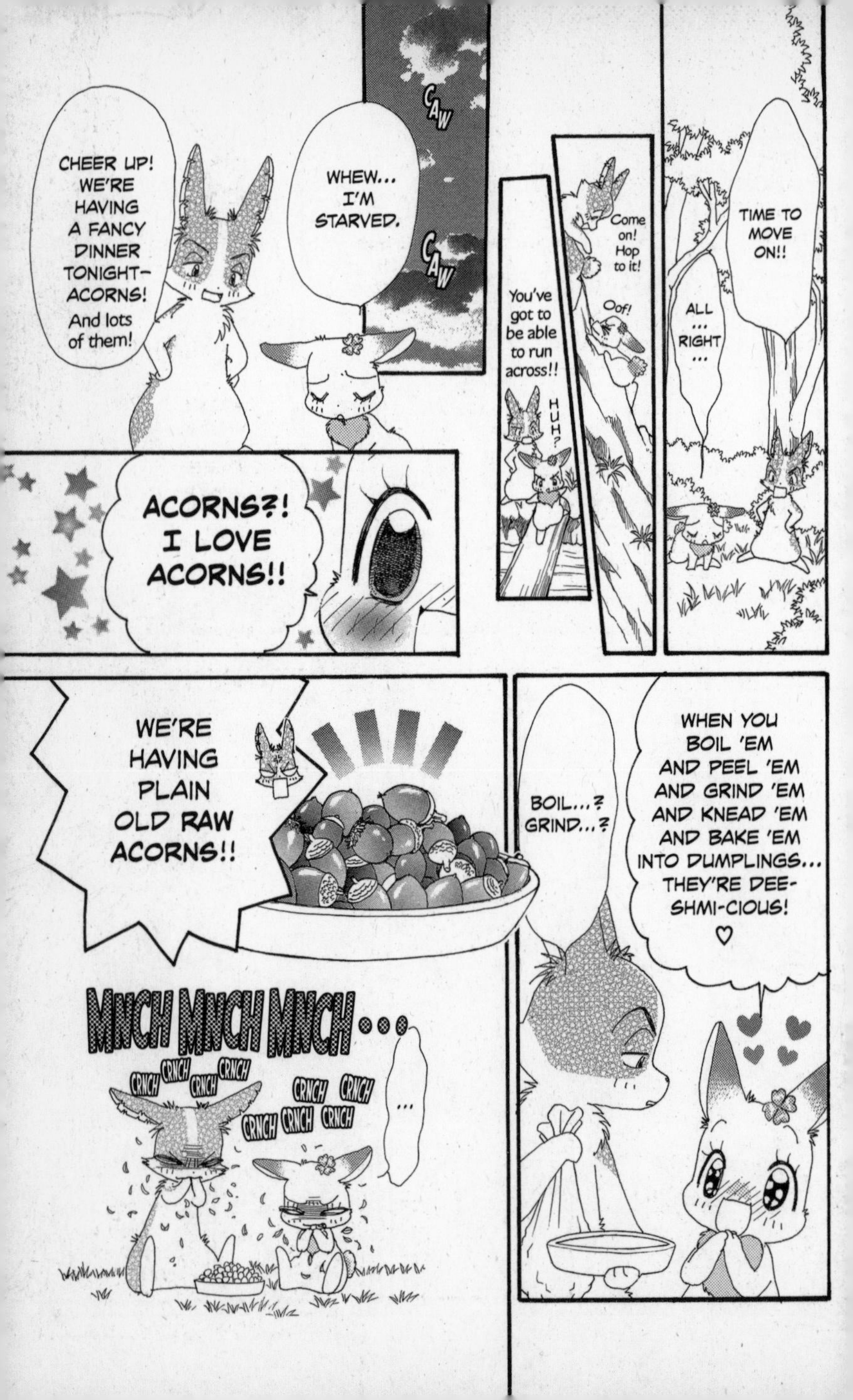
TIME TO MOVE ON!!
ALL... RIGHT...
Come on! Hop to it!
Oof!
You've got to be able to run across!!
HUH?
CAW
CAW
WHEW... I'M STARVED.
CHEER UP! WE'RE HAVING A FANCY DINNER TONIGHT—ACORNS! And lots of them!
ACORNS?! I LOVE ACORNS!!
WHEN YOU BOIL 'EM AND PEEL 'EM AND GRIND 'EM AND KNEAD 'EM AND BAKE 'EM INTO DUMPLINGS... THEY'RE DEE-SHMI-CIOUS! ♡
BOIL...? GRIND...?
WE'RE HAVING PLAIN OLD RAW ACORNS!!
MNCH MNCH MNCH...
CRNCH CRNCH CRNCH CRNCH
CRNCH CRNCH CRNCH CRNCH CRNCH
...

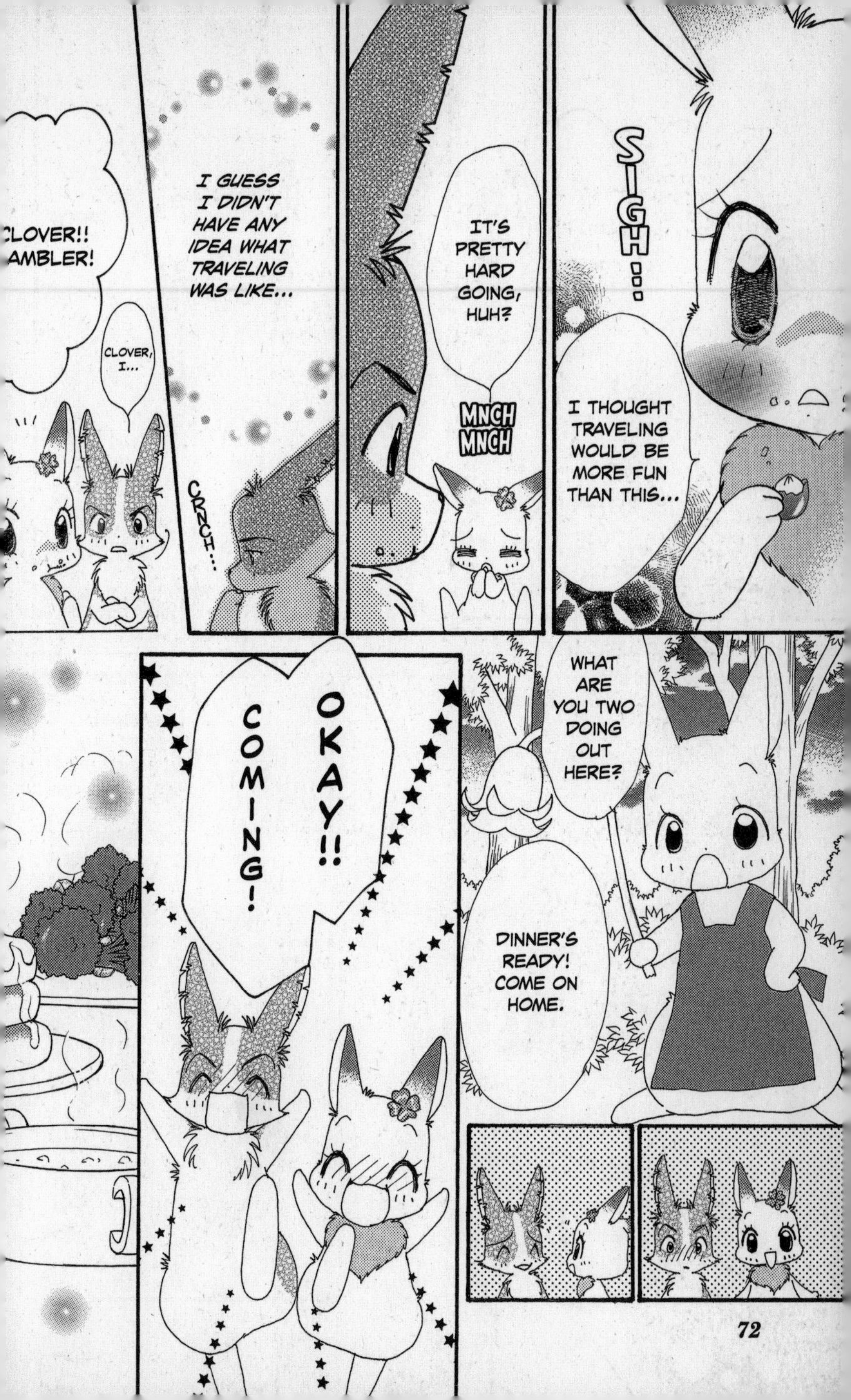
SIGH...
I THOUGHT TRAVELING WOULD BE MORE FUN THAN THIS...
IT'S PRETTY HARD GOING, HUH?
MNCH MNCH
I GUESS I DIDN'T HAVE ANY IDEA WHAT TRAVELING WAS LIKE...
CRNCH...
CLOVER, I...
CLOVER!! AMBLER!
WHAT ARE YOU TWO DOING OUT HERE?
DINNER'S READY! COME ON HOME.
OKAY!!
COMING!

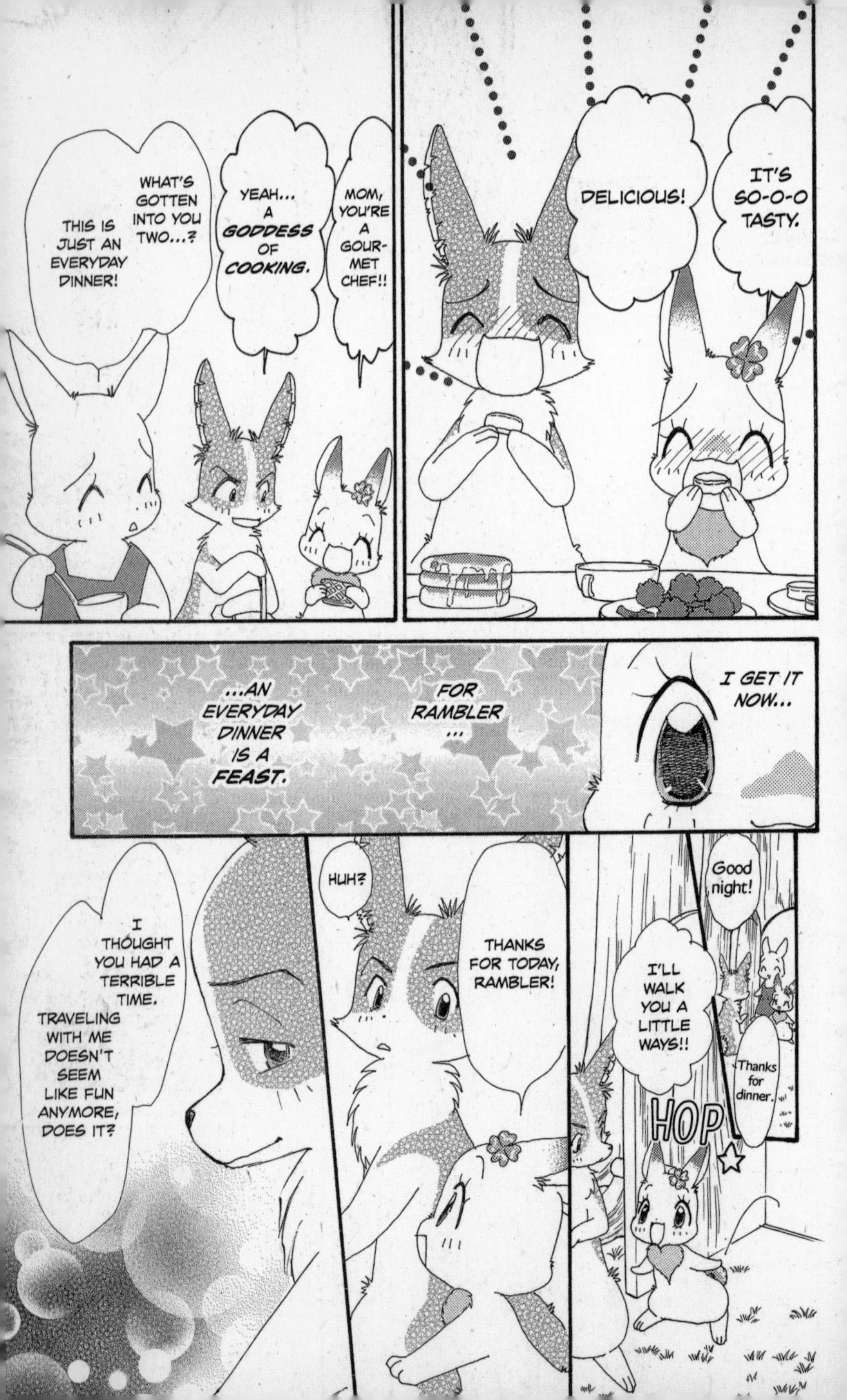
IT'S SO-O-O TASTY.
DELICIOUS!
MOM, YOU'RE A GOURMET CHEF!!
YEAH... A GODDESS OF COOKING.
WHAT'S GOTTEN INTO YOU TWO...?
THIS IS JUST AN EVERYDAY DINNER!
I GET IT NOW...
FOR RAMBLER...
...AN EVERYDAY DINNER IS A FEAST.
Good night!
I'LL WALK YOU A LITTLE WAYS!!
Thanks for dinner.
HOP
THANKS FOR TODAY, RAMBLER!
HUH?
I THOUGHT YOU HAD A TERRIBLE TIME.
TRAVELING WITH ME DOESN'T SEEM LIKE FUN ANYMORE, DOES IT?

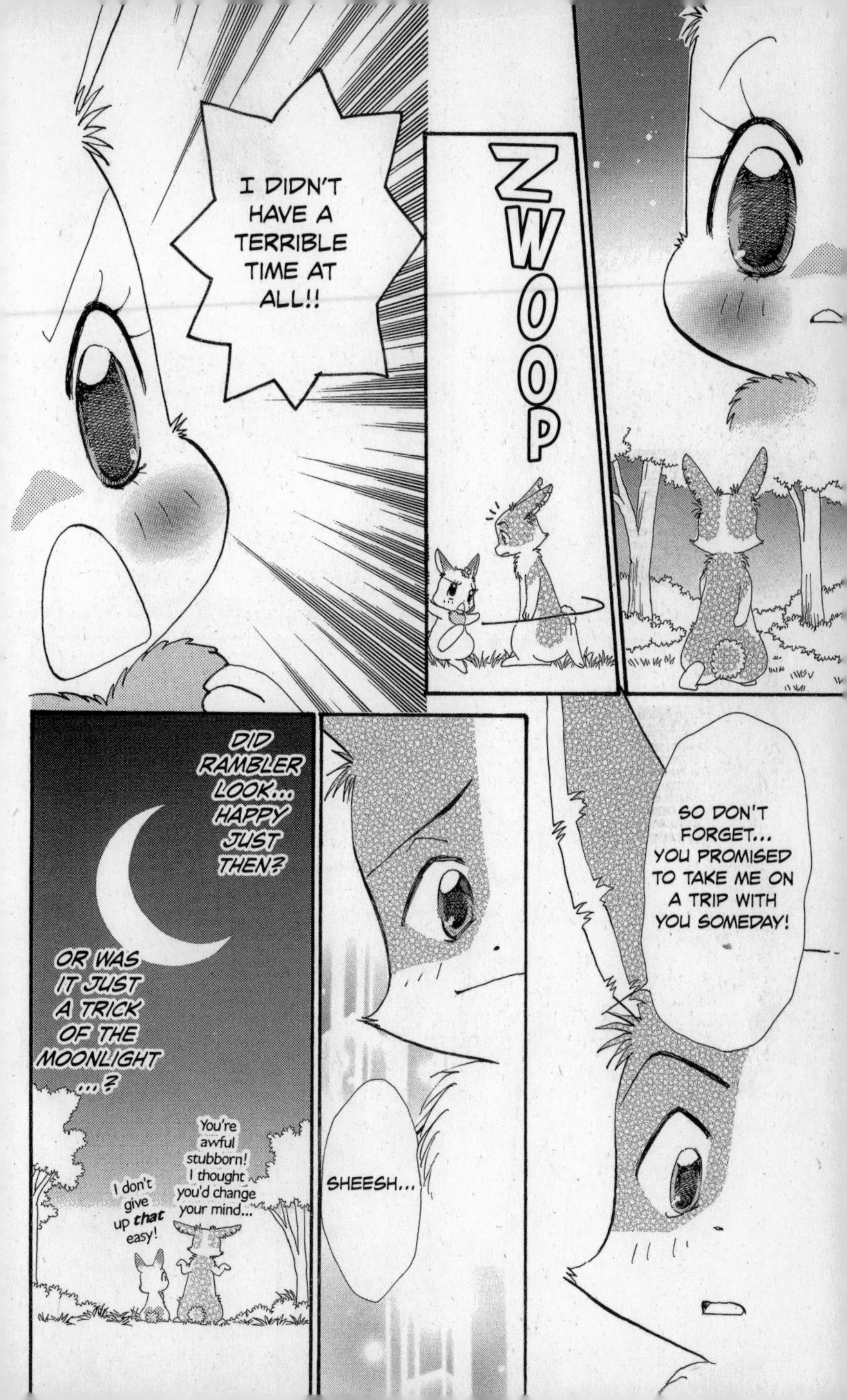
ZWOOP
I DIDN'T HAVE A TERRIBLE TIME AT ALL!!
SO DON'T FORGET... YOU PROMISED TO TAKE ME ON A TRIP WITH YOU SOMEDAY!
SHEESH...
DID RAMBLER LOOK... HAPPY JUST THEN?
OR WAS IT JUST A TRICK OF THE MOONLIGHT...?
You're awful stubborn! I thought you'd change your mind...
I don't give up *that* easy!

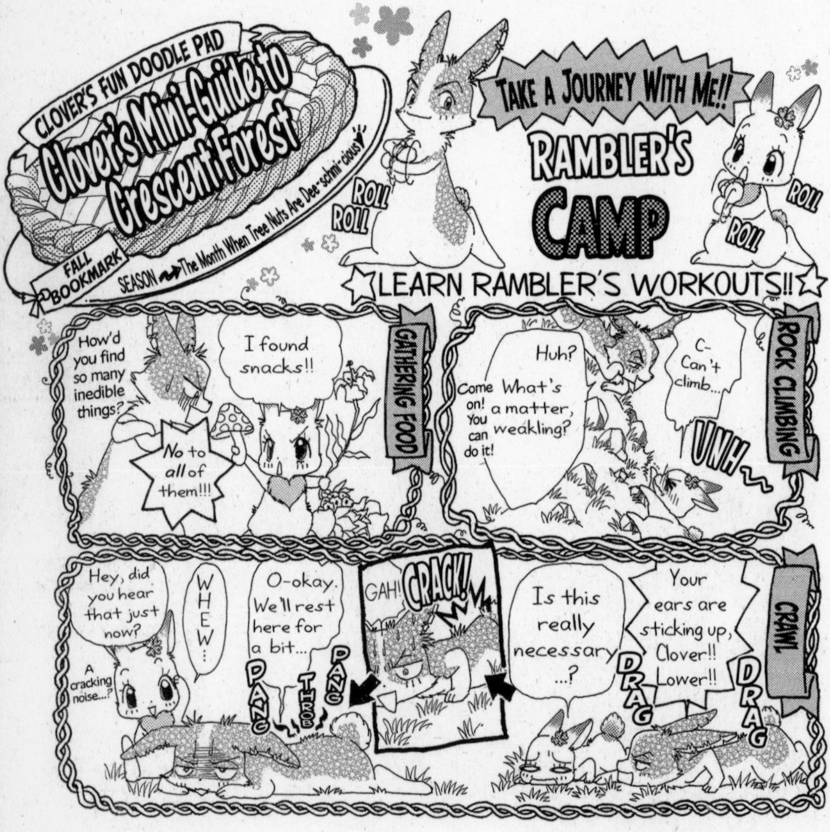
TAKE A JOURNEY WITH ME!!
RAMBLER'S CAMP
ROLL ROLL
ROLL ROLL
LEARN RAMBLER'S WORKOUTS!!
CLOVER'S FUN DOODLE PAD
Clover's Mini-Guide to Crescent Forest
FALL BOOKMARK
SEASON The Month When Tree Nuts Are Dee-schmi-cious
ROCK CLIMBING
C- Can't climb...
UNH~
Huh?
What's a matter, weakling?
Come on! You can do it!
GATHERING FOOD
I found snacks!!
How'd you find so many inedible things?
No to all of them!!!
CRAWL
Your ears are sticking up, Clover!! Lower!!
DRAG
Is this really necessary ...?
DRAG
CRACK!!
GAH!
O-okay. We'll rest here for a bit...
PANG
THROB
PANG
WHEW...
Hey, did you hear that just now?
A cracking noise...?

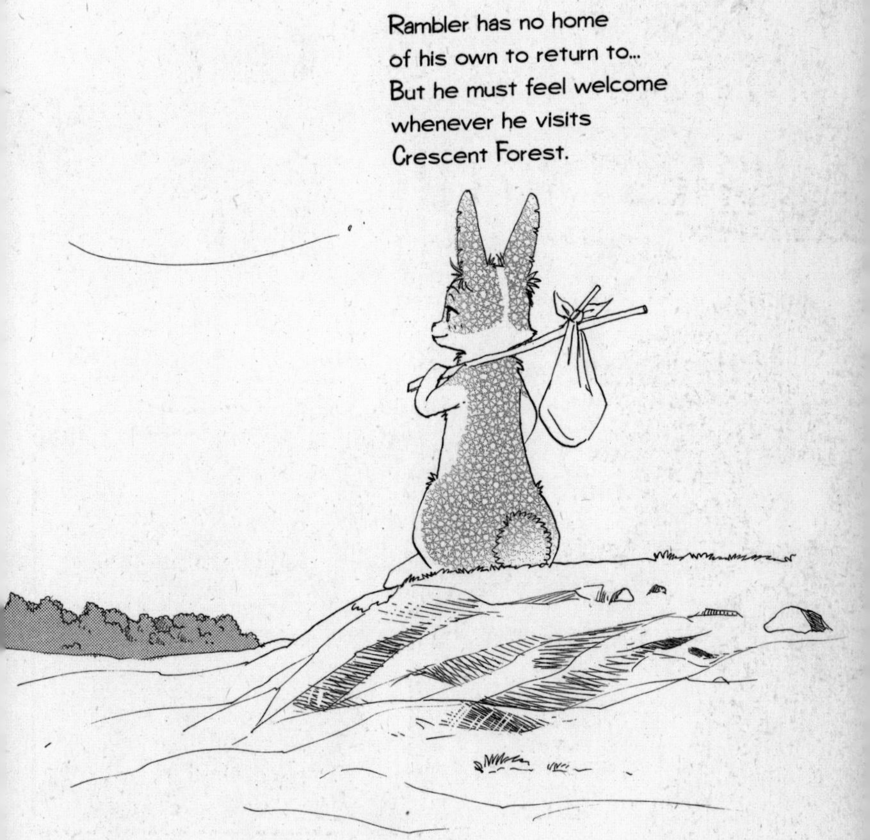
Rambler has no home
of his own to return to...
But he must feel welcome
whenever he visits
Crescent Forest.

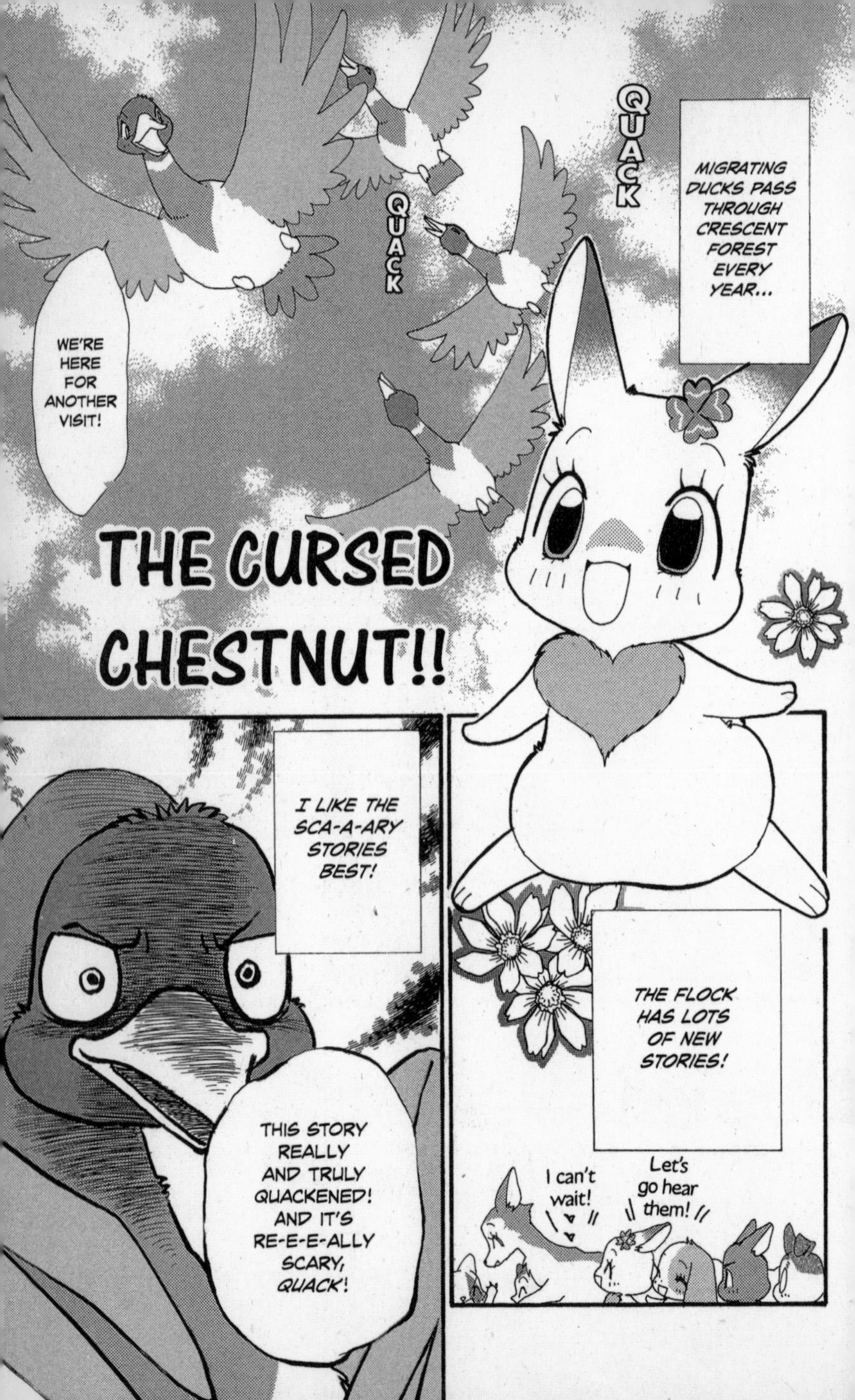
MIGRATING DUCKS PASS THROUGH CRESCENT FOREST EVERY YEAR...
QUACK
QUACK
WE'RE HERE FOR ANOTHER VISIT!
THE CURSED CHESTNUT!!
THE FLOCK HAS LOTS OF NEW STORIES!
Let's go hear them!
I can't wait!
I LIKE THE SCA-A-ARY STORIES BEST!
THIS STORY REALLY AND TRULY QUACKENED! AND IT'S RE-E-E-ALLY SCARY, QUACK!

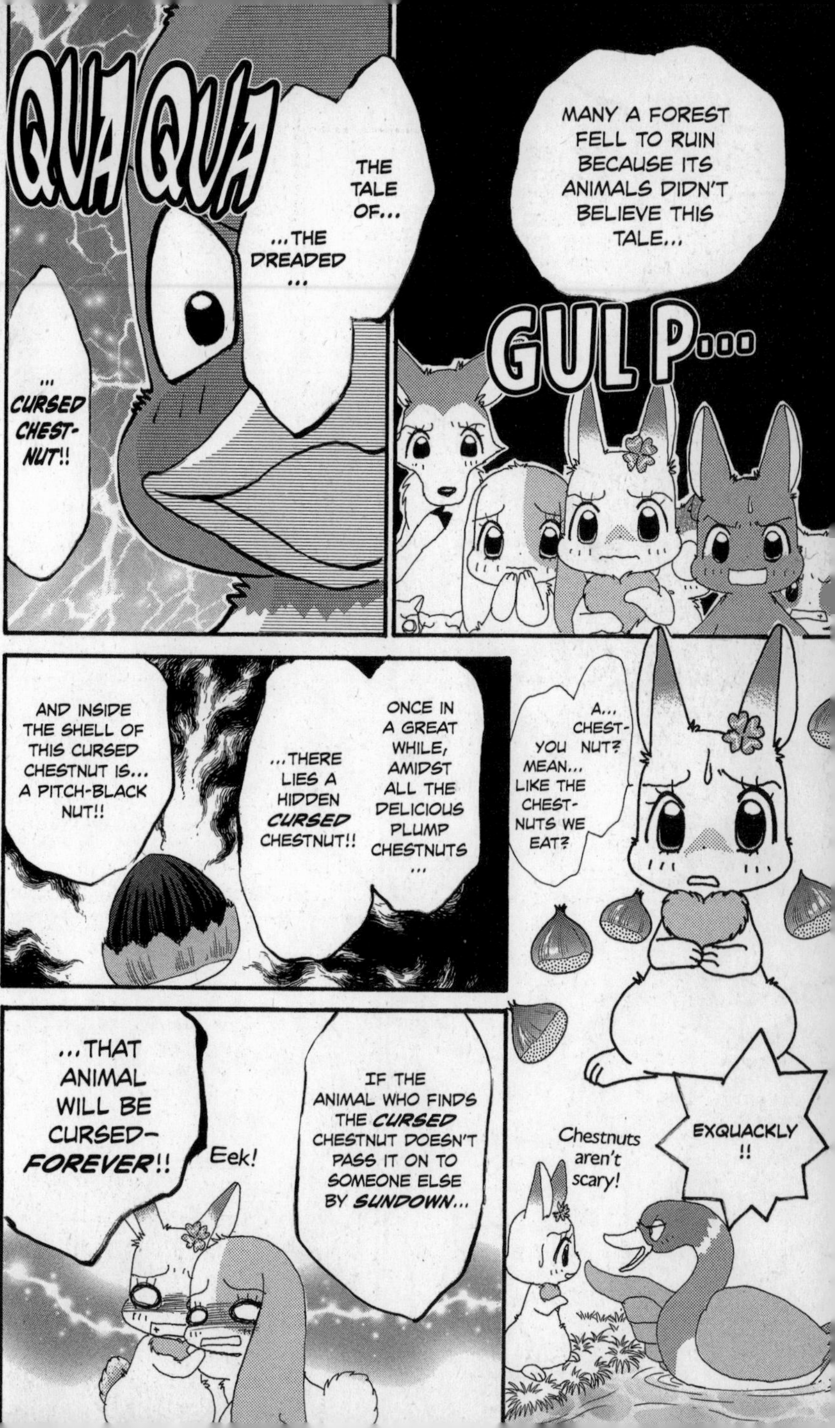
MANY A FOREST FELL TO RUIN BECAUSE ITS ANIMALS DIDN'T BELIEVE THIS TALE...
GULP...
QUA QUA
THE TALE OF...
...THE DREADED ...
... CURSED CHESTNUT!!
A... CHESTNUT?
YOU MEAN... LIKE THE CHESTNUTS WE EAT?
EXQUACKLY!!
Chestnuts aren't scary!
ONCE IN A GREAT WHILE, AMIDST ALL THE DELICIOUS PLUMP CHESTNUTS ...
...THERE LIES A HIDDEN CURSED CHESTNUT!!
AND INSIDE THE SHELL OF THIS CURSED CHESTNUT IS... A PITCH-BLACK NUT!!
IF THE ANIMAL WHO FINDS THE CURSED CHESTNUT DOESN'T PASS IT ON TO SOMEONE ELSE BY SUNDOWN...
...THAT ANIMAL WILL BE CURSED—FOREVER!!
Eek!

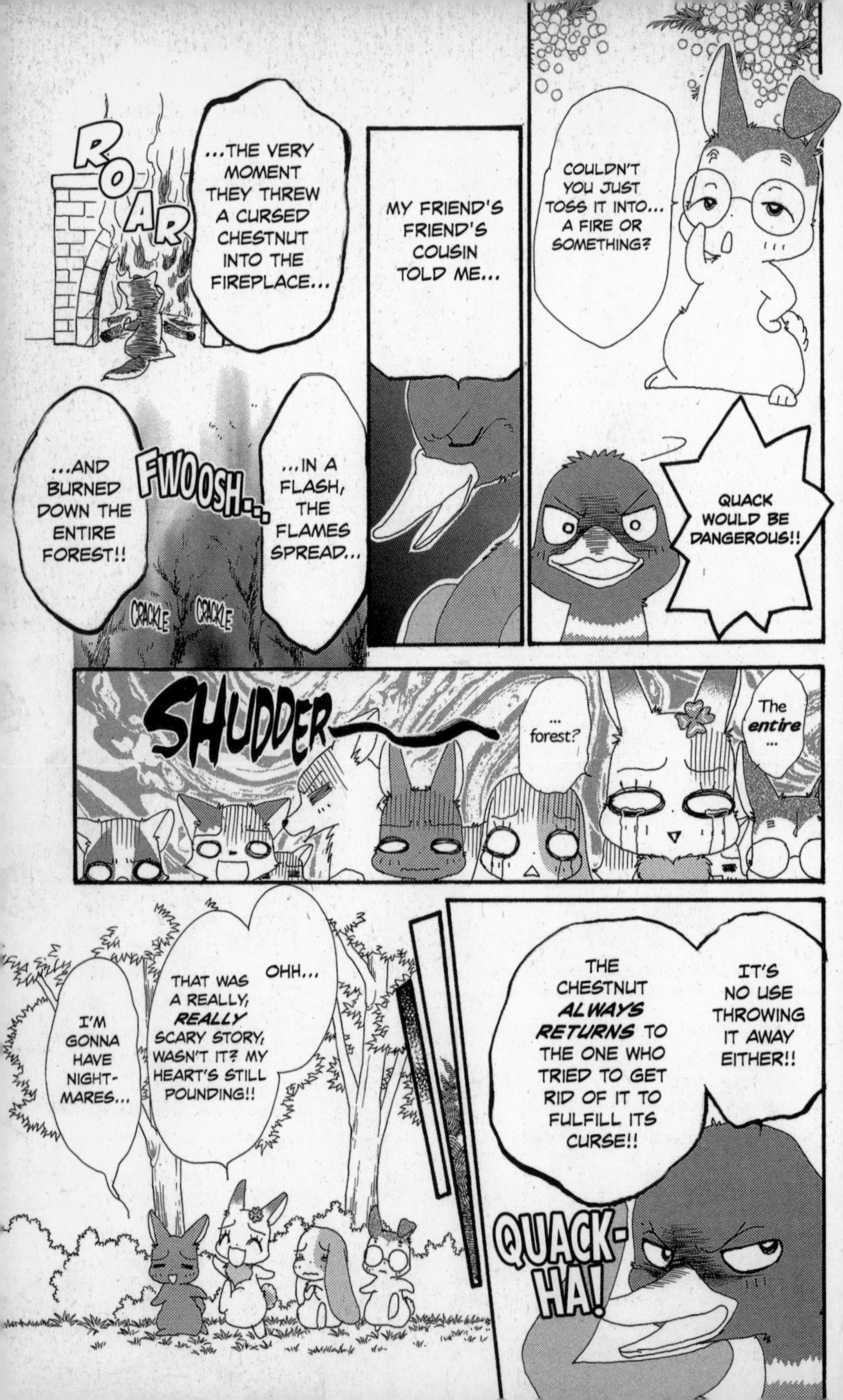
COULDN'T YOU JUST TOSS IT INTO... A FIRE OR SOMETHING?
QUACK WOULD BE DANGEROUS!!
MY FRIEND'S FRIEND'S COUSIN TOLD ME...
...THE VERY MOMENT THEY THREW A CURSED CHESTNUT INTO THE FIREPLACE...
ROAR
...IN A FLASH, THE FLAMES SPREAD...
FWOOSH...
...AND BURNED DOWN THE ENTIRE FOREST!!
CRACKLE CRACKLE
The *entire* ...
... forest?
SHUDDER
IT'S NO USE THROWING IT AWAY EITHER!!
THE CHESTNUT ***ALWAYS RETURNS*** TO THE ONE WHO TRIED TO GET RID OF IT TO FULFILL ITS CURSE!!
QUACK-HA!
OHH...
THAT WAS A REALLY, ***REALLY*** SCARY STORY, WASN'T IT? MY HEART'S STILL POUNDING!!
I'M GONNA HAVE NIGHT-MARES...

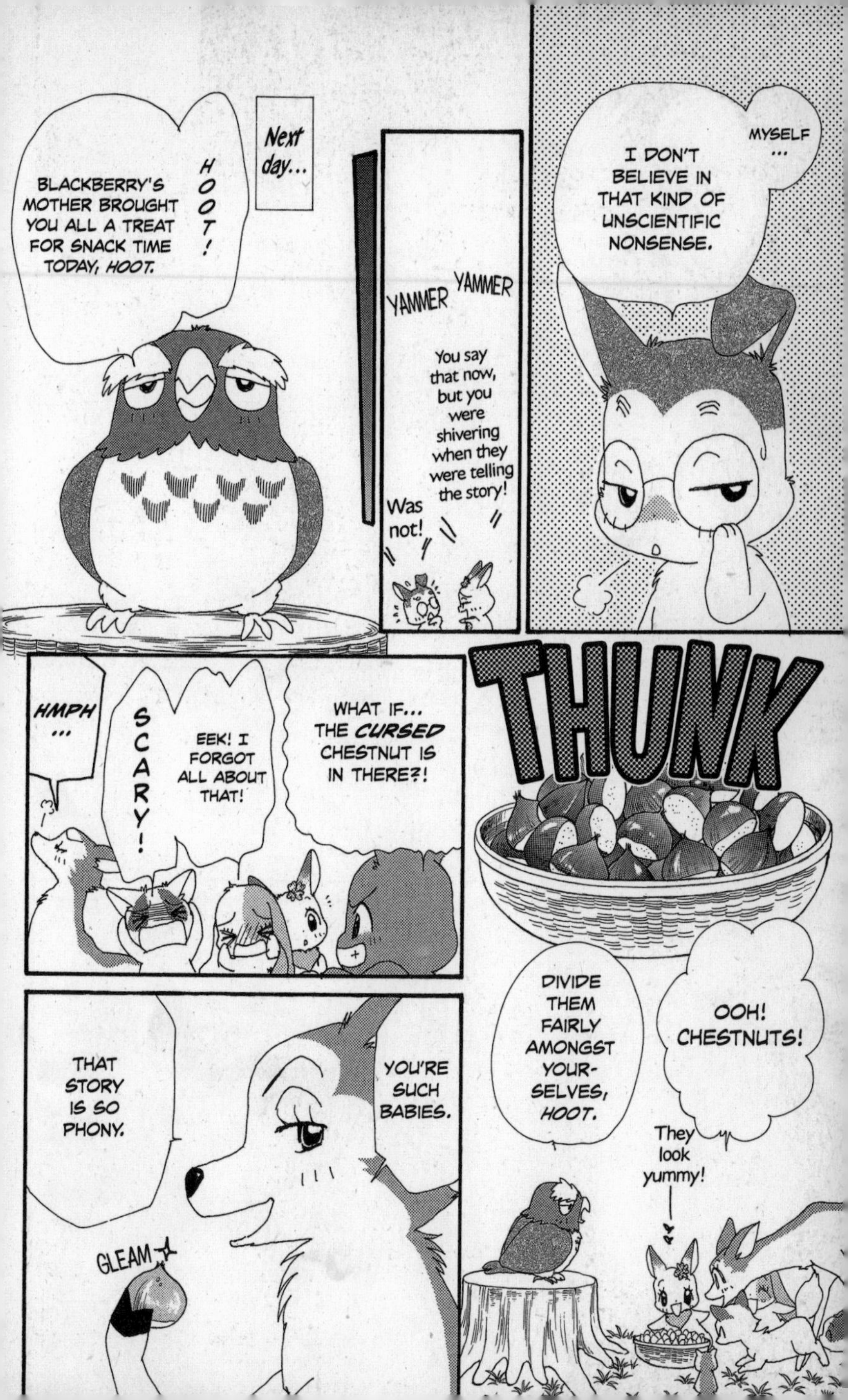
I DON'T BELIEVE IN THAT KIND OF UNSCIENTIFIC NONSENSE. MYSELF...
YAMMER YAMMER
You say that now, but you were shivering when they were telling the story!
Was not!
Next day...
HOOT!
BLACKBERRY'S MOTHER BROUGHT YOU ALL A TREAT FOR SNACK TIME TODAY, HOOT.
THUNK
OOH! CHESTNUTS!
DIVIDE THEM FAIRLY AMONGST YOUR-SELVES, HOOT.
They look yummy!
WHAT IF... THE CURSED CHESTNUT IS IN THERE?!
EEK! I FORGOT ALL ABOUT THAT!
SCARY!
HMPH...
YOU'RE SUCH BABIES.
THAT STORY IS SO PHONY.
GLEAM

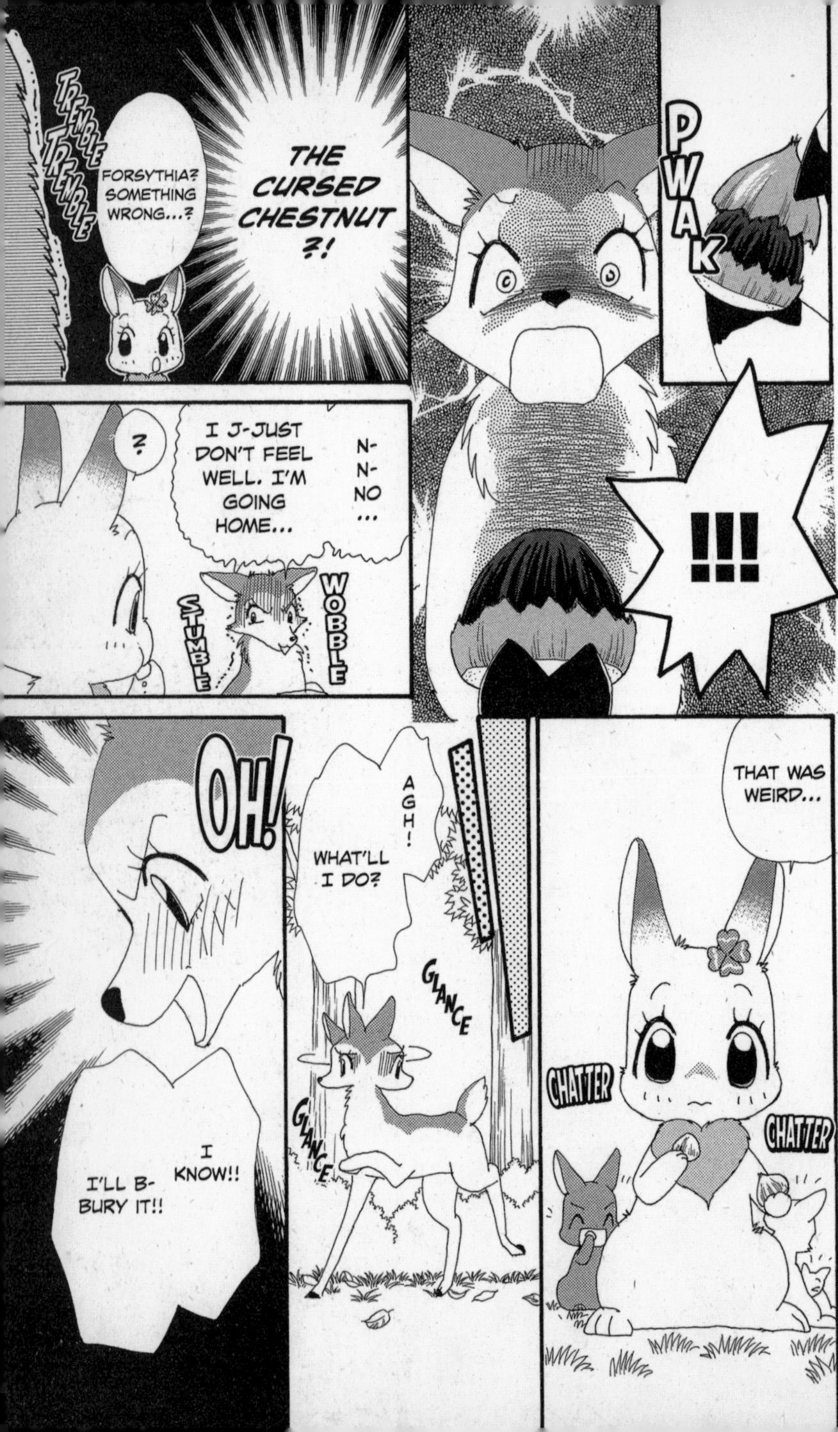
PWAK
!!!
THE CURSED CHESTNUT?!
TREMBLE TREMBLE
FORSYTHIA? SOMETHING WRONG...?
N-N-NO...
I J-JUST DON'T FEEL WELL. I'M GOING HOME...
?
WOBBLE
STUMBLE
THAT WAS WEIRD...
CHATTER
CHATTER
AGH!
WHAT'LL I DO?
GLANCE
GLANCE
OH!
I KNOW!!
I'LL B-BURY IT!!

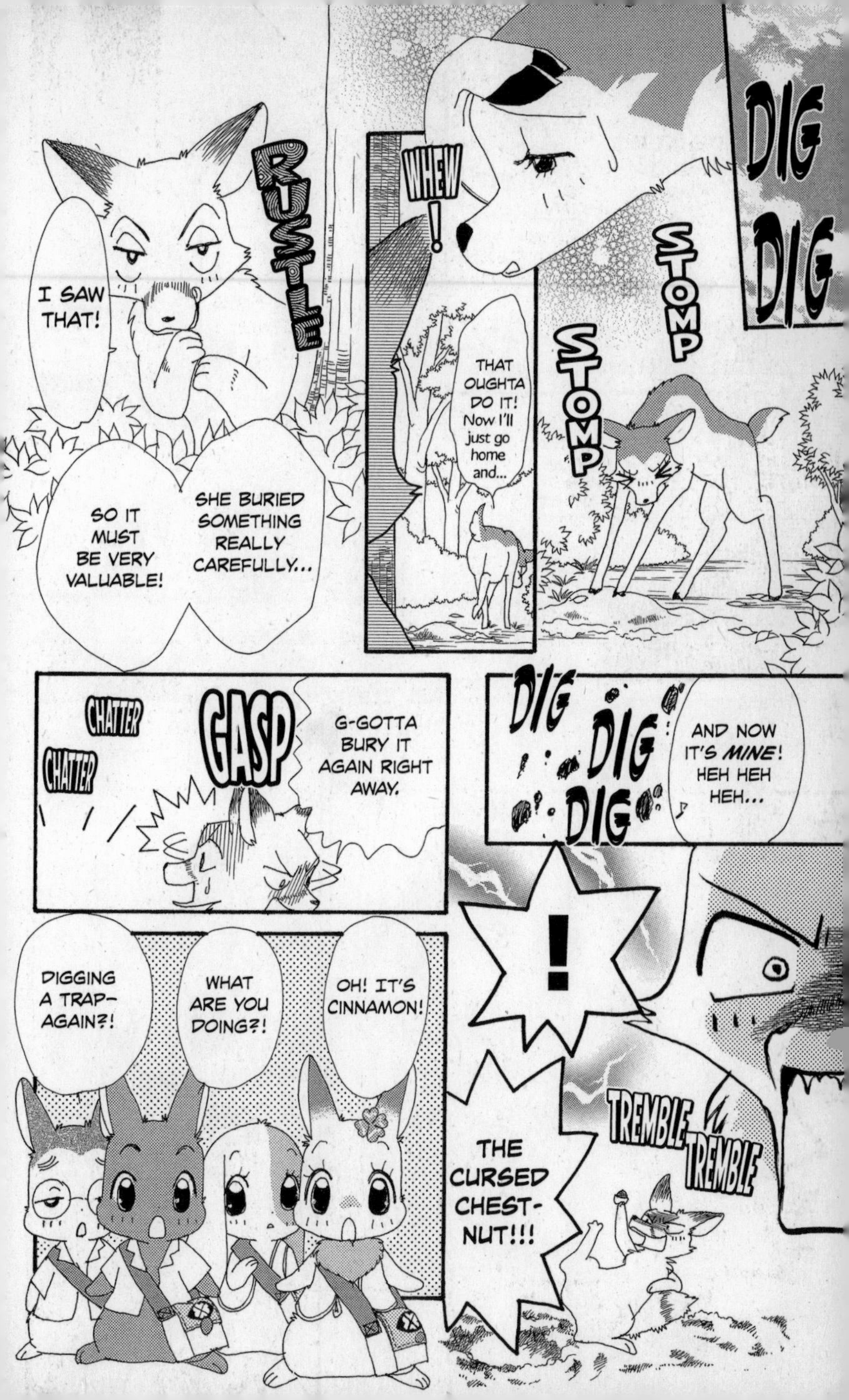
DIG DIG
STOMP
STOMP
WHEW !
THAT OUGHTA DO IT! Now I'll just go home and...
RUSTLE
I SAW THAT!
SHE BURIED SOMETHING REALLY CAREFULLY...
SO IT MUST BE VERY VALUABLE!
DIG DIG DIG
AND NOW IT'S *MINE*! HEH HEH HEH...
GASP
G-GOTTA BURY IT AGAIN RIGHT AWAY.
CHATTER
CHATTER
!
TREMBLE TREMBLE
THE CURSED CHEST-NUT!!!
OH! IT'S CINNAMON!
WHAT ARE YOU DOING?!
DIGGING A TRAP-AGAIN?!

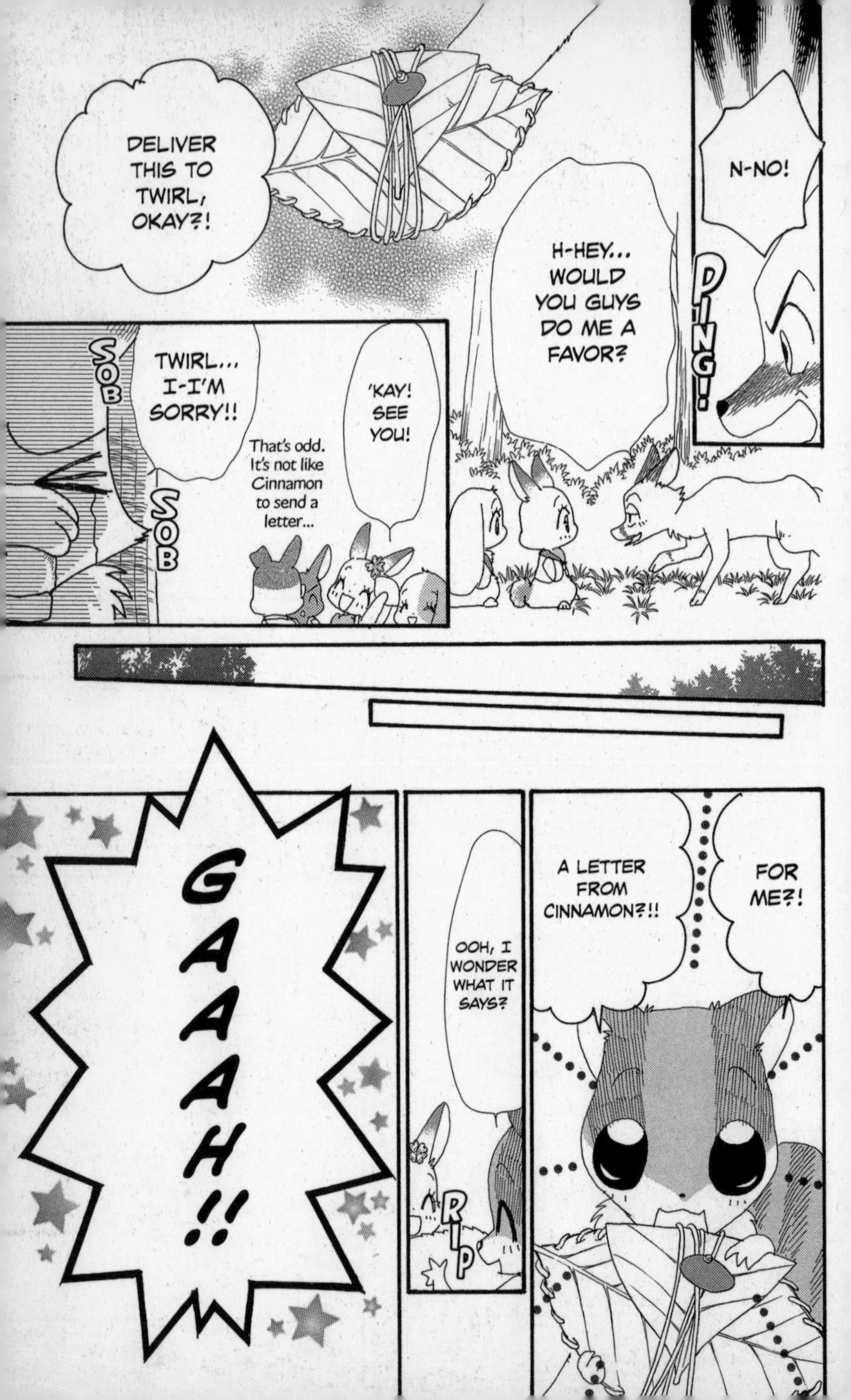
N-NO!
PING!
H-HEY... WOULD YOU GUYS DO ME A FAVOR?
DELIVER THIS TO TWIRL, OKAY?!
'KAY! SEE YOU!
That's odd. It's not like Cinnamon to send a letter...
TWIRL... I-I'M SORRY!!
SOB
SOB
FOR ME?!
A LETTER FROM CINNAMON?!!
OOH, I WONDER WHAT IT SAYS?
RIP
GAAAH!!

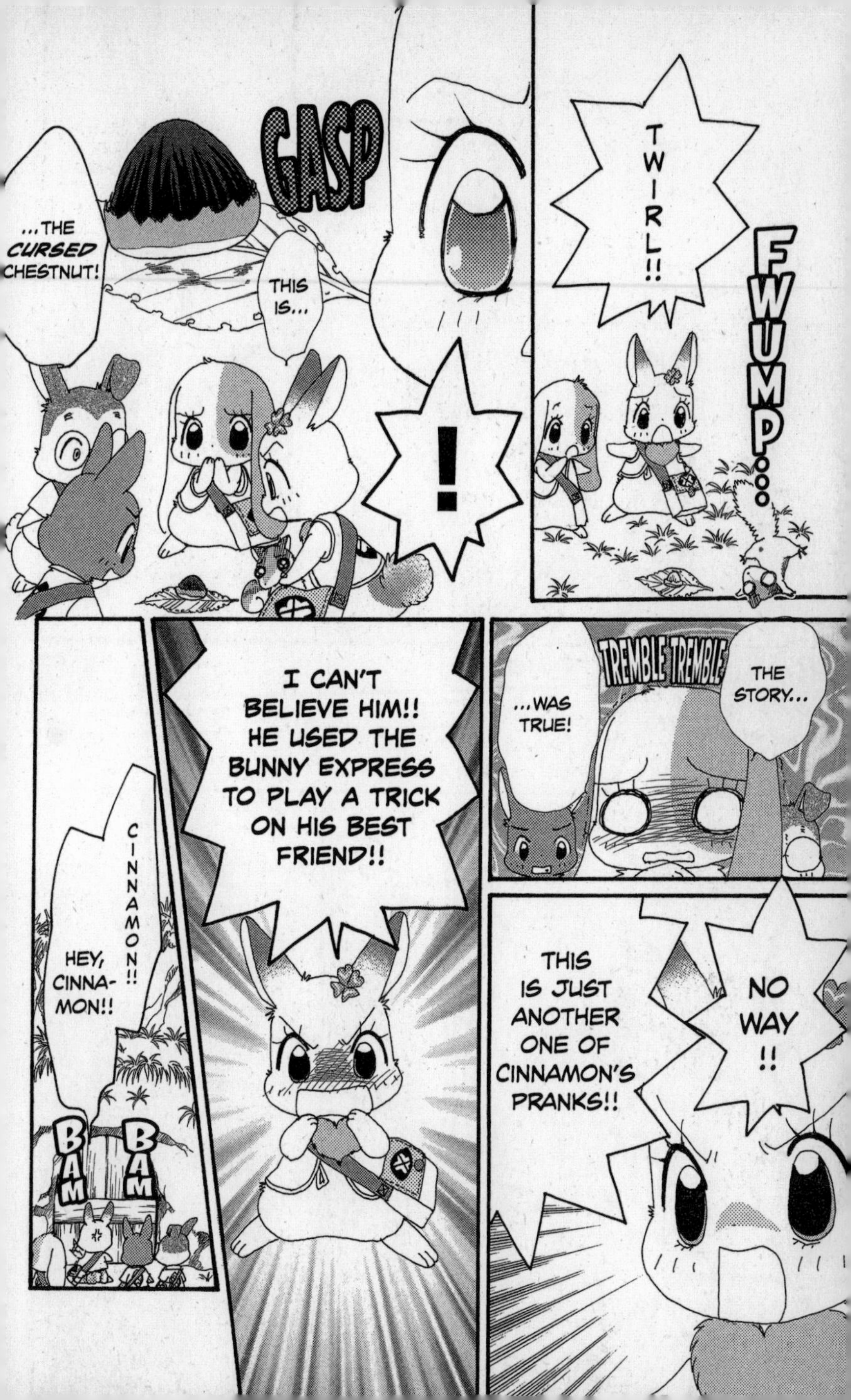
TWIRL!!
FWUMP...
GASP
THIS IS...
...THE CURSED CHESTNUT!
!
THE STORY...
TREMBLE TREMBLE
...WAS TRUE!
NO WAY!!
THIS IS JUST ANOTHER ONE OF CINNAMON'S PRANKS!!
I CAN'T BELIEVE HIM!! HE USED THE BUNNY EXPRESS TO PLAY A TRICK ON HIS BEST FRIEND!!
CINNAMON!!
HEY, CINNA-MON!!
BAM
BAM

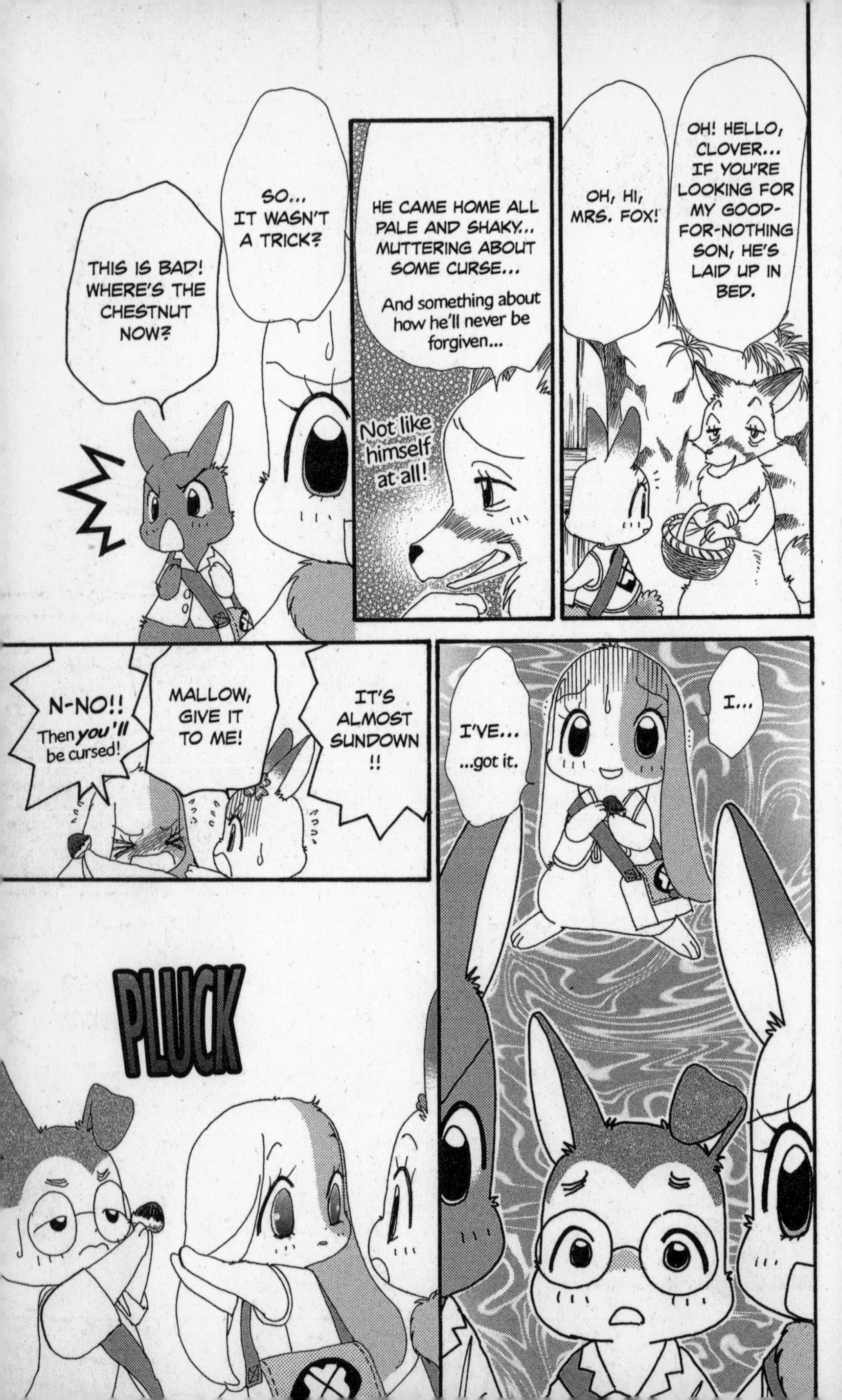
OH! HELLO, CLOVER... IF YOU'RE LOOKING FOR MY GOOD-FOR-NOTHING SON, HE'S LAID UP IN BED.
OH, HI, MRS. FOX!
HE CAME HOME ALL PALE AND SHAKY... MUTTERING ABOUT SOME CURSE...
And something about how he'll never be forgiven...
Not like himself at all!
SO... IT WASN'T A TRICK?
THIS IS BAD! WHERE'S THE CHESTNUT NOW?
I...
I'VE...
...got it.
IT'S ALMOST SUNDOWN !!
MALLOW, GIVE IT TO ME!
N-NO!!
Then *you'll* be cursed!
PLUCK

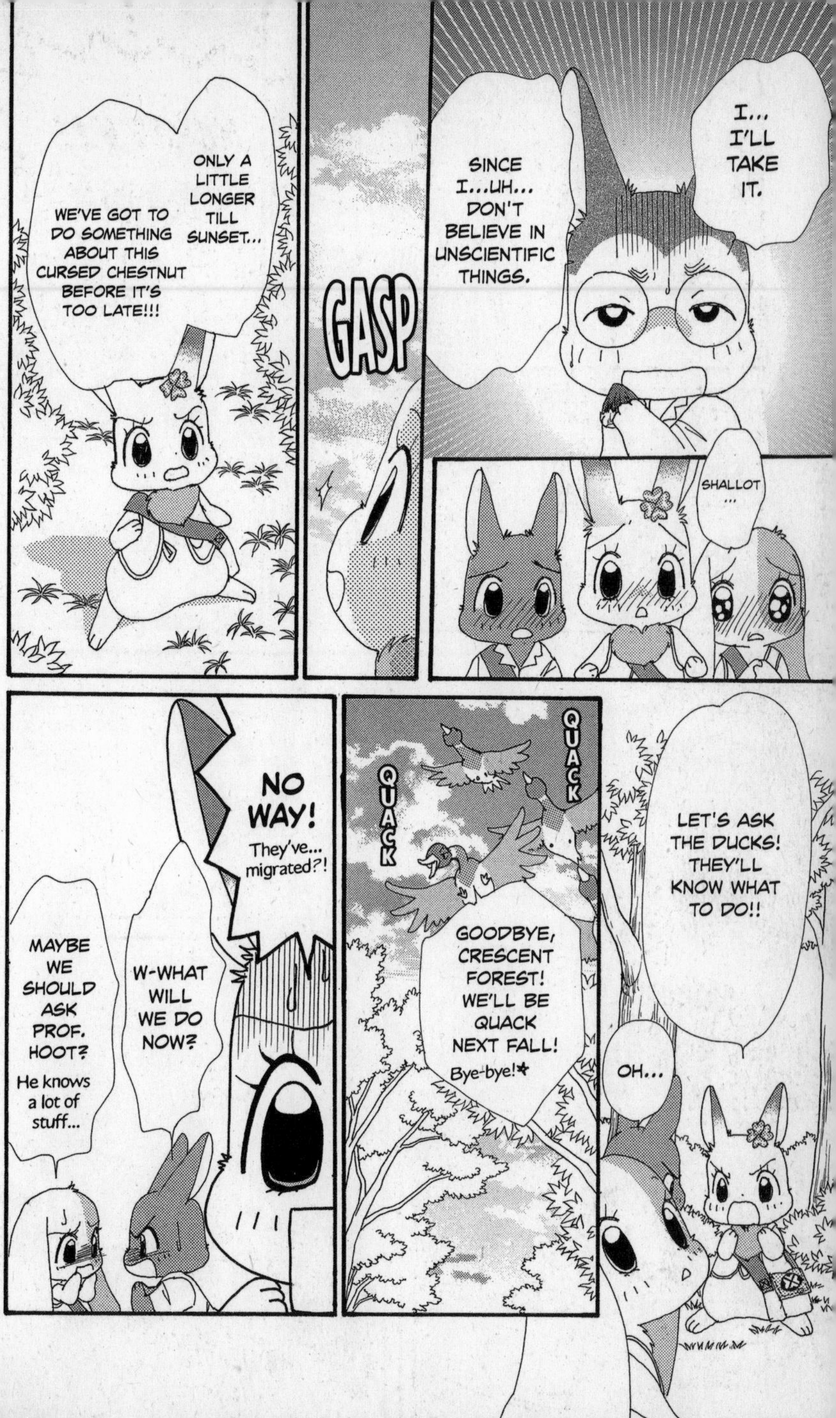
I... I'LL TAKE IT.
SINCE I...UH... DON'T BELIEVE IN UNSCIENTIFIC THINGS.
SHALLOT ...
GASP
ONLY A LITTLE LONGER TILL SUNSET...
WE'VE GOT TO DO SOMETHING ABOUT THIS CURSED CHESTNUT BEFORE IT'S TOO LATE!!!
LET'S ASK THE DUCKS! THEY'LL KNOW WHAT TO DO!!
OH...
QUACK
QUACK
GOODBYE, CRESCENT FOREST! WE'LL BE QUACK NEXT FALL!
Bye-bye!✬
NO WAY!
They've... migrated?!
W-WHAT WILL WE DO NOW?
MAYBE WE SHOULD ASK PROF. HOOT?
He knows a lot of stuff...

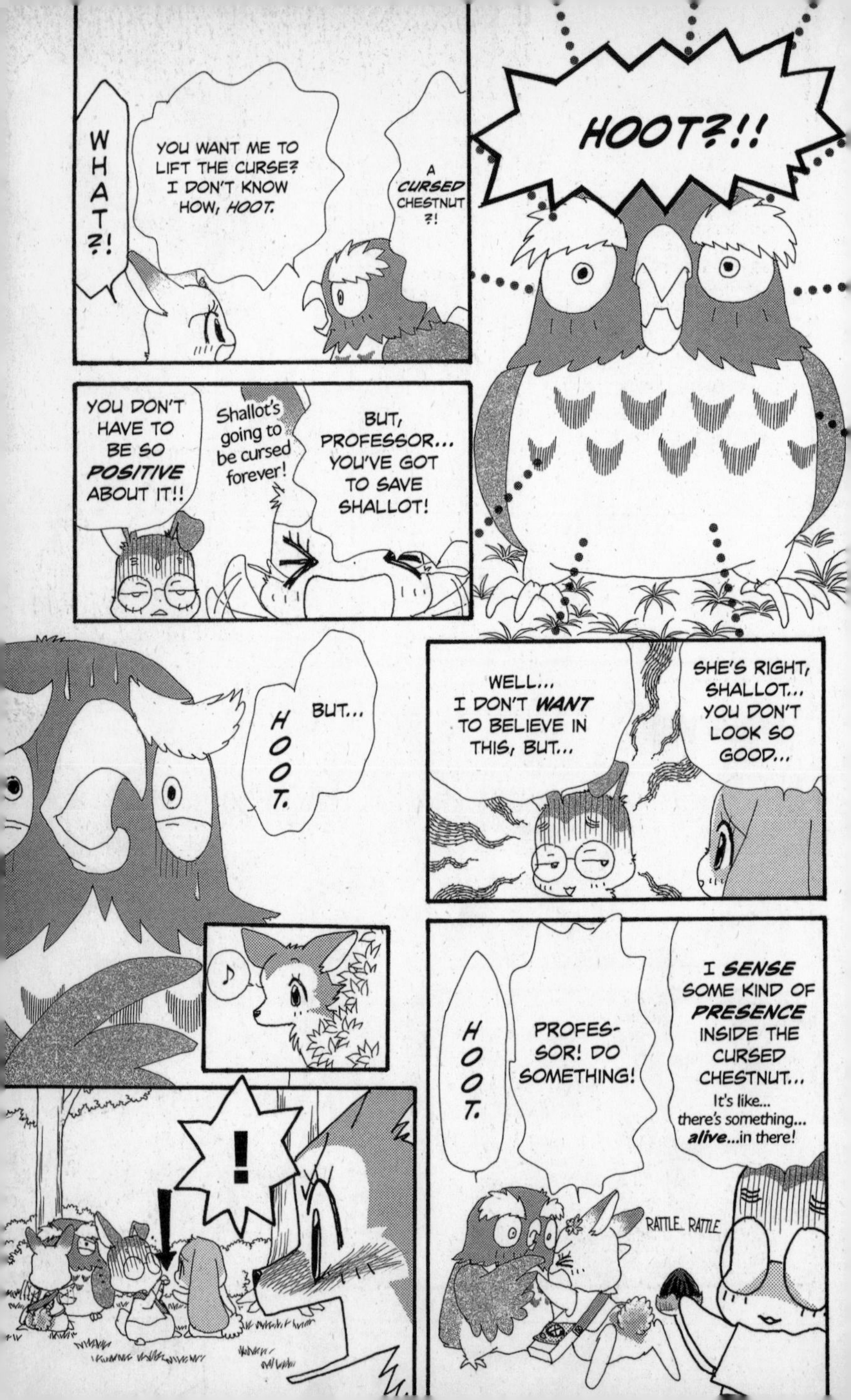
HOOT?!!
A CURSED CHESTNUT?!
YOU WANT ME TO LIFT THE CURSE? I DON'T KNOW HOW, HOOT.
WHAT?!
BUT, PROFESSOR... YOU'VE GOT TO SAVE SHALLOT!
Shallot's going to be cursed forever!
YOU DON'T HAVE TO BE SO POSITIVE ABOUT IT!!
SHE'S RIGHT, SHALLOT... YOU DON'T LOOK SO GOOD...
WELL... I DON'T WANT TO BELIEVE IN THIS, BUT...
BUT...
HOOT.
♪
I SENSE SOME KIND OF PRESENCE INSIDE THE CURSED CHESTNUT...
It's like... there's something... alive...in there!
PROFES-SOR! DO SOMETHING!
HOOT.
RATTLE... RATTLE
!

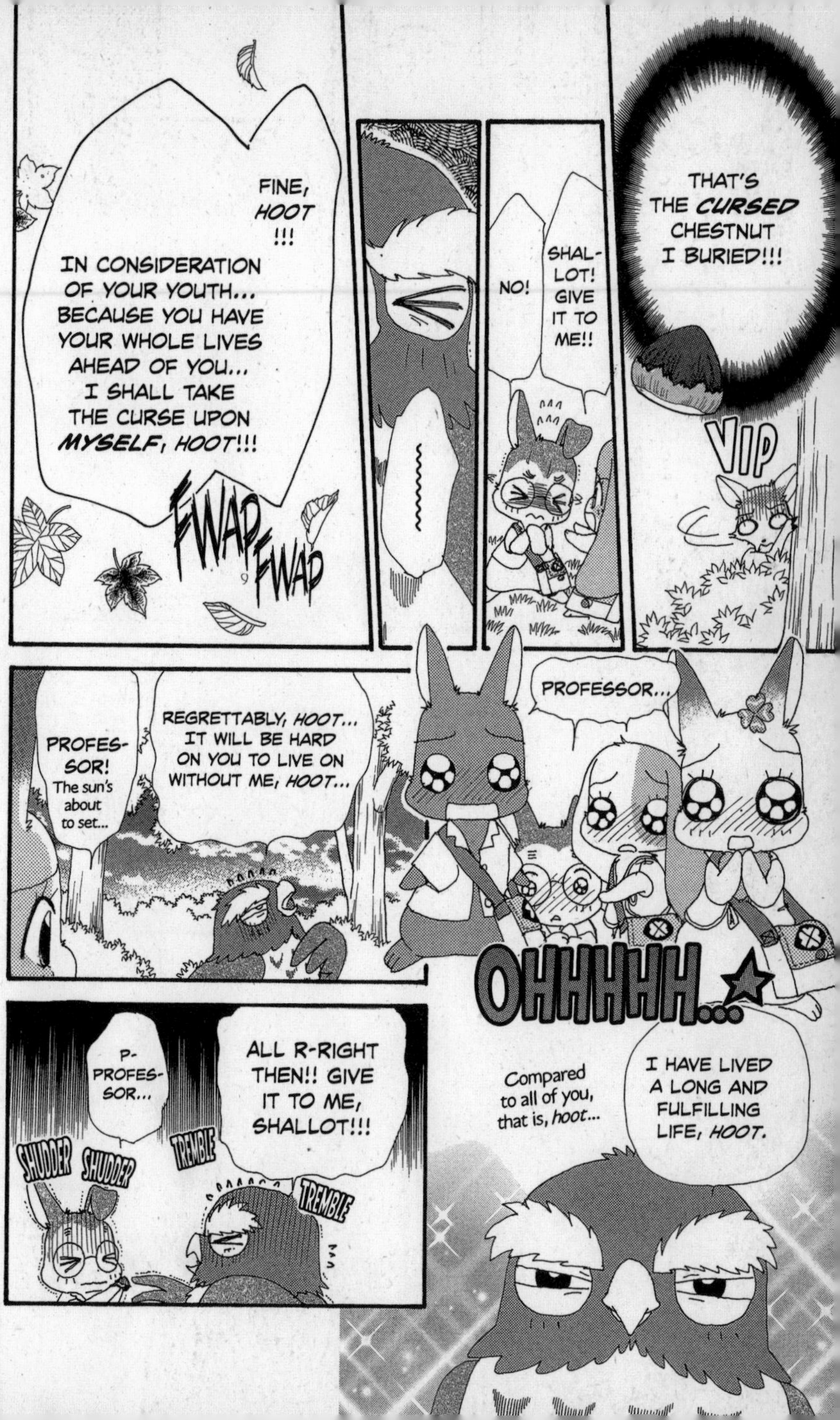
THAT'S THE *CURSED* CHESTNUT I BURIED!!!
VIP
SHAL-LOT! GIVE IT TO ME!!
NO!
FINE, *HOOT* !!!
IN CONSIDERATION OF YOUR YOUTH... BECAUSE YOU HAVE YOUR WHOLE LIVES AHEAD OF YOU... I SHALL TAKE THE CURSE UPON *MYSELF*, *HOOT*!!!
FWAP FWAP
PROFESSOR...
OHHHHH...
REGRETTABLY, *HOOT*... IT WILL BE HARD ON YOU TO LIVE ON WITHOUT ME, *HOOT*...
PROFES-SOR! The sun's about to set...
I HAVE LIVED A LONG AND FULFILLING LIFE, *HOOT*.
Compared to all of you, that is, *hoot*...
ALL R-RIGHT THEN!! GIVE IT TO ME, SHALLOT!!!
P-PROFES-SOR...
TREMBLE
TREMBLE
SHUDDER
SHUDDER

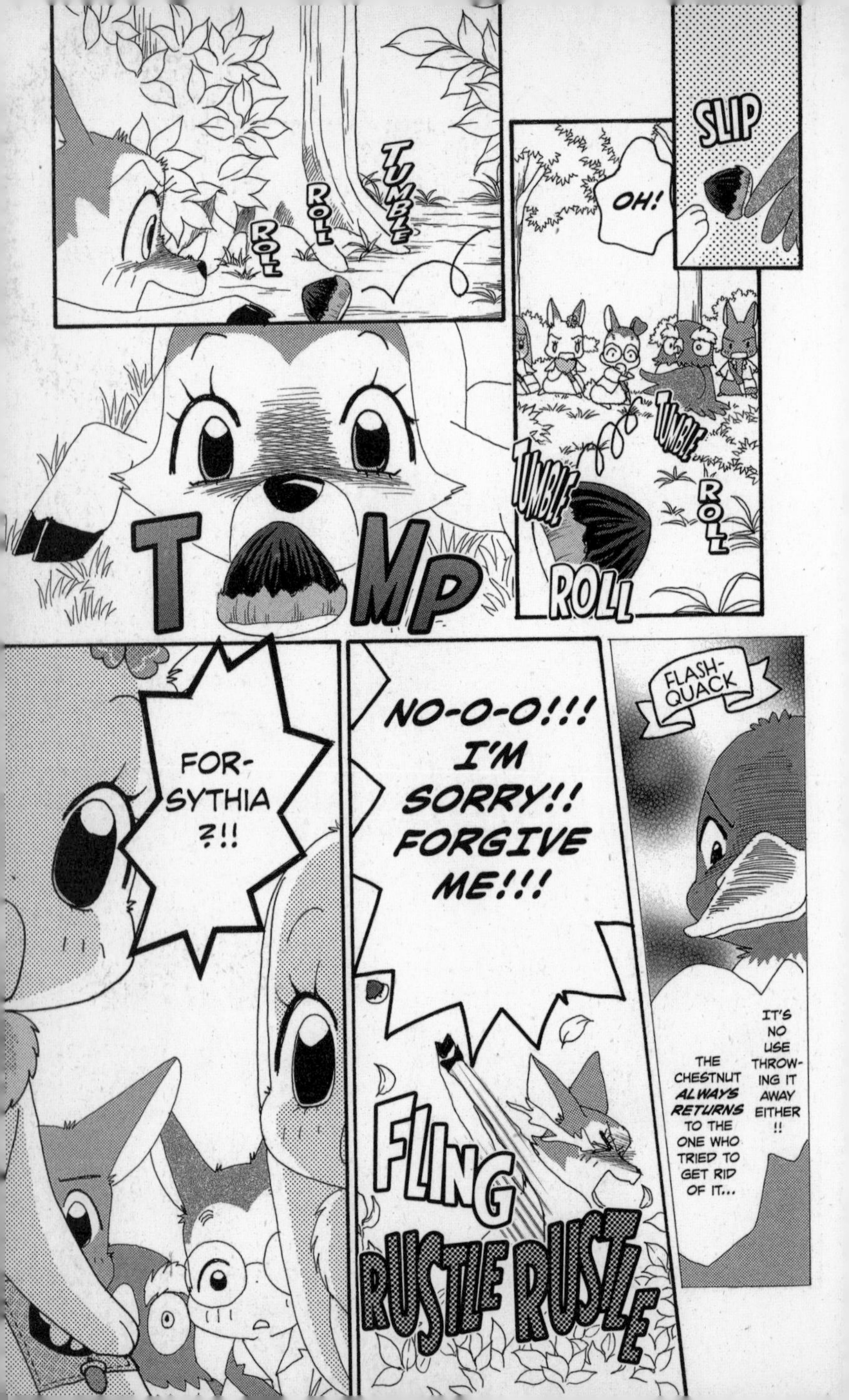
SLIP
OH!
TUMBLE
TUMBLE
ROLL
ROLL
TUMBLE
ROLL
ROLL
TOMP
FLASH-QUACK
IT'S NO USE THROWING IT AWAY EITHER!!
THE CHESTNUT *ALWAYS RETURNS* TO THE ONE WHO TRIED TO GET RID OF IT...
NO-O-O!!! I'M SORRY!! FORGIVE ME!!!
FLING
RUSTLE RUSTLE
FOR-SYTHIA?!!

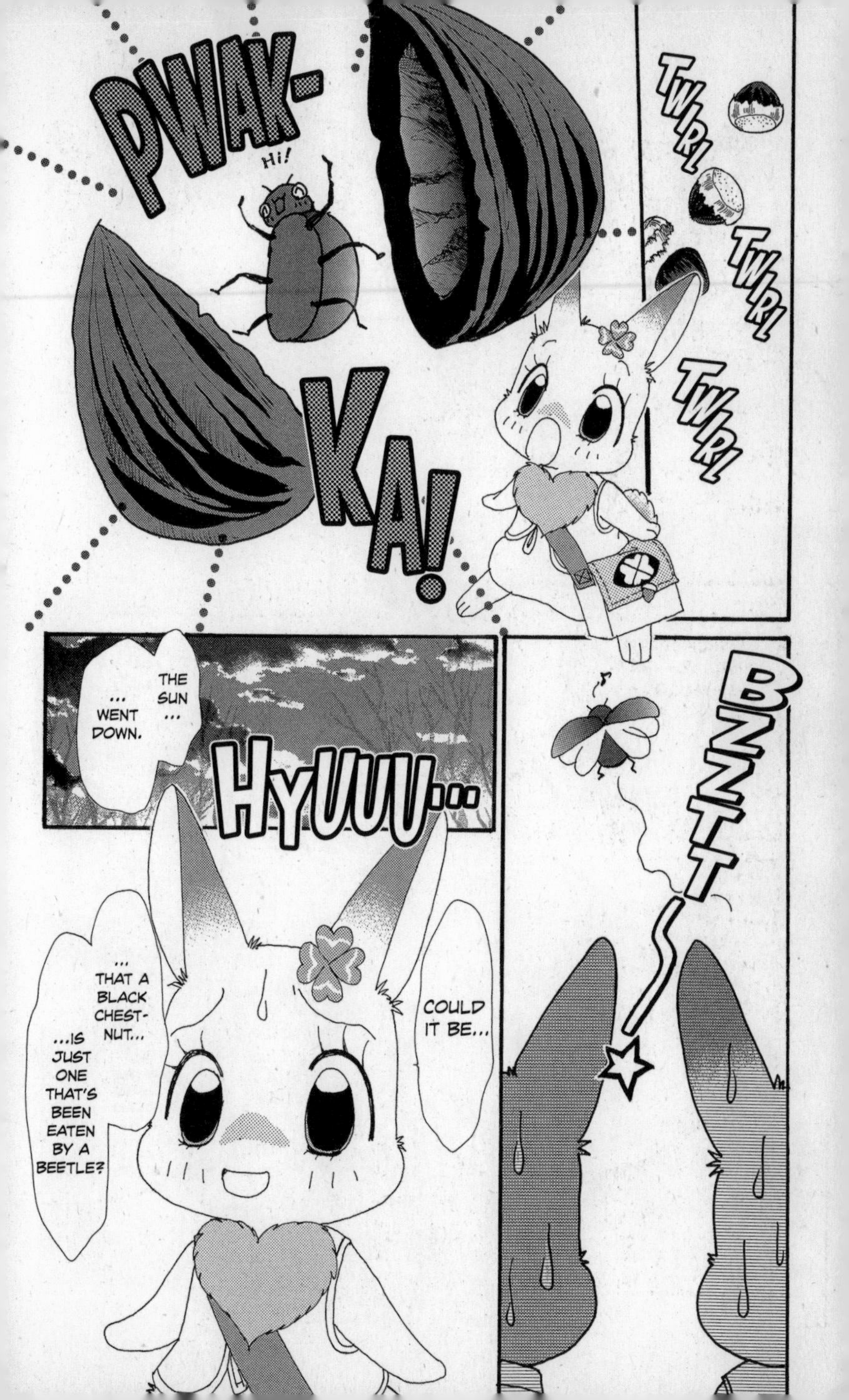
TWIRL
TWIRL
TWIRL
PWAK-
Hi!
KA!
BZZTT
THE SUN...
...WENT DOWN.
HYUUU...
COULD IT BE...
...THAT A BLACK CHESTNUT...
...IS JUST ONE THAT'S BEEN EATEN BY A BEETLE?

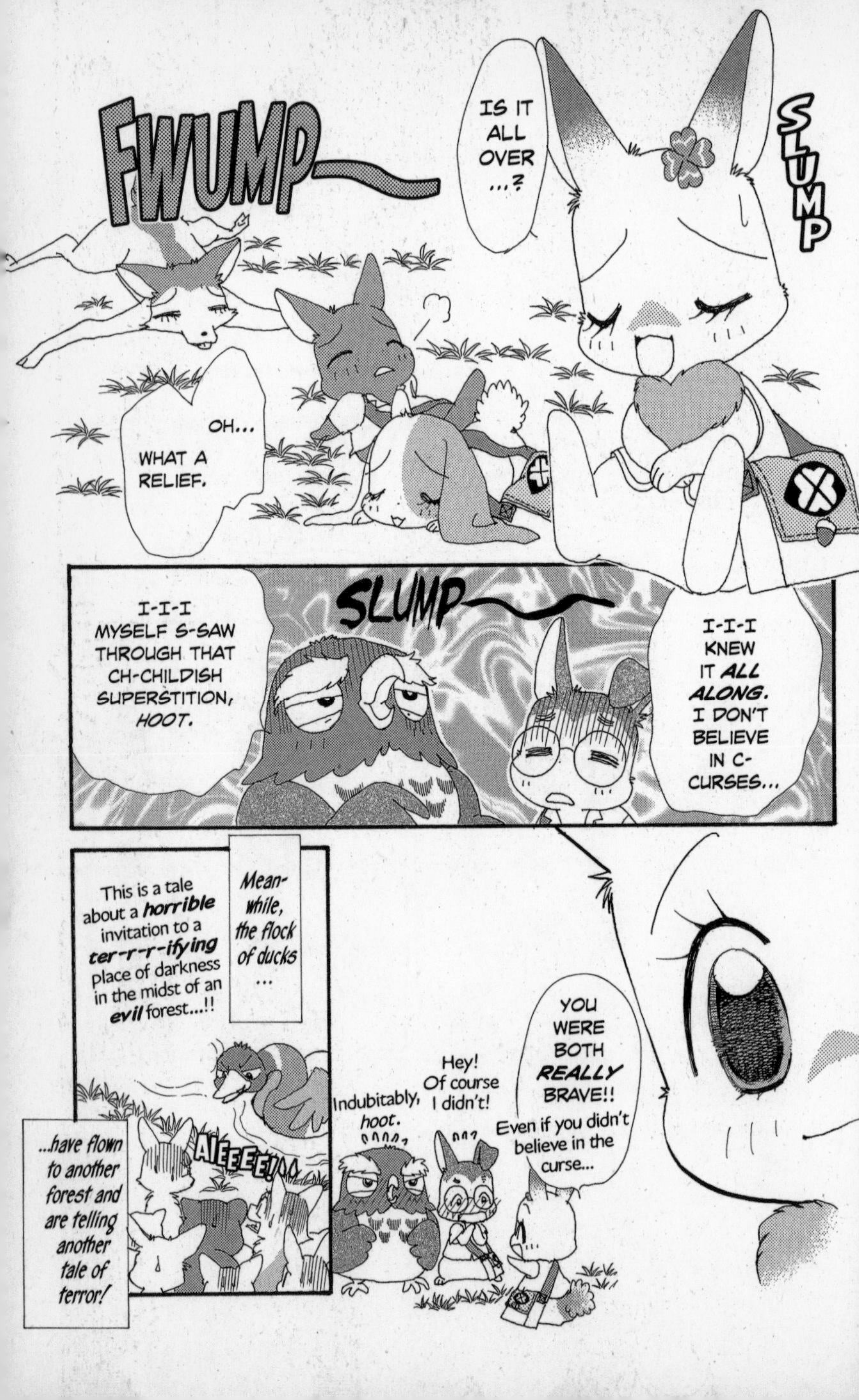

IS IT ALL OVER ...?
SLUMP
FWUMP—
OH... WHAT A RELIEF.
I-I-I KNEW IT ALL ALONG. I DON'T BELIEVE IN C-CURSES...
SLUMP—
I-I-I MYSELF S-SAW THROUGH THAT CH-CHILDISH SUPERSTITION, HOOT.
YOU WERE BOTH REALLY BRAVE!!
Even if you didn't believe in the curse...
Hey! Of course I didn't!
Indubitably, hoot.
Mean-while, the flock of ducks ...
This is a tale about a horrible invitation to a ter-r-r-ifying place of darkness in the midst of an evil forest...!!
AIEEEE!
...have flown to another forest and are telling another tale of terror!

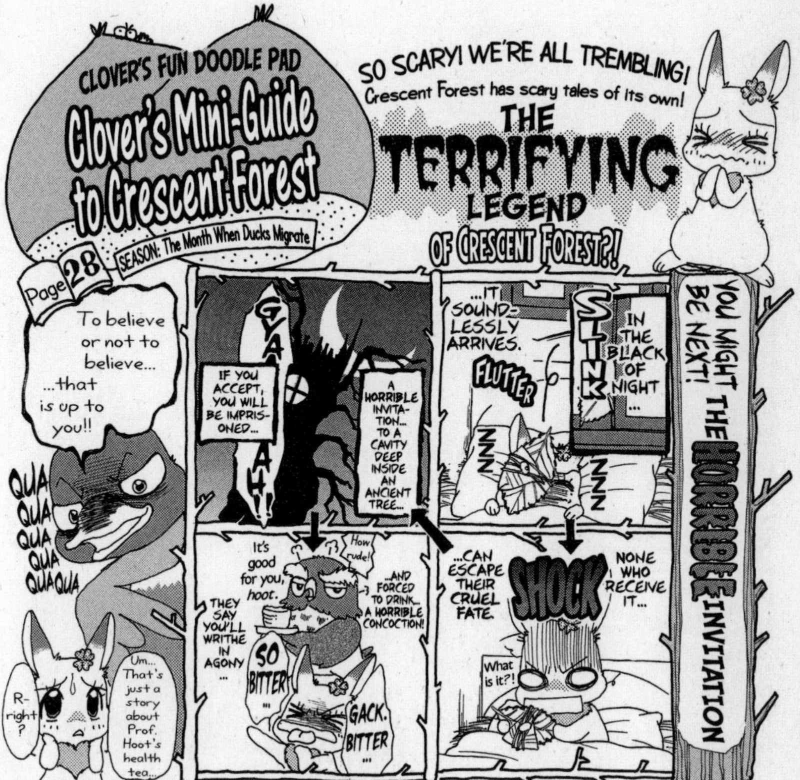
CLOVER'S FUN DOODLE PAD
Clover's Mini-Guide to Crescent Forest
SEASON: The Month When Ducks Migrate
Page 28
SO SCARY! WE'RE ALL TREMBLING!
Crescent Forest has scary tales of its own!
THE TERRIFYING LEGEND OF CRESCENT FOREST?!
YOU MIGHT BE NEXT! THE HORRIBLE INVITATION
IN THE BLACK OF NIGHT...
SLINK
...IT SOUNDLESSLY ARRIVES.
FLUTTER
ZZZ
ZZZ
A HORRIBLE INVITATION... TO A CAVITY DEEP INSIDE AN ANCIENT TREE...
GYAAH!!
IF YOU ACCEPT, YOU WILL BE IMPRISONED...
NONE WHO RECEIVE IT...
SHOCK
...CAN ESCAPE THEIR CRUEL FATE.
What is it?!
...AND FORCED TO DRINK... A HORRIBLE CONCOCTION!
How rude!
It's good for you, hoot.
THEY SAY YOU'LL WRITHE IN AGONY...
SO BITTER...
GACK. BITTER...
To believe or not to believe... ...that is up to you!!
QUA QUA QUA QUA QUAQUA
Um... That's just a story about Prof. Hoot's health tea...
R-right?

The next tale is about
Kale's little brothers! ☆

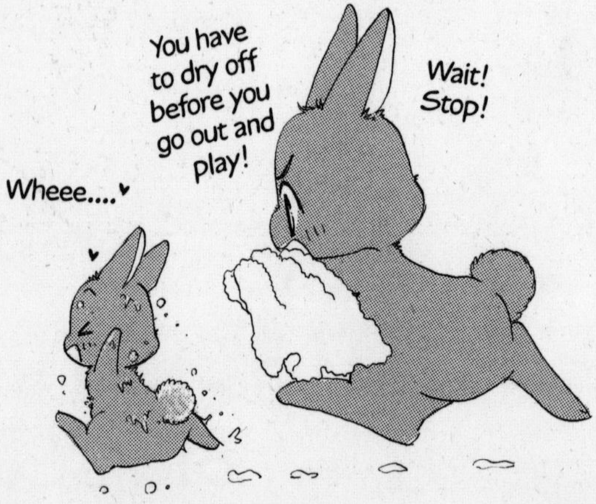
Wait! Stop!
You have to dry off before you go out and play!
Wheee....♥

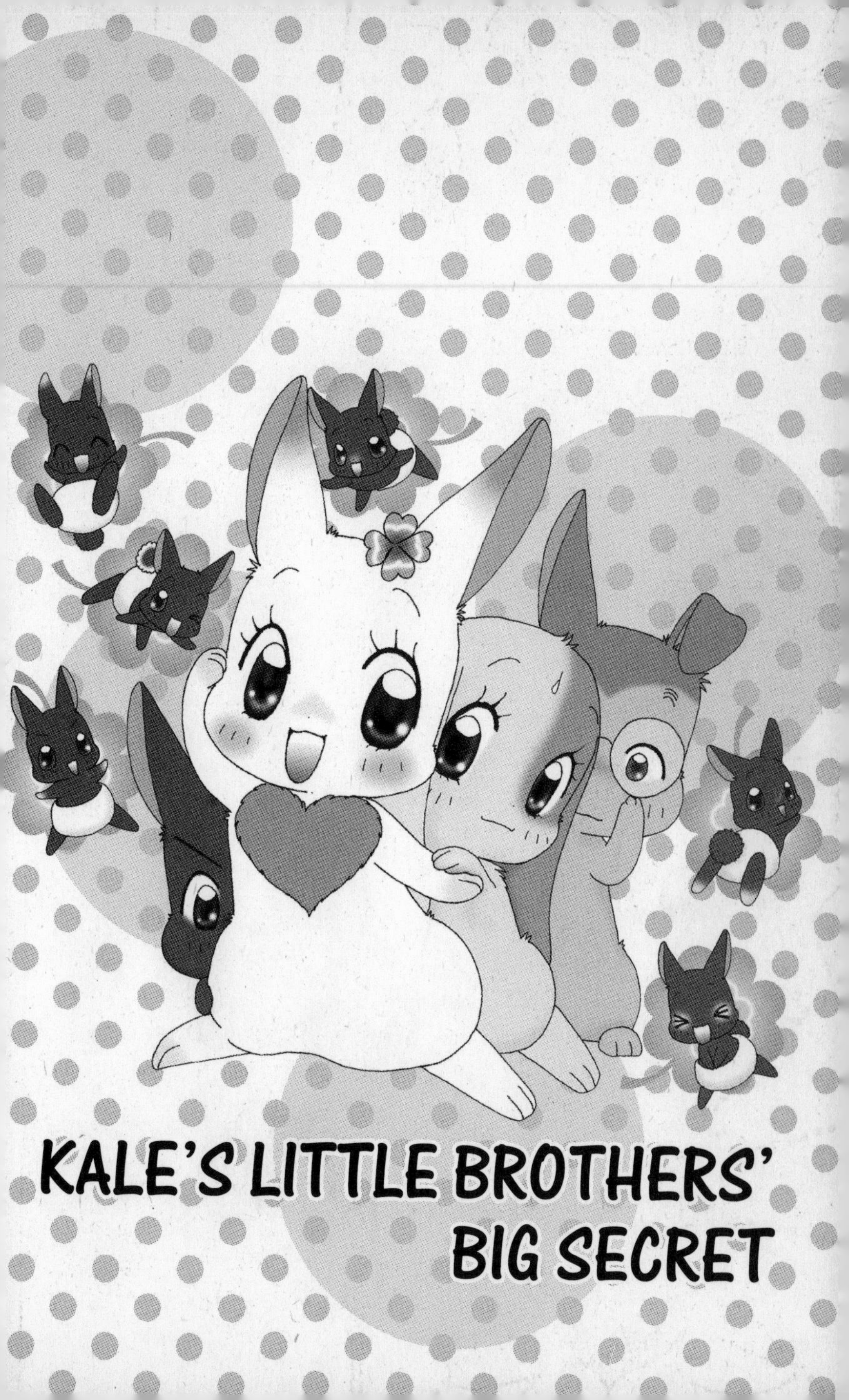
KALE'S LITTLE BROTHERS'
BIG SECRET

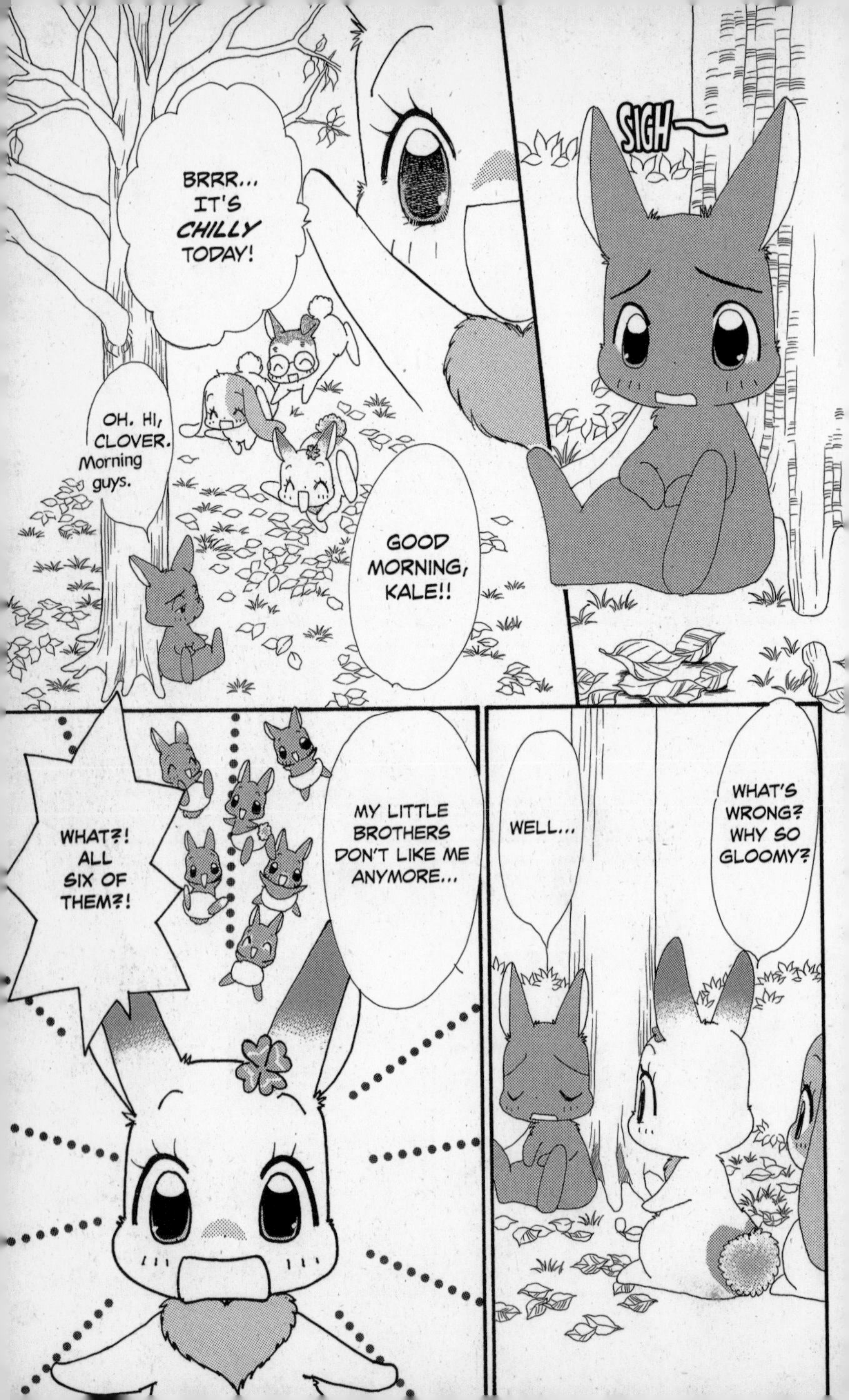
SIGH~
BRRR... IT'S *CHILLY* TODAY!
GOOD MORNING, KALE!!
OH. HI, CLOVER. Morning guys.
WHAT'S WRONG? WHY SO GLOOMY?
WELL...
MY LITTLE BROTHERS DON'T LIKE ME ANYMORE...
WHAT?! ALL SIX OF THEM?!

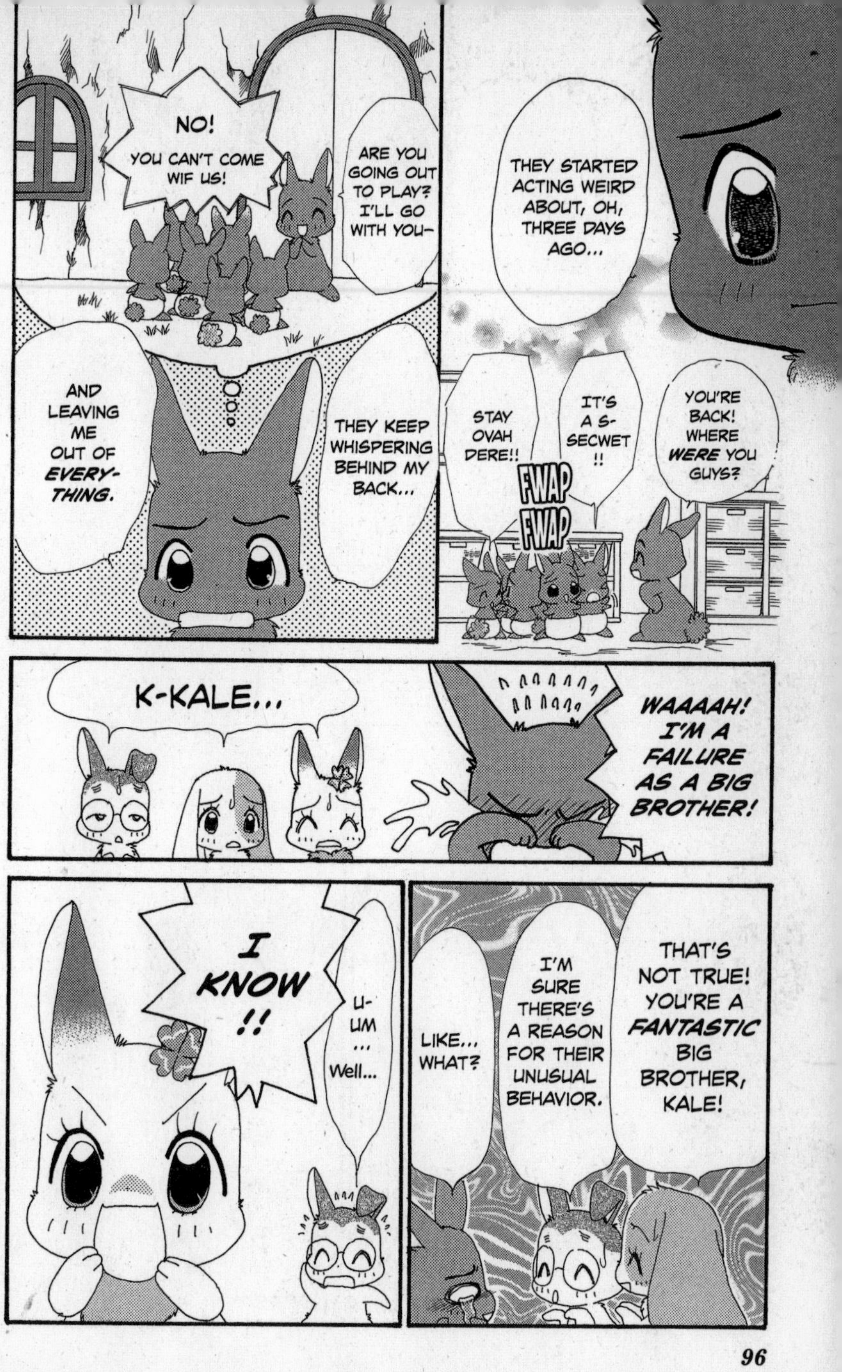
THEY STARTED ACTING WEIRD ABOUT, OH, THREE DAYS AGO...
YOU'RE BACK! WHERE *WERE* YOU GUYS?
IT'S A S-SECWET!!
STAY OVAH DERE!!
FWAP FWAP
ARE YOU GOING OUT TO PLAY? I'LL GO WITH YOU—
NO! YOU CAN'T COME WIF US!
THEY KEEP WHISPERING BEHIND MY BACK...
AND LEAVING ME OUT OF *EVERYTHING.*
WAAAAH! I'M A FAILURE AS A BIG BROTHER!
K-KALE...
THAT'S NOT TRUE! YOU'RE A *FANTASTIC* BIG BROTHER, KALE!
I'M SURE THERE'S A REASON FOR THEIR UNUSUAL BEHAVIOR.
LIKE... WHAT?
U-UM... Well...
I KNOW!!

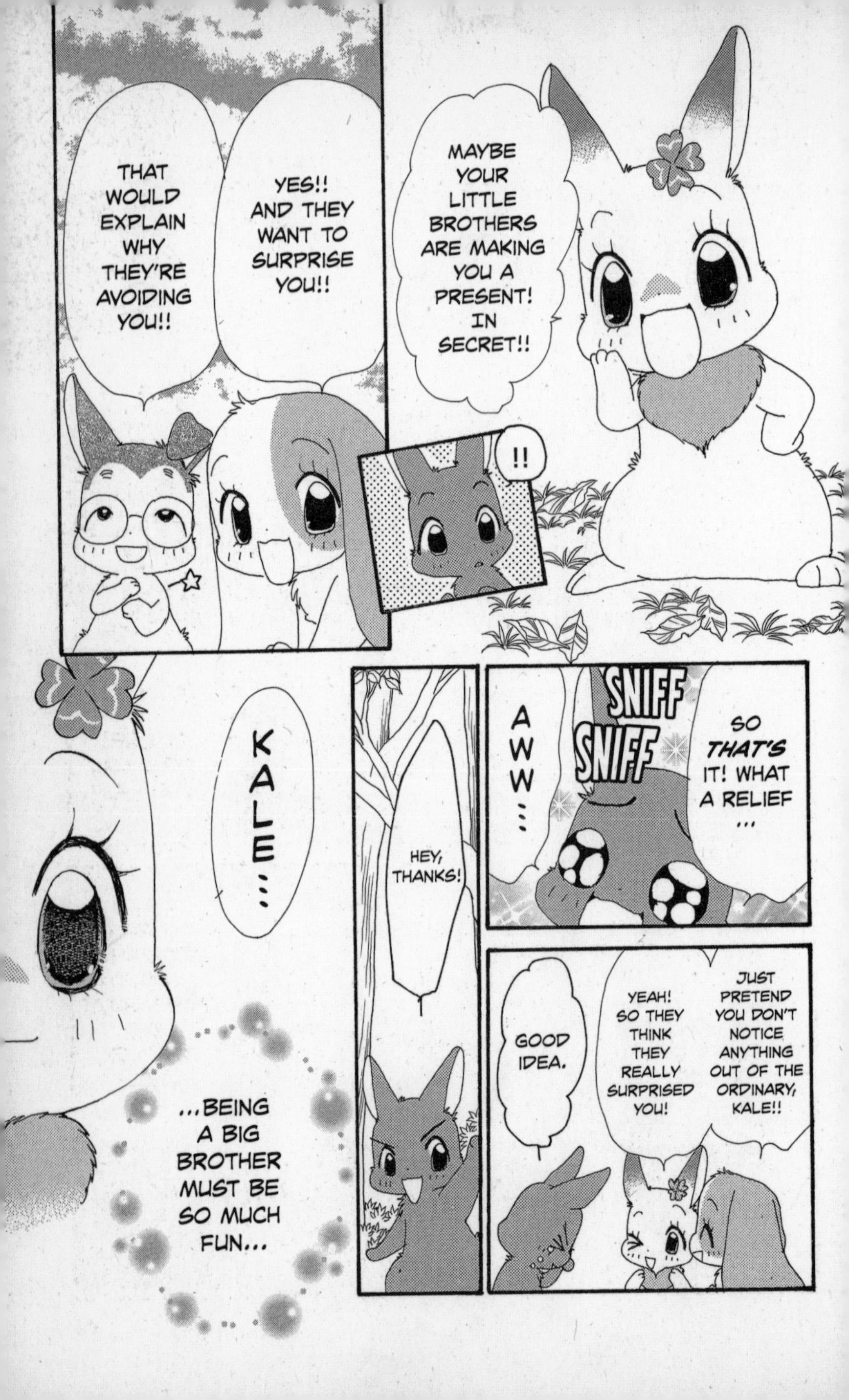
MAYBE YOUR LITTLE BROTHERS ARE MAKING YOU A PRESENT! IN SECRET!!
!!
YES!! AND THEY WANT TO SURPRISE YOU!!
THAT WOULD EXPLAIN WHY THEY'RE AVOIDING YOU!!
SO *THAT'S* IT! WHAT A RELIEF ...
SNIFF SNIFF
AWW...
JUST PRETEND YOU DON'T NOTICE ANYTHING OUT OF THE ORDINARY, KALE!!
YEAH! SO THEY THINK THEY REALLY SURPRISED YOU!
GOOD IDEA.
HEY, THANKS!
KALE...
...BEING A BIG BROTHER MUST BE SO MUCH FUN...

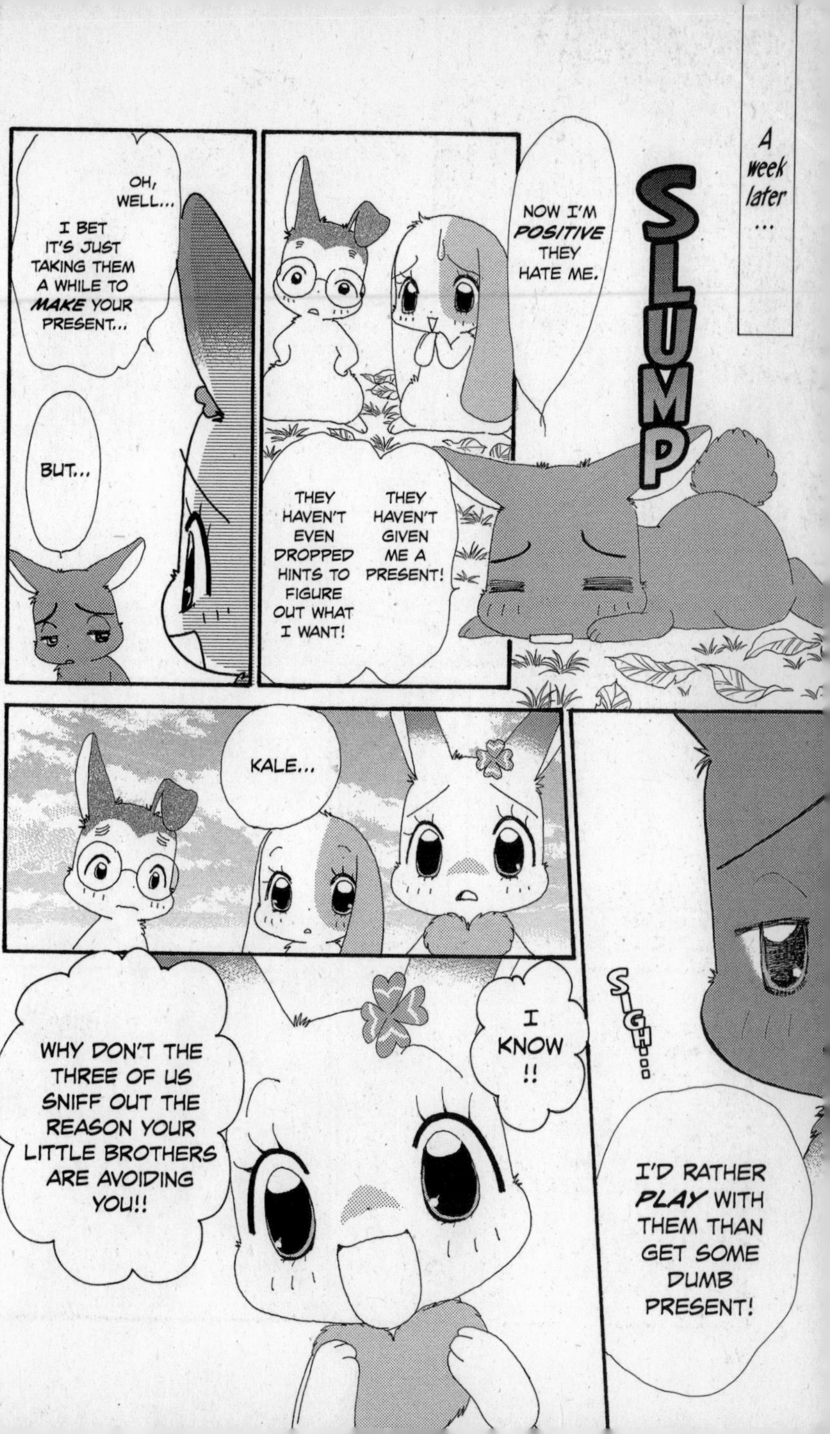
A week later...
SLUMP
NOW I'M POSITIVE THEY HATE ME.
THEY HAVEN'T GIVEN ME A PRESENT!
THEY HAVEN'T EVEN DROPPED HINTS TO FIGURE OUT WHAT I WANT!
OH, WELL...
I BET IT'S JUST TAKING THEM A WHILE TO MAKE YOUR PRESENT...
BUT...
SIGH...
I'D RATHER PLAY WITH THEM THAN GET SOME DUMB PRESENT!
KALE...
I KNOW!!
WHY DON'T THE THREE OF US SNIFF OUT THE REASON YOUR LITTLE BROTHERS ARE AVOIDING YOU!!

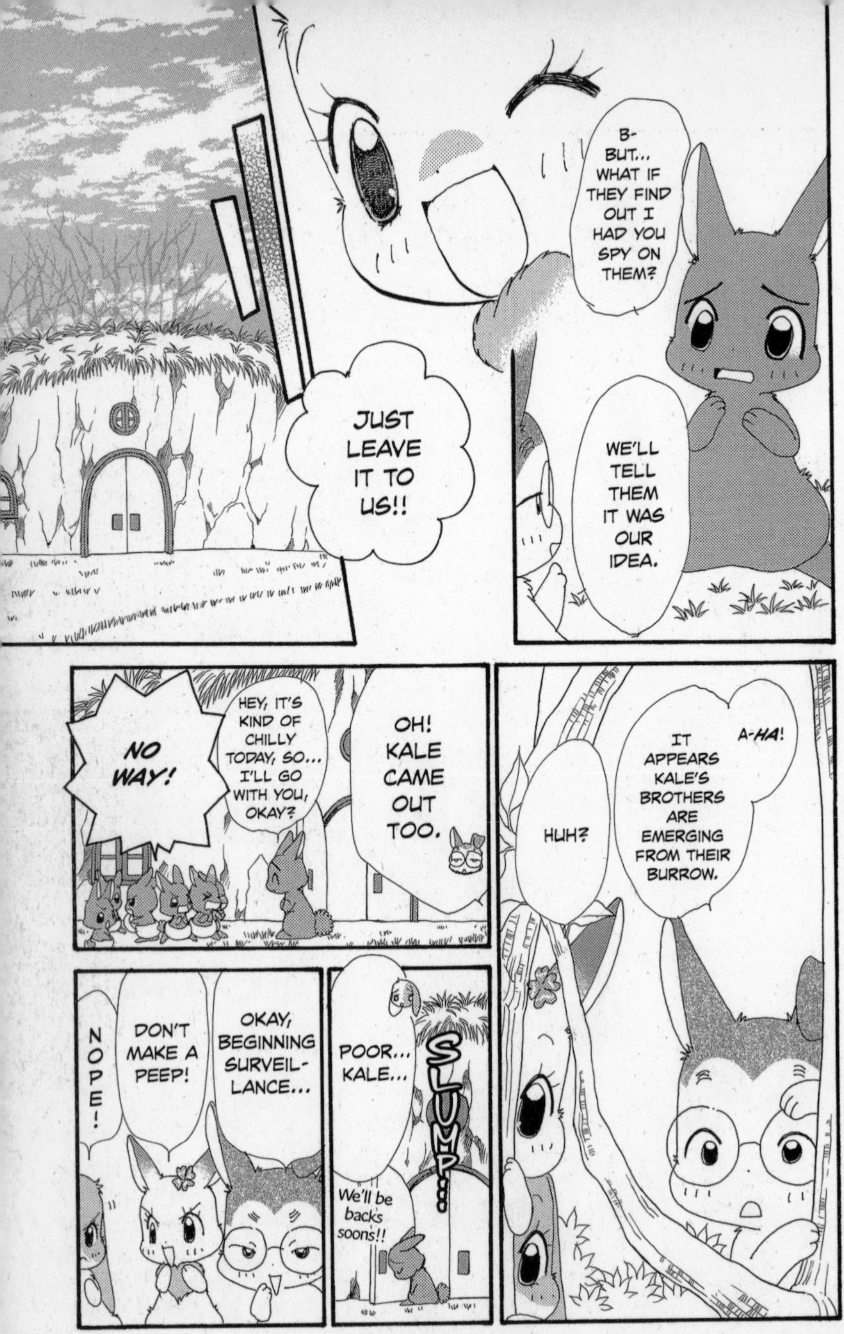
B-BUT... WHAT IF THEY FIND OUT I HAD YOU SPY ON THEM?
WE'LL TELL THEM IT WAS OUR IDEA.
JUST LEAVE IT TO US!!
A-HA! IT APPEARS KALE'S BROTHERS ARE EMERGING FROM THEIR BURROW.
HUH?
OH! KALE CAME OUT TOO.
HEY, IT'S KIND OF CHILLY TODAY, SO... I'LL GO WITH YOU, OKAY?
NO WAY!
POOR... KALE...
SLUMP...
We'll be backs soons!!
OKAY, BEGINNING SURVEIL-LANCE...
DON'T MAKE A PEEP!
NOPE!

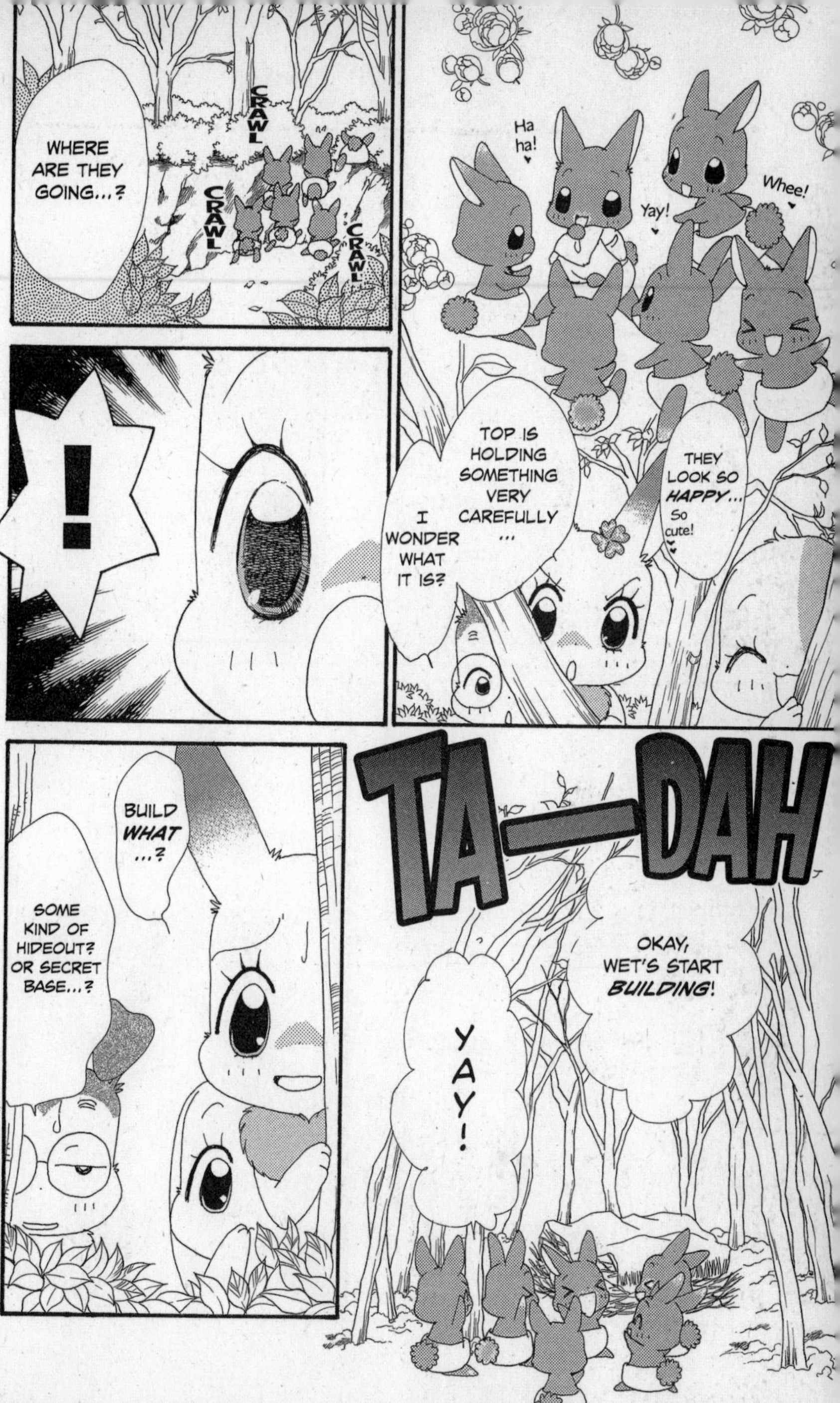

Whee!
Yay!
Ha ha!
THEY LOOK SO *HAPPY*...
So cute!
TOP IS HOLDING SOMETHING VERY CAREFULLY...
I WONDER WHAT IT IS?
CRAWL
CRAWL
CRAWL
WHERE ARE THEY GOING...?
!
TA—DAH
OKAY, WET'S START *BUILDING*!
YAY!
BUILD *WHAT*...?
SOME KIND OF HIDEOUT? OR SECRET BASE...?

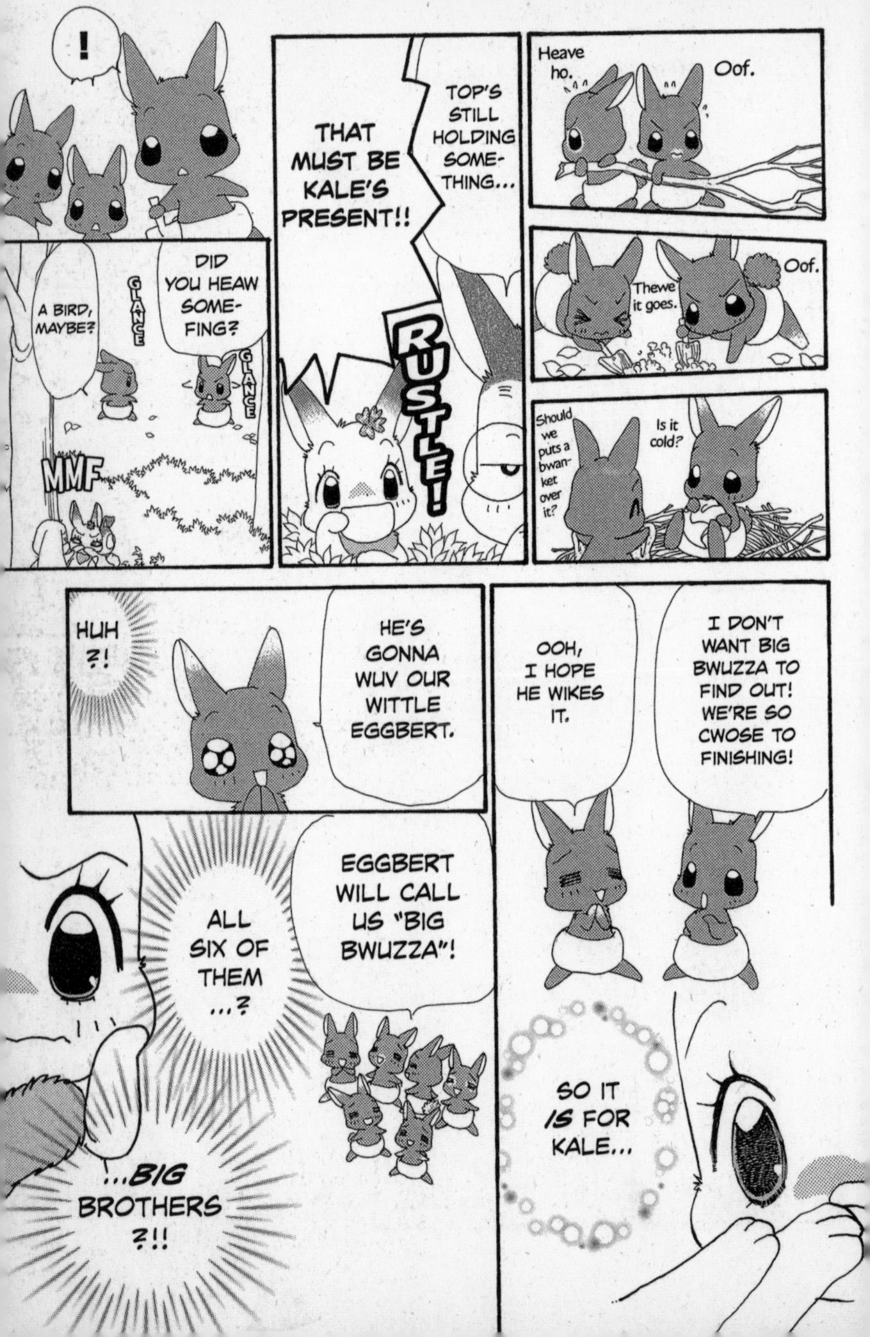
Oof.
Heave ho.
Oof.
Thewe it goes.
Is it cold?
Should we puts a bwanket over it?
TOP'S STILL HOLDING SOMETHING...
THAT MUST BE KALE'S PRESENT!!
RUSTLE!
!
DID YOU HEAW SOMEFING?
GLANCE
GLANCE
A BIRD, MAYBE?
MMF
I DON'T WANT BIG BWUZZA TO FIND OUT! WE'RE SO CWOSE TO FINISHING!
OOH, I HOPE HE WIKES IT.
SO IT *IS* FOR KALE...
HE'S GONNA WUV OUR WITTLE EGGBERT.
HUH ?!
EGGBERT WILL CALL US "BIG BWUZZA"!
ALL SIX OF THEM ...?
...*BIG* BROTHERS ?!!

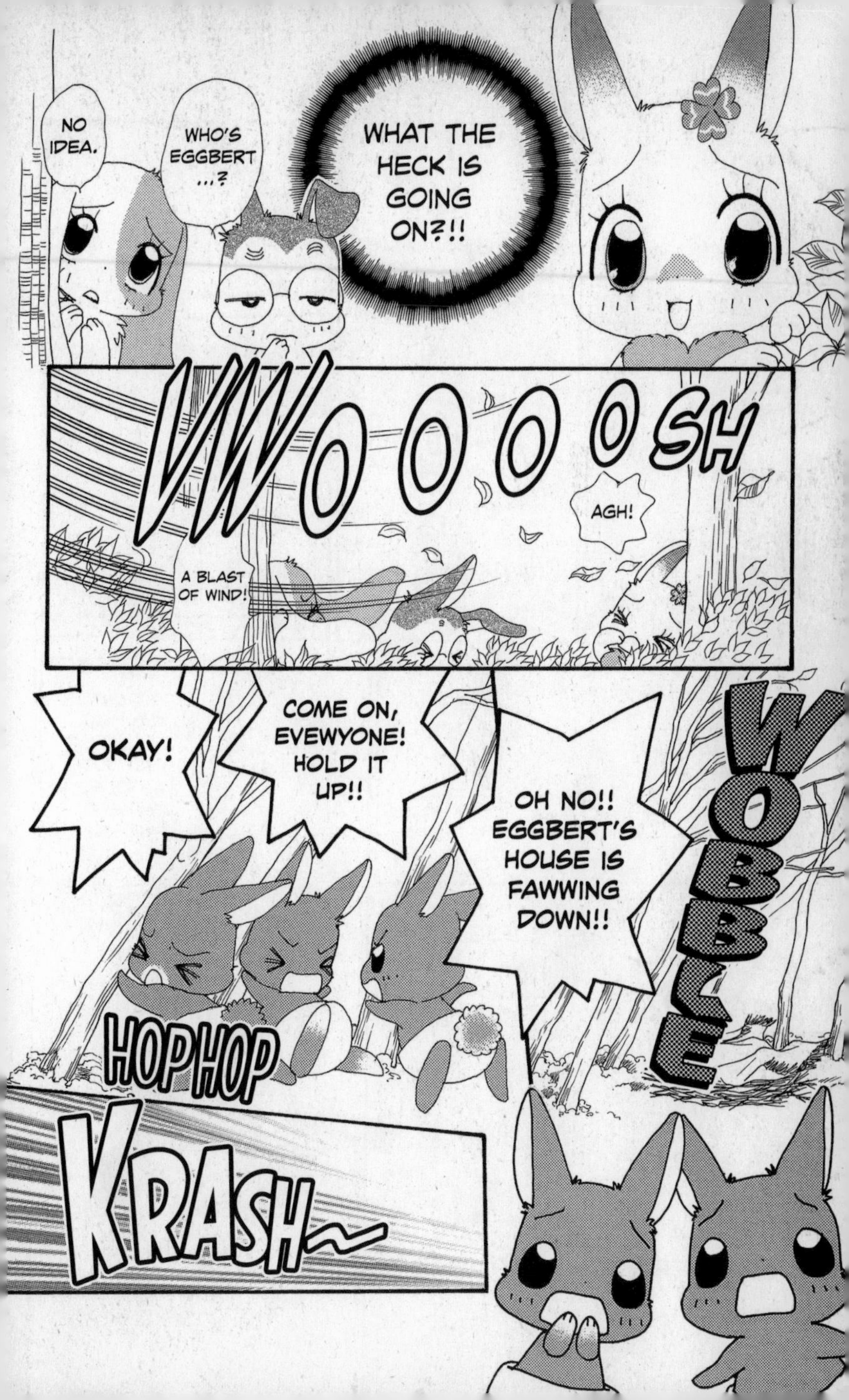
WHAT THE HECK IS GOING ON?!!
WHO'S EGGBERT ...?
NO IDEA.
VWOOOOOSH
AGH!
A BLAST OF WIND!
WOBBLE
OH NO!! EGGBERT'S HOUSE IS FAWWING DOWN!!
COME ON, EVEWYONE! HOLD IT UP!!
OKAY!
HOP HOP
KRASH~

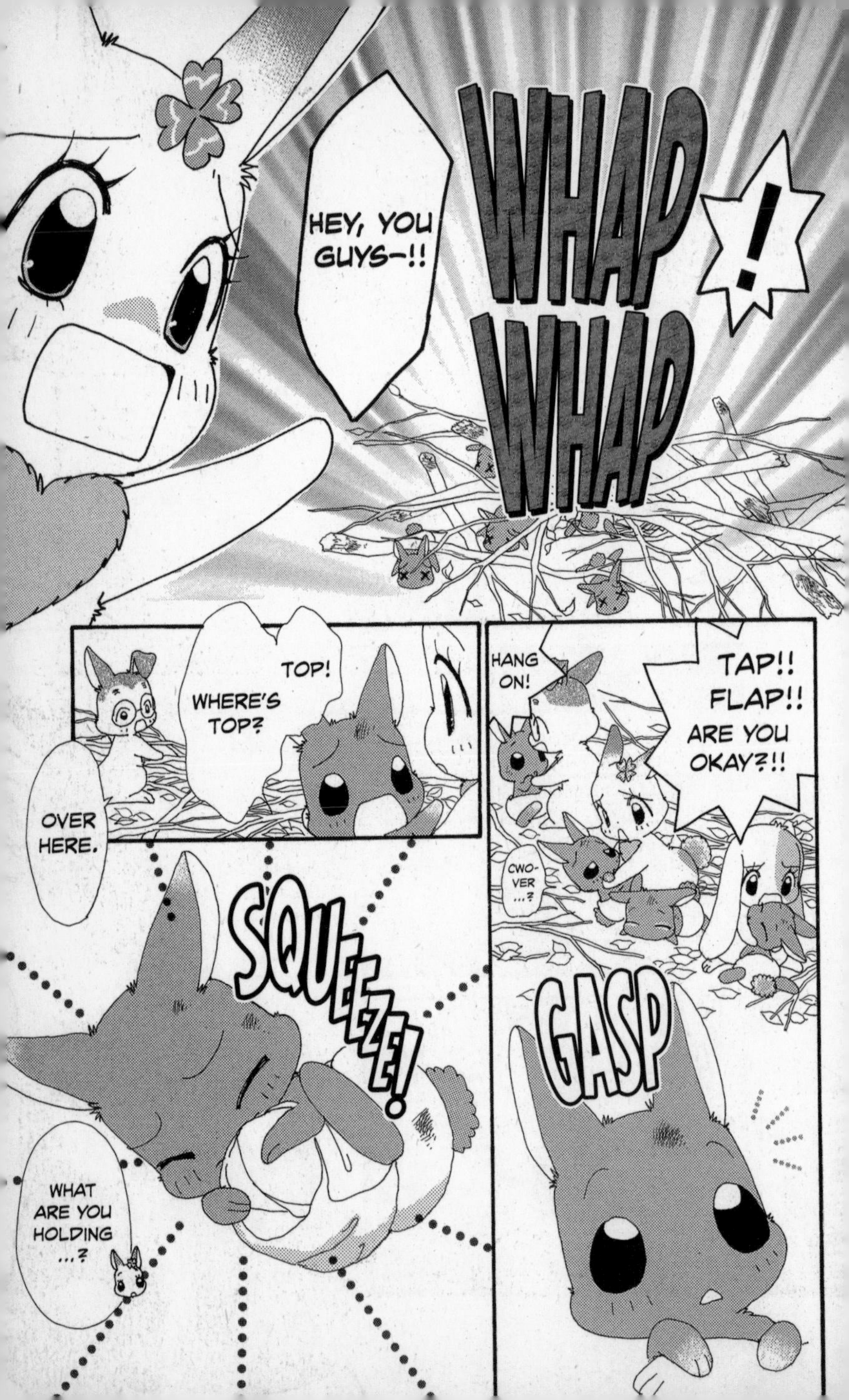
!
WHAP WHAP
HEY, YOU GUYS—!!
TAP!! FLAP!! ARE YOU OKAY?!!
HANG ON!
CWO-VER ...?
TOP! WHERE'S TOP?
OVER HERE.
GASP
SQUEEZE!
WHAT ARE YOU HOLDING ...?

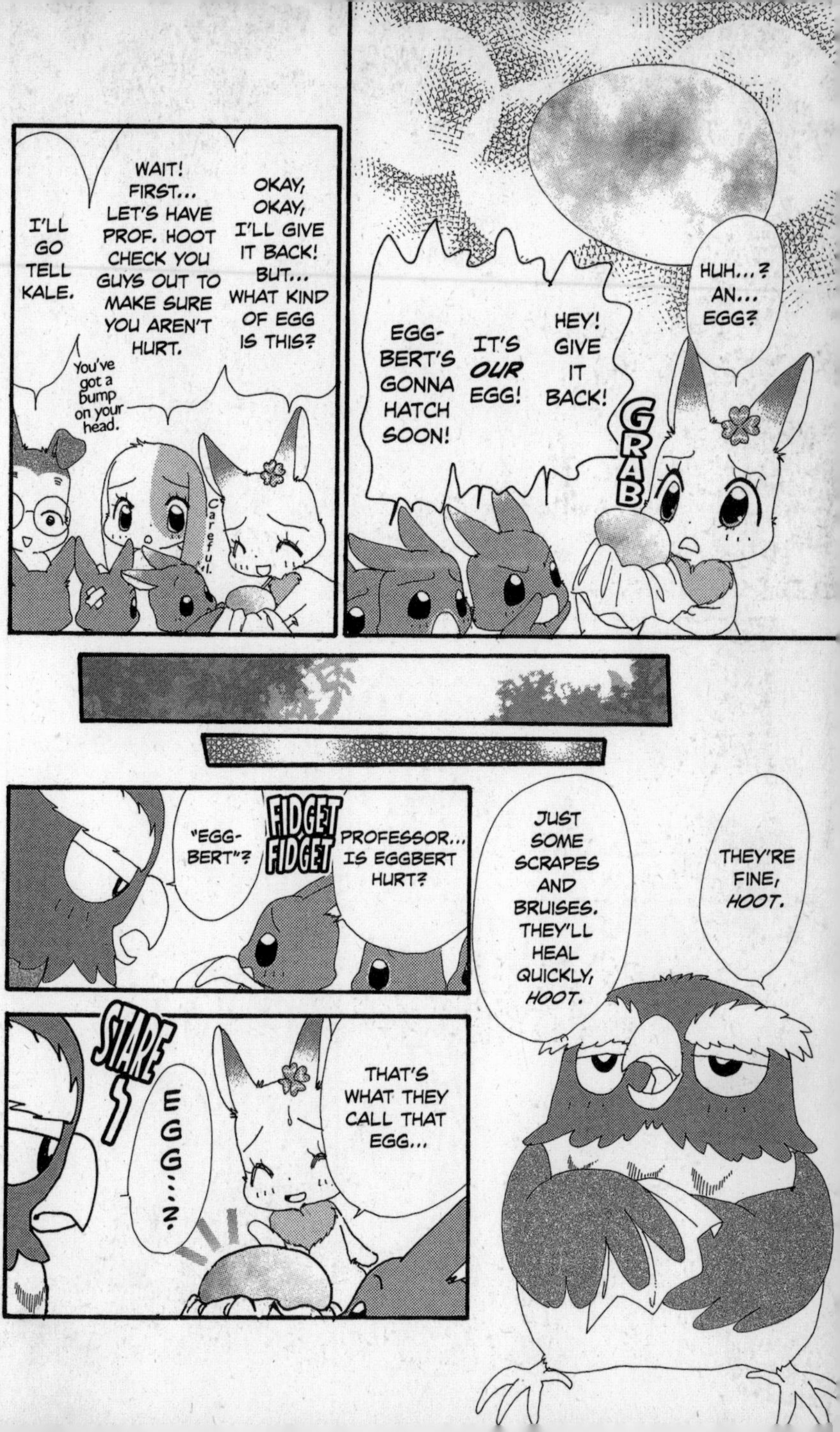
HUH...? AN... EGG?
GRAB
HEY! GIVE IT BACK!
IT'S *OUR* EGG!
EGG-BERT'S GONNA HATCH SOON!
OKAY, OKAY, I'LL GIVE IT BACK! BUT... WHAT KIND OF EGG IS THIS?
Careful.
WAIT! FIRST... LET'S HAVE PROF. HOOT CHECK YOU GUYS OUT TO MAKE SURE YOU AREN'T HURT.
You've got a bump on your head.
I'LL GO TELL KALE.
THEY'RE FINE, *HOOT*.
JUST SOME SCRAPES AND BRUISES. THEY'LL HEAL QUICKLY, *HOOT*.
PROFESSOR... IS EGGBERT HURT?
FIDGET FIDGET
"EGG-BERT"?
THAT'S WHAT THEY CALL THAT EGG...
EGG...?
STARE

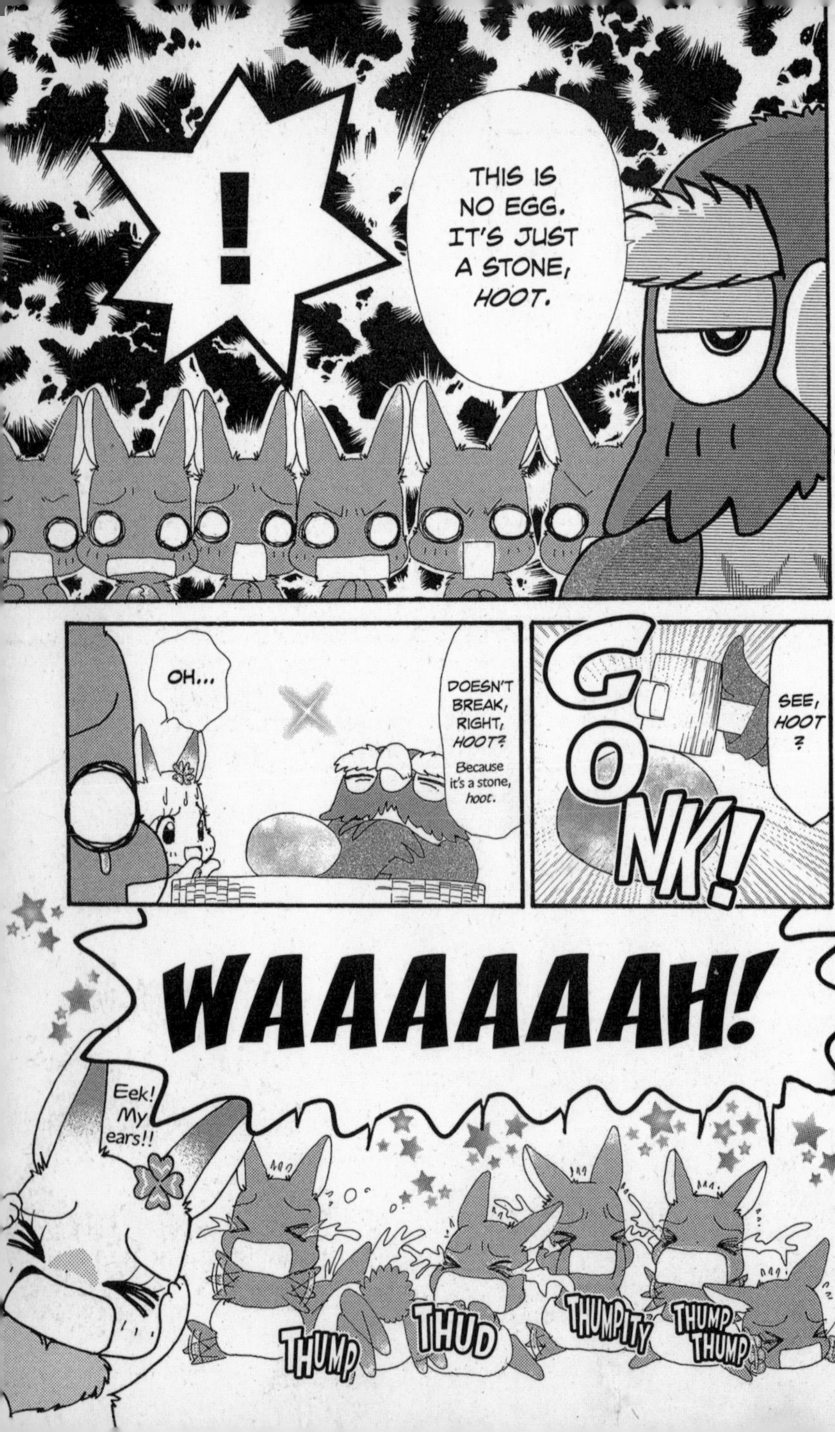
THIS IS NO EGG. IT'S JUST A STONE, *HOOT.*
!
SEE, *HOOT*?
GONK!
DOESN'T BREAK, RIGHT, *HOOT*?
Because it's a stone, *hoot.*
OH...
WAAAAAAH!
Eek! My ears!!
THUMP THUMP
THUMPITY
THUD
THUMP

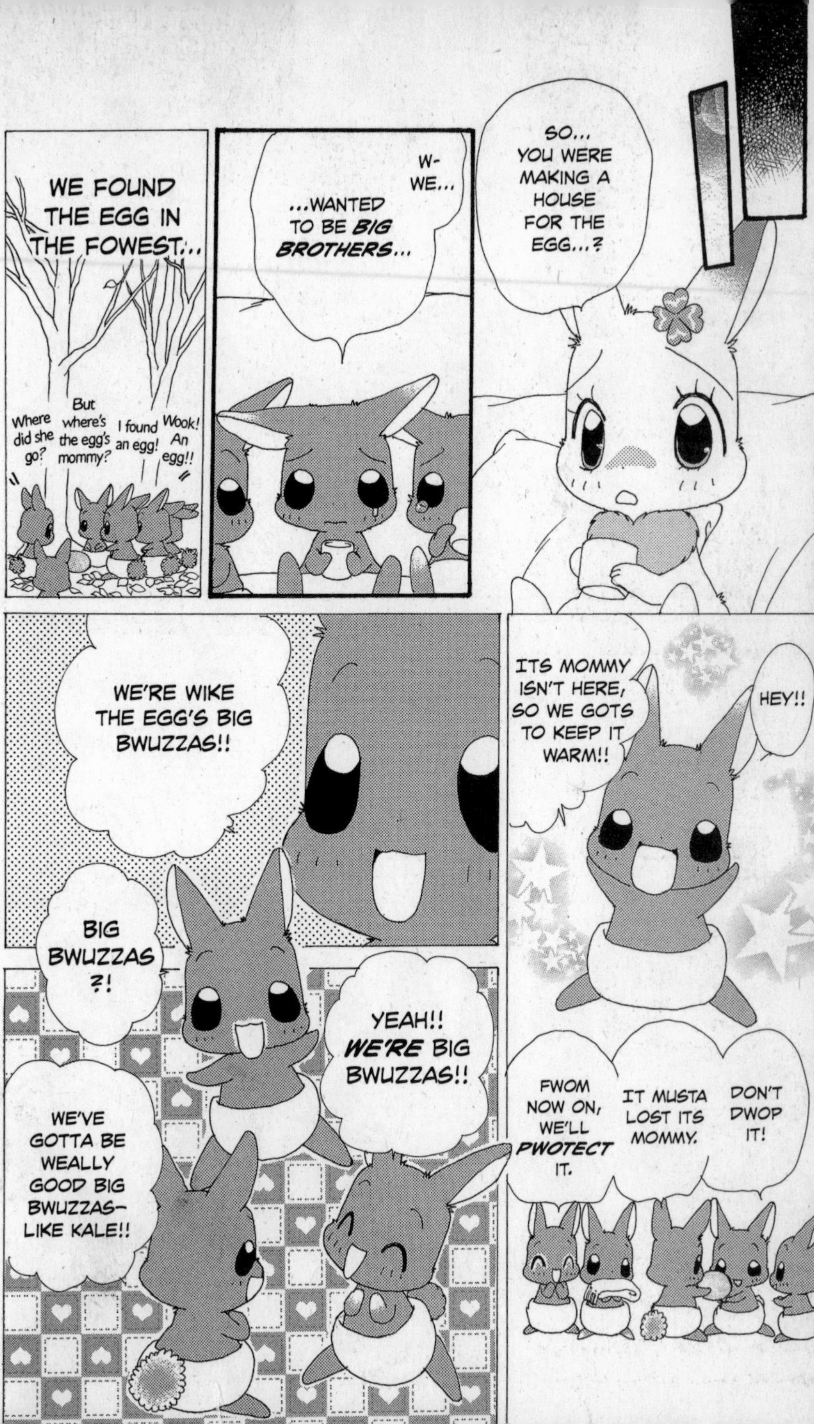
SO... YOU WERE MAKING A HOUSE FOR THE EGG...?
W- WE...
...WANTED TO BE *BIG BROTHERS*...
WE FOUND THE EGG IN THE FOWEST...
Wook! An egg!!
I found an egg!
But where's the egg's mommy?
Where did she go?
HEY!!
ITS MOMMY ISN'T HERE, SO WE GOTS TO KEEP IT WARM!!
DON'T DWOP IT!
IT MUSTA LOST ITS MOMMY.
FWOM NOW ON, WE'LL *PWOTECT* IT.
WE'RE WIKE THE EGG'S BIG BWUZZAS!!
BIG BWUZZAS ?!
YEAH!! *WE'RE* BIG BWUZZAS!!
WE'VE GOTTA BE WEALLY GOOD BIG BWUZZAS— LIKE KALE!!

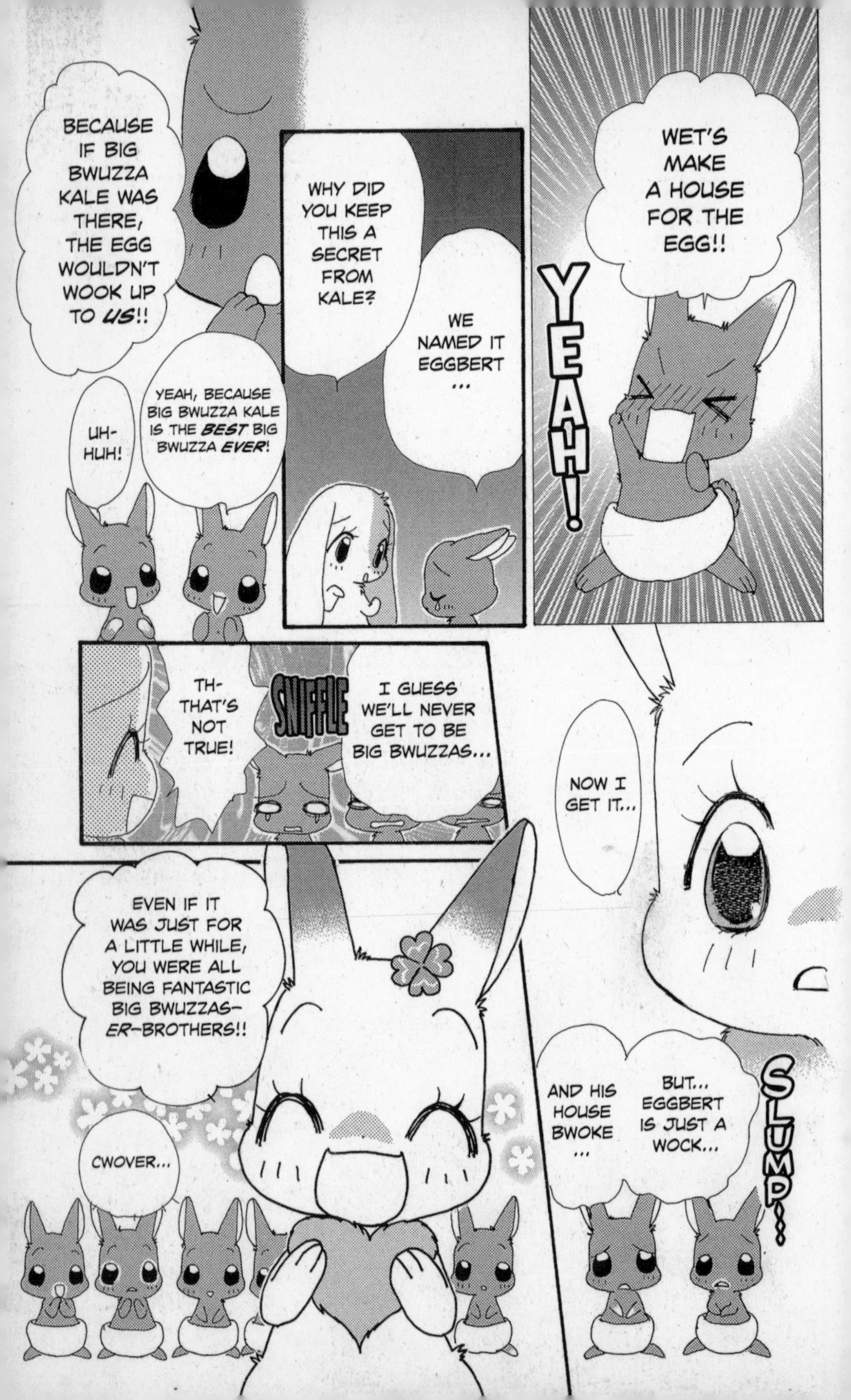
WET'S MAKE A HOUSE FOR THE EGG!!
YEAH!
WHY DID YOU KEEP THIS A SECRET FROM KALE?
WE NAMED IT EGGBERT ...
BECAUSE IF BIG BWUZZA KALE WAS THERE, THE EGG WOULDN'T WOOK UP TO *US*!!
YEAH, BECAUSE BIG BWUZZA KALE IS THE *BEST* BIG BWUZZA *EVER*!
UH-HUH!
NOW I GET IT...
BUT... EGGBERT IS JUST A WOCK...
AND HIS HOUSE BWOKE ...
SLUMP...
I GUESS WE'LL NEVER GET TO BE BIG BWUZZAS...
SNIFFLE
TH-THAT'S NOT TRUE!
EVEN IF IT WAS JUST FOR A LITTLE WHILE, YOU WERE ALL BEING FANTASTIC BIG BWUZZAS—*ER*—BROTHERS!!
CWOVER...

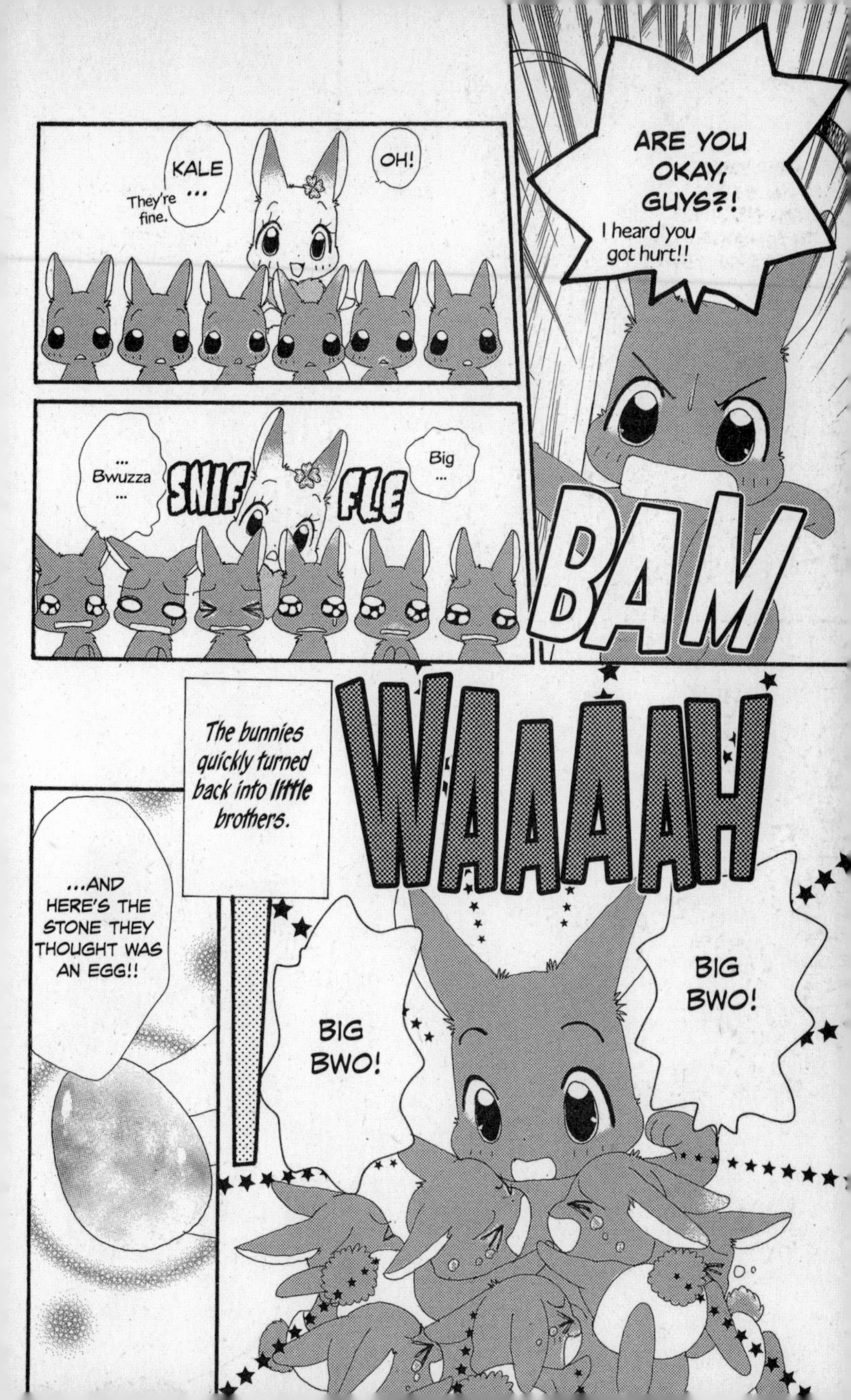
ARE YOU OKAY, GUYS?!
I heard you got hurt!!
BAM
OH!
KALE...
They're fine.
Big...
SNIF FLE
...Bwuzza...
WAAAAH
BIG BWO!
The bunnies quickly turned back into little brothers.
BIG BWO!
...AND HERE'S THE STONE THEY THOUGHT WAS AN EGG!!

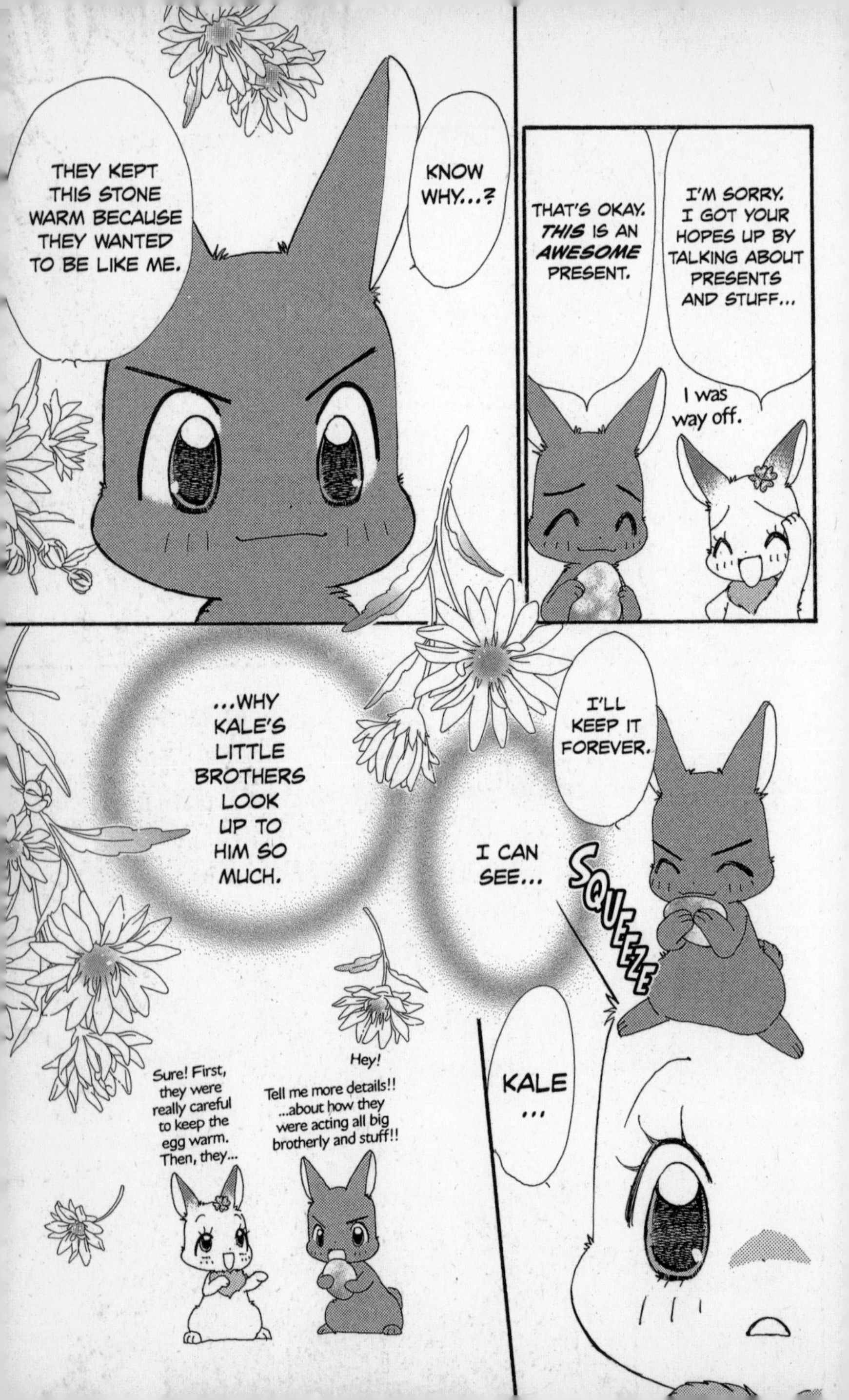
I'M SORRY. I GOT YOUR HOPES UP BY TALKING ABOUT PRESENTS AND STUFF...
I was way off.
THAT'S OKAY. *THIS* IS AN *AWESOME* PRESENT.
KNOW WHY...?
THEY KEPT THIS STONE WARM BECAUSE THEY WANTED TO BE LIKE ME.
I'LL KEEP IT FOREVER.
SQUEEZE
I CAN SEE...
...WHY KALE'S LITTLE BROTHERS LOOK UP TO HIM SO MUCH.
KALE ...
Hey!
Tell me more details!! ...about how they were acting all big brotherly and stuff!!
Sure! First, they were really careful to keep the egg warm. Then, they...

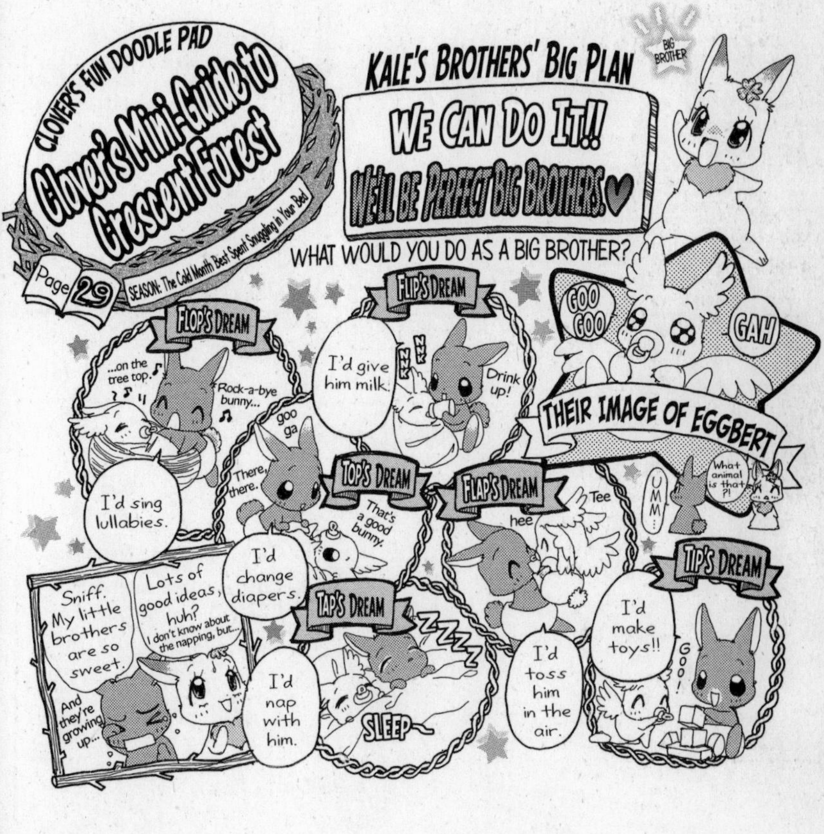
CLOVER'S FUN DOODLE PAD
Clover's Mini-Guide to Crescent Forest
Page 29
SEASON: The Cold Month Best Spent Snuggling in Your Bed
KALE'S BROTHERS' BIG PLAN
WE CAN DO IT!!
WE'LL BE PERFECT BIG BROTHERS♥
BIG BROTHER
WHAT WOULD YOU DO AS A BIG BROTHER?
THEIR IMAGE OF EGGBERT
GOO GOO
GAH
What animal is that?!
UMM...
FLIP'S DREAM
Drink up!
NNK NNK
I'd give him milk.
FLOP'S DREAM
Rock-a-bye bunny...
...on the tree top.
I'd sing lullabies.
FLAP'S DREAM
Tee hee
I'd toss him in the air.
TOP'S DREAM
That's a good bunny.
goo ga
There, there.
I'd change diapers.
TIP'S DREAM
GOO!
I'd make toys!!
TAP'S DREAM
ZZZZ
SLEEP
I'd nap with him.
Lots of good ideas, huh?
I don't know about the napping, but...
Sniff. My little brothers are so sweet.
And they're growing up...

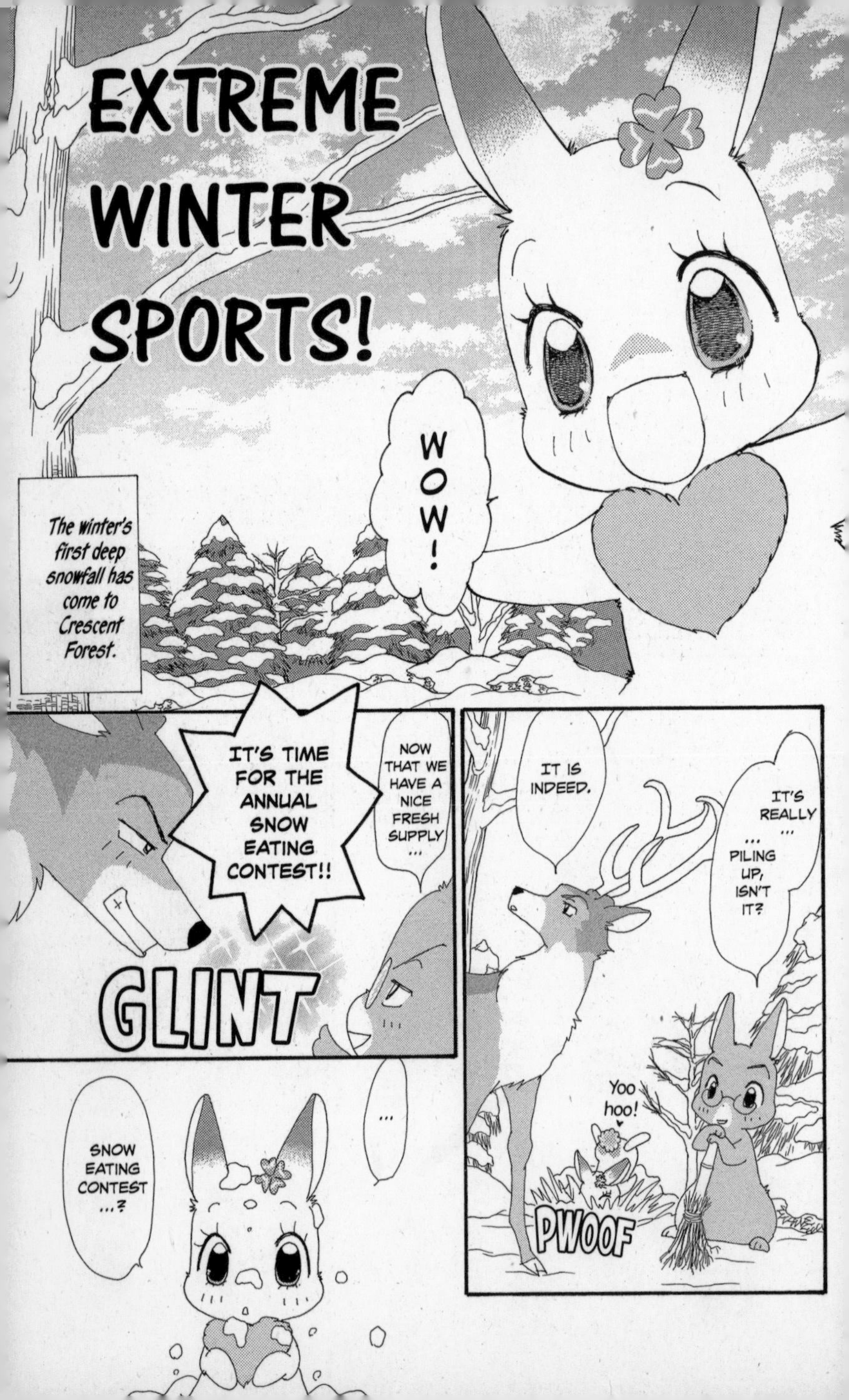
EXTREME WINTER SPORTS!
WOW!
The winter's first deep snowfall has come to Crescent Forest.
IT'S REALLY ... ... PILING UP, ISN'T IT?
IT IS INDEED.
Yoo hoo!
PWOOF
NOW THAT WE HAVE A NICE FRESH SUPPLY ...
IT'S TIME FOR THE ANNUAL SNOW EATING CONTEST!!
GLINT
...
SNOW EATING CONTEST ...?

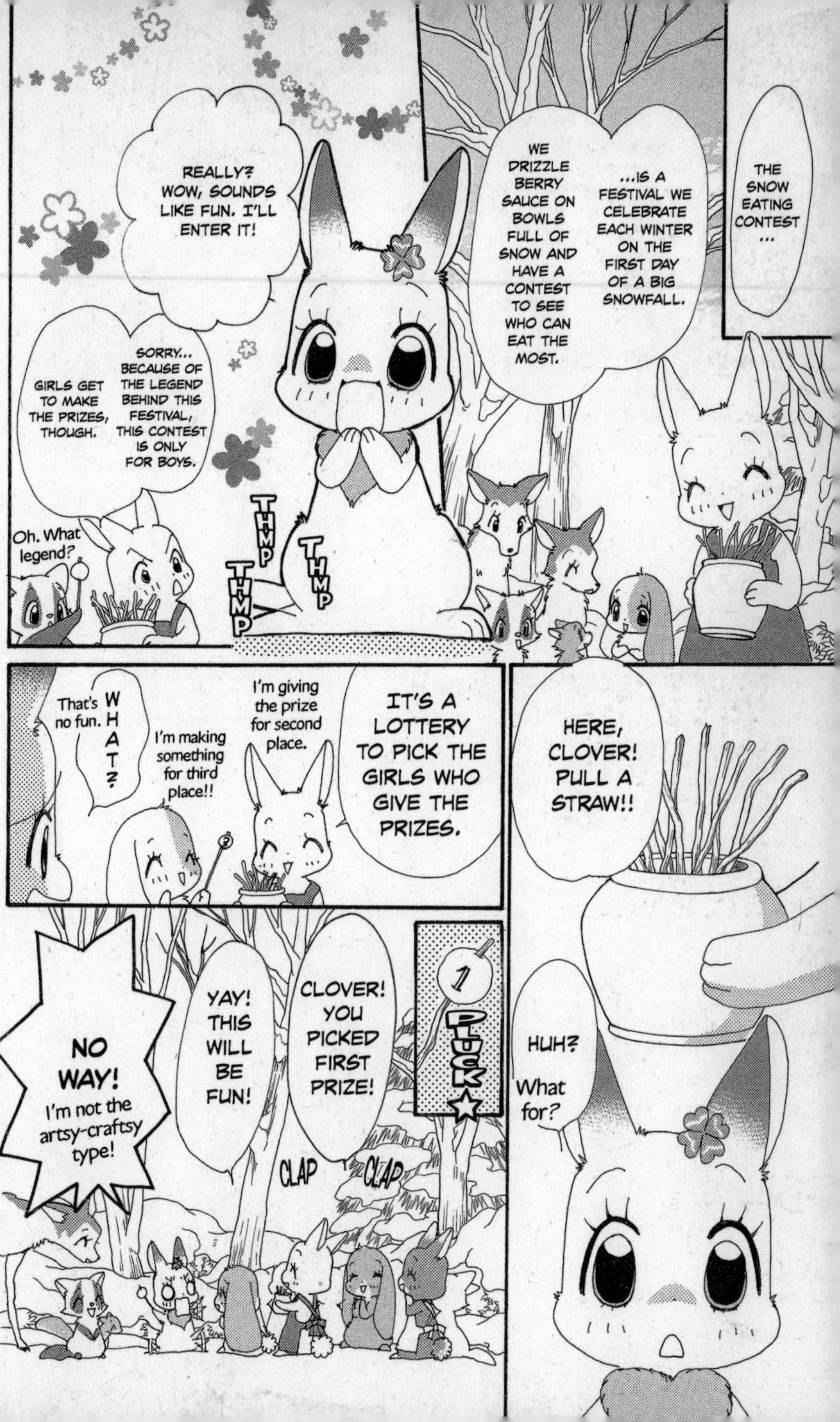
THE SNOW EATING CONTEST...
...IS A FESTIVAL WE CELEBRATE EACH WINTER ON THE FIRST DAY OF A BIG SNOWFALL.
WE DRIZZLE BERRY SAUCE ON BOWLS FULL OF SNOW AND HAVE A CONTEST TO SEE WHO CAN EAT THE MOST.
REALLY? WOW, SOUNDS LIKE FUN. I'LL ENTER IT!
SORRY... BECAUSE OF THE LEGEND BEHIND THIS FESTIVAL, THIS CONTEST IS ONLY FOR BOYS.
GIRLS GET TO MAKE THE PRIZES, THOUGH.
THMP THMP THMP
Oh. What legend?
HERE, CLOVER! PULL A STRAW!!
HUH?
What for?
IT'S A LOTTERY TO PICK THE GIRLS WHO GIVE THE PRIZES.
I'm giving the prize for second place.
I'm making something for third place!!
WHAT?
That's no fun.
PLUCK
CLOVER! YOU PICKED FIRST PRIZE!
YAY! THIS WILL BE FUN!
CLAP CLAP
NO WAY! I'm not the artsy-craftsy type!

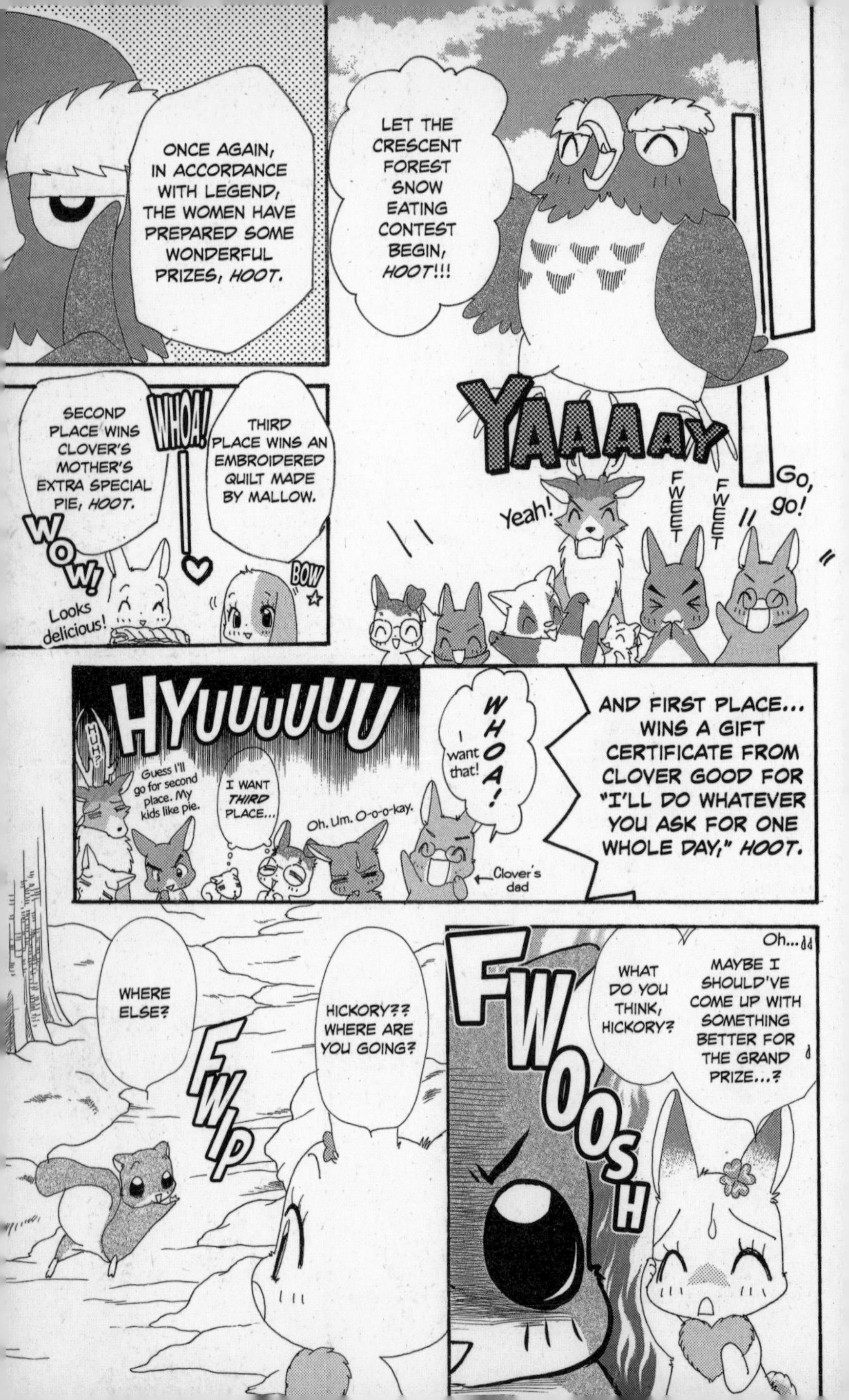
LET THE CRESCENT FOREST SNOW EATING CONTEST BEGIN, HOOT!!!
YAAAAY
Go, go!
FWEET
FWEET
Yeah!
ONCE AGAIN, IN ACCORDANCE WITH LEGEND, THE WOMEN HAVE PREPARED SOME WONDERFUL PRIZES, HOOT.
THIRD PLACE WINS AN EMBROIDERED QUILT MADE BY MALLOW.
BOW
WHOA!
SECOND PLACE WINS CLOVER'S MOTHER'S EXTRA SPECIAL PIE, HOOT.
WOW!
Looks delicious!
AND FIRST PLACE... WINS A GIFT CERTIFICATE FROM CLOVER GOOD FOR "I'LL DO WHATEVER YOU ASK FOR ONE WHOLE DAY," HOOT.
WHOA!
I want that!
Clover's dad
Oh. Um. O-o-o-kay.
I WANT THIRD PLACE...
Guess I'll go for second place. My kids like pie.
HUH?
HYUUUUUU
Oh...
MAYBE I SHOULD'VE COME UP WITH SOMETHING BETTER FOR THE GRAND PRIZE...?
WHAT DO YOU THINK, HICKORY?
FWOOSH
HICKORY?? WHERE ARE YOU GOING?
FWIP
WHERE ELSE?

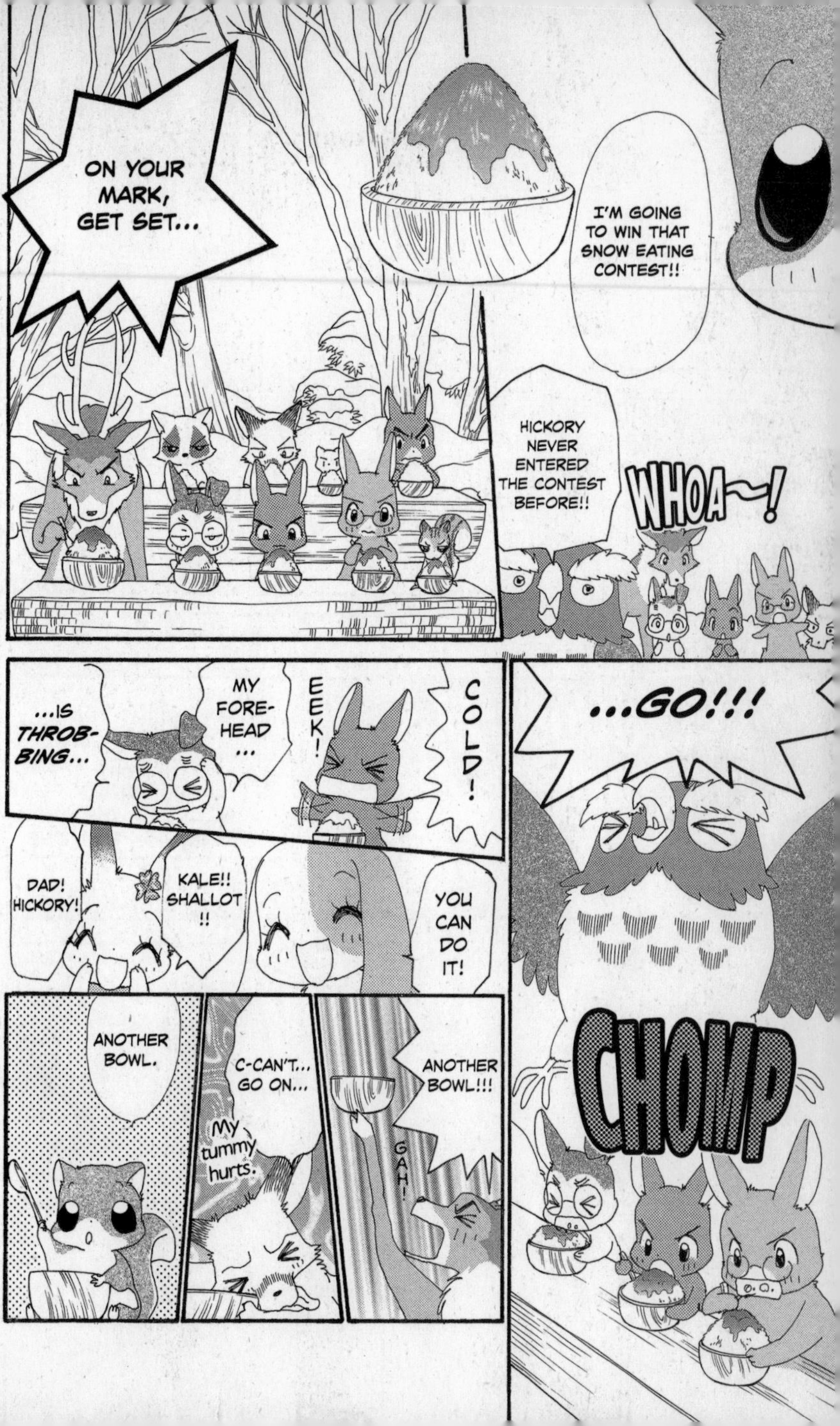

I'M GOING TO WIN THAT SNOW EATING CONTEST!!
WHOA~!
HICKORY NEVER ENTERED THE CONTEST BEFORE!!
ON YOUR MARK, GET SET...
...GO!!!
CHOMP
COLD!
EEK!
MY FOREHEAD ...
...IS THROBBING...
YOU CAN DO IT!
KALE!! SHALLOT!!
DAD! HICKORY!
ANOTHER BOWL!!!
GAH!
C-CAN'T... GO ON...
My tummy hurts.
ANOTHER BOWL.

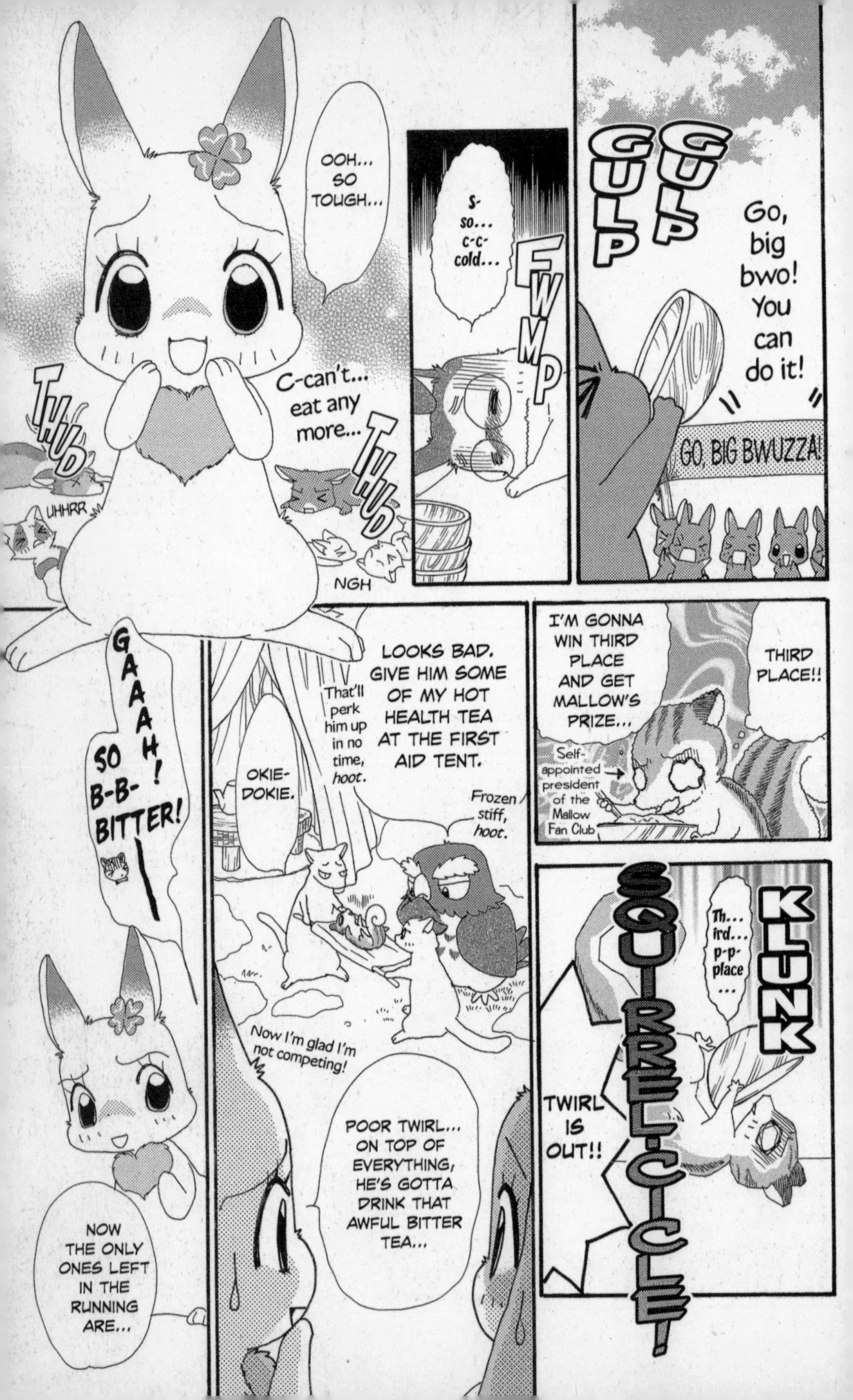
GULP
GULP
Go, big bwo! You can do it!
GO, BIG BWUZZA!
S-so... c-c-cold...
FWMP
OOH... SO TOUGH...
C-can't... eat any more...
THUD
THUD
UHHRR
NGH
THIRD PLACE!!
I'M GONNA WIN THIRD PLACE AND GET MALLOW'S PRIZE...
Self-appointed president of the Mallow Fan Club
KLUNK
Th... ird... p-p-place...
SQUIRREL-CICLE!
TWIRL IS OUT!!
LOOKS BAD. GIVE HIM SOME OF MY HOT HEALTH TEA AT THE FIRST AID TENT.
That'll perk him up in no time, hoot.
OKIE-DOKIE.
Frozen stiff, hoot.
Now I'm glad I'm not competing!
POOR TWIRL... ON TOP OF EVERYTHING, HE'S GOTTA DRINK THAT AWFUL BITTER TEA...
GAAAAH! SO B-B-BITTER!
NOW THE ONLY ONES LEFT IN THE RUNNING ARE...

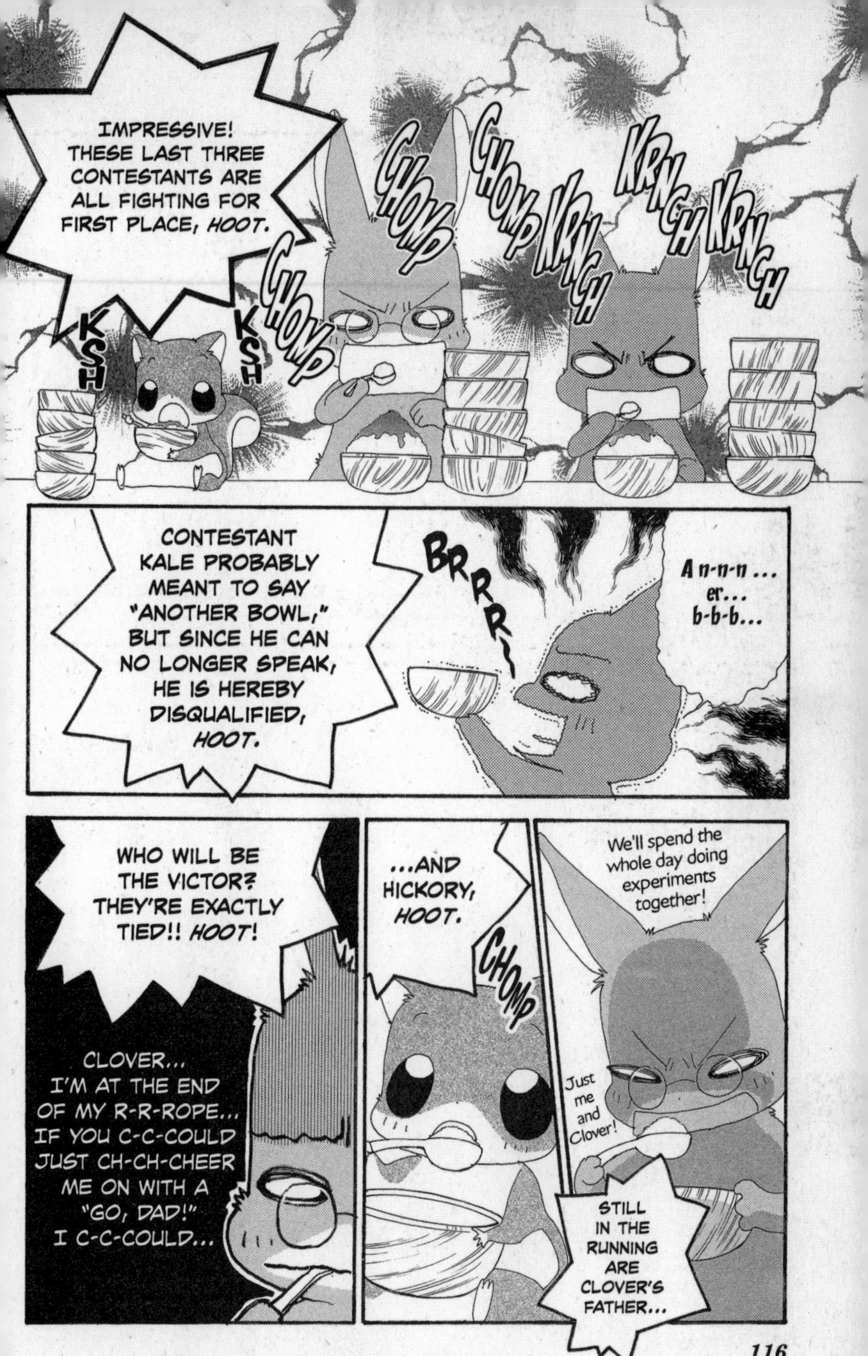
KRNCH KRNCH
CHOMP KRNCH
CHOMP
CHOMP
IMPRESSIVE! THESE LAST THREE CONTESTANTS ARE ALL FIGHTING FOR FIRST PLACE, *HOOT.*
KSH KSH
A n-n-n ... er... b-b-b...
BRRRR
CONTESTANT KALE PROBABLY MEANT TO SAY "ANOTHER BOWL," BUT SINCE HE CAN NO LONGER SPEAK, HE IS HEREBY DISQUALIFIED, *HOOT.*
We'll spend the whole day doing experiments together!
Just me and Clover!
STILL IN THE RUNNING ARE CLOVER'S FATHER...
...AND HICKORY, *HOOT.*
CHOMP
WHO WILL BE THE VICTOR? THEY'RE EXACTLY TIED!! *HOOT*!
CLOVER... I'M AT THE END OF MY R-R-ROPE... IF YOU C-C-COULD JUST CH-CH-CHEER ME ON WITH A "GO, DAD!" I C-C-COULD...

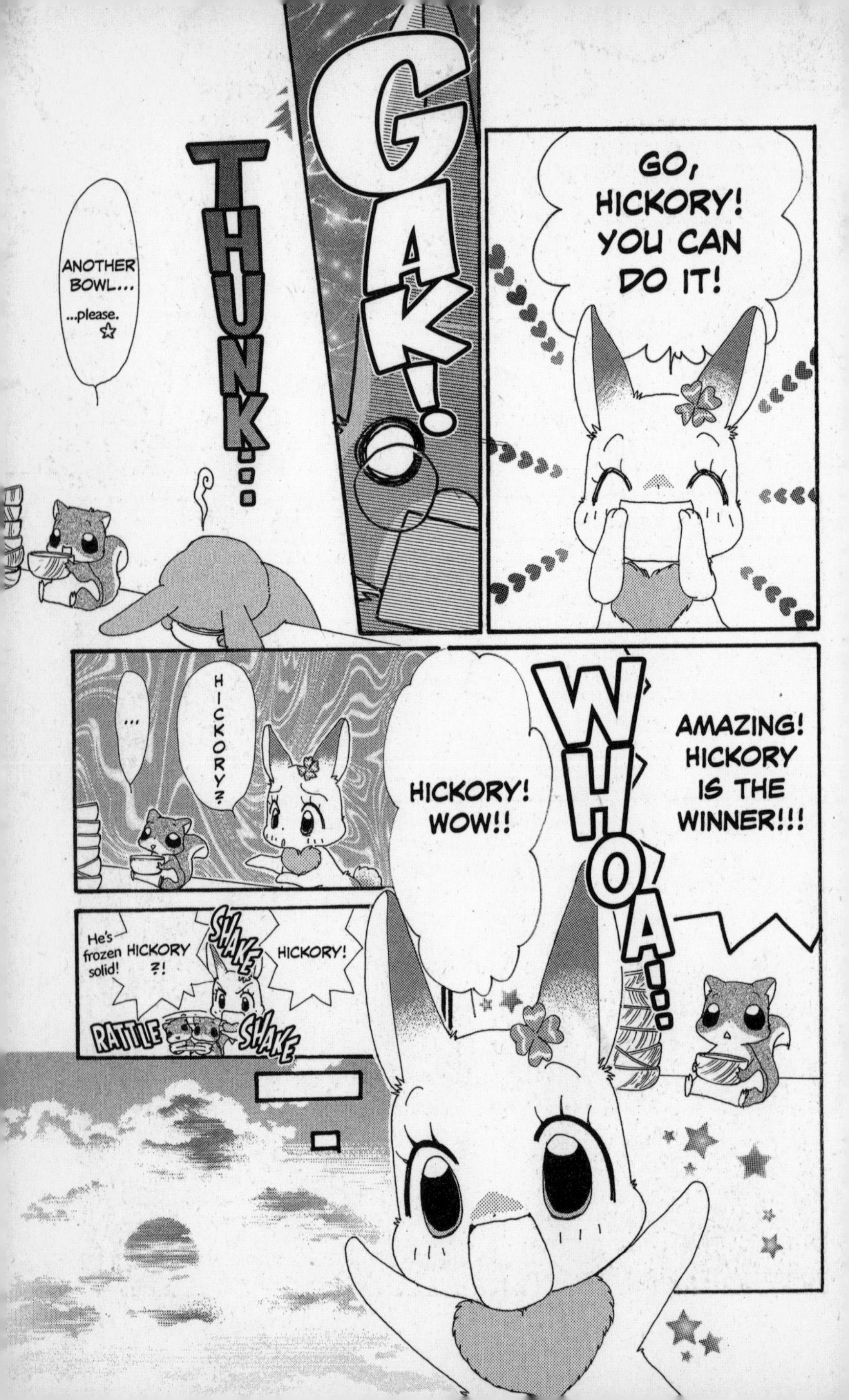

GO, HICKORY! YOU CAN DO IT!
GAK!
THUNK...
ANOTHER BOWL...
...please. ☆
WHOA...
AMAZING! HICKORY IS THE WINNER!!!
HICKORY! WOW!!
HICKORY?
...
HICKORY!
SHAKE
HICKORY?!
He's frozen solid!
RATTLE
SHAKE

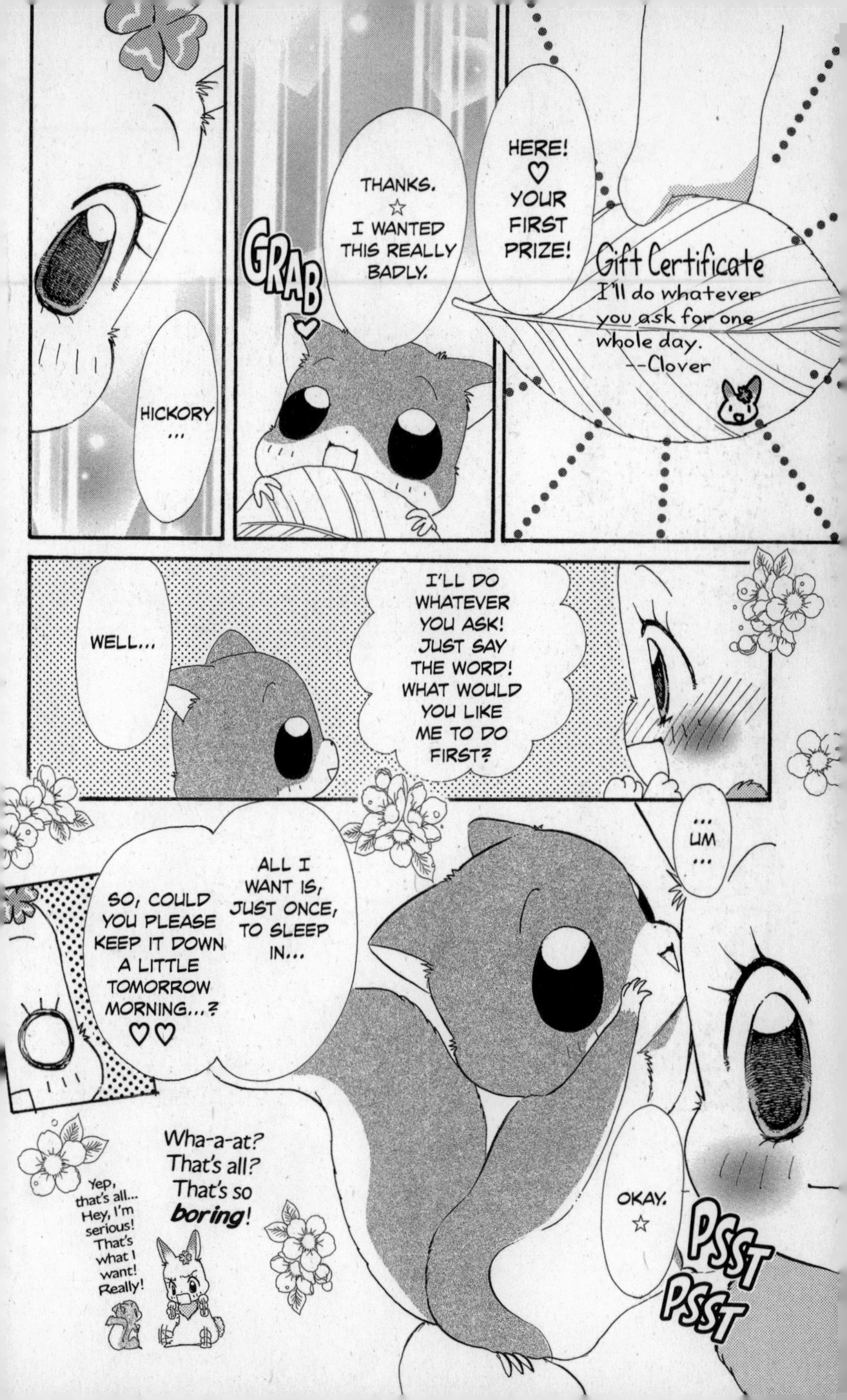
HERE! ♡ YOUR FIRST PRIZE!
Gift Certificate
I'll do whatever you ask for one whole day.
--Clover
GRAB
THANKS. ☆ I WANTED THIS REALLY BADLY.
HICKORY ...
I'LL DO WHATEVER YOU ASK! JUST SAY THE WORD! WHAT WOULD YOU LIKE ME TO DO FIRST?
WELL...
... UM ...
ALL I WANT IS, JUST ONCE, TO SLEEP IN...
SO, COULD YOU PLEASE KEEP IT DOWN A LITTLE TOMORROW MORNING...? ♡♡
OKAY. ☆
PSST PSST
Wha-a-at? That's all? That's so **boring**!
Yep, that's all... Hey, I'm serious! That's what I want! Really!

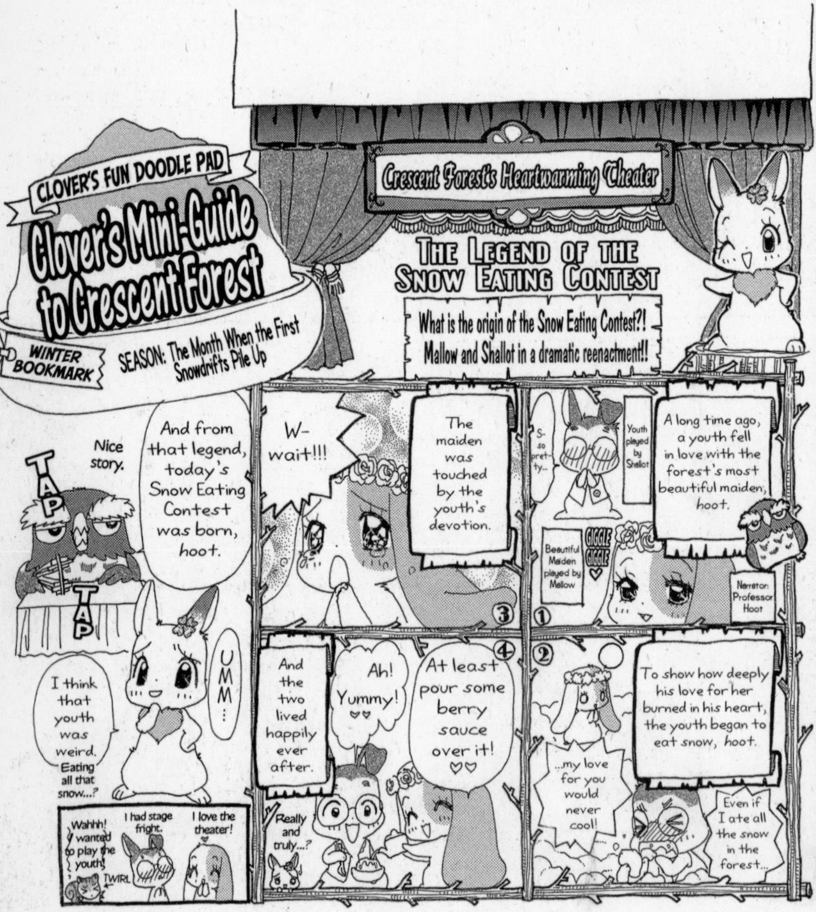
CLOVER'S FUN DOODLE PAD
Clover's Mini-Guide to Crescent Forest
WINTER BOOKMARK
SEASON: The Month When the First Snowdrifts Pile Up
Crescent Forest's Heartwarming Theater
THE LEGEND OF THE SNOW EATING CONTEST
What is the origin of the Snow Eating Contest?! Mallow and Shallot in a dramatic reenactment!!
A long time ago, a youth fell in love with the forest's most beautiful maiden, hoot.
Narrator: Professor Hoot
Youth played by Shallot
S-so pret-ty...
GIGGLE GIGGLE ♡
Beautiful Maiden played by Mellow
To show how deeply his love for her burned in his heart, the youth began to eat snow, hoot.
Even if I ate all the snow in the forest...
...my love for you would never cool!
The maiden was touched by the youth's devotion.
W-wait!!!
At least pour some berry sauce over it! ♡♡
Ah! Yummy! ♡♡
And the two lived happily ever after.
Really and truly...?
And from that legend, today's Snow Eating Contest was born, hoot.
Nice story.
TAP TAP
UMM...
I think that youth was weird. Eating all that snow...?
I love the theater!
I had stage fright.
Wahhh! I wanted to play the youth!
TWIRL

Clover & Mallow

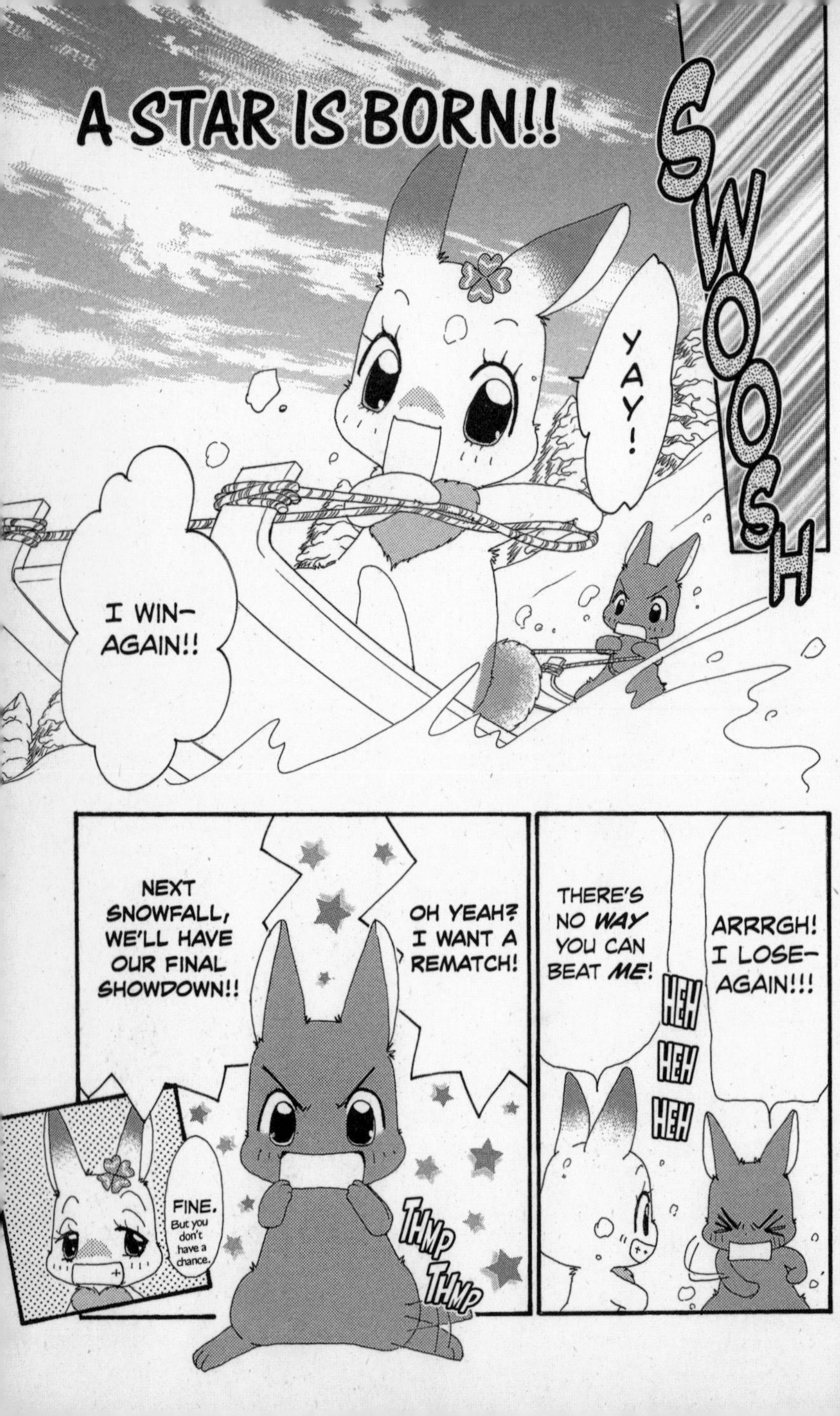
A STAR IS BORN!!
SWOOSH
YAY!
I WIN—AGAIN!!
ARRRGH! I LOSE—AGAIN!!!
HEH HEH HEH
THERE'S NO *WAY* YOU CAN BEAT *ME*!
OH YEAH? I WANT A REMATCH!
NEXT SNOWFALL, WE'LL HAVE OUR FINAL SHOWDOWN!!
THMP THMP
FINE. But you don't have a chance.

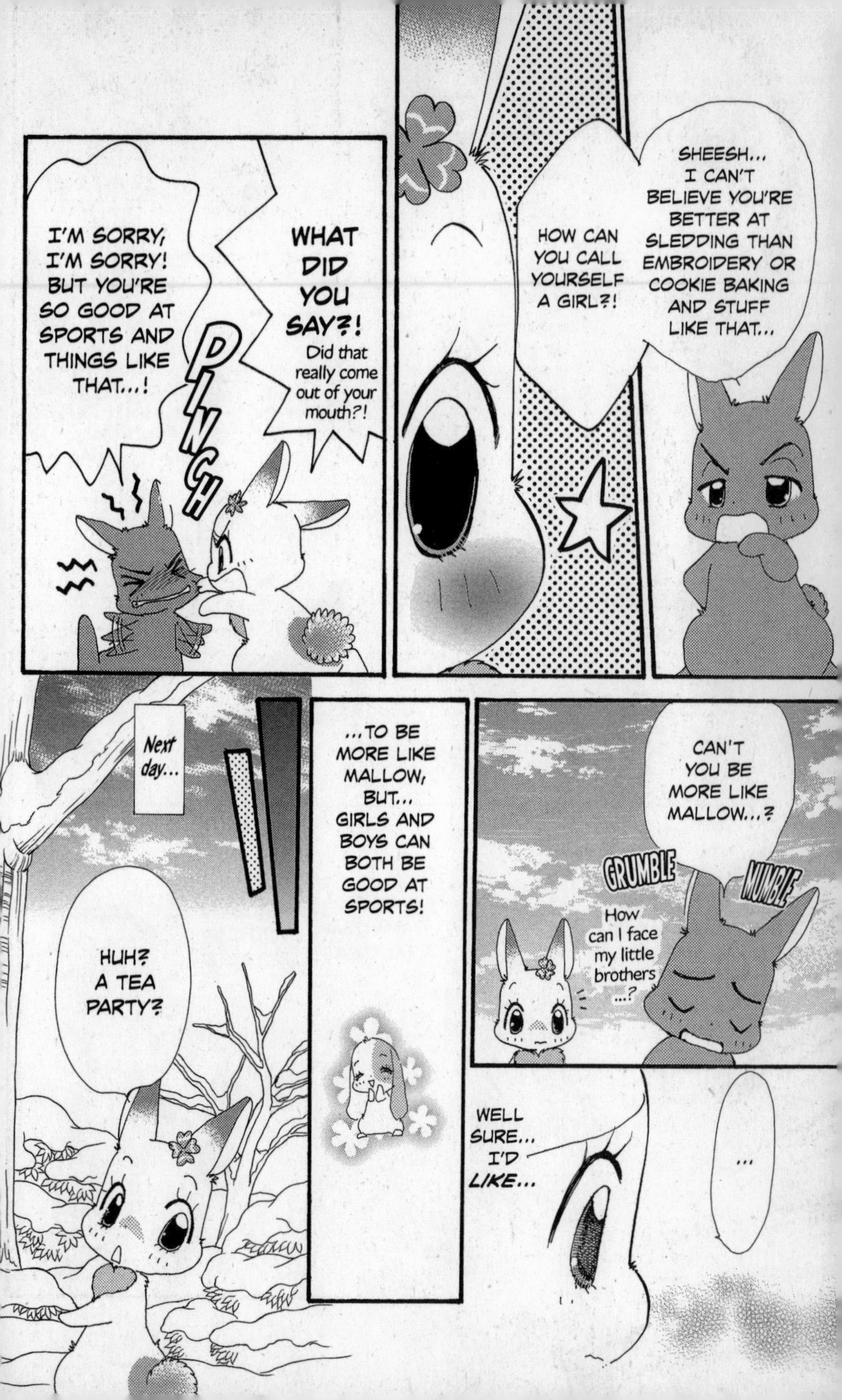
SHEESH... I CAN'T BELIEVE YOU'RE BETTER AT SLEDDING THAN EMBROIDERY OR COOKIE BAKING AND STUFF LIKE THAT...
HOW CAN YOU CALL YOURSELF A GIRL?!
WHAT DID YOU SAY?!
Did that really come out of your mouth?!
PINCH
I'M SORRY, I'M SORRY! BUT YOU'RE SO GOOD AT SPORTS AND THINGS LIKE THAT...!
CAN'T YOU BE MORE LIKE MALLOW...?
MUMBLE
GRUMBLE
How can I face my little brothers ...?
...
WELL SURE... I'D LIKE...
...TO BE MORE LIKE MALLOW, BUT... GIRLS AND BOYS CAN BOTH BE GOOD AT SPORTS!
Next day...
HUH? A TEA PARTY?

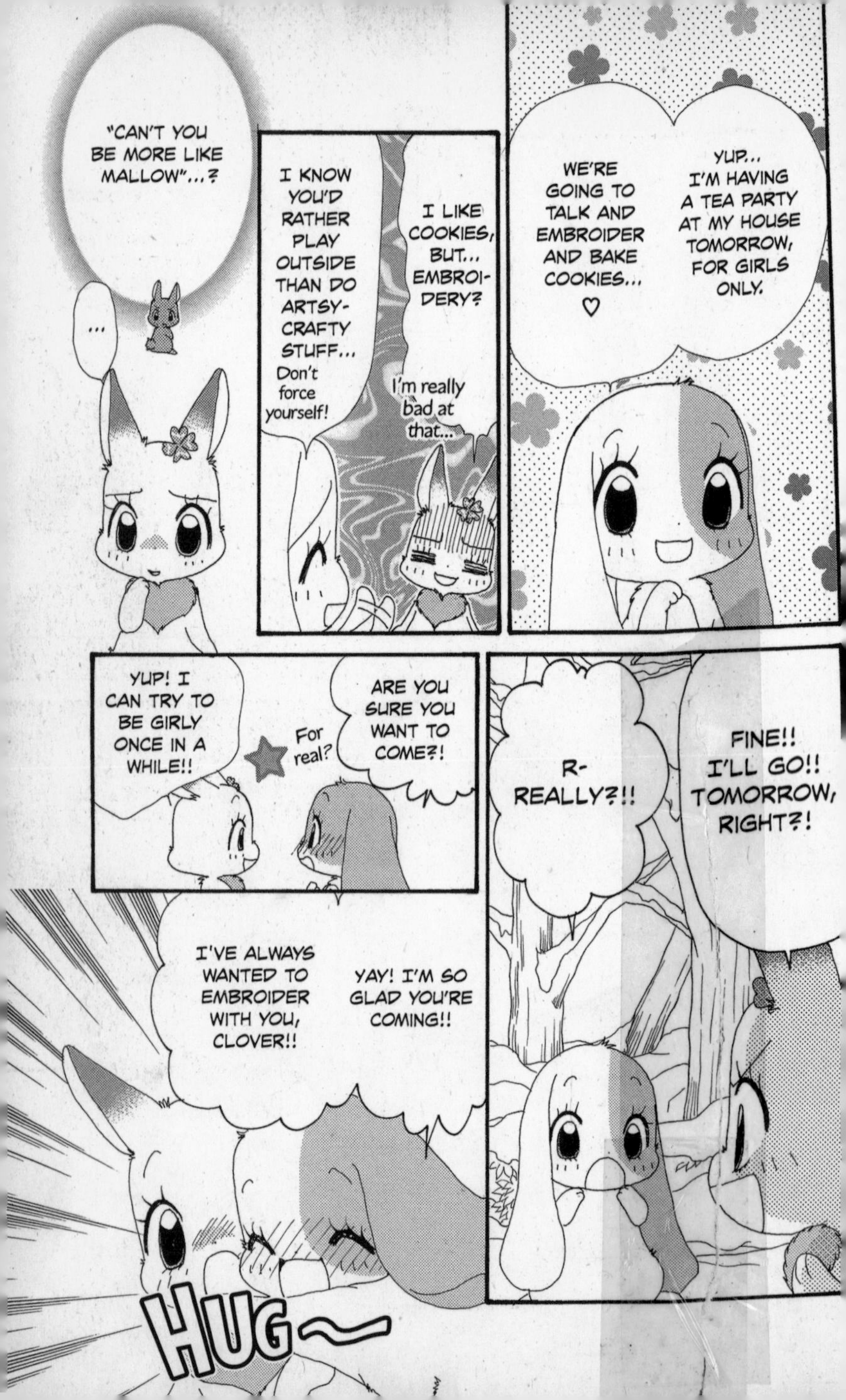

YUP... I'M HAVING A TEA PARTY AT MY HOUSE TOMORROW, FOR GIRLS ONLY.
WE'RE GOING TO TALK AND EMBROIDER AND BAKE COOKIES... ♡
I LIKE COOKIES, BUT... EMBROIDERY?
I'm really bad at that...
I KNOW YOU'D RATHER PLAY OUTSIDE THAN DO ARTSY-CRAFTY STUFF...
Don't force yourself!
"CAN'T YOU BE MORE LIKE MALLOW"...?
...
FINE!! I'LL GO!! TOMORROW, RIGHT?!
R-REALLY?!!
ARE YOU SURE YOU WANT TO COME?!
For real?
YUP! I CAN TRY TO BE GIRLY ONCE IN A WHILE!!
YAY! I'M SO GLAD YOU'RE COMING!!
I'VE ALWAYS WANTED TO EMBROIDER WITH YOU, CLOVER!!
HUG~

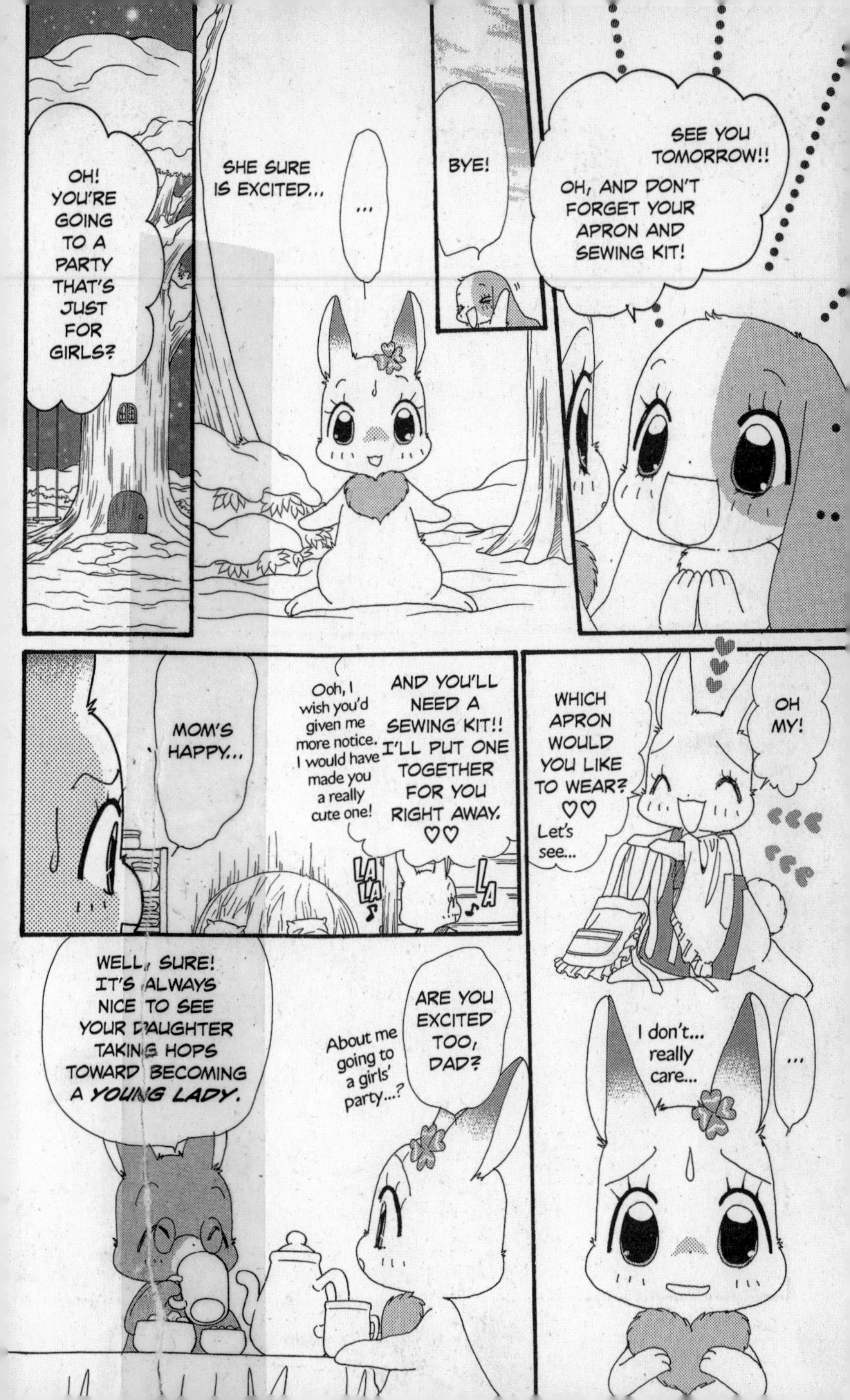
SEE YOU TOMORROW!!
OH, AND DON'T FORGET YOUR APRON AND SEWING KIT!
BYE!
...
SHE SURE IS EXCITED...
OH! YOU'RE GOING TO A PARTY THAT'S JUST FOR GIRLS?
OH MY!
WHICH APRON WOULD YOU LIKE TO WEAR? ♡♡
Let's see...
AND YOU'LL NEED A SEWING KIT!! I'LL PUT ONE TOGETHER FOR YOU RIGHT AWAY. ♡♡
Ooh, I wish you'd given me more notice. I would have made you a really cute one!
LA LA LA
MOM'S HAPPY...
...
I don't... really care...
ARE YOU EXCITED TOO, DAD?
About me going to a girls' party...?
WELL, SURE! IT'S ALWAYS NICE TO SEE YOUR DAUGHTER TAKING HOPS TOWARD BECOMING A *YOUNG LADY*.

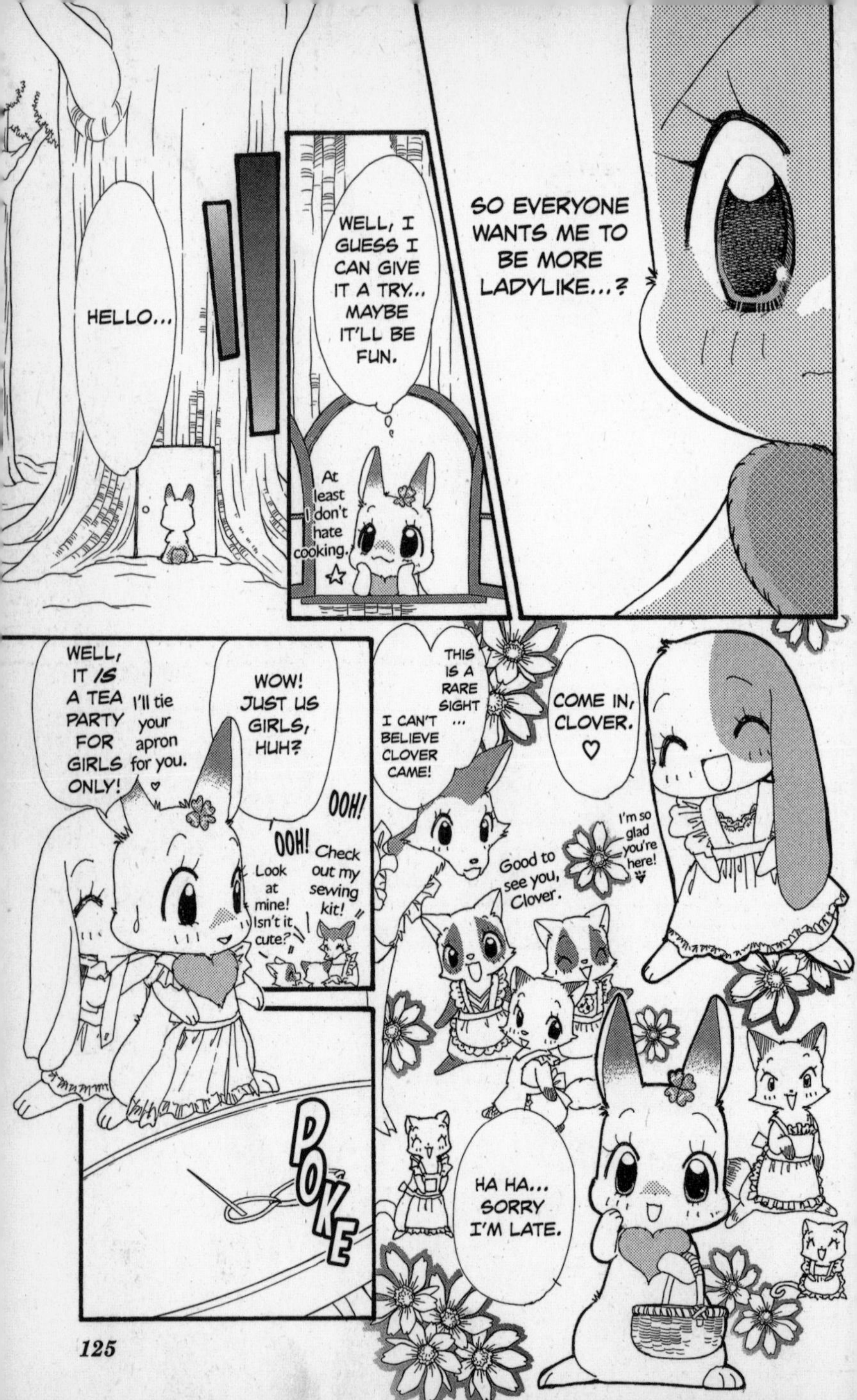
SO EVERYONE WANTS ME TO BE MORE LADYLIKE...?
WELL, I GUESS I CAN GIVE IT A TRY... MAYBE IT'LL BE FUN.
At least I don't hate cooking.
HELLO...
COME IN, CLOVER.
I'm so glad you're here!
Good to see you, Clover.
THIS IS A RARE SIGHT...
I CAN'T BELIEVE CLOVER CAME!
HA HA... SORRY I'M LATE.
WOW! JUST US GIRLS, HUH?
WELL, IT IS A TEA PARTY FOR GIRLS ONLY!
I'll tie your apron for you.
OOH!
OOH!
Check out my sewing kit!
Look at mine! Isn't it cute?
POKE

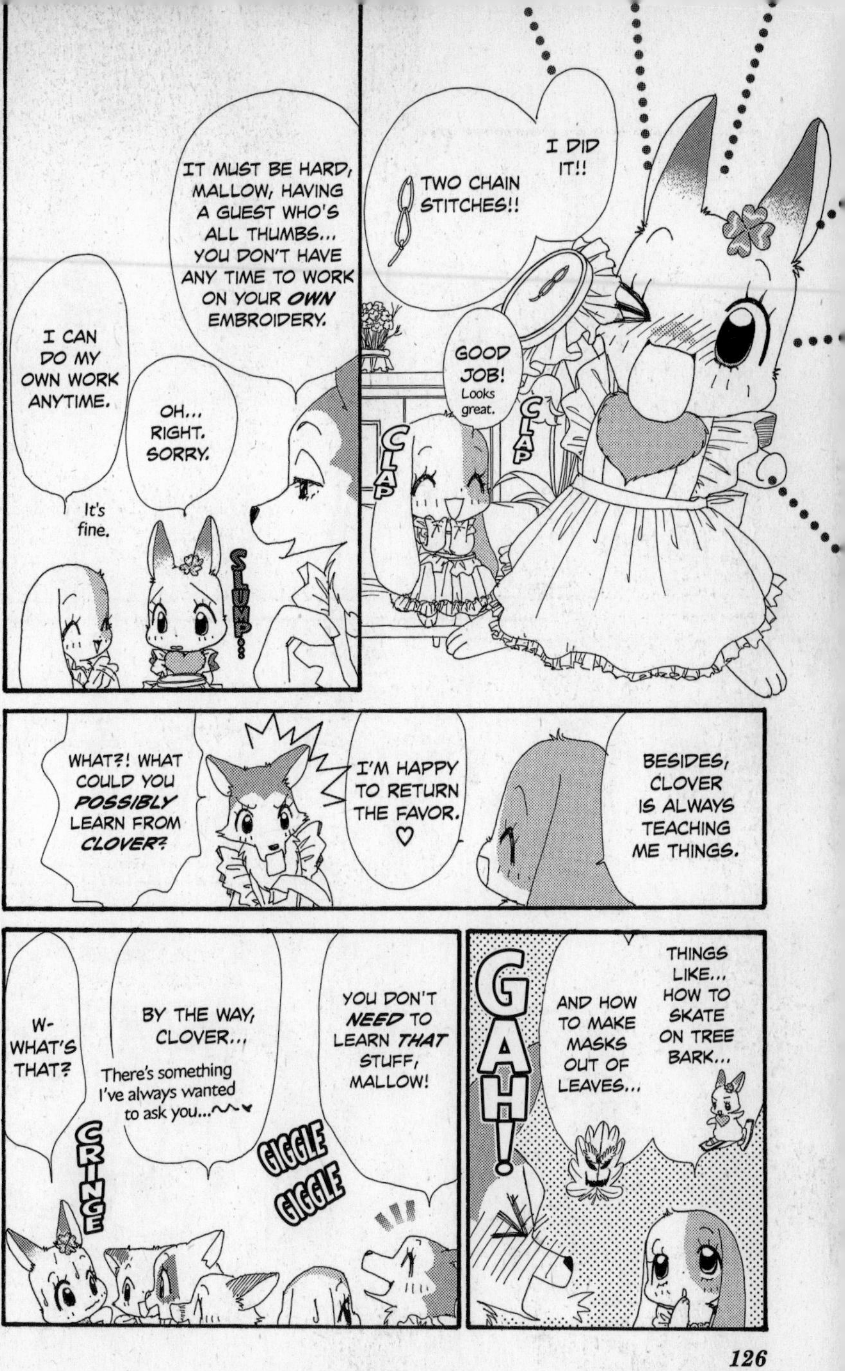
I DID IT!!
TWO CHAIN STITCHES!!
GOOD JOB! Looks great.
CLAP
CLAP
IT MUST BE HARD, MALLOW, HAVING A GUEST WHO'S ALL THUMBS... YOU DON'T HAVE ANY TIME TO WORK ON YOUR ***OWN*** EMBROIDERY.
I CAN DO MY OWN WORK ANYTIME.
It's fine.
OH... RIGHT. SORRY.
SLUMP...
BESIDES, CLOVER IS ALWAYS TEACHING ME THINGS.
I'M HAPPY TO RETURN THE FAVOR. ♡
WHAT?! WHAT COULD YOU ***POSSIBLY*** LEARN FROM ***CLOVER?***
THINGS LIKE... HOW TO SKATE ON TREE BARK...
AND HOW TO MAKE MASKS OUT OF LEAVES...
GAH!
YOU DON'T ***NEED*** TO LEARN ***THAT*** STUFF, MALLOW!
GIGGLE GIGGLE
BY THE WAY, CLOVER...
There's something I've always wanted to ask you...
W- WHAT'S THAT?
CRINGE

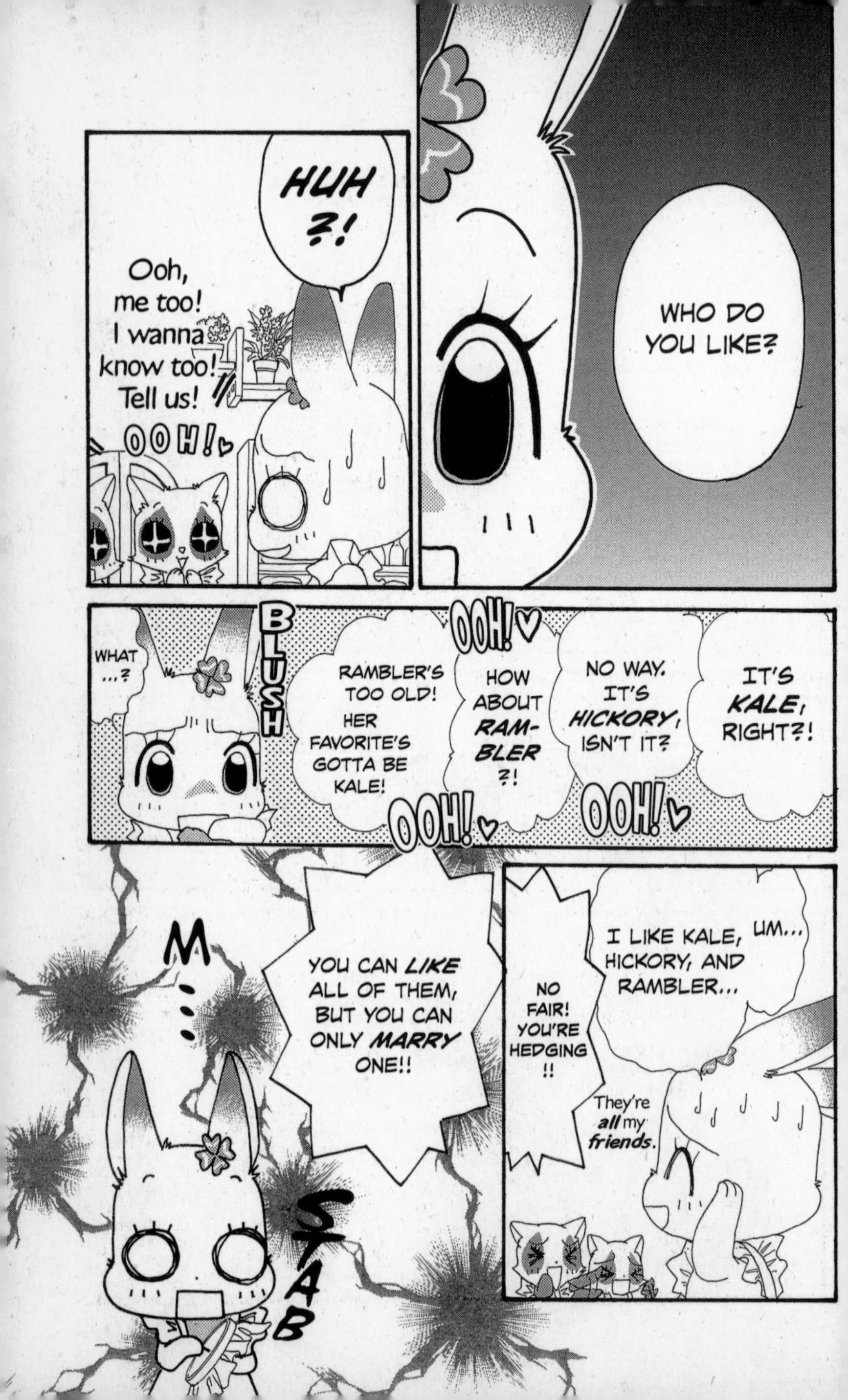
WHO DO YOU LIKE?
HUH ?!
Ooh, me too! I wanna know too! Tell us!
OOH!♥
IT'S KALE, RIGHT?!
NO WAY. IT'S HICKORY, ISN'T IT?
OOH!♥
HOW ABOUT RAMBLER ?!
OOH!♥
RAMBLER'S TOO OLD! HER FAVORITE'S GOTTA BE KALE!
OOH!♥
BLUSH
WHAT ...?
UM...
I LIKE KALE, HICKORY, AND RAMBLER...
They're all my friends.
NO FAIR! YOU'RE HEDGING !!
YOU CAN LIKE ALL OF THEM, BUT YOU CAN ONLY MARRY ONE!!
M...
STAB

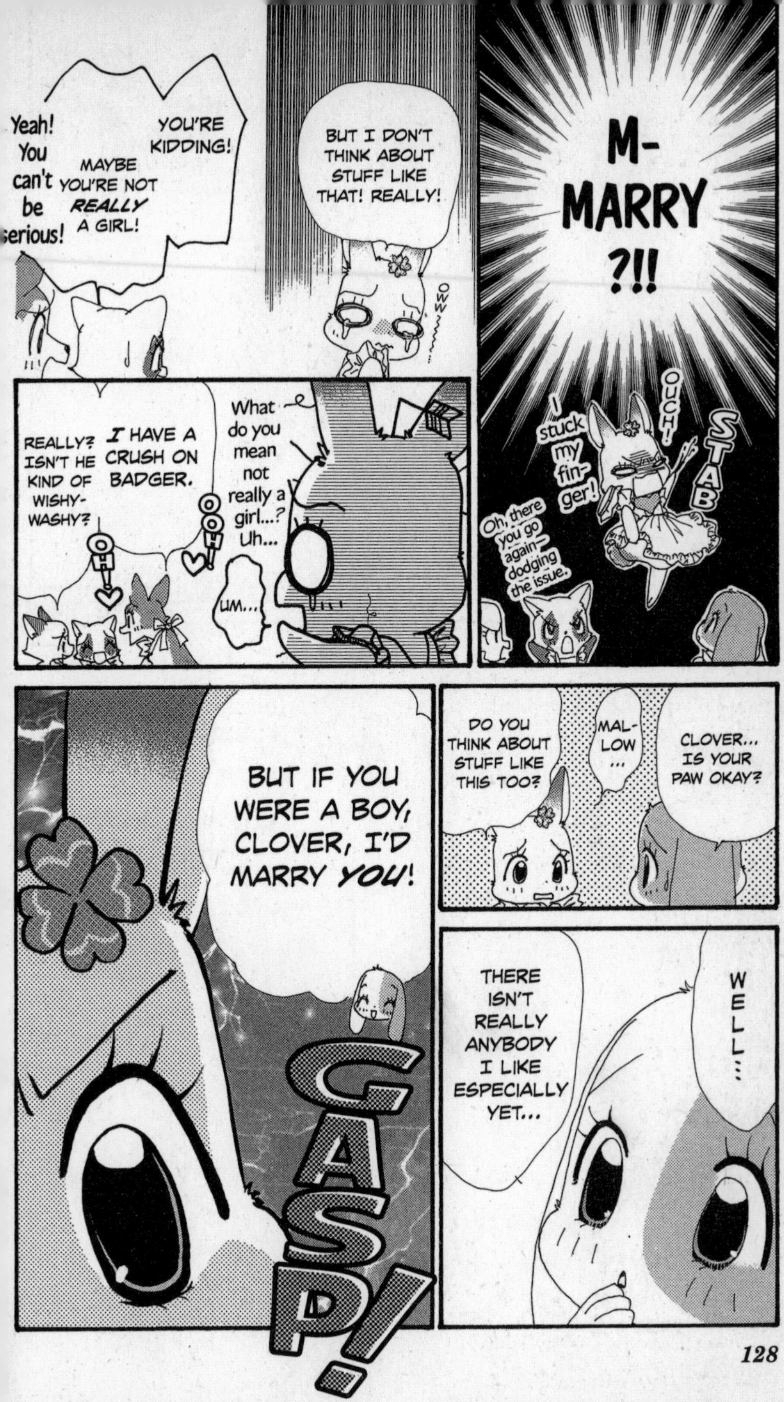
M-MARRY?!!
OUCH!
STAB
I stuck my finger!
Oh, there you go again—dodging the issue.
BUT I DON'T THINK ABOUT STUFF LIKE THAT! REALLY!
OWW~
YOU'RE KIDDING! MAYBE YOU'RE NOT REALLY A GIRL!
Yeah! You can't be serious!
What do you mean not really a girl...? Uh...
I HAVE A CRUSH ON BADGER.
REALLY? ISN'T HE KIND OF WISHY-WASHY?
OOH!
OH!
UM...
CLOVER... IS YOUR PAW OKAY?
MAL-LOW...
DO YOU THINK ABOUT STUFF LIKE THIS TOO?
WELL...
THERE ISN'T REALLY ANYBODY I LIKE ESPECIALLY YET...
BUT IF YOU WERE A BOY, CLOVER, I'D MARRY YOU!
GASP!

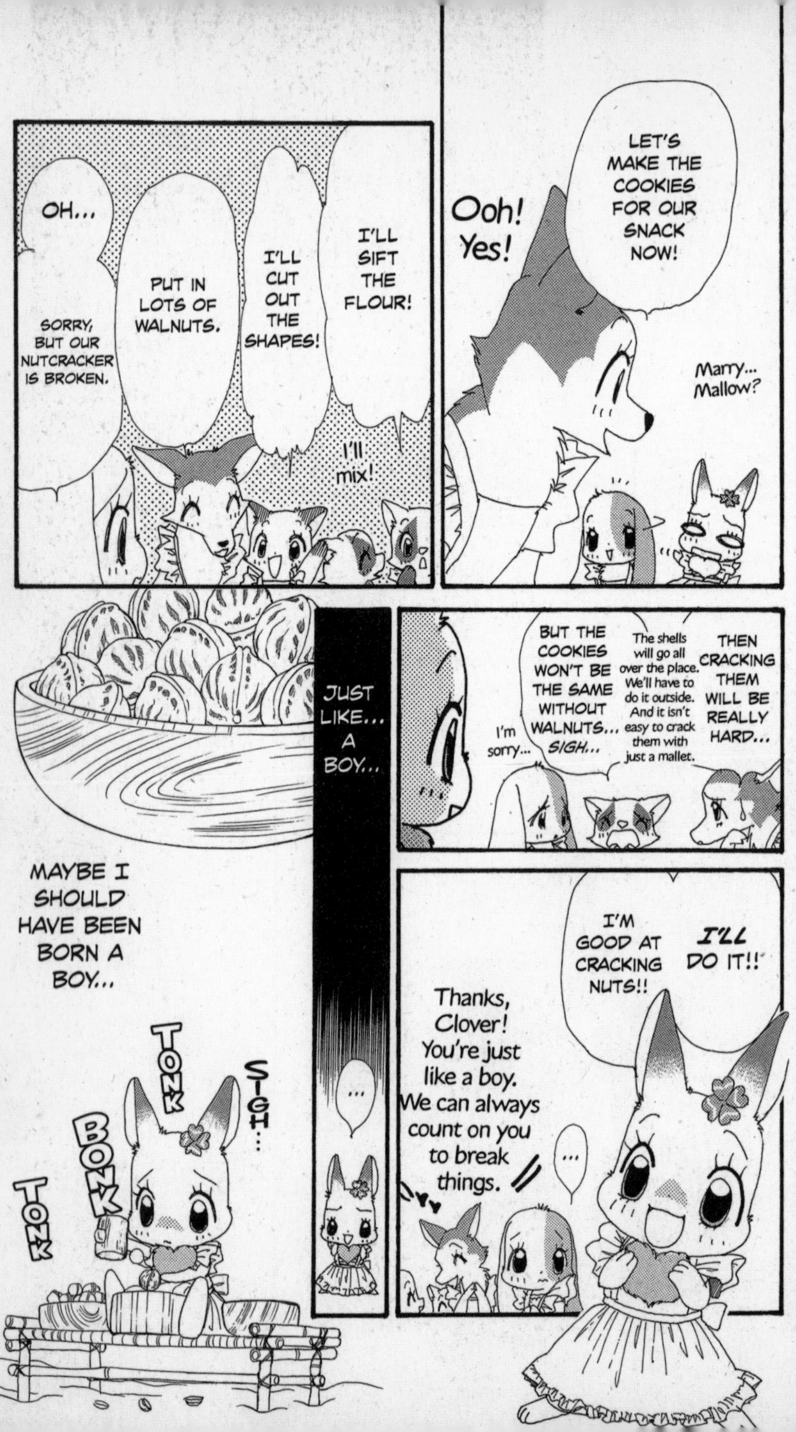
LET'S MAKE THE COOKIES FOR OUR SNACK NOW!
Ooh! Yes!
Marry... Mallow?
I'LL SIFT THE FLOUR!
I'LL CUT OUT THE SHAPES!
PUT IN LOTS OF WALNUTS.
OH...
SORRY, BUT OUR NUTCRACKER IS BROKEN.
I'll mix!
THEN CRACKING THEM WILL BE REALLY HARD...
The shells will go all over the place. We'll have to do it outside. And it isn't easy to crack them with just a mallet.
BUT THE COOKIES WON'T BE THE SAME WITHOUT WALNUTS... SIGH...
I'm sorry...
I'LL DO IT!!
I'M GOOD AT CRACKING NUTS!!
Thanks, Clover! You're just like a boy. We can always count on you to break things.
...
JUST LIKE... A BOY...
...
MAYBE I SHOULD HAVE BEEN BORN A BOY...
TONK
SIGH...
BONK
TONK

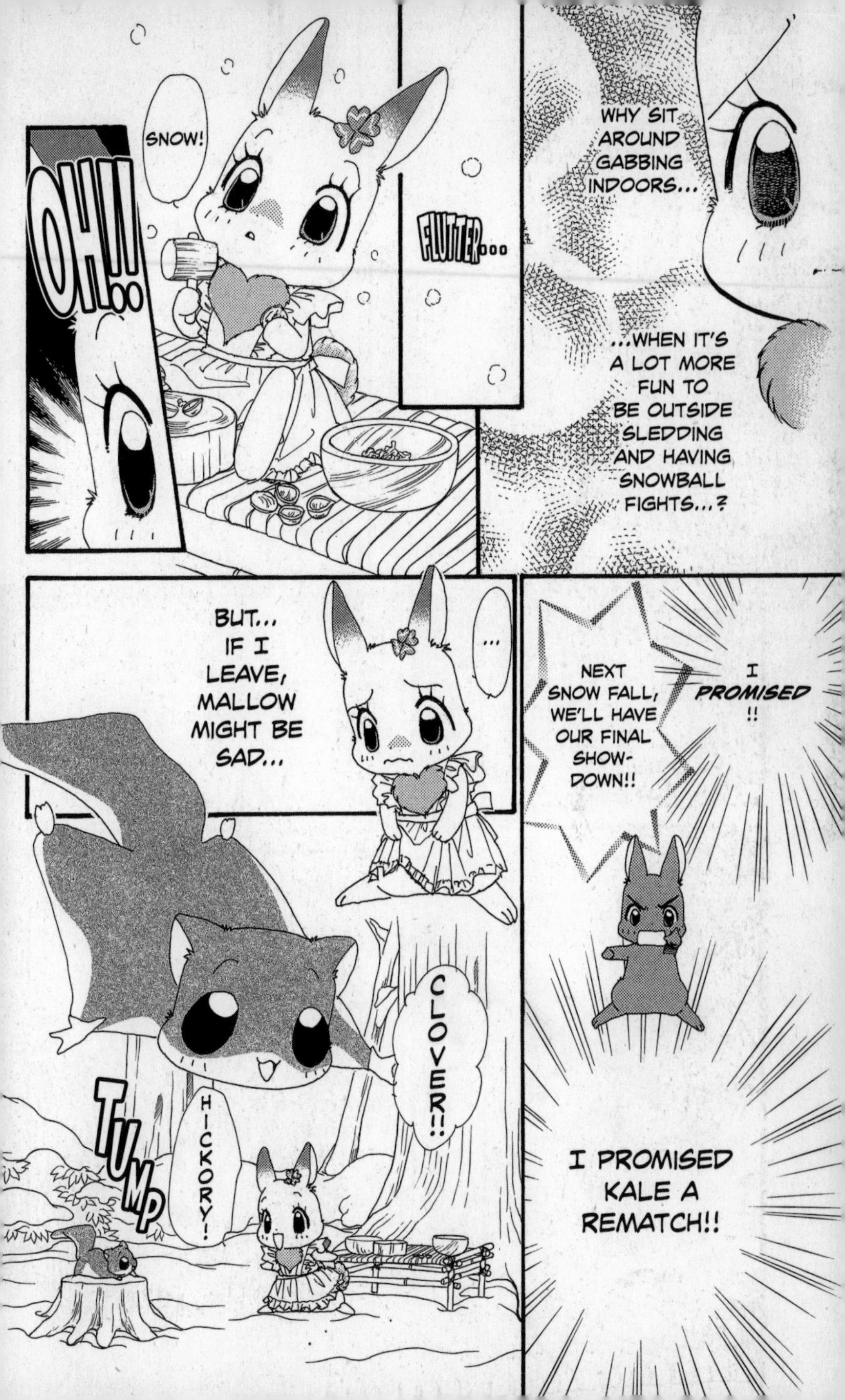
WHY SIT AROUND GABBING INDOORS...
...WHEN IT'S A LOT MORE FUN TO BE OUTSIDE SLEDDING AND HAVING SNOWBALL FIGHTS...?
FLUTTER...
OH!!..
SNOW!
I PROMISED!!
NEXT SNOW FALL, WE'LL HAVE OUR FINAL SHOW-DOWN!!
I PROMISED KALE A REMATCH!!
...
BUT... IF I LEAVE, MALLOW MIGHT BE SAD...
CLOVER!!
TUMP
HICKORY!

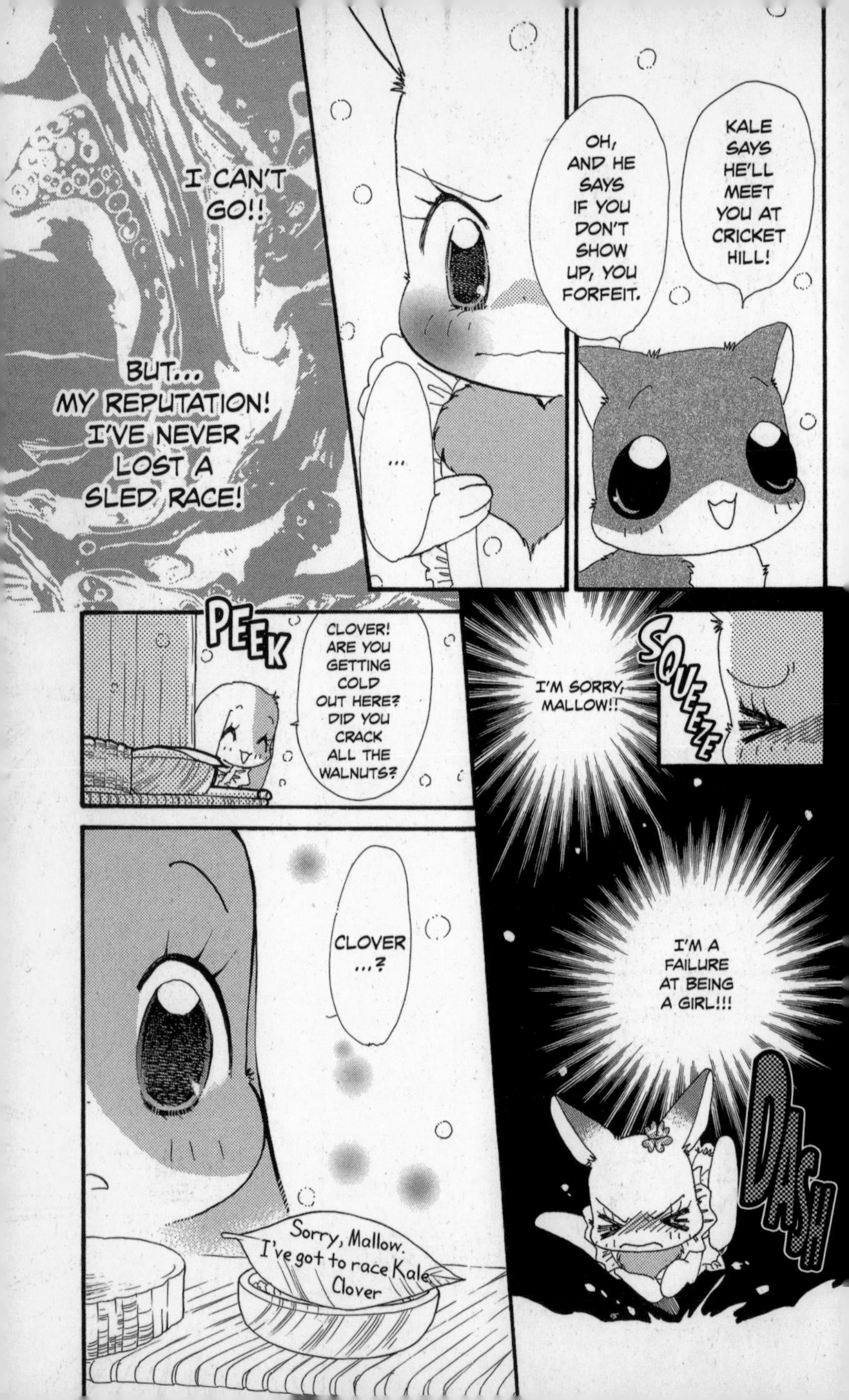
KALE SAYS HE'LL MEET YOU AT CRICKET HILL!
OH, AND HE SAYS IF YOU DON'T SHOW UP, YOU FORFEIT.
...
I CAN'T GO!!
BUT... MY REPUTATION! I'VE NEVER LOST A SLED RACE!
SQUEEZE
I'M SORRY, MALLOW!!
I'M A FAILURE AT BEING A GIRL!!!
DASH
PEEK
CLOVER! ARE YOU GETTING COLD OUT HERE? DID YOU CRACK ALL THE WALNUTS?
CLOVER ...?
Sorry, Mallow. I've got to race Kale. Clover

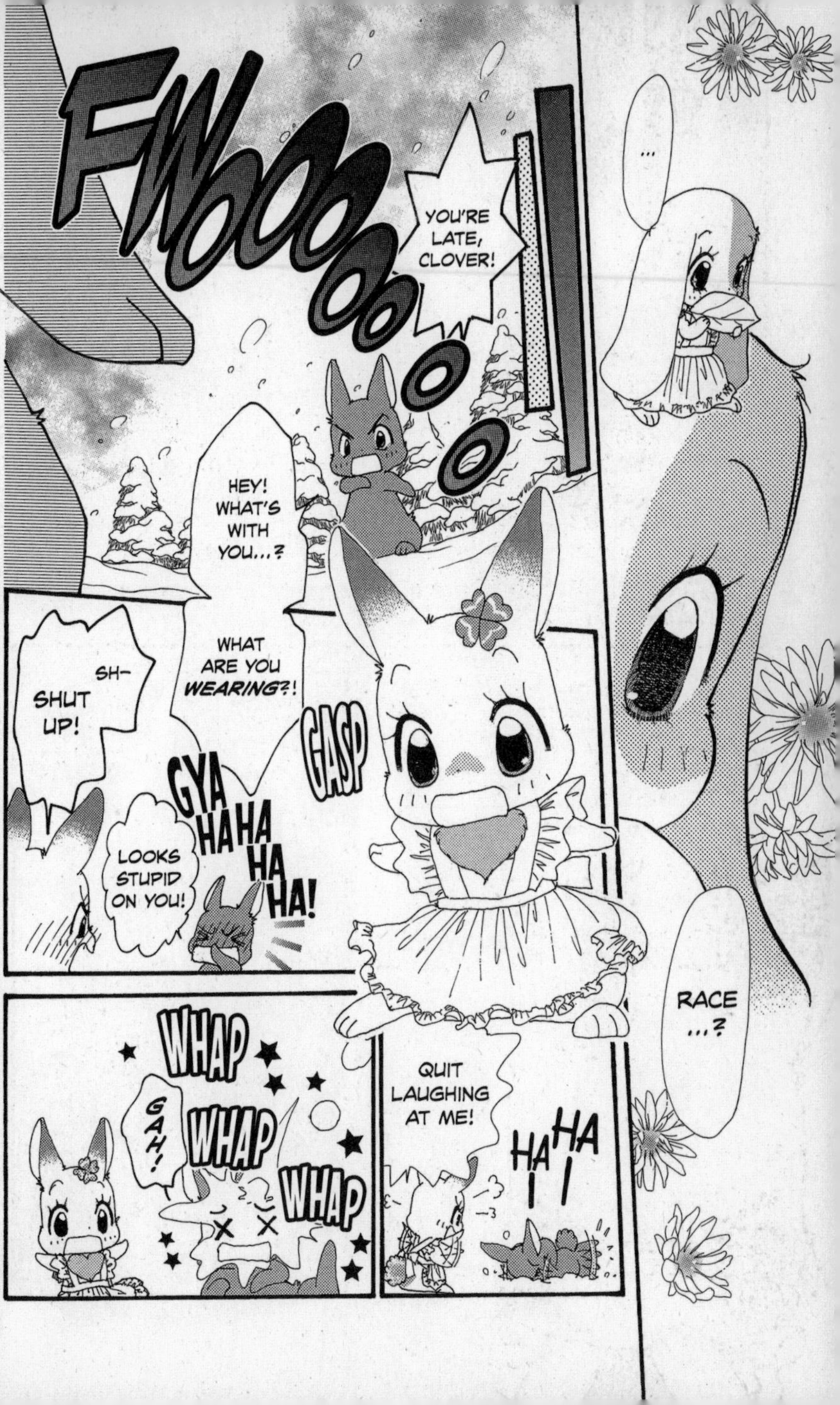
...
RACE ...?
FWOOOOOOOO
YOU'RE LATE, CLOVER!
HEY! WHAT'S WITH YOU...?
WHAT ARE YOU WEARING?!
GASP
SH- SHUT UP!
GYAHAHAHAHA!
LOOKS STUPID ON YOU!
QUIT LAUGHING AT ME!
HAHA
WHAP
GAH!
WHAP
WHAP

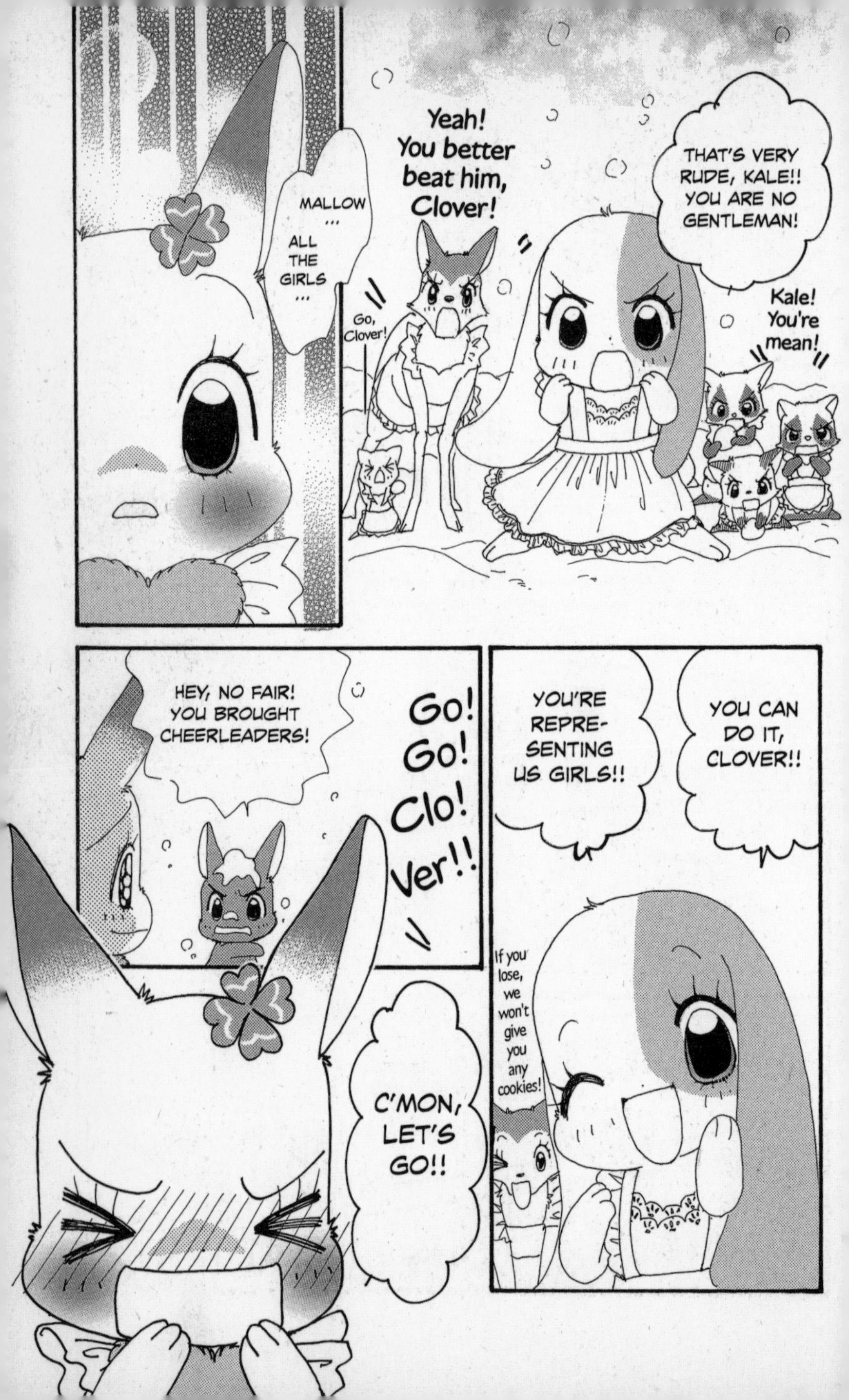
THAT'S VERY RUDE, KALE!! YOU ARE NO GENTLEMAN!
Kale! You're mean!
Yeah! You better beat him, Clover!
Go, Clover!
MALLOW... ALL THE GIRLS...
YOU CAN DO IT, CLOVER!!
YOU'RE REPRESENTING US GIRLS!!
If you lose, we won't give you any cookies!
Go! Go! Clo! Ver!!
HEY, NO FAIR! YOU BROUGHT CHEERLEADERS!
C'MON, LET'S GO!!

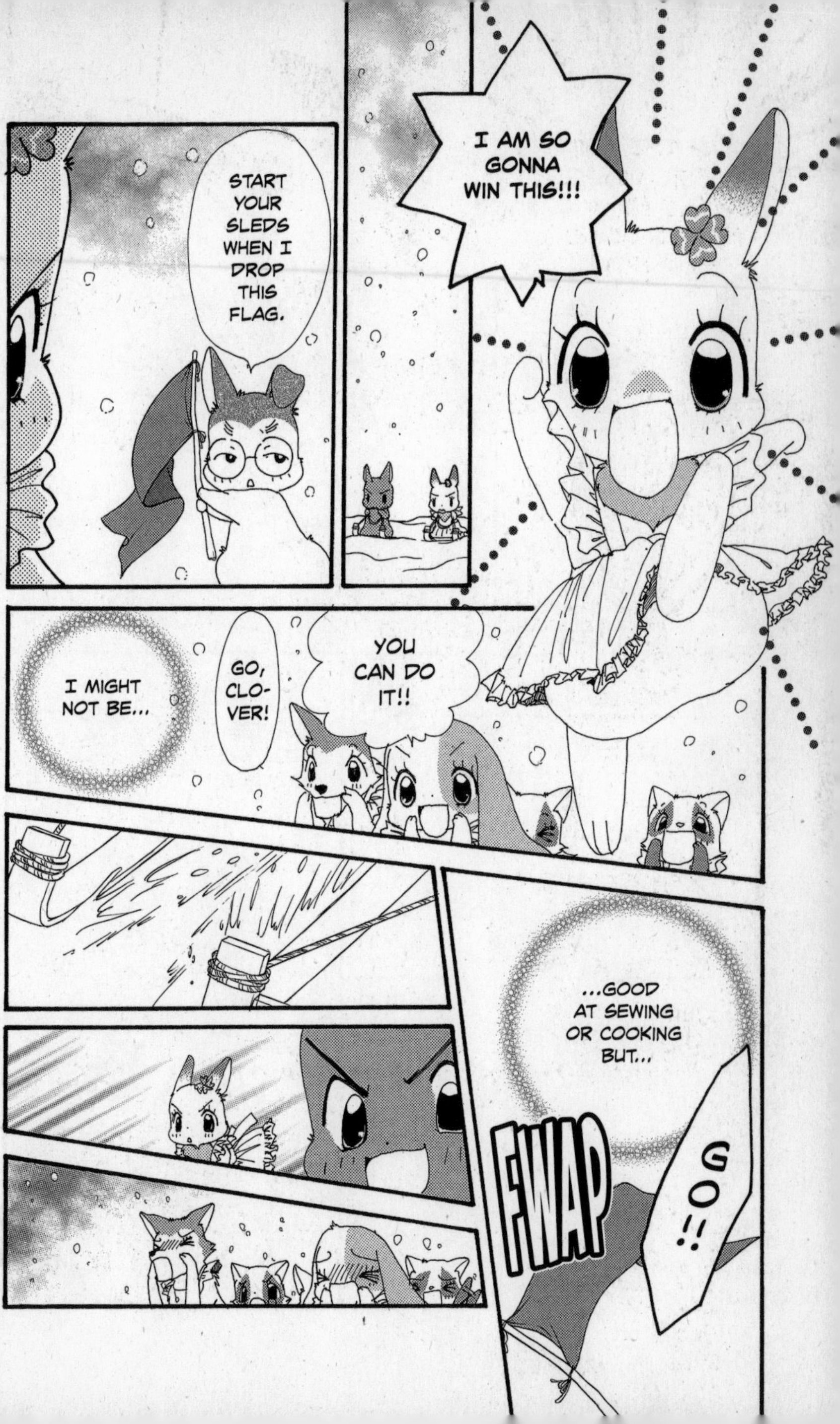
I AM SO GONNA WIN THIS!!!
START YOUR SLEDS WHEN I DROP THIS FLAG.
YOU CAN DO IT!!
GO, CLO-VER!
I MIGHT NOT BE...
...GOOD AT SEWING OR COOKING BUT...
GO!!
FWAP

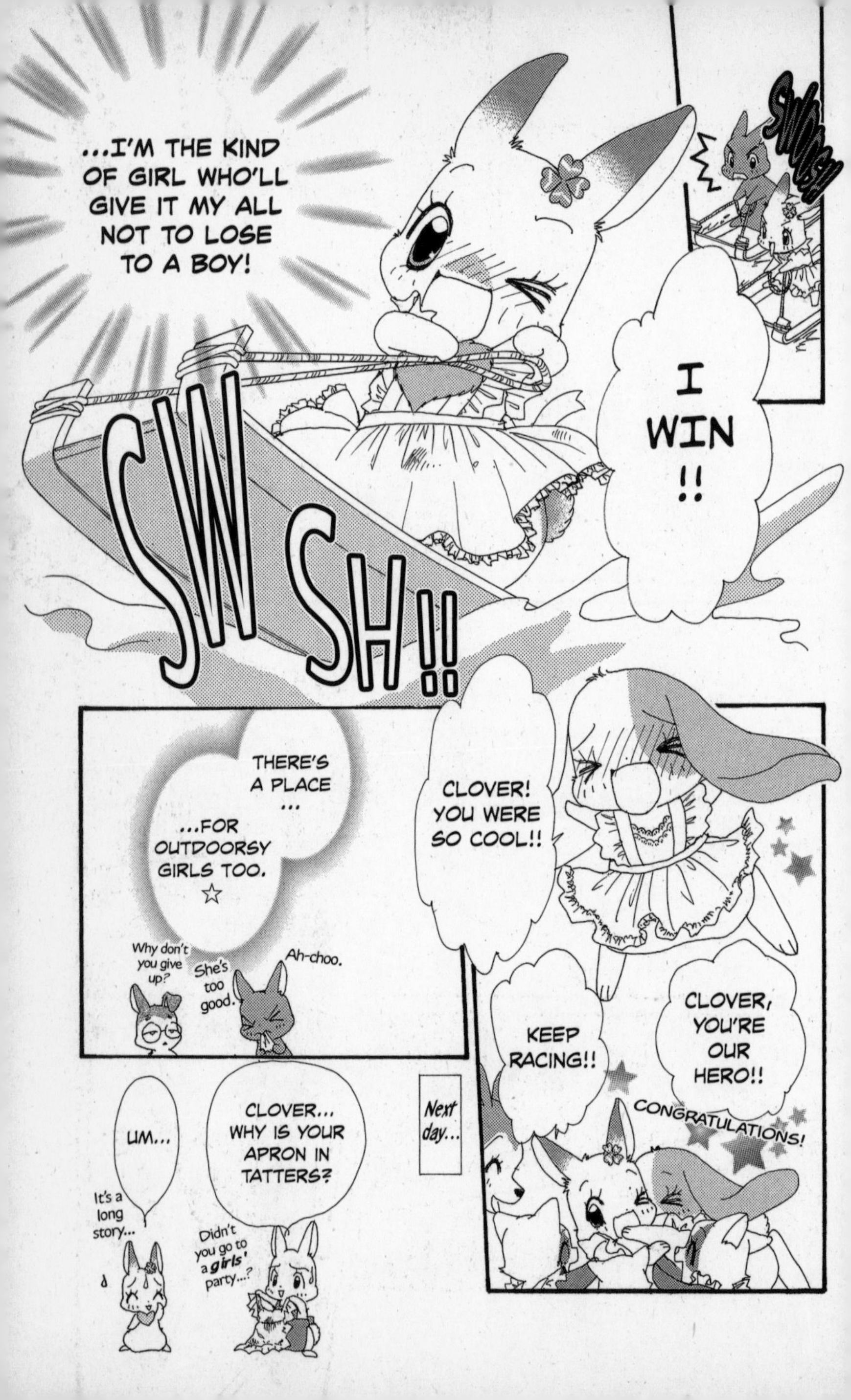
SWOOSH!!
I WIN!!
...I'M THE KIND OF GIRL WHO'LL GIVE IT MY ALL NOT TO LOSE TO A BOY!
SW SH!!
CLOVER! YOU WERE SO COOL!!
CLOVER, YOU'RE OUR HERO!!
KEEP RACING!!
CONGRATULATIONS!
THERE'S A PLACE...
...FOR OUTDOORSY GIRLS TOO. ☆
Ah-choo.
She's too good.
Why don't you give up?
Next day...
CLOVER... WHY IS YOUR APRON IN TATTERS?
Didn't you go to a girls' party...?
UM...
It's a long story...

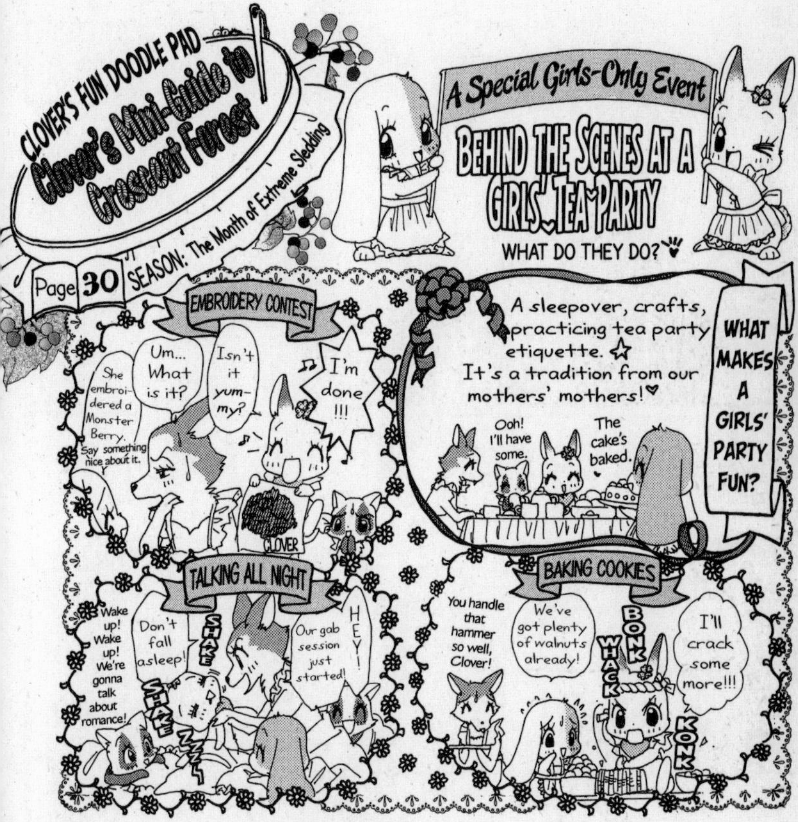

A Special Girls-Only Event
BEHIND THE SCENES AT A GIRLS' TEA PARTY
WHAT DO THEY DO?
CLOVER'S FUN DOODLE PAD
Clover's Mini-Guide to Crescent Forest
Page 30
SEASON: The Month of Extreme Sledding
WHAT MAKES A GIRLS' PARTY FUN?
A sleepover, crafts, practicing tea party etiquette. ☆ It's a tradition from our mothers' mothers!♡
The cake's baked.
Ooh! I'll have some.
EMBROIDERY CONTEST
I'm done!!!
Isn't it yum-my?
Um... What is it?
She embroi-dered a Monster Berry. Say something nice about it.
CLOVER
BAKING COOKIES
I'll crack some more!!!
BONK
WHACK
KONK
We've got plenty of walnuts already!
You handle that hammer so well, Clover!
TALKING ALL NIGHT
HEY!
Our gab session just started!
SHAKE
Don't fall asleep!
SHAKE
Wake up! Wake up! We're gonna talk about romance!
ZZZ

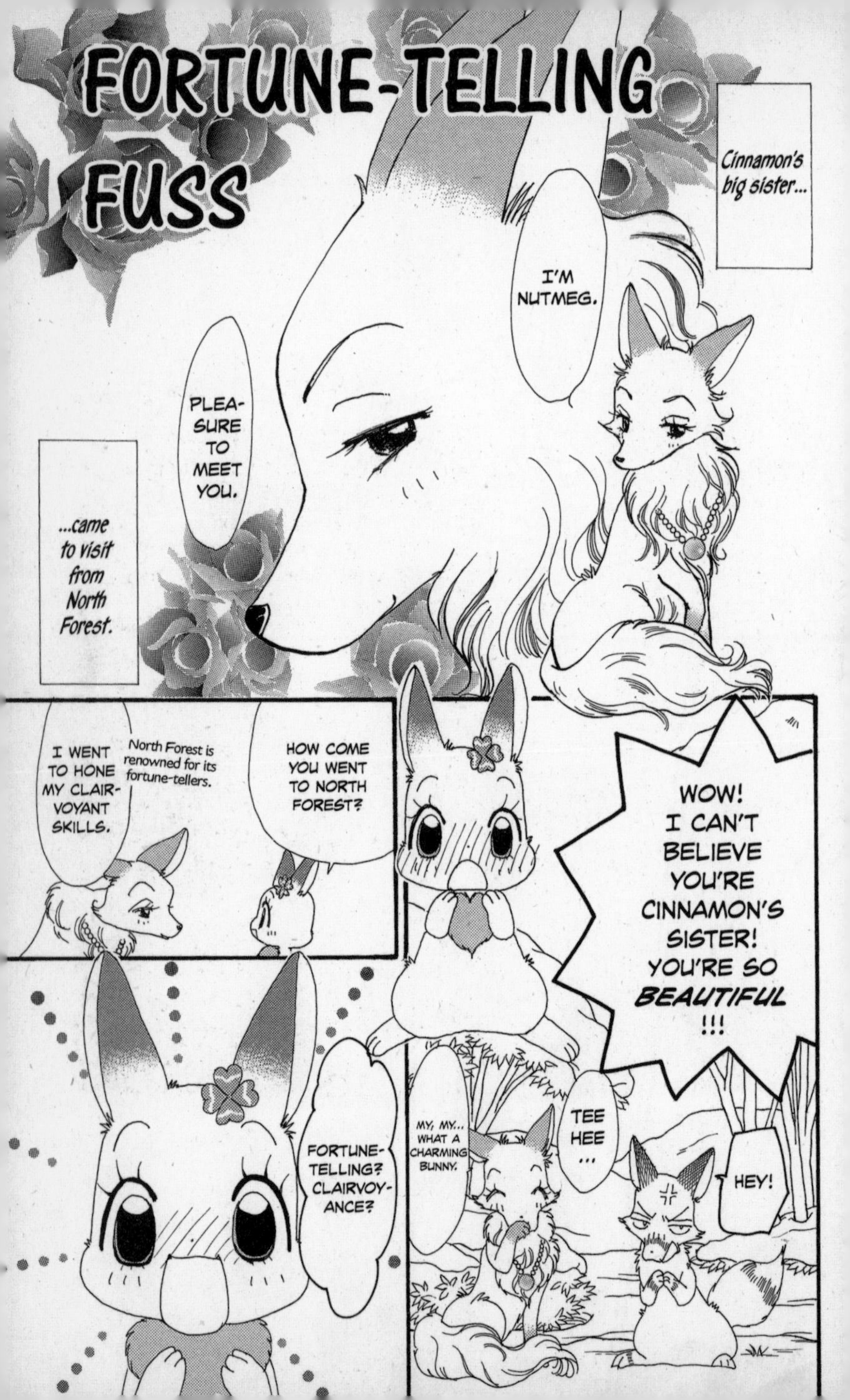
FORTUNE-TELLING FUSS
Cinnamon's big sister...
I'M NUTMEG.
PLEA-SURE TO MEET YOU.
...came to visit from North Forest.
WOW! I CAN'T BELIEVE YOU'RE CINNAMON'S SISTER! YOU'RE SO BEAUTIFUL!!!
HOW COME YOU WENT TO NORTH FOREST?
North Forest is renowned for its fortune-tellers.
I WENT TO HONE MY CLAIR-VOYANT SKILLS.
HEY!
TEE HEE...
MY, MY... WHAT A CHARMING BUNNY.
FORTUNE-TELLING? CLAIRVOY-ANCE?

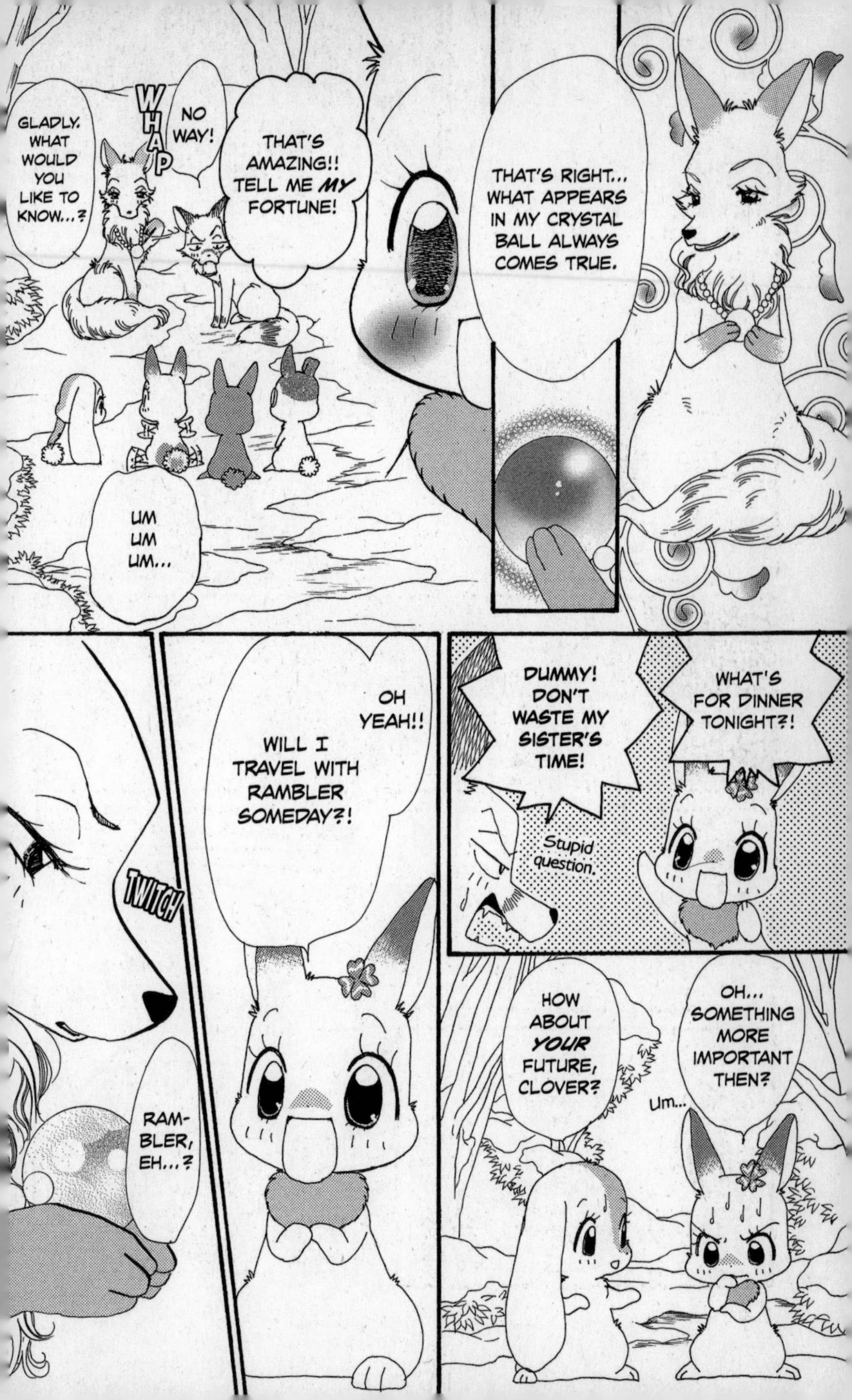
THAT'S RIGHT... WHAT APPEARS IN MY CRYSTAL BALL ALWAYS COMES TRUE.
THAT'S AMAZING!! TELL ME MY FORTUNE!
NO WAY!
WHAP
GLADLY. WHAT WOULD YOU LIKE TO KNOW...?
UM UM UM...
WHAT'S FOR DINNER TONIGHT?!
DUMMY! DON'T WASTE MY SISTER'S TIME!
Stupid question.
OH... SOMETHING MORE IMPORTANT THEN?
HOW ABOUT YOUR FUTURE, CLOVER?
Um...
OH YEAH!!
WILL I TRAVEL WITH RAMBLER SOMEDAY?!
TWITCH
RAM-BLER, EH...?

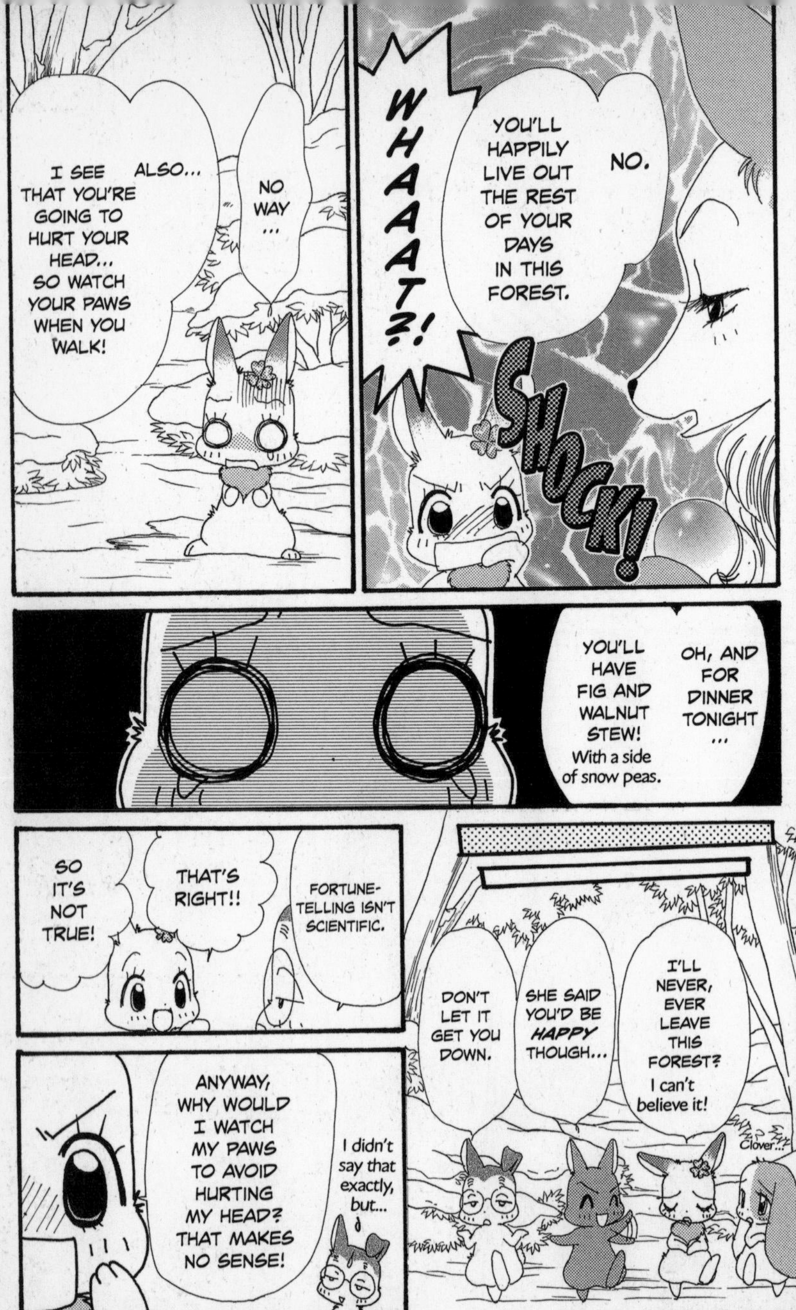
NO.
YOU'LL HAPPILY LIVE OUT THE REST OF YOUR DAYS IN THIS FOREST.
WHAAAT?!
SHOCK!
NO WAY...
ALSO... I SEE THAT YOU'RE GOING TO HURT YOUR HEAD... SO WATCH YOUR PAWS WHEN YOU WALK!
OH, AND FOR DINNER TONIGHT...
YOU'LL HAVE FIG AND WALNUT STEW! With a side of snow peas.
I'LL NEVER, EVER LEAVE THIS FOREST? I can't believe it!
SHE SAID YOU'D BE *HAPPY* THOUGH...
DON'T LET IT GET YOU DOWN.
Clover...?
FORTUNE-TELLING ISN'T SCIENTIFIC.
THAT'S RIGHT!!
SO IT'S NOT TRUE!
ANYWAY, WHY WOULD I WATCH MY PAWS TO AVOID HURTING MY HEAD? THAT MAKES NO SENSE!
I didn't say that exactly, but...

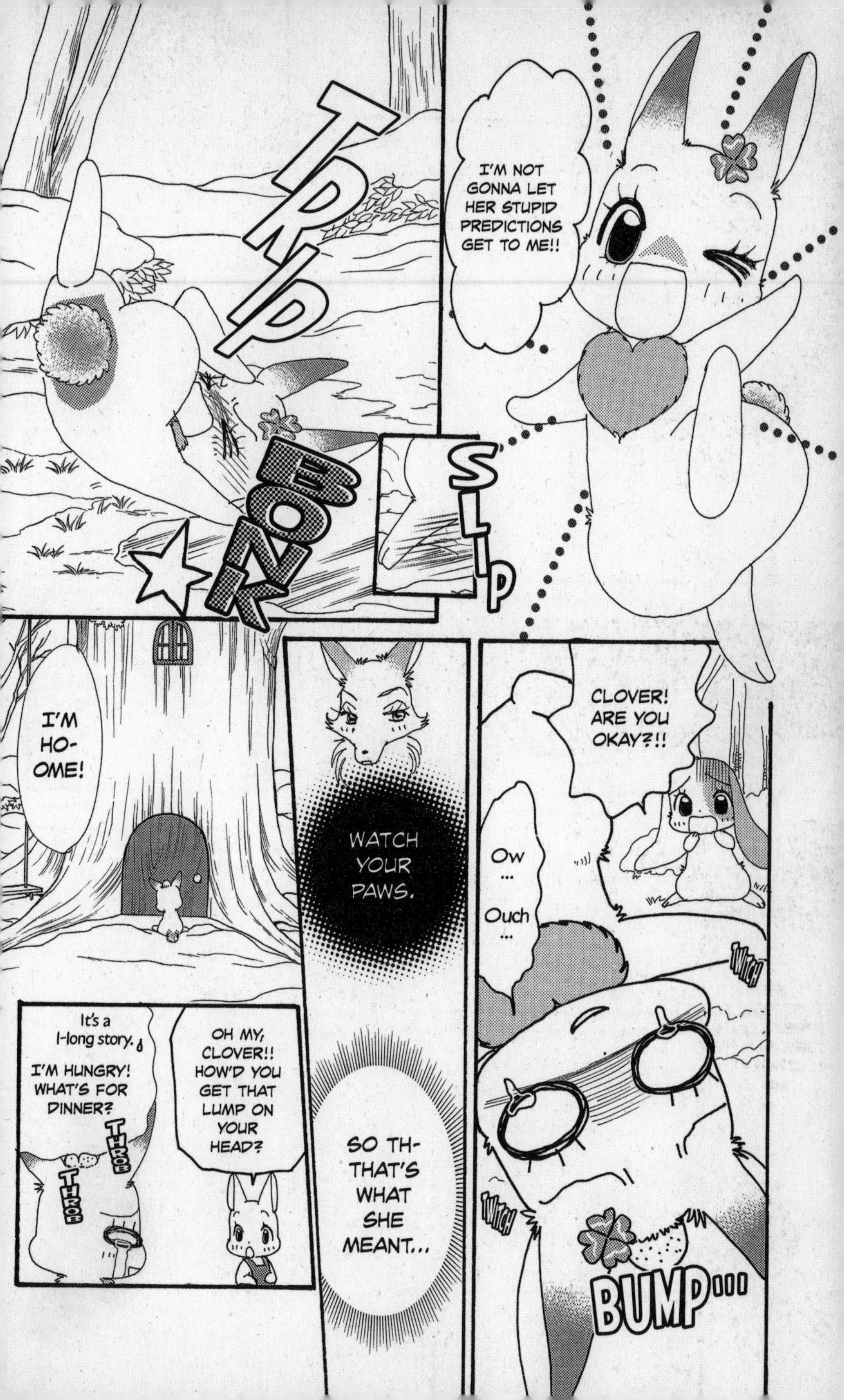
I'M NOT GONNA LET HER STUPID PREDICTIONS GET TO ME!!
SLIP
TRIP
BONK
CLOVER! ARE YOU OKAY?!!
Ow... Ouch...
TWITCH
TWITCH
BUMP...
WATCH YOUR PAWS.
SO TH-THAT'S WHAT SHE MEANT...
I'M HO-OME!
OH MY, CLOVER!! HOW'D YOU GET THAT LUMP ON YOUR HEAD?
It's a l-long story.
I'M HUNGRY! WHAT'S FOR DINNER?
THROB
THROB

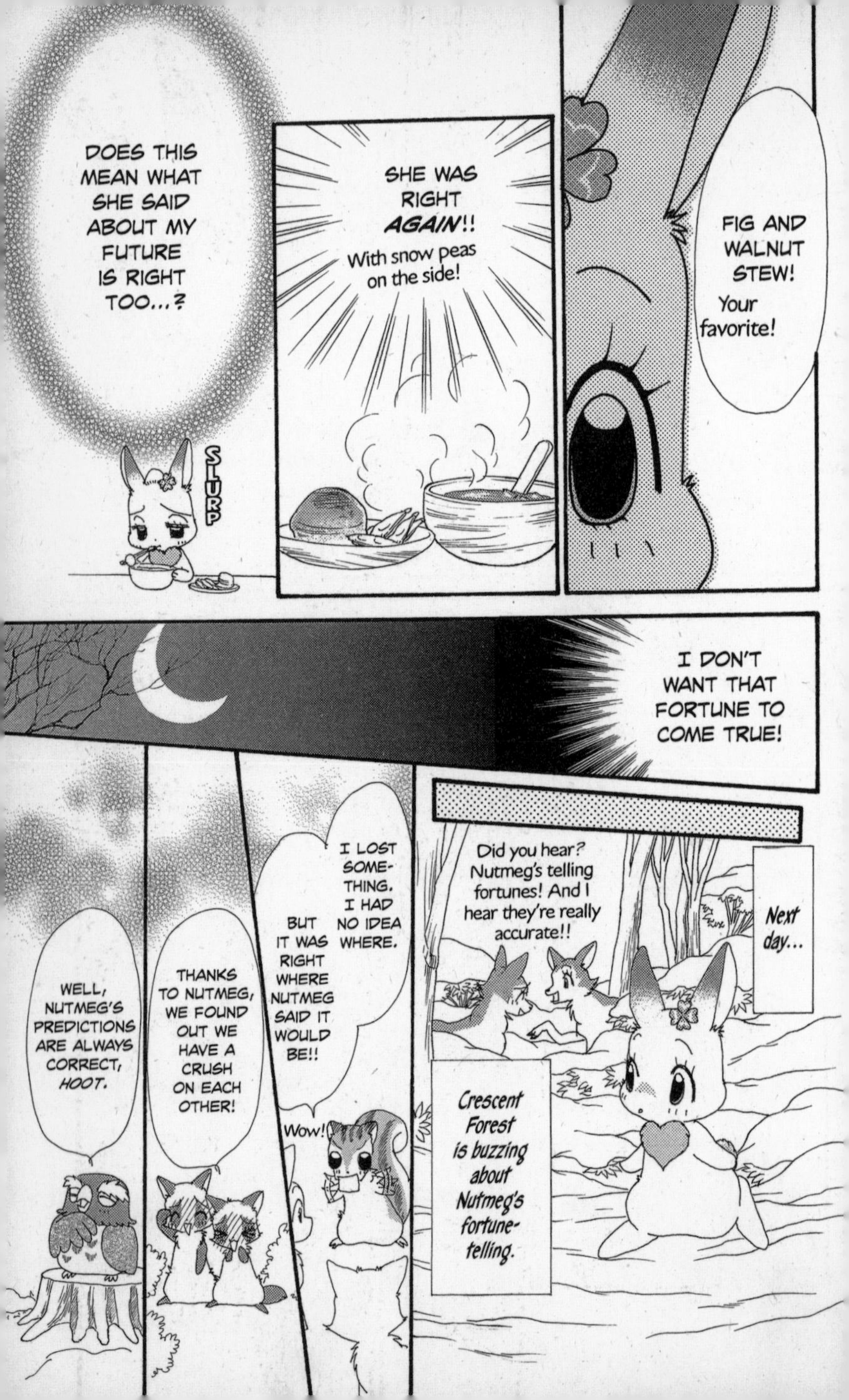
FIG AND WALNUT STEW!
Your favorite!
SHE WAS RIGHT AGAIN!!
With snow peas on the side!
DOES THIS MEAN WHAT SHE SAID ABOUT MY FUTURE IS RIGHT TOO...?
SLURP
I DON'T WANT THAT FORTUNE TO COME TRUE!
Next day...
Did you hear? Nutmeg's telling fortunes! And I hear they're really accurate!!
Crescent Forest is buzzing about Nutmeg's fortune-telling.
I LOST SOMETHING. I HAD NO IDEA WHERE.
BUT IT WAS RIGHT WHERE NUTMEG SAID IT WOULD BE!!
Wow!
THANKS TO NUTMEG, WE FOUND OUT WE HAVE A CRUSH ON EACH OTHER!
WELL, NUTMEG'S PREDICTIONS ARE ALWAYS CORRECT, HOOT.

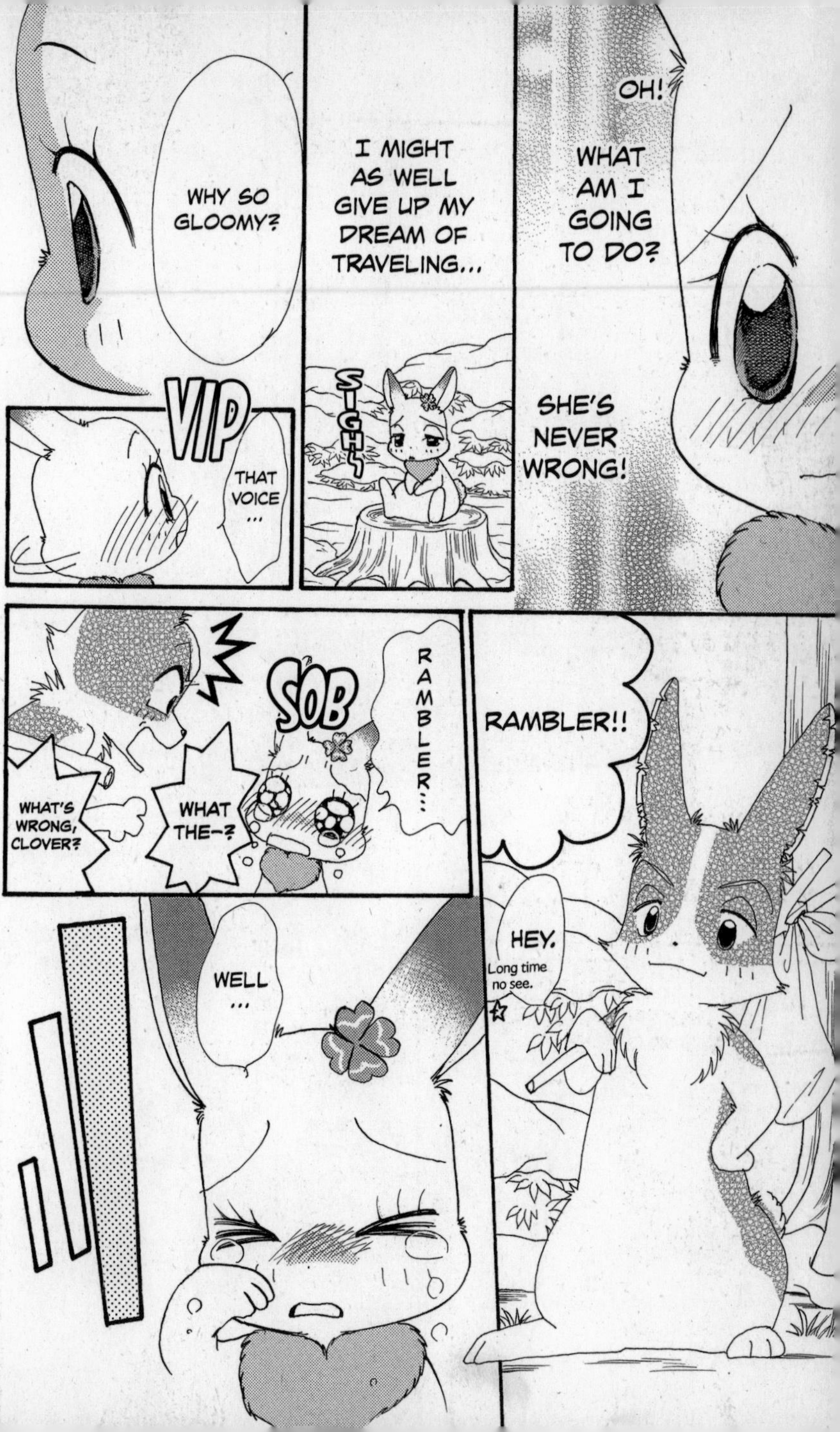
OH!
WHAT AM I GOING TO DO?
SHE'S NEVER WRONG!
I MIGHT AS WELL GIVE UP MY DREAM OF TRAVELING...
SIGH
WHY SO GLOOMY?
VIP
THAT VOICE ...
RAMBLER!!
HEY.
Long time no see.
RAMBLER...
SOB
WHAT THE-?
WHAT'S WRONG, CLOVER?
WELL ...

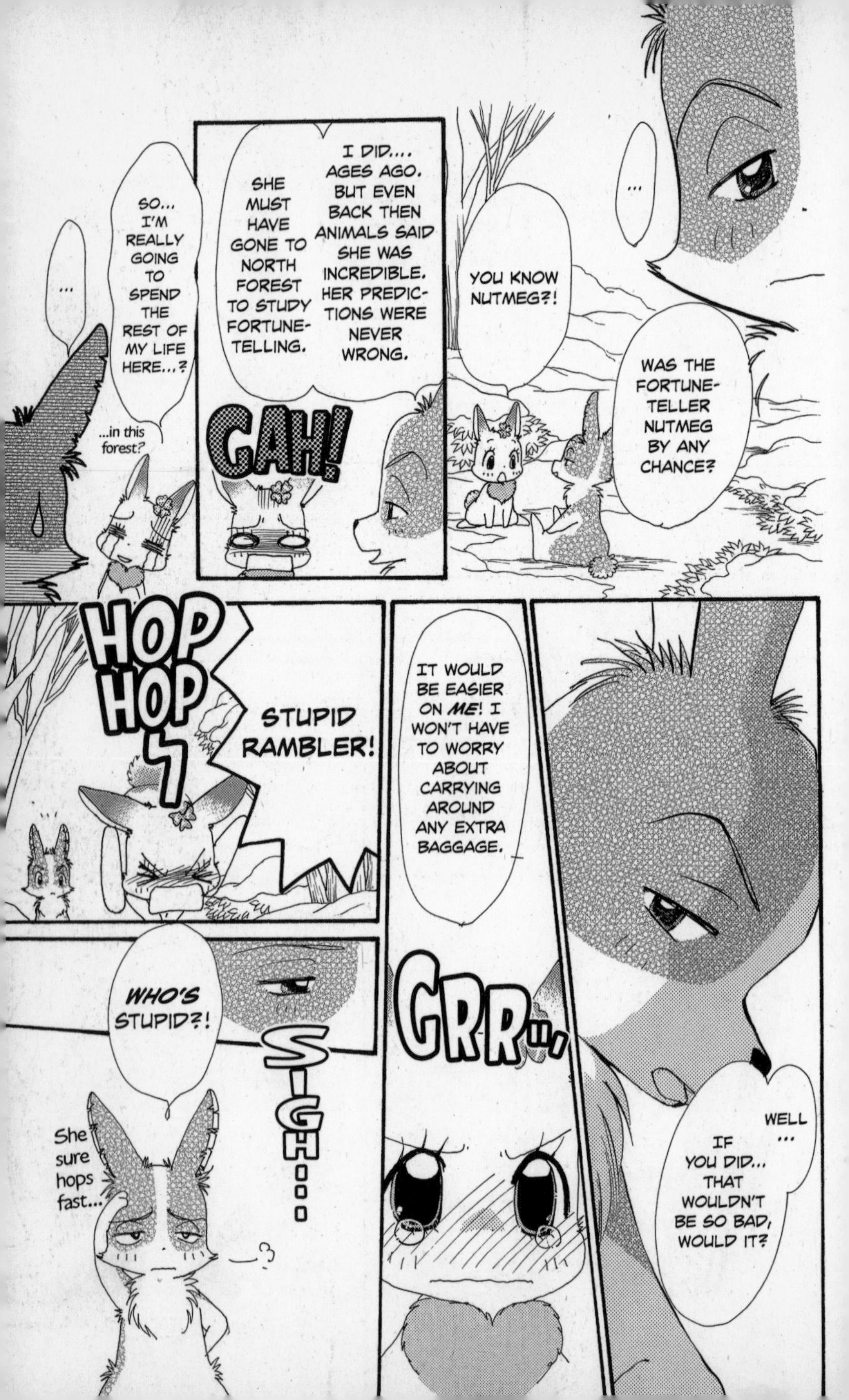
...
WAS THE FORTUNE-TELLER NUTMEG BY ANY CHANCE?
YOU KNOW NUTMEG?!
I DID.... AGES AGO. BUT EVEN BACK THEN ANIMALS SAID SHE WAS INCREDIBLE. HER PREDICTIONS WERE NEVER WRONG.
SHE MUST HAVE GONE TO NORTH FOREST TO STUDY FORTUNE-TELLING.
GAH!
SO... I'M REALLY GOING TO SPEND THE REST OF MY LIFE HERE...?
...in this forest?
...
WELL... IF YOU DID... THAT WOULDN'T BE SO BAD, WOULD IT?
IT WOULD BE EASIER ON *ME*! I WON'T HAVE TO WORRY ABOUT CARRYING AROUND ANY EXTRA BAGGAGE.
GRR...
HOP HOP
STUPID RAMBLER!
WHO'S STUPID?!
SIGH...
She sure hops fast...

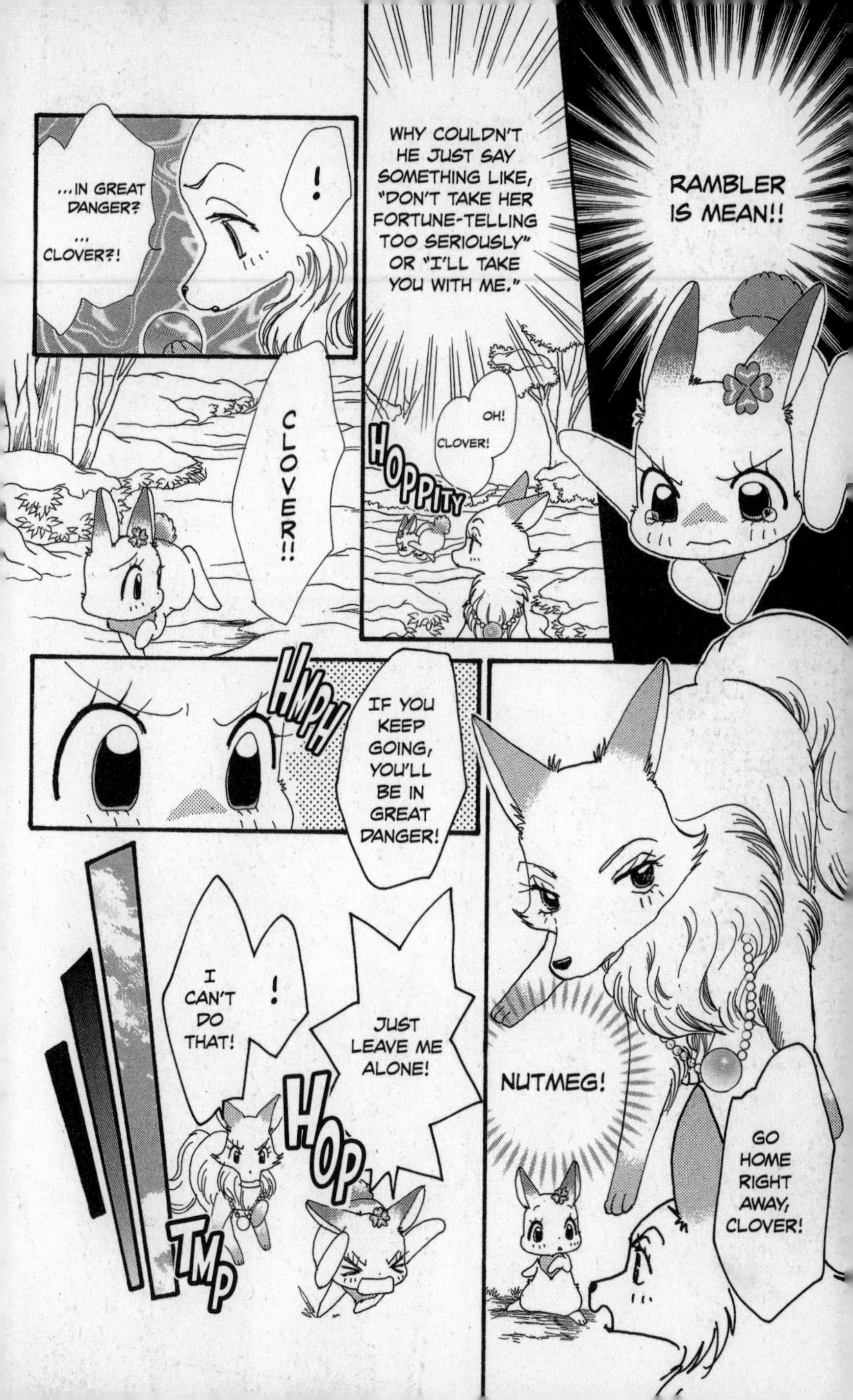
RAMBLER IS MEAN!!
WHY COULDN'T HE JUST SAY SOMETHING LIKE, "DON'T TAKE HER FORTUNE-TELLING TOO SERIOUSLY" OR "I'LL TAKE YOU WITH ME."
OH! CLOVER!
HOPPITY
!
...IN GREAT DANGER? ... CLOVER?!
CLOVER!!
NUTMEG!
GO HOME RIGHT AWAY, CLOVER!
...
HMPH
IF YOU KEEP GOING, YOU'LL BE IN GREAT DANGER!
JUST LEAVE ME ALONE!
HOP
!
I CAN'T DO THAT!
TMP

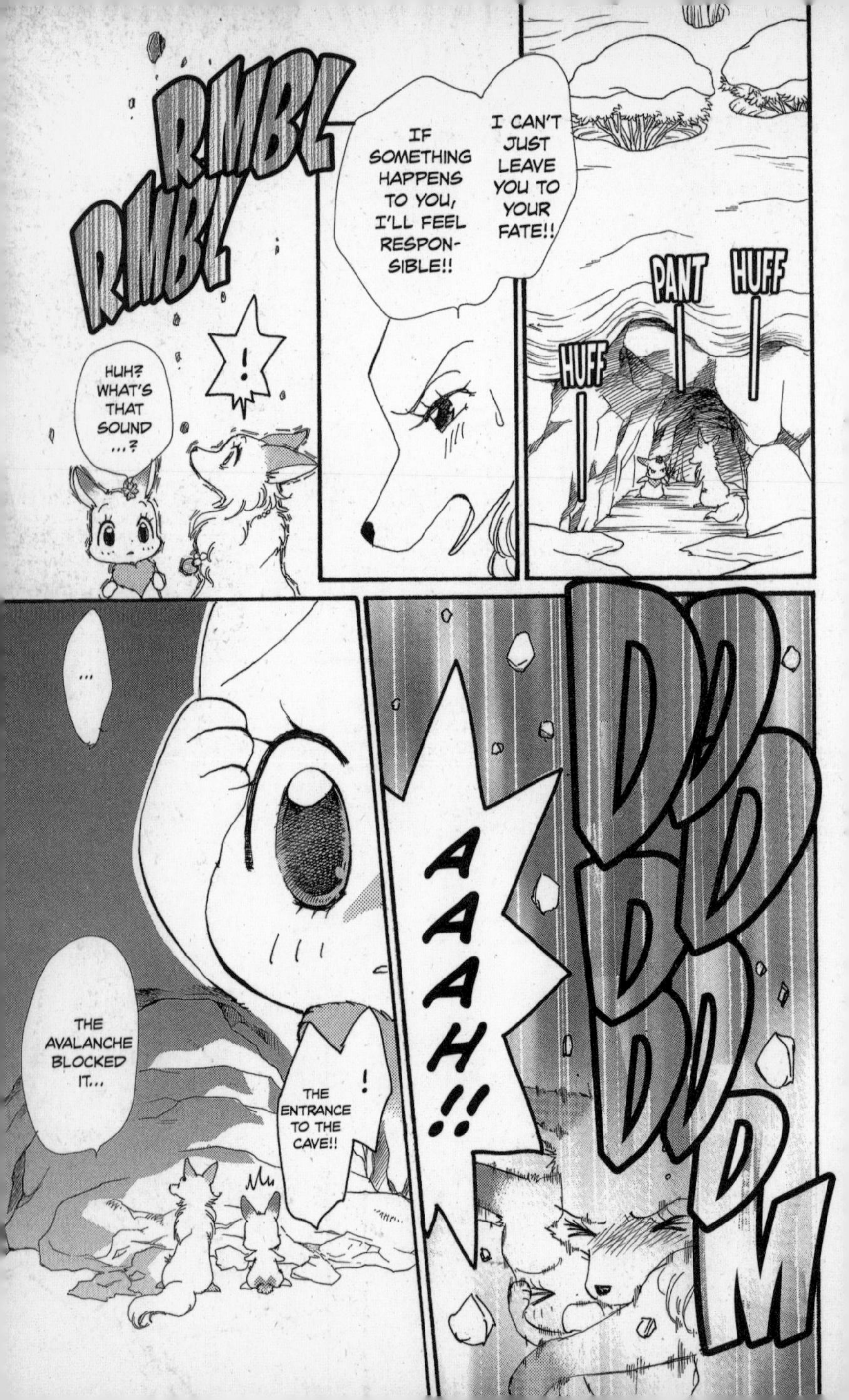
HUFF
PANT
HUFF
I CAN'T JUST LEAVE YOU TO YOUR FATE!!
IF SOMETHING HAPPENS TO YOU, I'LL FEEL RESPON-SIBLE!!
RMBL
RMBL
!
HUH? WHAT'S THAT SOUND ...?
DDDDDDDM
AAAAH!!
...
!
THE ENTRANCE TO THE CAVE!!
THE AVALANCHE BLOCKED IT...

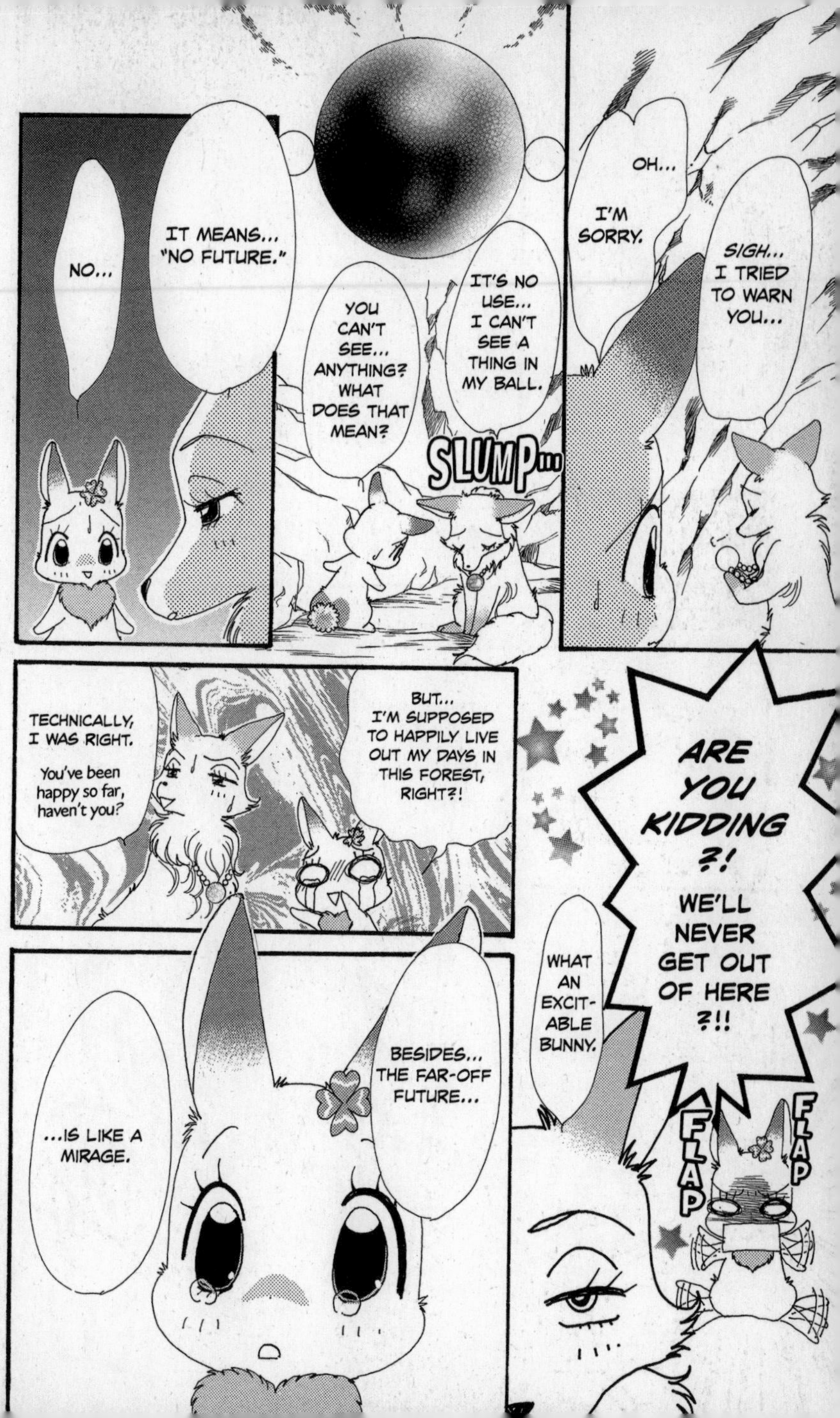
SIGH... I TRIED TO WARN YOU...
OH... I'M SORRY.
IT'S NO USE... I CAN'T SEE A THING IN MY BALL.
YOU CAN'T SEE... ANYTHING? WHAT DOES THAT MEAN?
SLUMP...
IT MEANS... "NO FUTURE."
NO...
ARE YOU KIDDING?! WE'LL NEVER GET OUT OF HERE?!!
BUT... I'M SUPPOSED TO HAPPILY LIVE OUT MY DAYS IN THIS FOREST, RIGHT?!
TECHNICALLY, I WAS RIGHT.
You've been happy so far, haven't you?
WHAT AN EXCITABLE BUNNY.
FLAP
FLAP
BESIDES... THE FAR-OFF FUTURE...
...IS LIKE A MIRAGE.

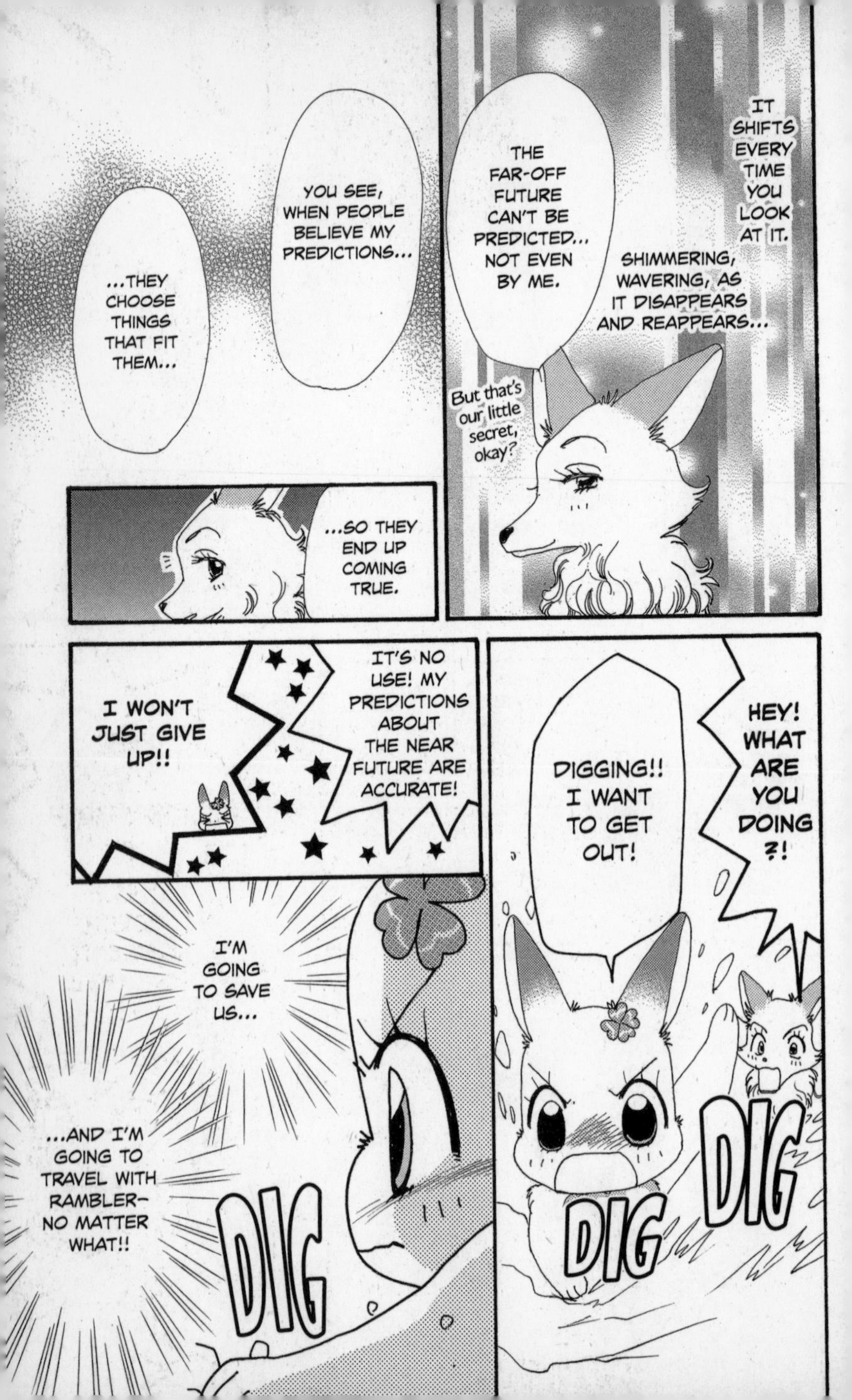
IT SHIFTS EVERY TIME YOU LOOK AT IT.
SHIMMERING, WAVERING, AS IT DISAPPEARS AND REAPPEARS...
THE FAR-OFF FUTURE CAN'T BE PREDICTED... NOT EVEN BY ME.
But that's our little secret, okay?
YOU SEE, WHEN PEOPLE BELIEVE MY PREDICTIONS...
...THEY CHOOSE THINGS THAT FIT THEM...
...SO THEY END UP COMING TRUE.
HEY! WHAT ARE YOU DOING?!
DIGGING!! I WANT TO GET OUT!
DIG
DIG
IT'S NO USE! MY PREDICTIONS ABOUT THE NEAR FUTURE ARE ACCURATE!
I WON'T JUST GIVE UP!!
I'M GOING TO SAVE US...
...AND I'M GOING TO TRAVEL WITH RAMBLER—NO MATTER WHAT!!
DIG

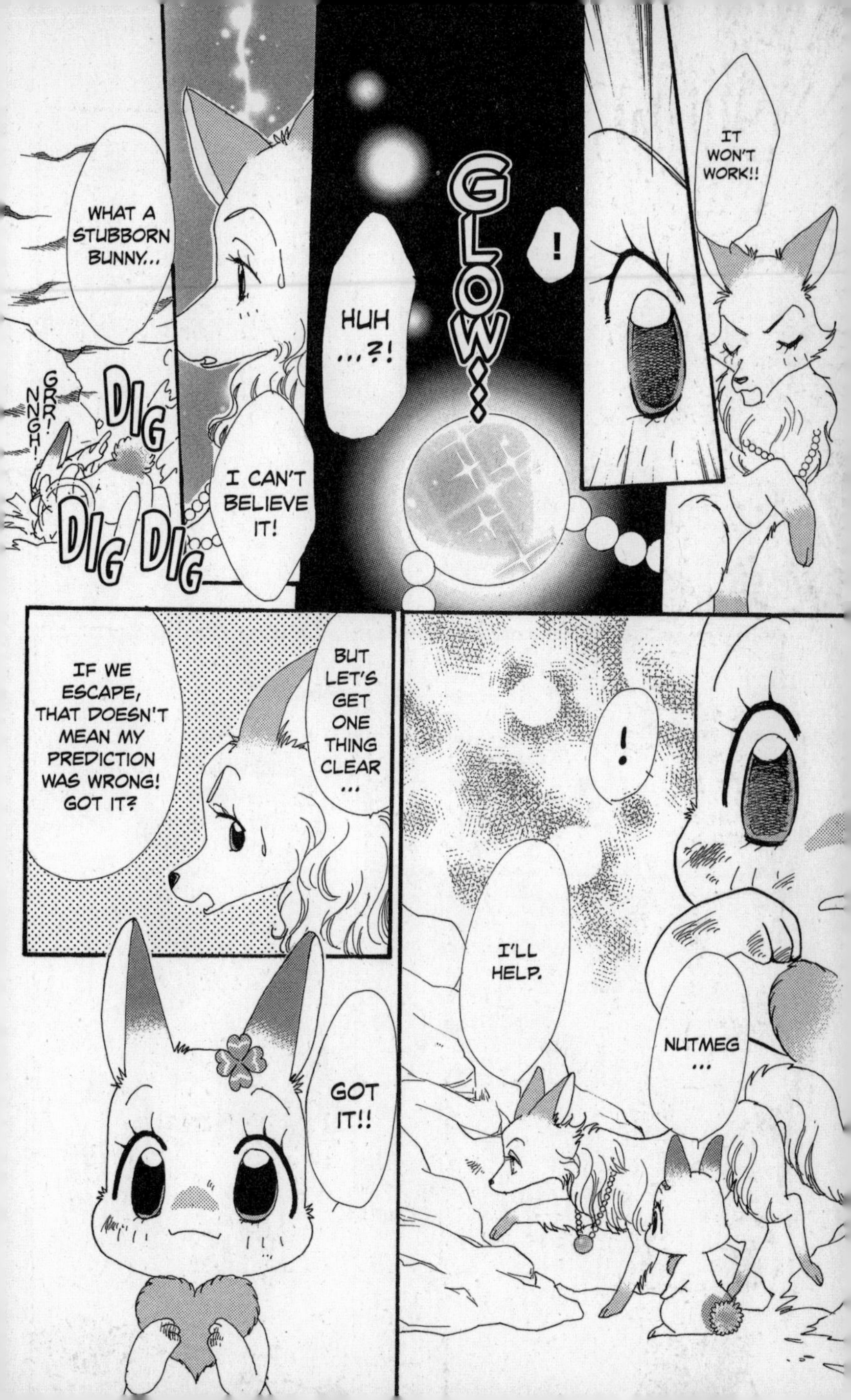
IT WON'T WORK!!
!
GLOW
HUH ...?!
WHAT A STUBBORN BUNNY...
I CAN'T BELIEVE IT!
DIG DIG DIG
GRR!
NNGH!
!
I'LL HELP.
NUTMEG ...
BUT LET'S GET ONE THING CLEAR ...
IF WE ESCAPE, THAT DOESN'T MEAN MY PREDICTION WAS WRONG! GOT IT?
GOT IT!!

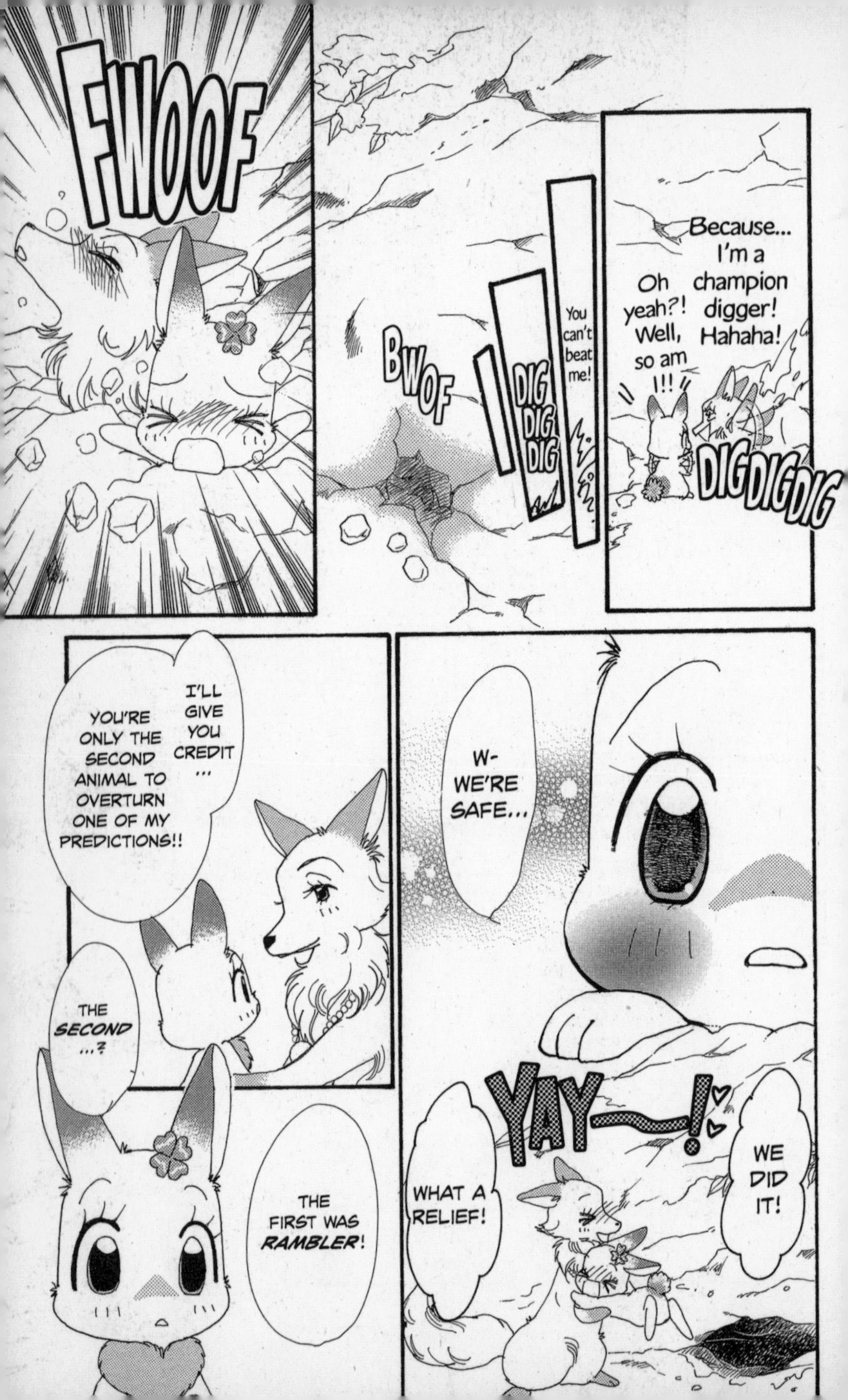
Because... I'm a champion digger! Hahaha!
Oh yeah?! Well, so am I!!!
DIGDIGDIG
You can't beat me!
DIG DIG DIG
BWOF
FWOOF
W-WE'RE SAFE...
YAY~~!
WE DID IT!
WHAT A RELIEF!
I'LL GIVE YOU CREDIT...
YOU'RE ONLY THE SECOND ANIMAL TO OVERTURN ONE OF MY PREDICTIONS!!
THE *SECOND*...?
THE FIRST WAS *RAMBLER*!

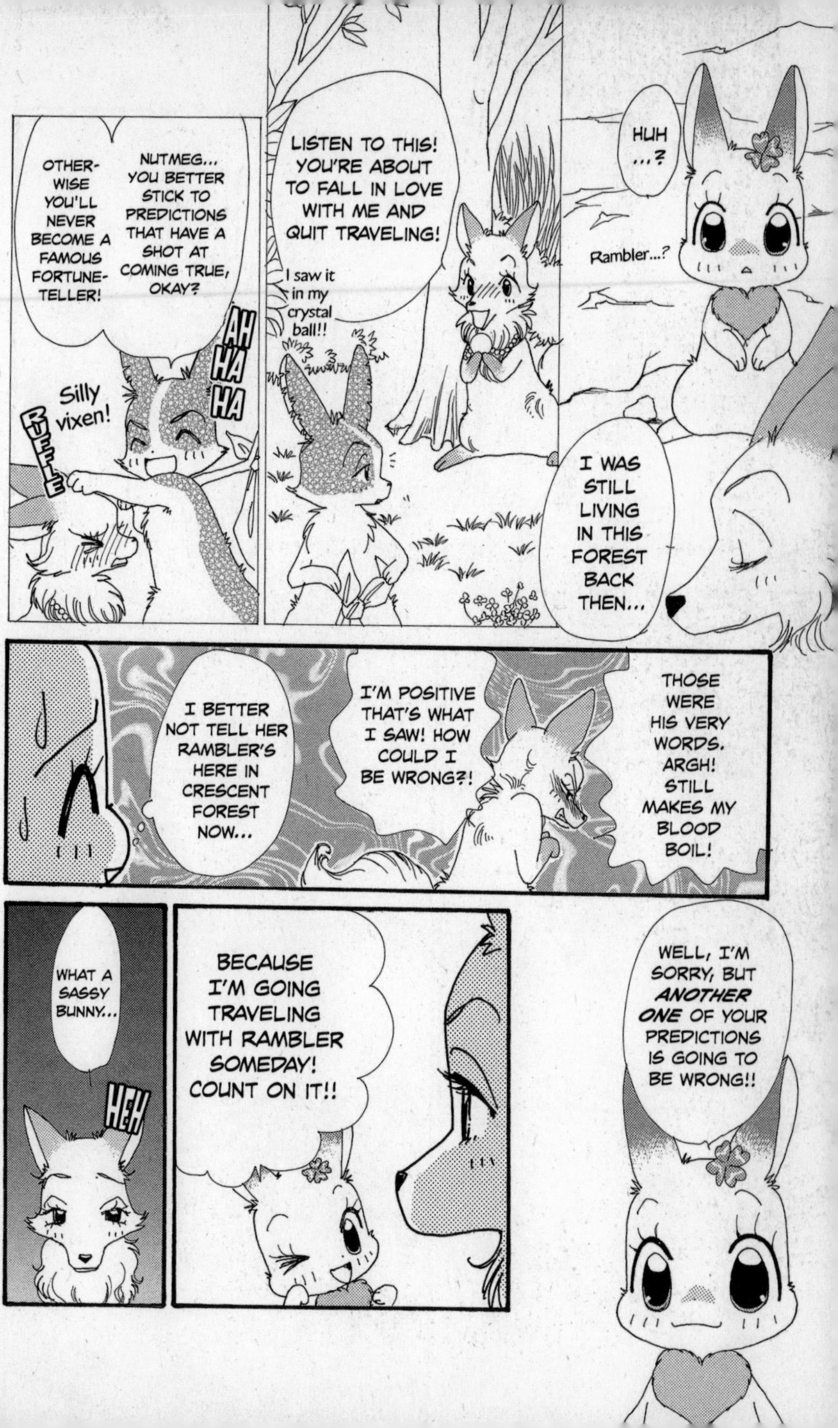
HUH ...?
Rambler...?
I WAS STILL LIVING IN THIS FOREST BACK THEN...
LISTEN TO THIS! YOU'RE ABOUT TO FALL IN LOVE WITH ME AND QUIT TRAVELING!
I saw it in my crystal ball!!
NUTMEG... YOU BETTER STICK TO PREDICTIONS THAT HAVE A SHOT AT COMING TRUE, OKAY?
OTHER-WISE YOU'LL NEVER BECOME A FAMOUS FORTUNE-TELLER!
AH HA HA
Silly vixen!
RUFFLE
THOSE WERE HIS VERY WORDS. ARGH! STILL MAKES MY BLOOD BOIL!
I'M POSITIVE THAT'S WHAT I SAW! HOW COULD I BE WRONG?!
I BETTER NOT TELL HER RAMBLER'S HERE IN CRESCENT FOREST NOW...
WELL, I'M SORRY, BUT ***ANOTHER ONE*** OF YOUR PREDICTIONS IS GOING TO BE WRONG!!
BECAUSE I'M GOING TRAVELING WITH RAMBLER SOMEDAY! COUNT ON IT!!
HEH
WHAT A SASSY BUNNY...

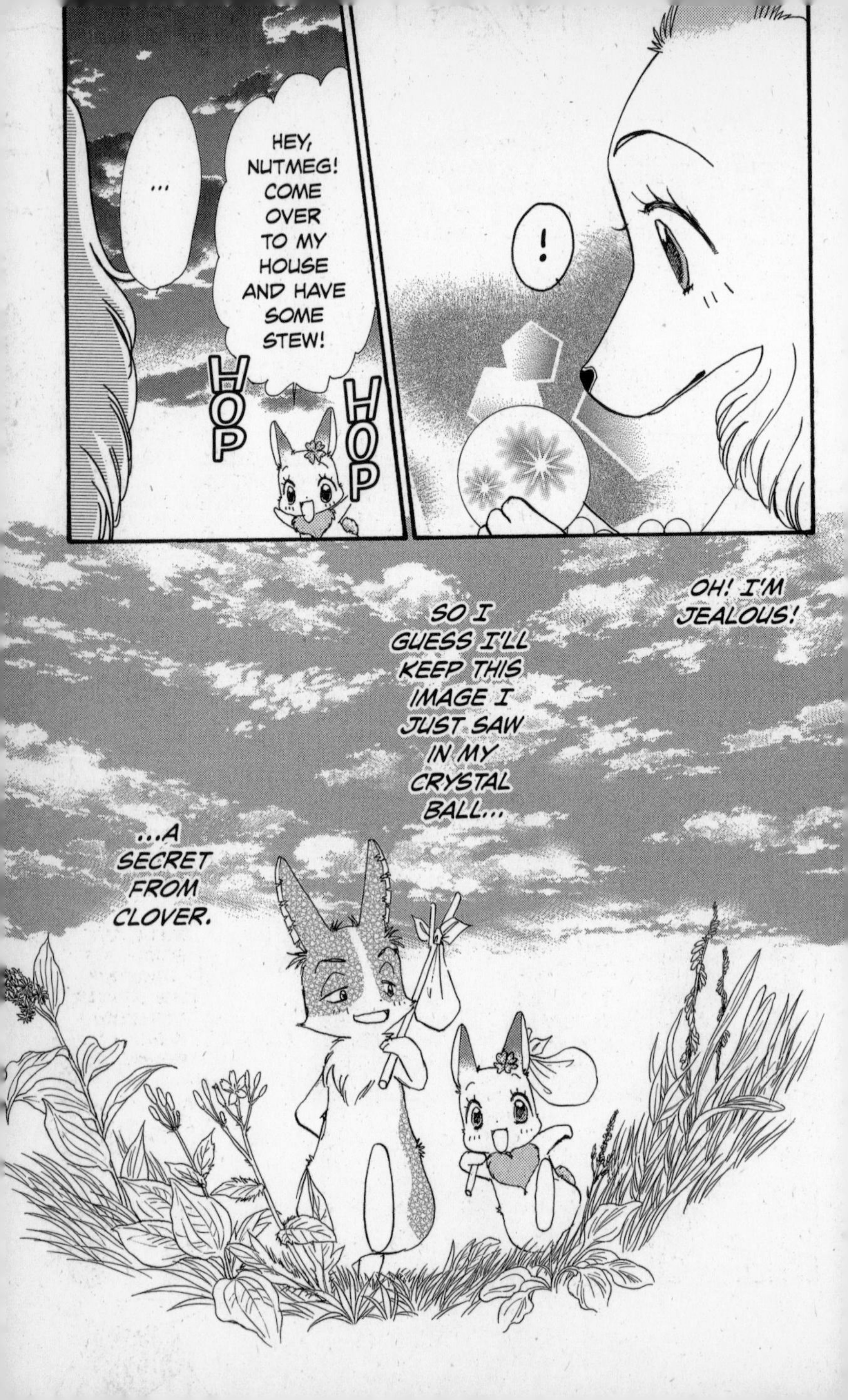
!
HEY, NUTMEG! COME OVER TO MY HOUSE AND HAVE SOME STEW!
...
HOP
HOP
OH! I'M JEALOUS!
SO I GUESS I'LL KEEP THIS IMAGE I JUST SAW IN MY CRYSTAL BALL...
...A SECRET FROM CLOVER.

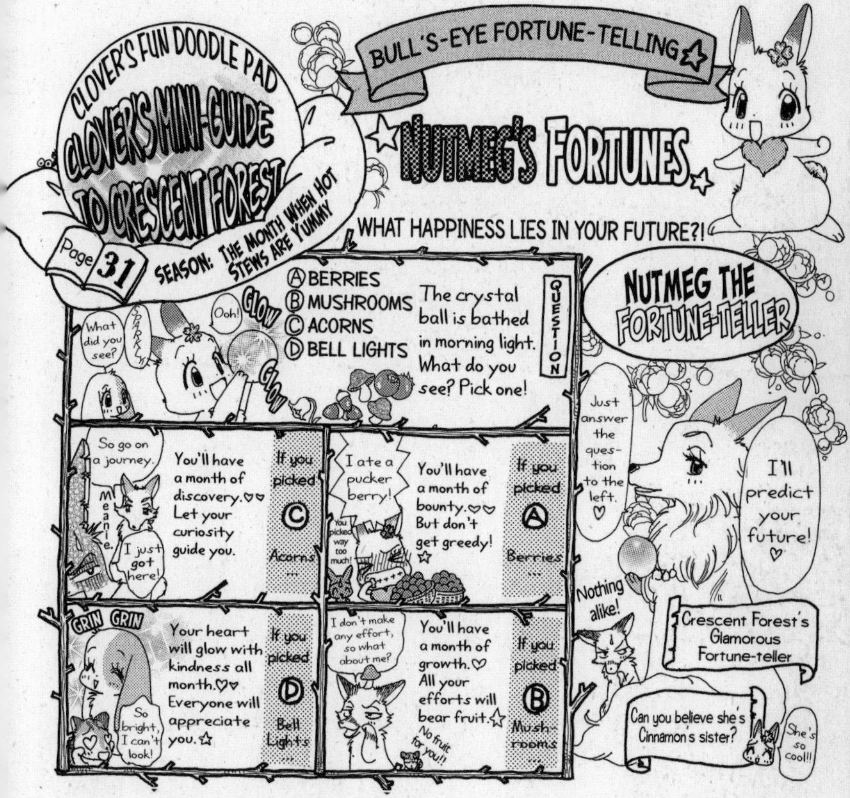

BULL'S-EYE FORTUNE-TELLING
NUTMEG'S FORTUNES
CLOVER'S FUN DOODLE PAD
CLOVER'S MINI-GUIDE TO CRESCENT FOREST
Page 31
SEASON: THE MONTH WHEN HOT STEWS ARE YUMMY
WHAT HAPPINESS LIES IN YOUR FUTURE?!
NUTMEG THE FORTUNE-TELLER
I'll predict your future! ♡
Just answer the question to the left. ♡
Crescent Forest's Glamorous Fortune-teller
Nothing alike!
She's so cool!!
Can you believe she's Cinnamon's sister?
QUESTION
The crystal ball is bathed in morning light. What do you see? Pick one!
Ⓐ BERRIES
Ⓑ MUSHROOMS
Ⓒ ACORNS
Ⓓ BELL LIGHTS
GLOW
Ooh!
GLOW
SPARKLY
What did you see?
If you picked Ⓐ Berries...
You'll have a month of bounty. ♡♡ But don't get greedy! ☆
I ate a pucker berry!
You picked way too much!
If you picked Ⓒ Acorns...
You'll have a month of discovery. ♡♡ Let your curiosity guide you.
So go on a journey.
Meanie.
I just got here!
If you picked Ⓑ Mushrooms...
You'll have a month of growth. ♡ All your efforts will bear fruit. ☆
I don't make any effort, so what about me?
No fruit for you!!
If you picked Ⓓ Bell Lights...
Your heart will glow with kindness all month. ♡♡ Everyone will appreciate you. ☆
GRIN GRIN
So bright, I can't look!

THE MAKING OF BIG BROTHER KALE!

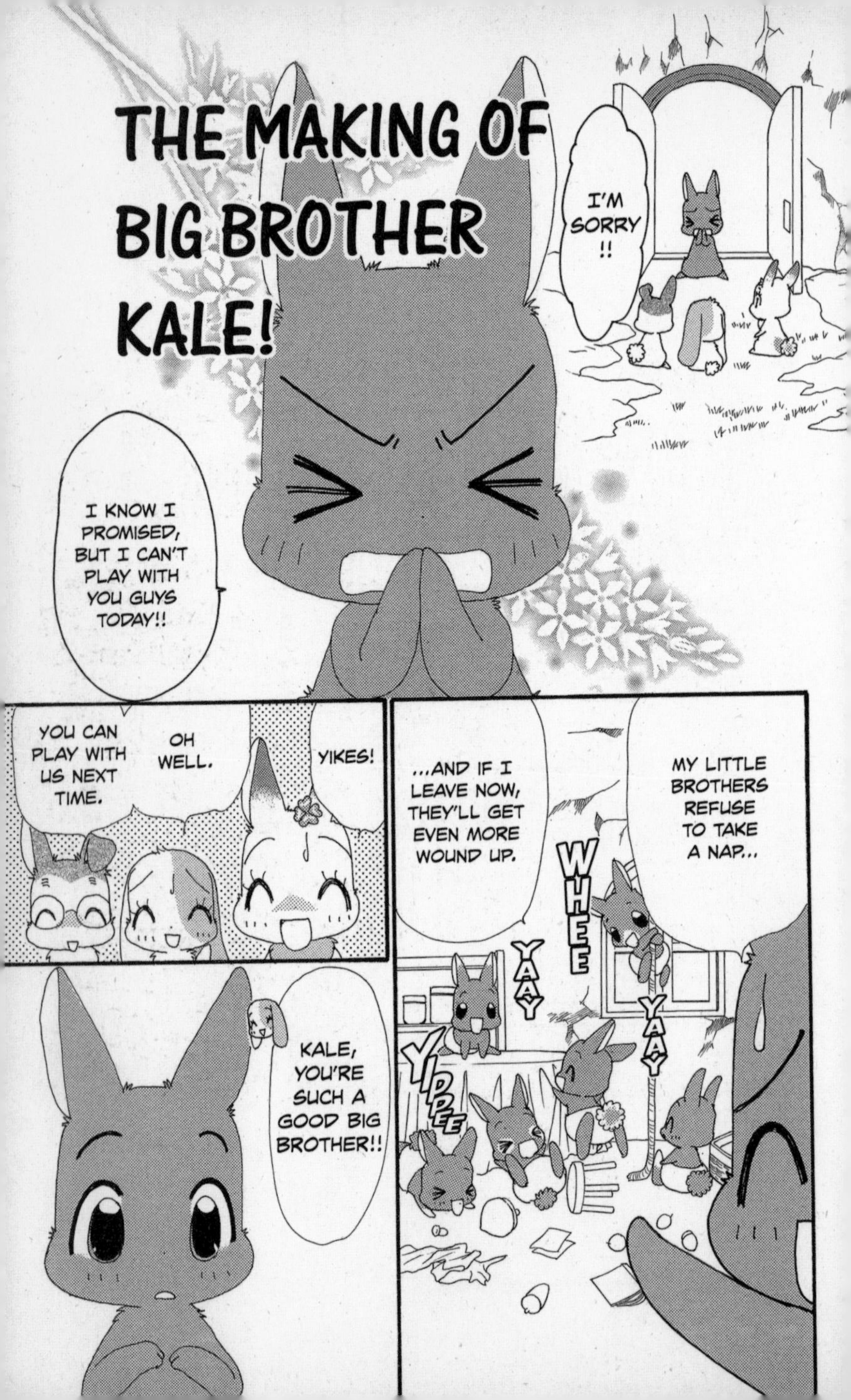
I'M SORRY!!
I KNOW I PROMISED, BUT I CAN'T PLAY WITH YOU GUYS TODAY!!
MY LITTLE BROTHERS REFUSE TO TAKE A NAP...
...AND IF I LEAVE NOW, THEY'LL GET EVEN MORE WOUND UP.
WHEE
YAAY
YAAY
YIPPEE
YIKES!
OH WELL.
YOU CAN PLAY WITH US NEXT TIME.
KALE, YOU'RE SUCH A GOOD BIG BROTHER!!

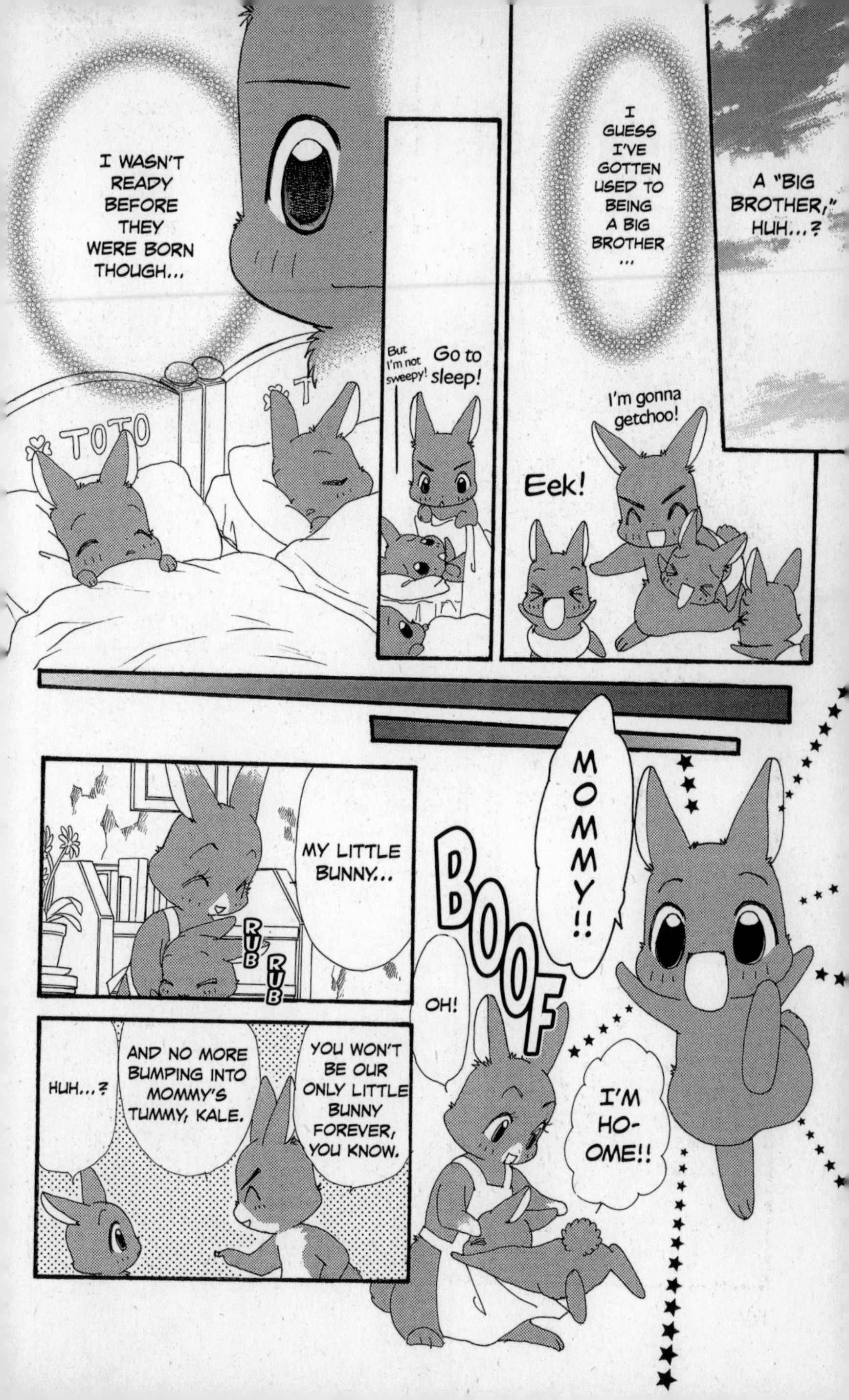
A "BIG BROTHER," HUH...?
I GUESS I'VE GOTTEN USED TO BEING A BIG BROTHER ...
I'm gonna getchoo!
Eek!
Go to sleep!
But I'm not sweepy!
I WASN'T READY BEFORE THEY WERE BORN THOUGH...
MOMMY!!
BOOF
I'M HO-OME!!
OH!
MY LITTLE BUNNY...
RUB RUB
YOU WON'T BE OUR ONLY LITTLE BUNNY FOREVER, YOU KNOW.
AND NO MORE BUMPING INTO MOMMY'S TUMMY, KALE.
HUH...?

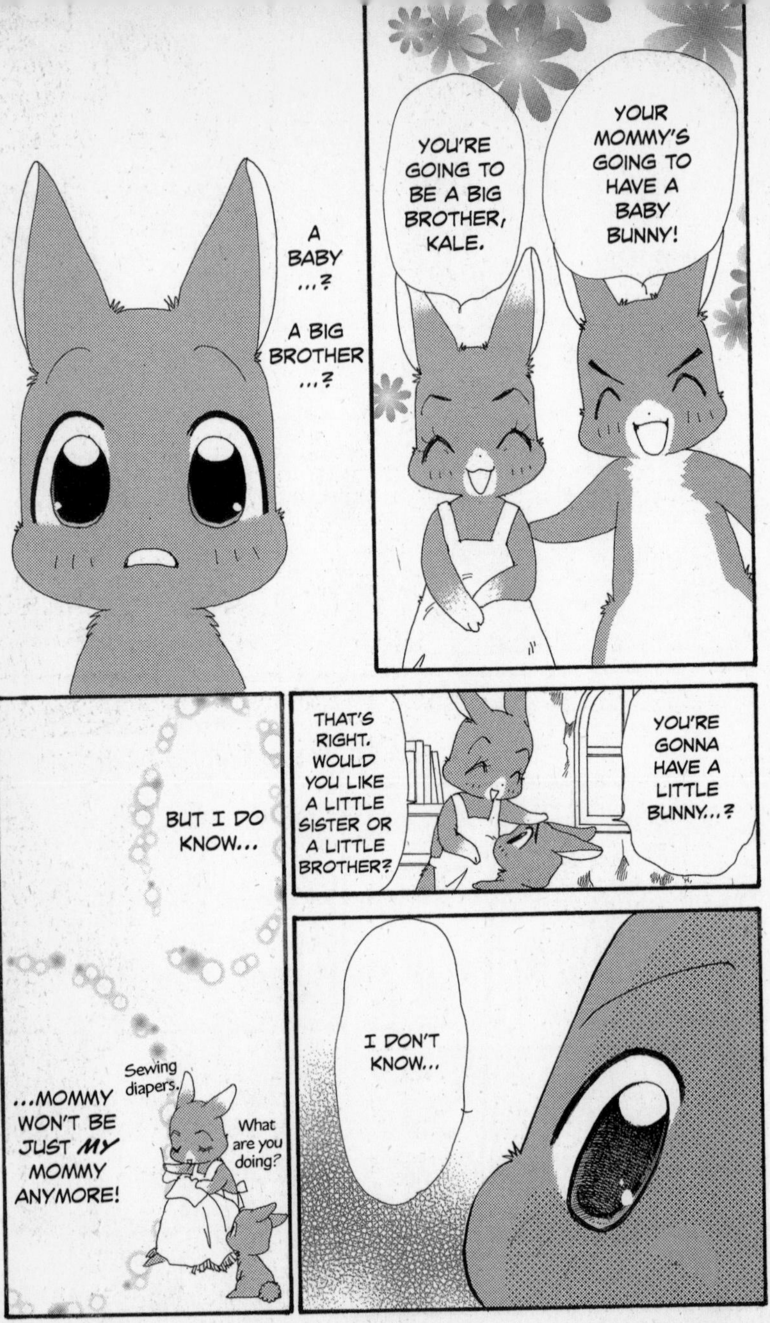
YOUR MOMMY'S GOING TO HAVE A BABY BUNNY!
YOU'RE GOING TO BE A BIG BROTHER, KALE.
A BABY ...?
A BIG BROTHER ...?
YOU'RE GONNA HAVE A LITTLE BUNNY...?
THAT'S RIGHT. WOULD YOU LIKE A LITTLE SISTER OR A LITTLE BROTHER?
I DON'T KNOW...
BUT I DO KNOW...
What are you doing?
Sewing diapers.
...MOMMY WON'T BE JUST *MY* MOMMY ANYMORE!

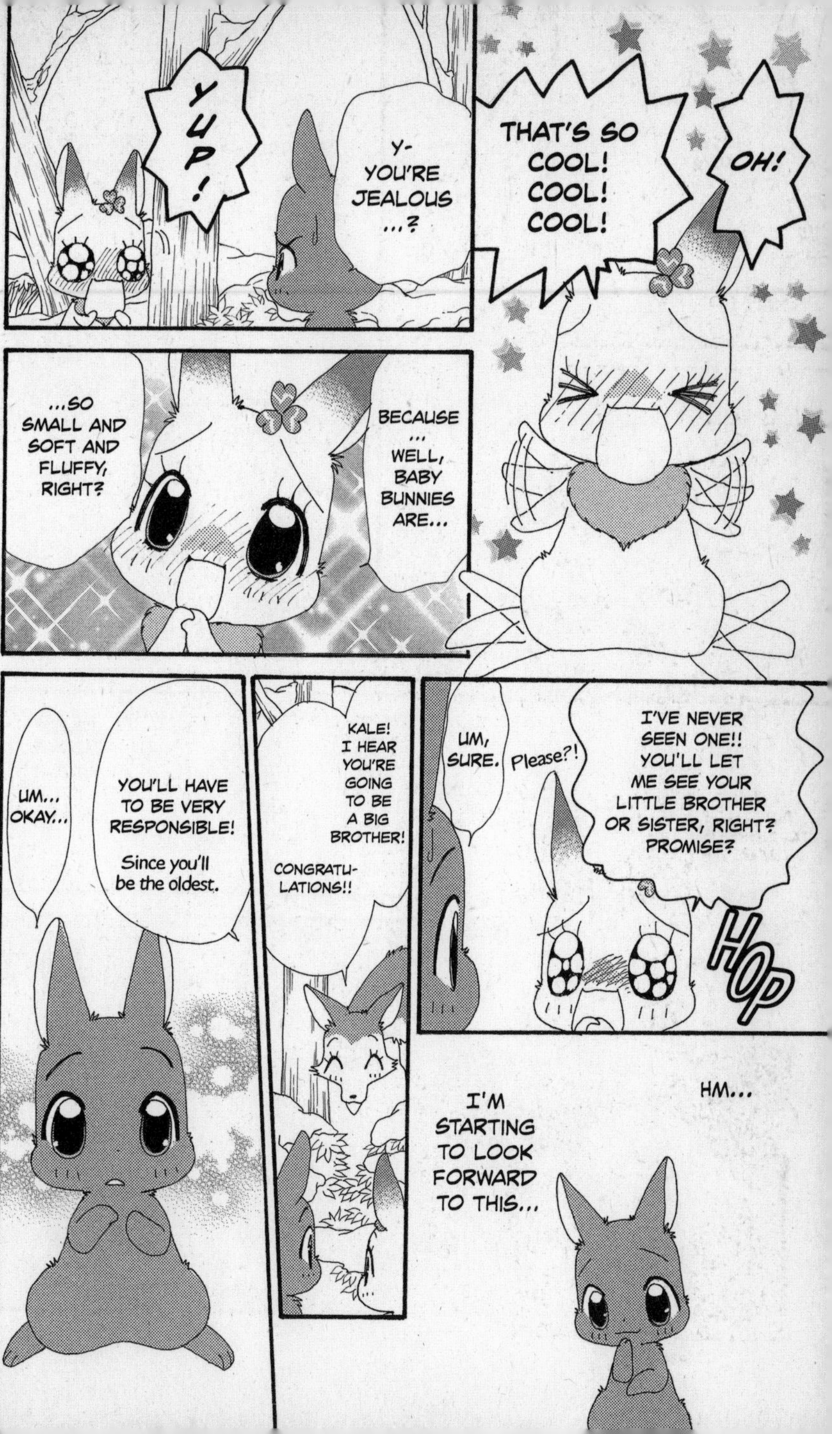
OH!
THAT'S SO COOL! COOL! COOL!
Y-YOU'RE JEALOUS...?
YUP!
BECAUSE... WELL, BABY BUNNIES ARE...
...SO SMALL AND SOFT AND FLUFFY, RIGHT?
I'VE NEVER SEEN ONE!! YOU'LL LET ME SEE YOUR LITTLE BROTHER OR SISTER, RIGHT? PROMISE?
Please?!
UM, SURE.
HOP
HM...
I'M STARTING TO LOOK FORWARD TO THIS...
KALE! I HEAR YOU'RE GOING TO BE A BIG BROTHER!
CONGRATULATIONS!!
YOU'LL HAVE TO BE VERY RESPONSIBLE!
Since you'll be the oldest.
UM... OKAY...

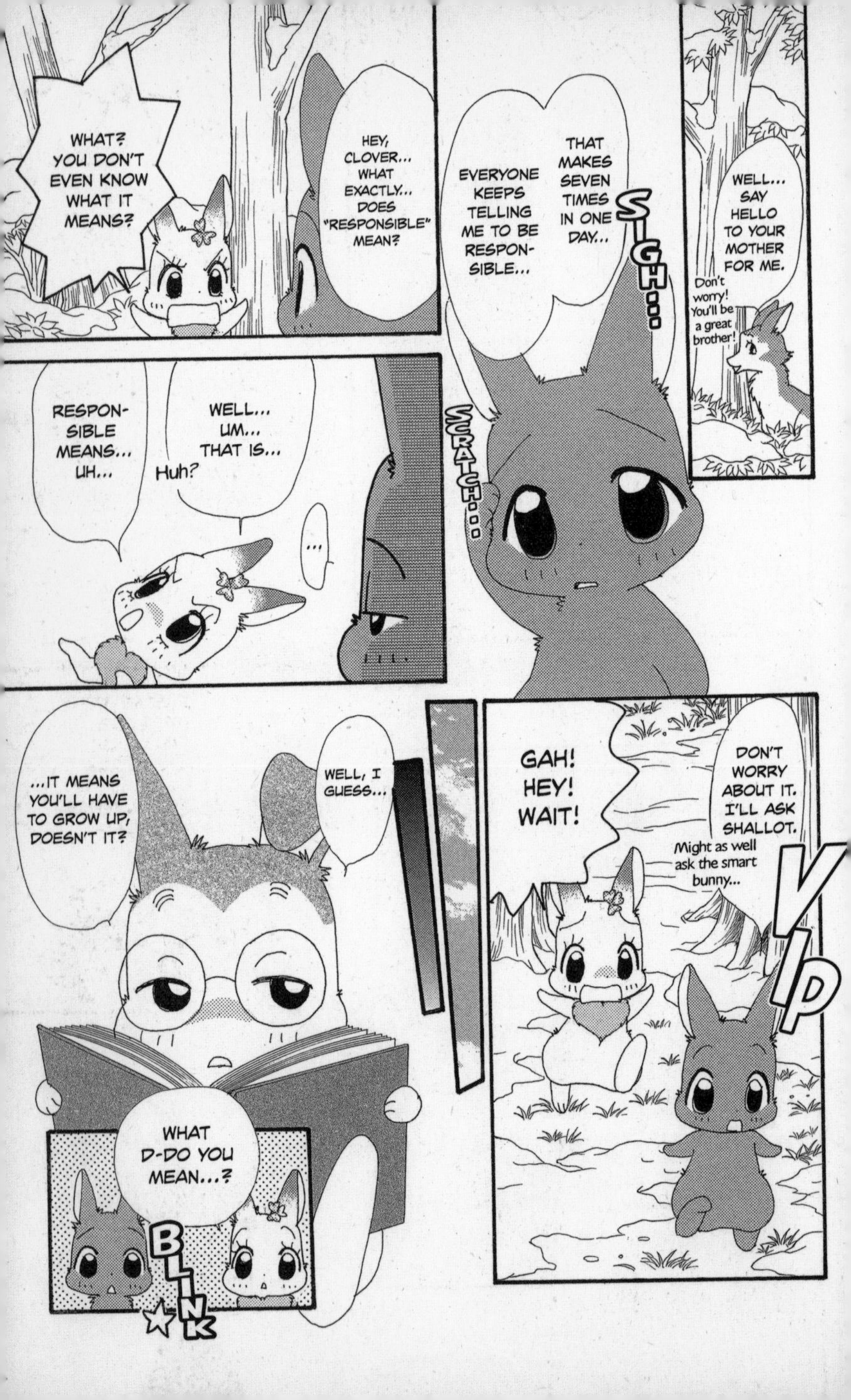
WELL... SAY HELLO TO YOUR MOTHER FOR ME.
Don't worry! You'll be a great brother!
THAT MAKES SEVEN TIMES IN ONE DAY...
EVERYONE KEEPS TELLING ME TO BE RESPON-SIBLE...
SIGH...
SCRATCH...
HEY, CLOVER... WHAT EXACTLY... DOES "RESPONSIBLE" MEAN?
WHAT? YOU DON'T EVEN KNOW WHAT IT MEANS?
WELL... UM... THAT IS...
RESPON-SIBLE MEANS... UH...
Huh?
...
DON'T WORRY ABOUT IT. I'LL ASK SHALLOT.
Might as well ask the smart bunny...
GAH! HEY! WAIT!
YIP
WELL, I GUESS...
...IT MEANS YOU'LL HAVE TO GROW UP, DOESN'T IT?
WHAT D-DO YOU MEAN...?
BLINK

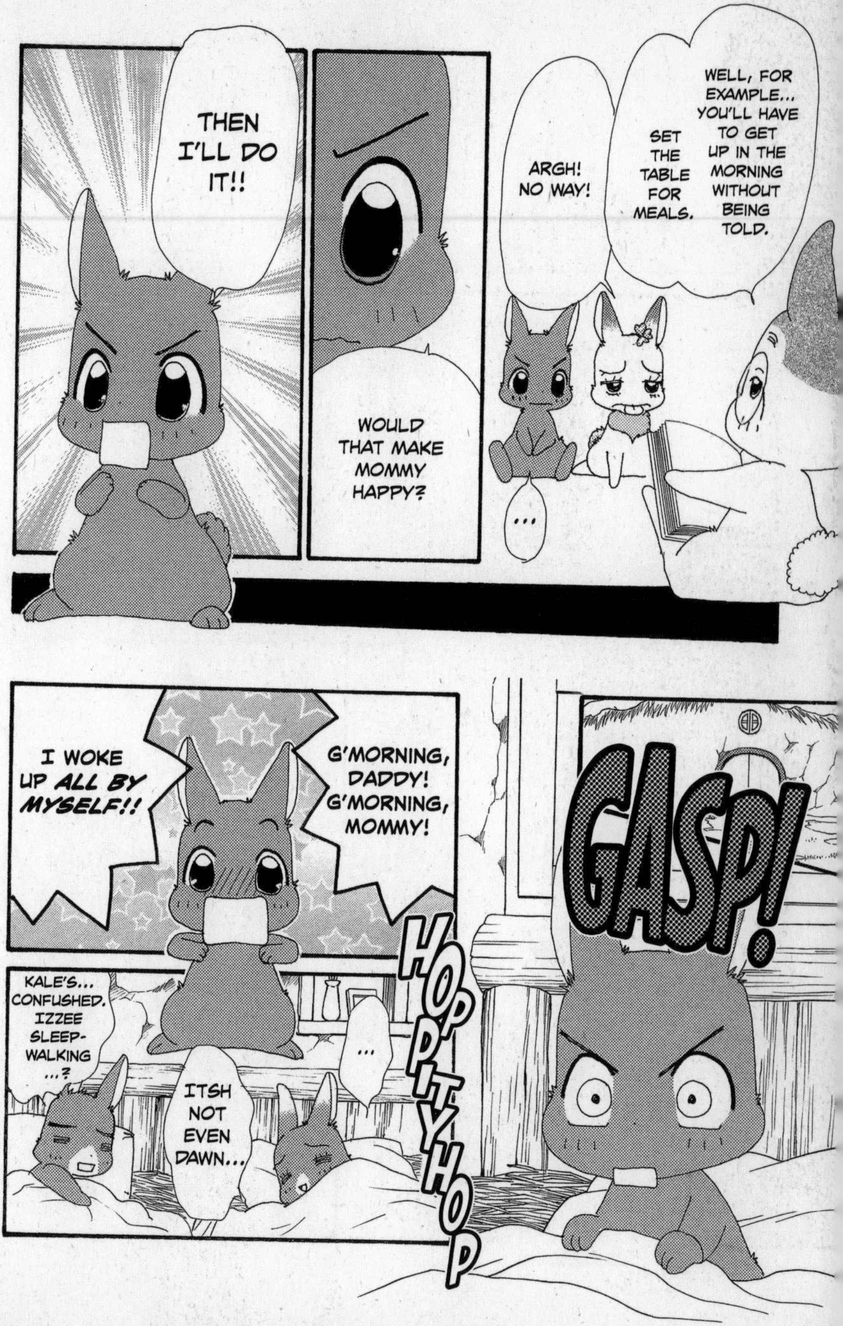
WELL, FOR EXAMPLE... YOU'LL HAVE TO GET UP IN THE MORNING WITHOUT BEING TOLD.
SET THE TABLE FOR MEALS.
ARGH! NO WAY!
...
WOULD THAT MAKE MOMMY HAPPY?
THEN I'LL DO IT!!
GASP!
HOPPITYHOP
G'MORNING, DADDY! G'MORNING, MOMMY!
I WOKE UP ALL BY MYSELF!!
...
ITSH NOT EVEN DAWN...
KALE'S... CONFUSHED. IZZEE SLEEP-WALKING ...?

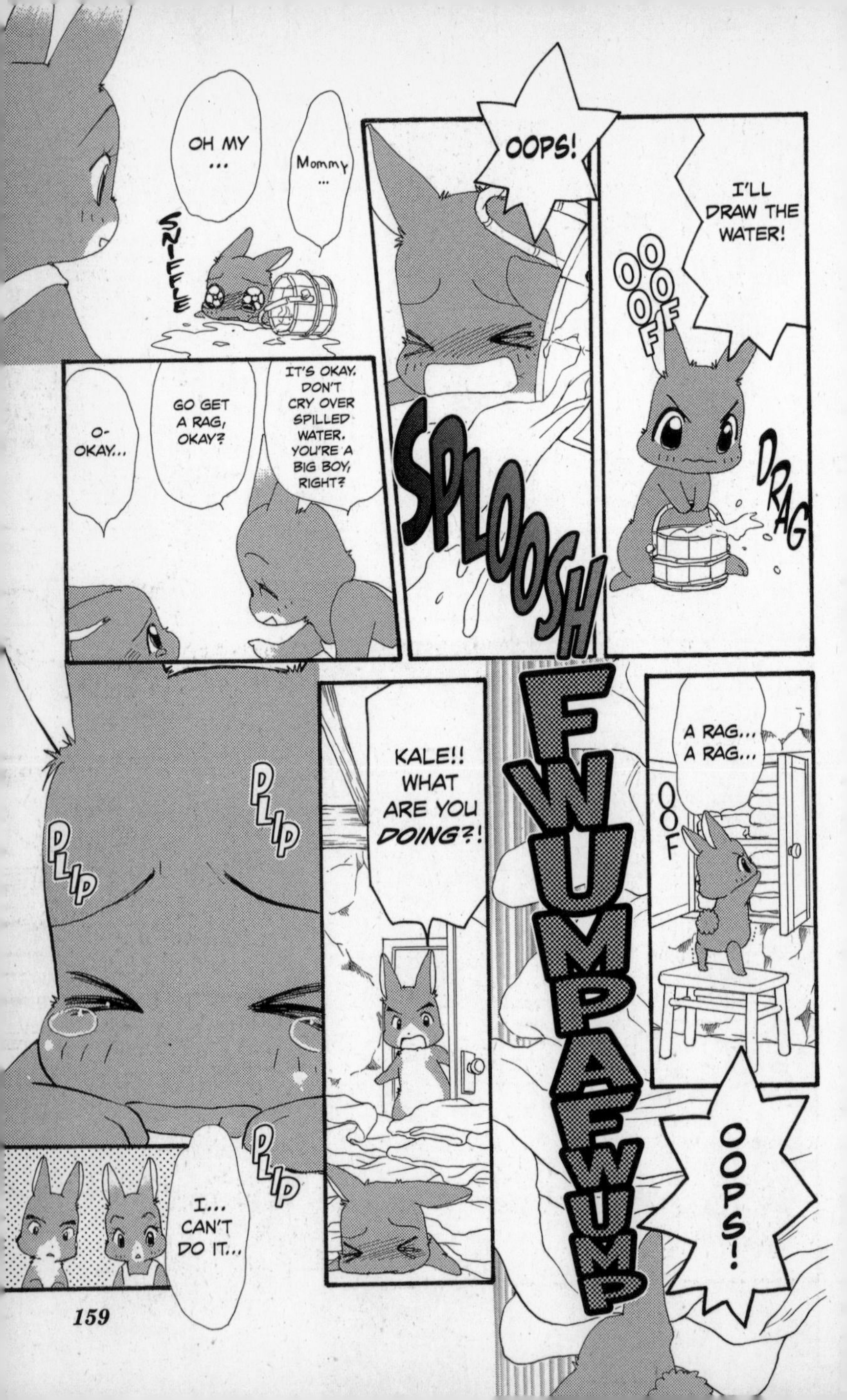
I'LL DRAW THE WATER!
OOOOF
DRAG
OOPS!
SPLOOSH
Mommy ...
OH MY ...
SNIFFLE
IT'S OKAY. DON'T CRY OVER SPILLED WATER. YOU'RE A BIG BOY, RIGHT?
GO GET A RAG, OKAY?
O-OKAY...
A RAG... A RAG...
OOF
FWUMPAFWUMP
OOPS!
KALE!! WHAT ARE YOU DOING?!
PLIP
PLIP
PLIP
I... CAN'T DO IT...

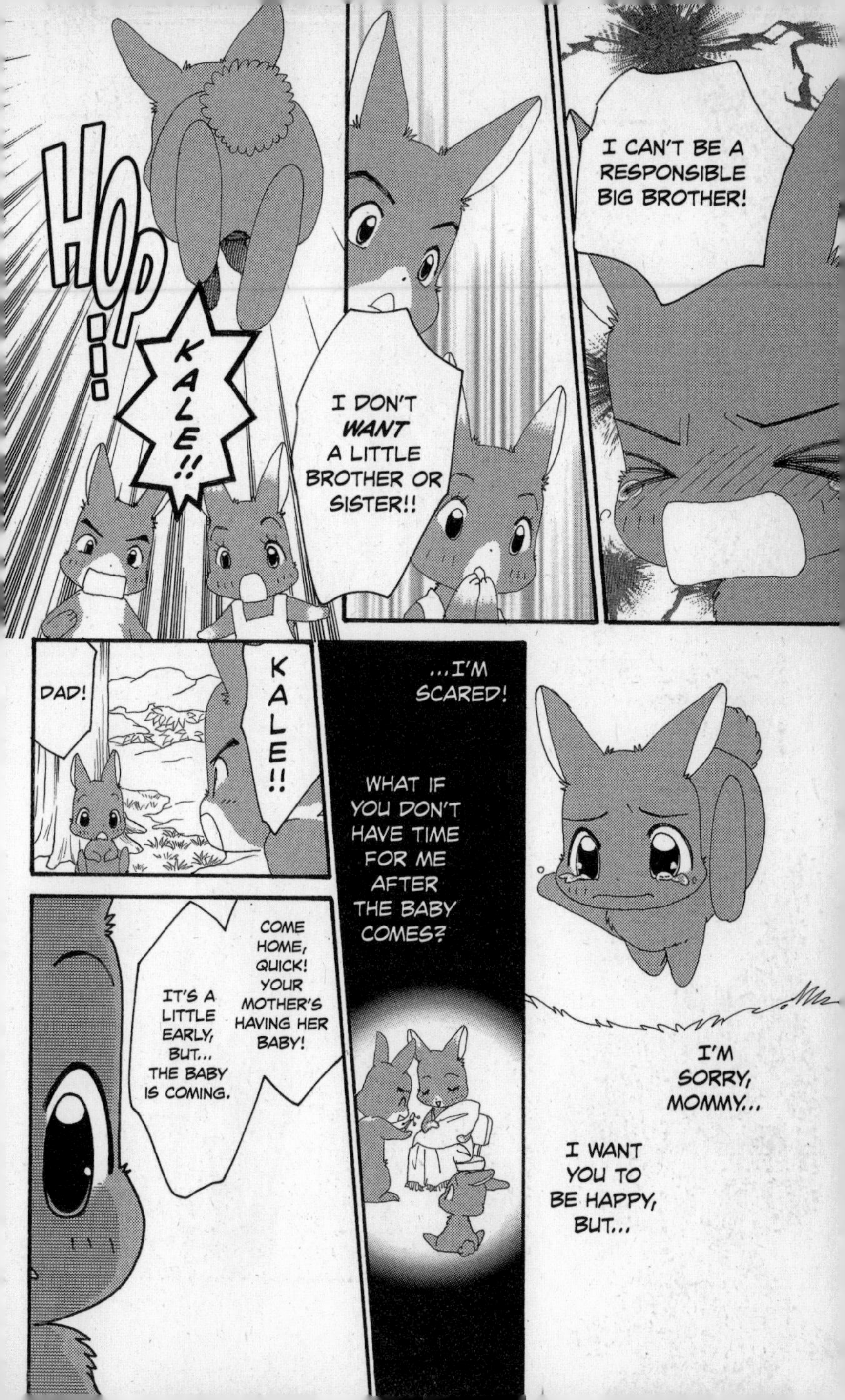
I CAN'T BE A RESPONSIBLE BIG BROTHER!
I DON'T *WANT* A LITTLE BROTHER OR SISTER!!
HOP!!!
KALE!!
I'M SORRY, MOMMY...
I WANT YOU TO BE HAPPY, BUT...
...I'M SCARED!
WHAT IF YOU DON'T HAVE TIME FOR ME AFTER THE BABY COMES?
KALE!!
DAD!
COME HOME, QUICK! YOUR MOTHER'S HAVING HER BABY!
IT'S A LITTLE EARLY, BUT... THE BABY IS COMING.

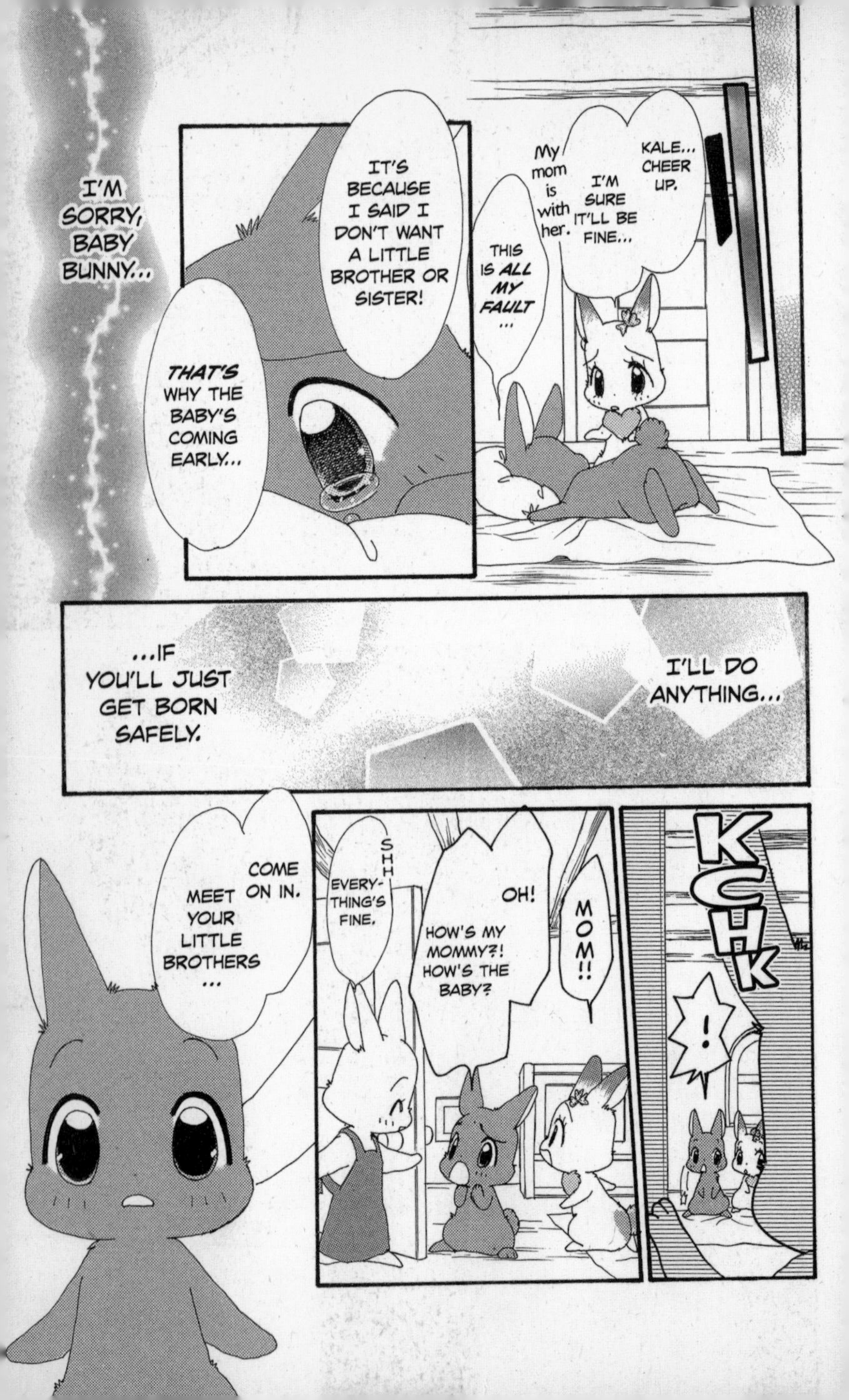
KALE... CHEER UP.
I'M SURE IT'LL BE FINE...
My mom is with her.
THIS IS ALL MY FAULT...
IT'S BECAUSE I SAID I DON'T WANT A LITTLE BROTHER OR SISTER!
THAT'S WHY THE BABY'S COMING EARLY...
I'M SORRY, BABY BUNNY...
I'LL DO ANYTHING...
...IF YOU'LL JUST GET BORN SAFELY.
KCHK
!
MOM!!
OH!
HOW'S MY MOMMY?! HOW'S THE BABY?
SHH
EVERY-THING'S FINE.
COME ON IN.
MEET YOUR LITTLE BROTHERS...

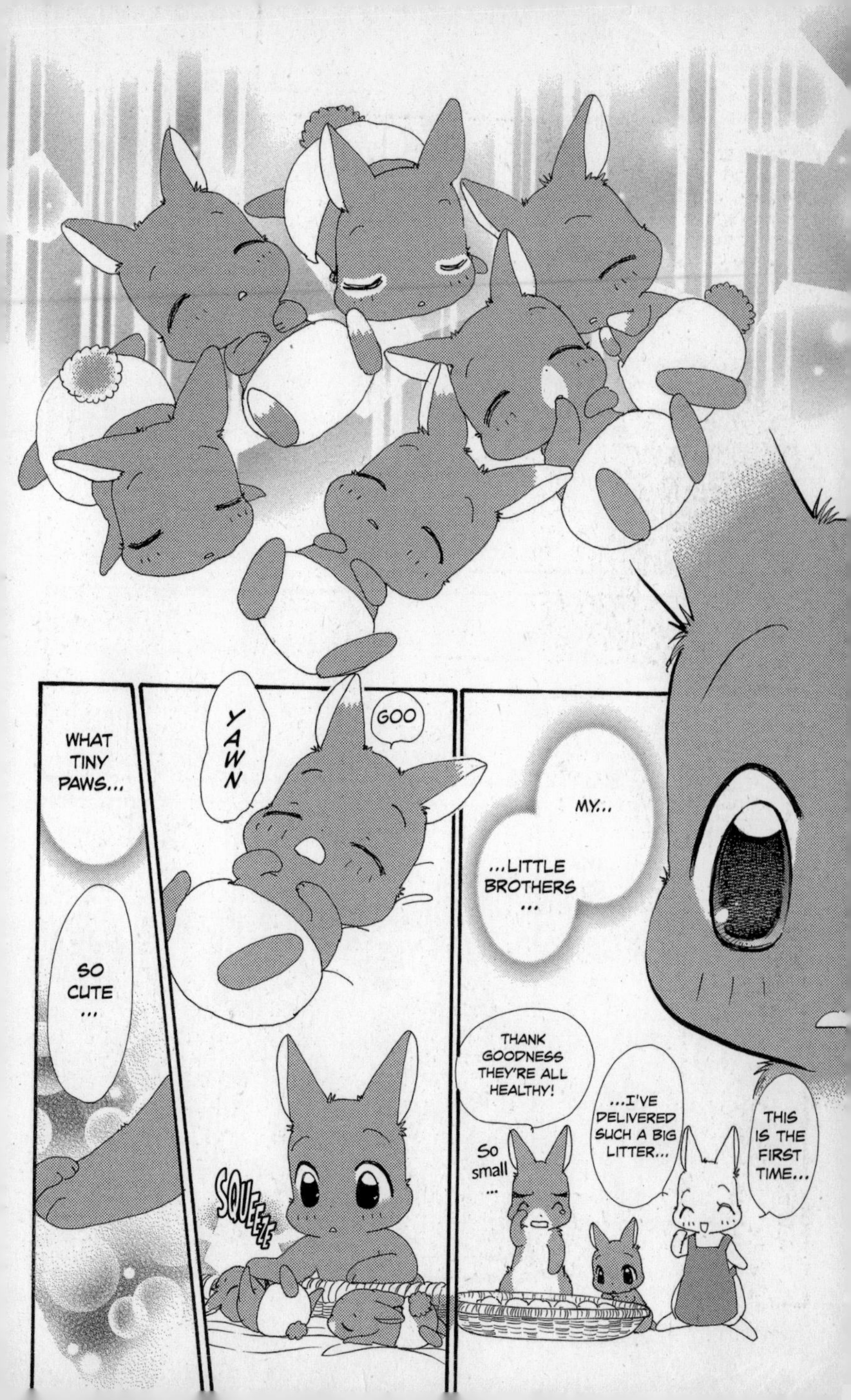
MY...
...LITTLE BROTHERS...
THIS IS THE FIRST TIME...
...I'VE DELIVERED SUCH A BIG LITTER...
THANK GOODNESS THEY'RE ALL HEALTHY!
So small...
GOO
YAWN
SQUEEZE
WHAT TINY PAWS...
SO CUTE...

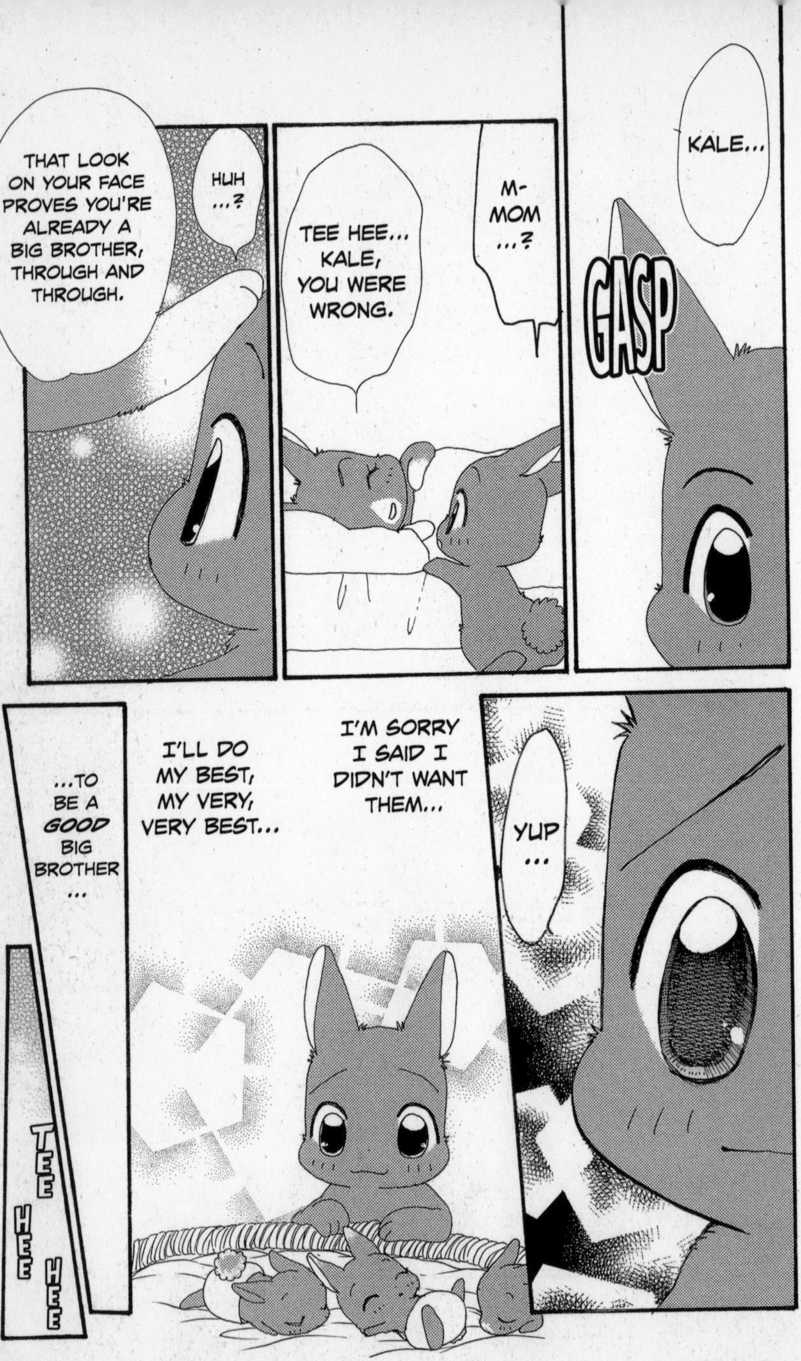
KALE...
GASP
M-MOM ...?
TEE HEE... KALE, YOU WERE WRONG.
HUH ...?
THAT LOOK ON YOUR FACE PROVES YOU'RE ALREADY A BIG BROTHER, THROUGH AND THROUGH.
YUP ...
I'M SORRY I SAID I DIDN'T WANT THEM...
I'LL DO MY BEST, MY VERY, VERY BEST...
...TO BE A GOOD BIG BROTHER ...
TEE HEE HEE HEE

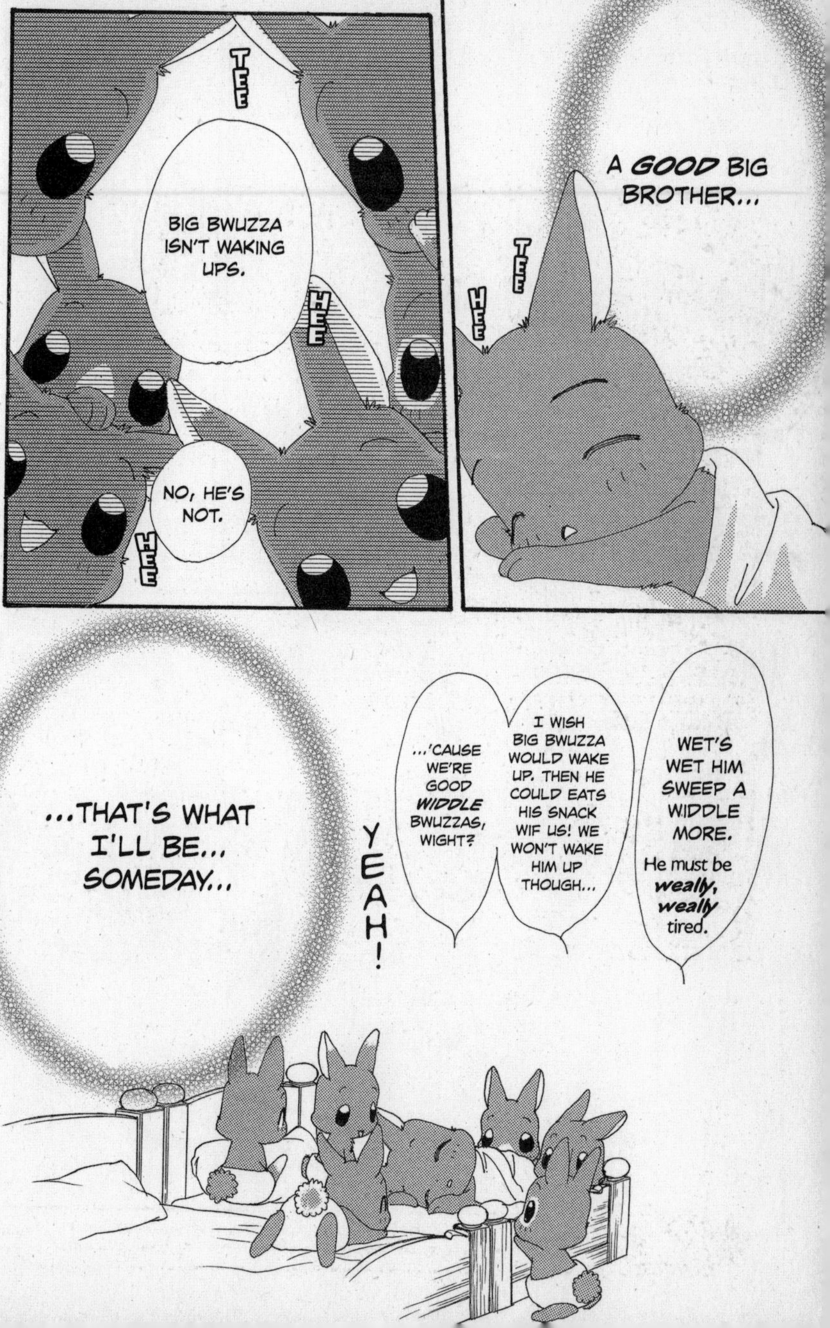
A *GOOD* BIG BROTHER...
TEE
HEE
TEE
BIG BWUZZA ISN'T WAKING UPS.
HEE
NO, HE'S NOT.
HEE
WET'S WET HIM SWEEP A WIDDLE MORE. He must be *weally, weally* tired.
I WISH BIG BWUZZA WOULD WAKE UP. THEN HE COULD EATS HIS SNACK WIF US! WE WON'T WAKE HIM UP THOUGH...
...'CAUSE WE'RE GOOD *WIDDLE* BWUZZAS, WIGHT?
YEAH!
...THAT'S WHAT I'LL BE... SOMEDAY...

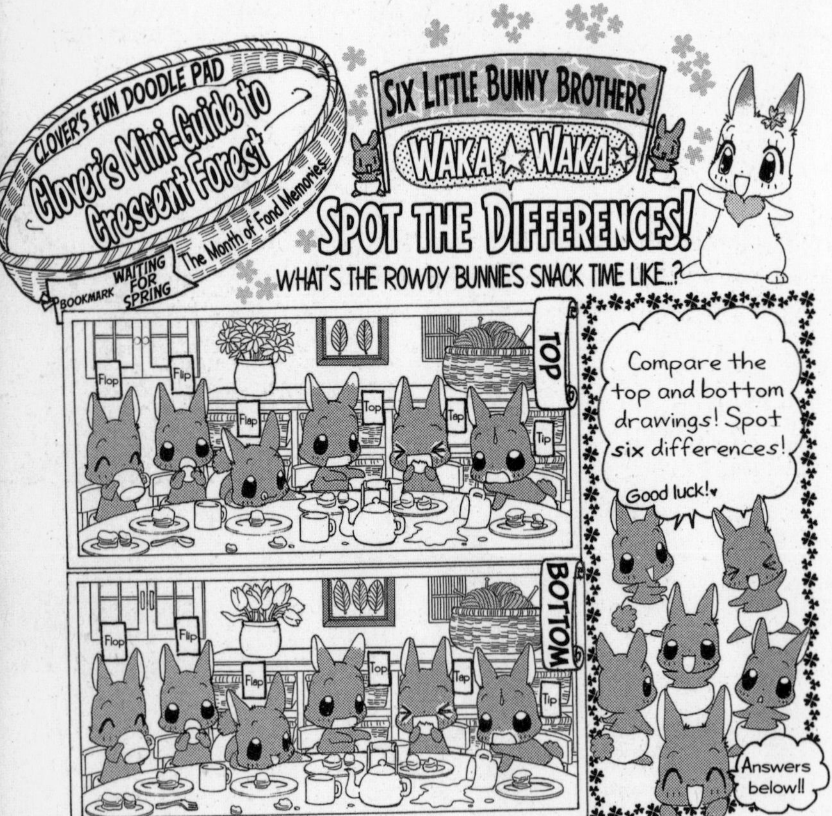

CLOVER'S FUN DOODLE PAD
Clover's Mini-Guide to Cresecent Forest
The Month of Fond Memories
WAITING FOR SPRING
BOOKMARK
SIX LITTLE BUNNY BROTHERS
WAKA★WAKA★
SPOT THE DIFFERENCES!
WHAT'S THE ROWDY BUNNIES SNACK TIME LIKE...?
TOP
Flop
Flip
Flap
Top
Tap
Tip
BOTTOM
Flop
Flip
Flap
Top
Tap
Tip
Compare the top and bottom drawings! Spot six differences!
Good luck!♥
Answers below!!

ANSWERS

1. Fewer snacks on Tip's plate 2. Number of leaves in picture 3. Flowers in vase 4. Flap's mouth 5. Window handles 6. Fork replaced spoon

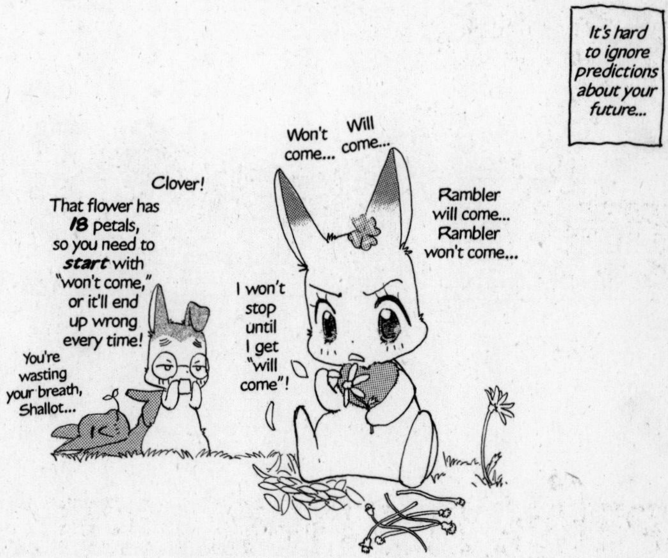
It's hard to ignore predictions about your future...
Won't come...
Will come...
Rambler will come... Rambler won't come...
I won't stop until I get "will come"!
Clover! That flower has 18 petals, so you need to start with "won't come," or it'll end up wrong every time!
You're wasting your breath, Shallot...

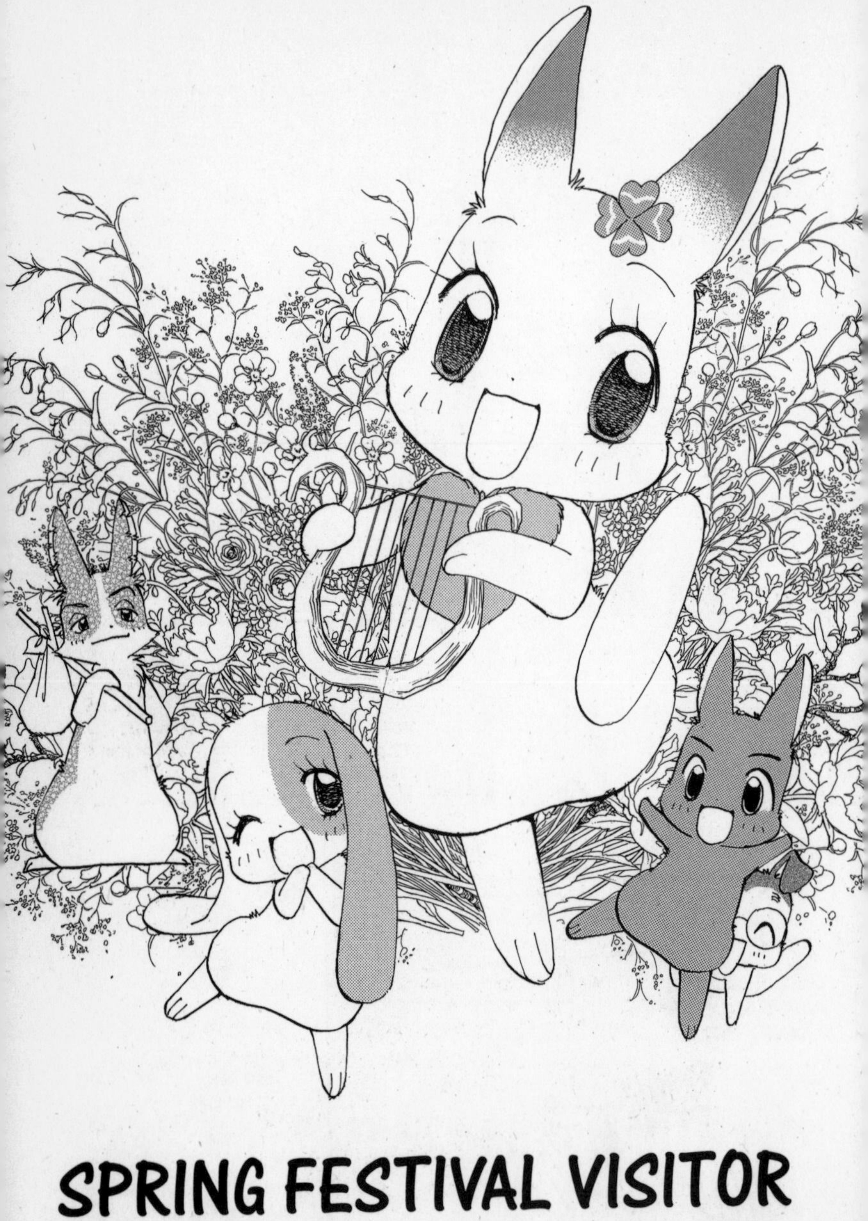

SPRING FESTIVAL VISITOR

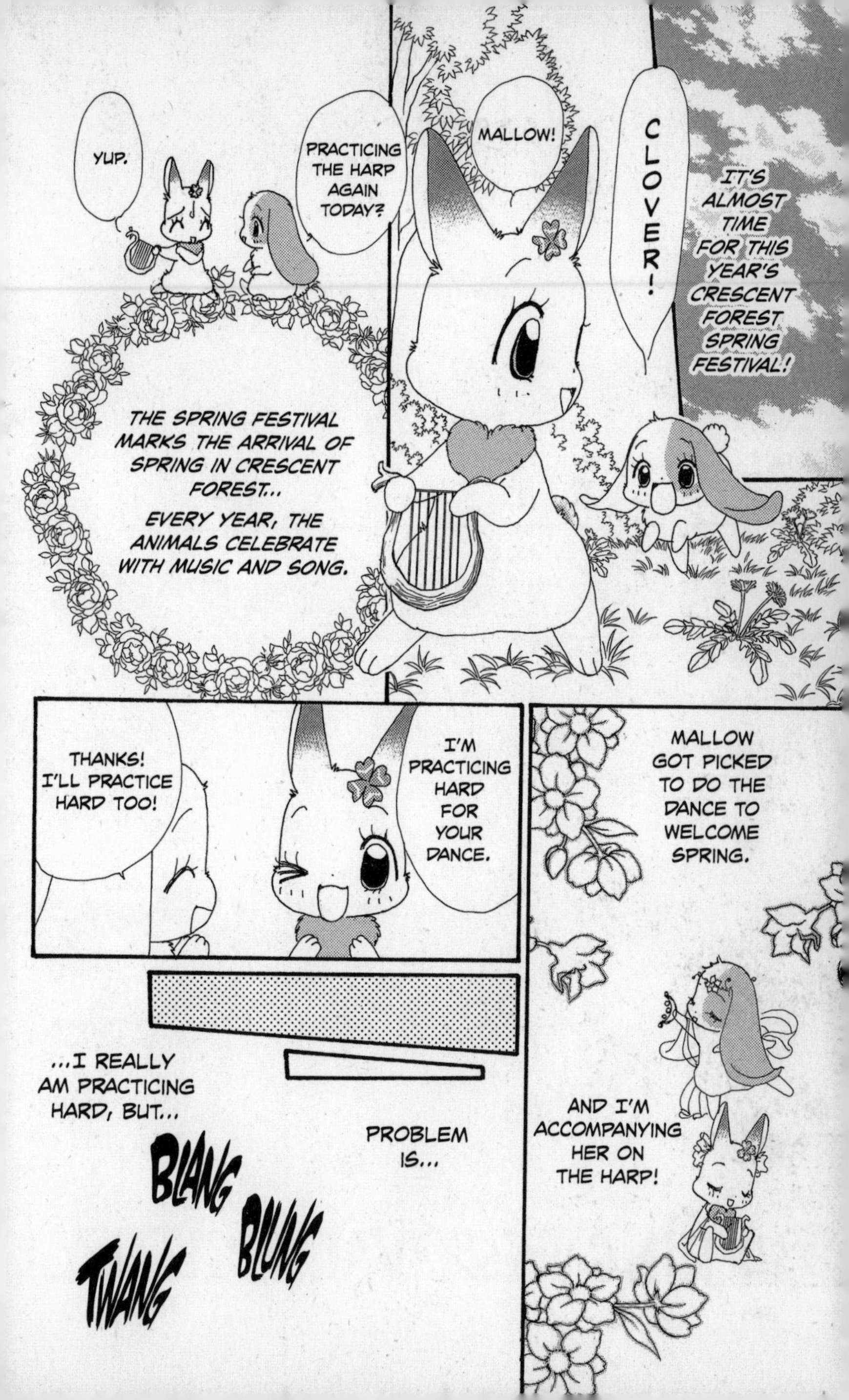
IT'S ALMOST TIME FOR THIS YEAR'S CRESCENT FOREST SPRING FESTIVAL!
CLOVER!
MALLOW!
PRACTICING THE HARP AGAIN TODAY?
YUP.
THE SPRING FESTIVAL MARKS THE ARRIVAL OF SPRING IN CRESCENT FOREST...
EVERY YEAR, THE ANIMALS CELEBRATE WITH MUSIC AND SONG.
MALLOW GOT PICKED TO DO THE DANCE TO WELCOME SPRING.
AND I'M ACCOMPANYING HER ON THE HARP!
I'M PRACTICING HARD FOR YOUR DANCE.
THANKS! I'LL PRACTICE HARD TOO!
PROBLEM IS...
...I REALLY AM PRACTICING HARD, BUT...
BLANG
BLUNG
TWANG

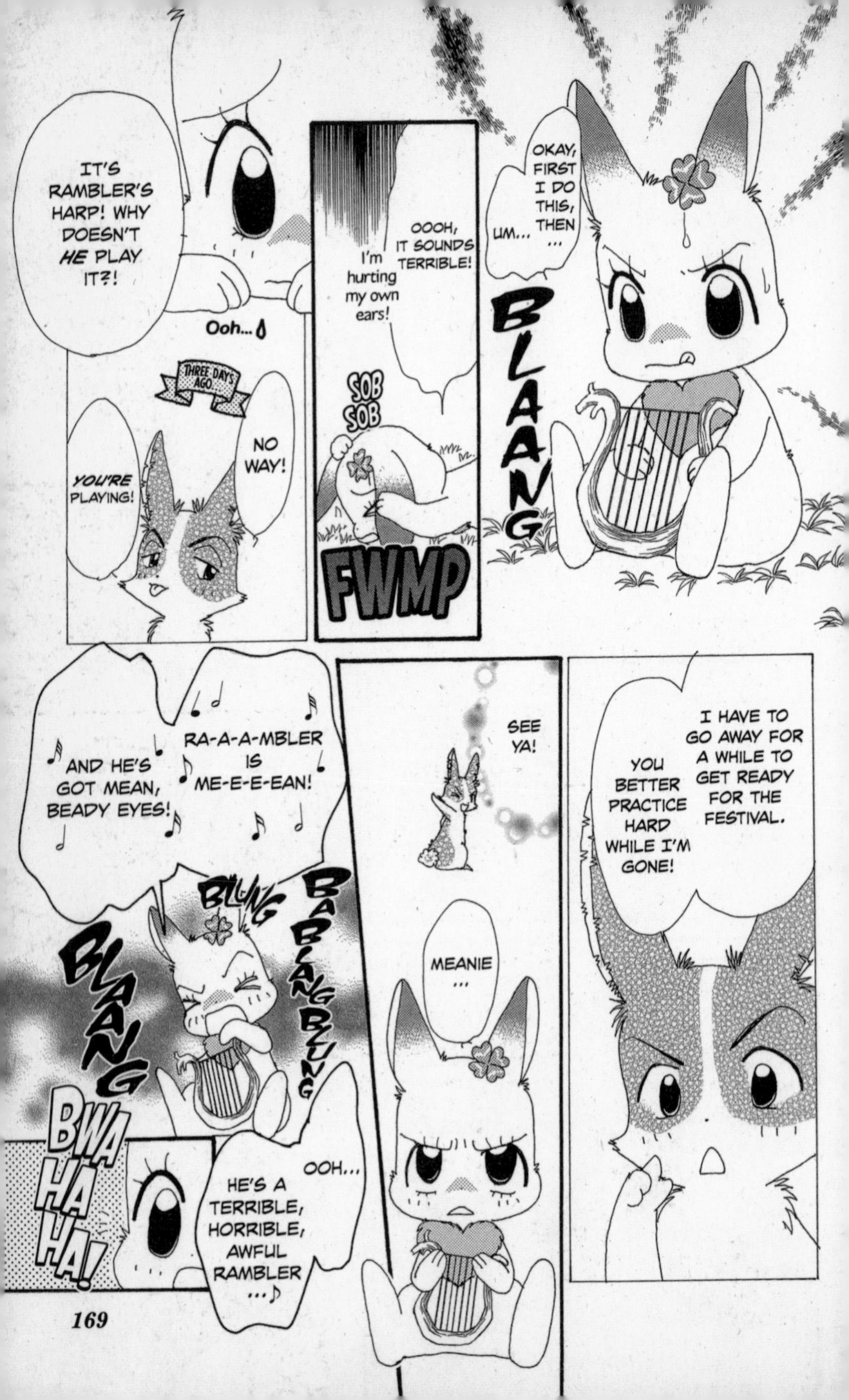

OKAY, FIRST I DO THIS, THEN ...
UM...
BLAANG
OOOH, IT SOUNDS TERRIBLE!
I'm hurting my own ears!
SOB SOB
FWMP
IT'S RAMBLER'S HARP! WHY DOESN'T HE PLAY IT?!
Ooh...
THREE DAYS AGO...
NO WAY!
YOU'RE PLAYING!
I HAVE TO GO AWAY FOR A WHILE TO GET READY FOR THE FESTIVAL.
YOU BETTER PRACTICE HARD WHILE I'M GONE!
SEE YA!
MEANIE ...
RA-A-A-MBLER IS ME-E-E-EAN!
AND HE'S GOT MEAN, BEADY EYES!
BLUNG
BABLANG BLUNG
BLANG
BWAHAHAHA!
OOH...
HE'S A TERRIBLE, HORRIBLE, AWFUL RAMBLER ...♪

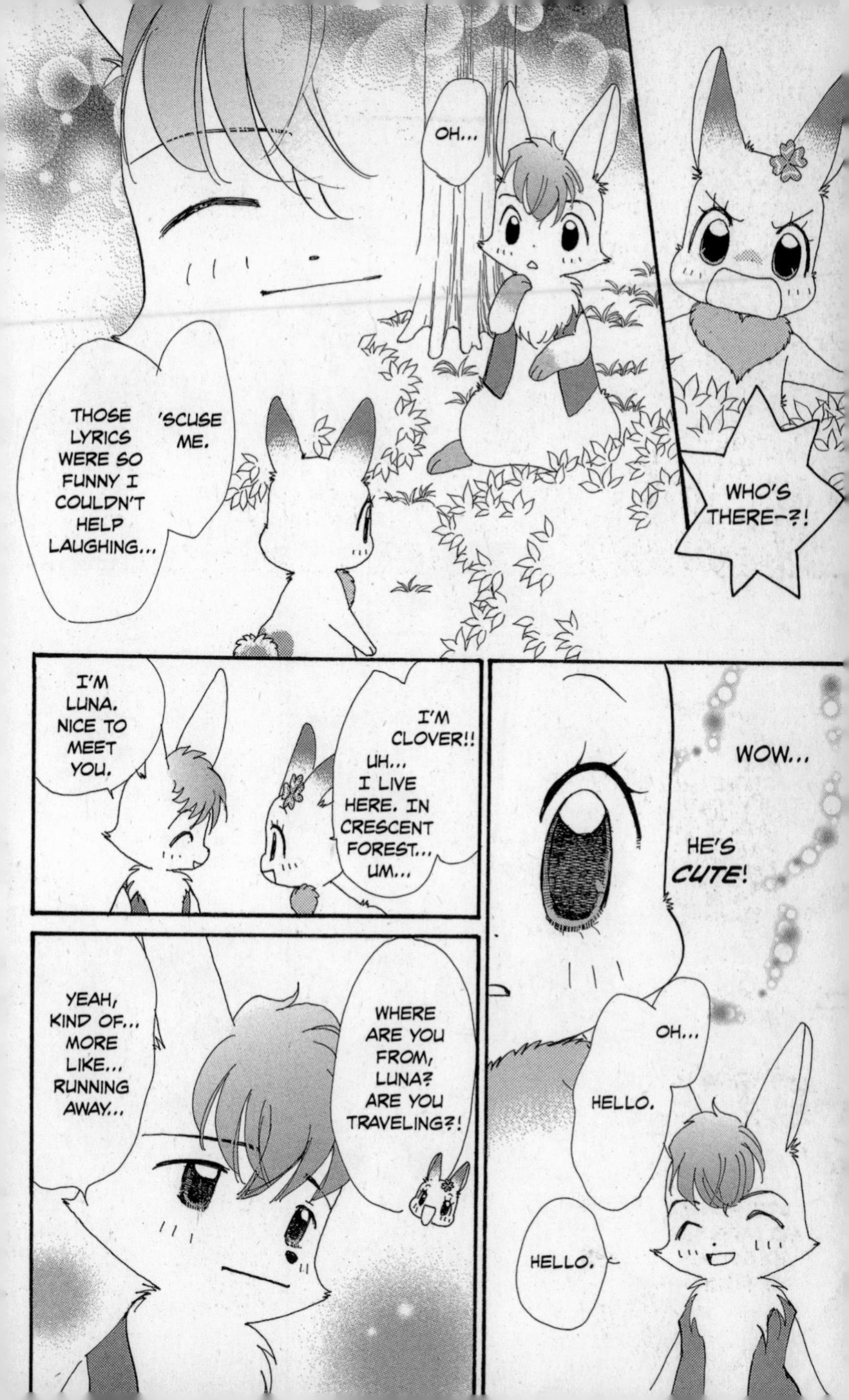

WHO'S THERE—?!
OH...
'SCUSE ME.
THOSE LYRICS WERE SO FUNNY I COULDN'T HELP LAUGHING...
WOW...
HE'S *CUTE*!
OH...
HELLO.
HELLO.
I'M CLOVER!! UH... I LIVE HERE. IN CRESCENT FOREST... UM...
I'M LUNA. NICE TO MEET YOU.
WHERE ARE YOU FROM, LUNA? ARE YOU TRAVELING?!
YEAH, KIND OF... MORE LIKE... RUNNING AWAY...

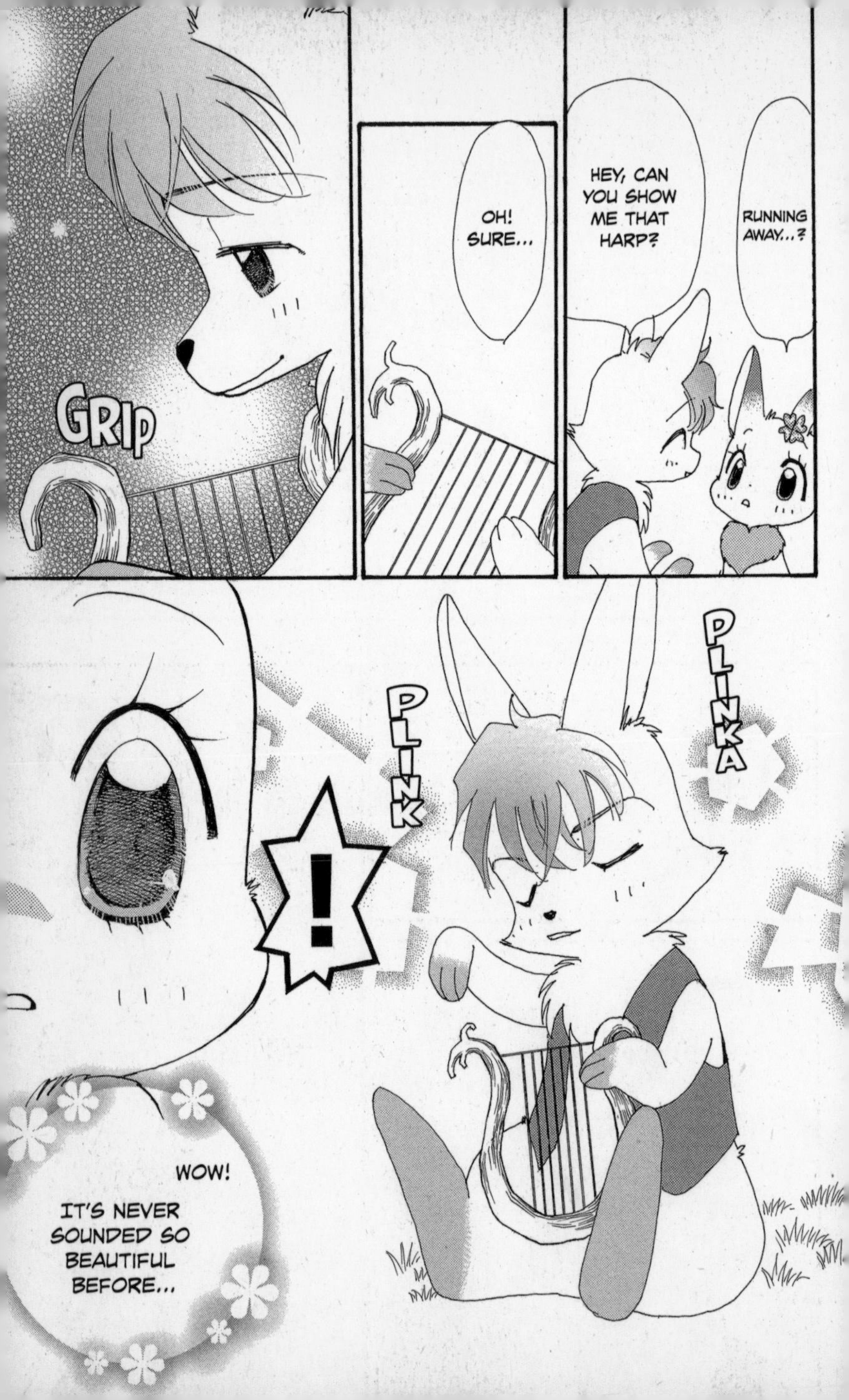
RUNNING AWAY...?
HEY, CAN YOU SHOW ME THAT HARP?
OH! SURE...
GRIP
PLINKA
PLINK
!
WOW!
IT'S NEVER SOUNDED SO BEAUTIFUL BEFORE...

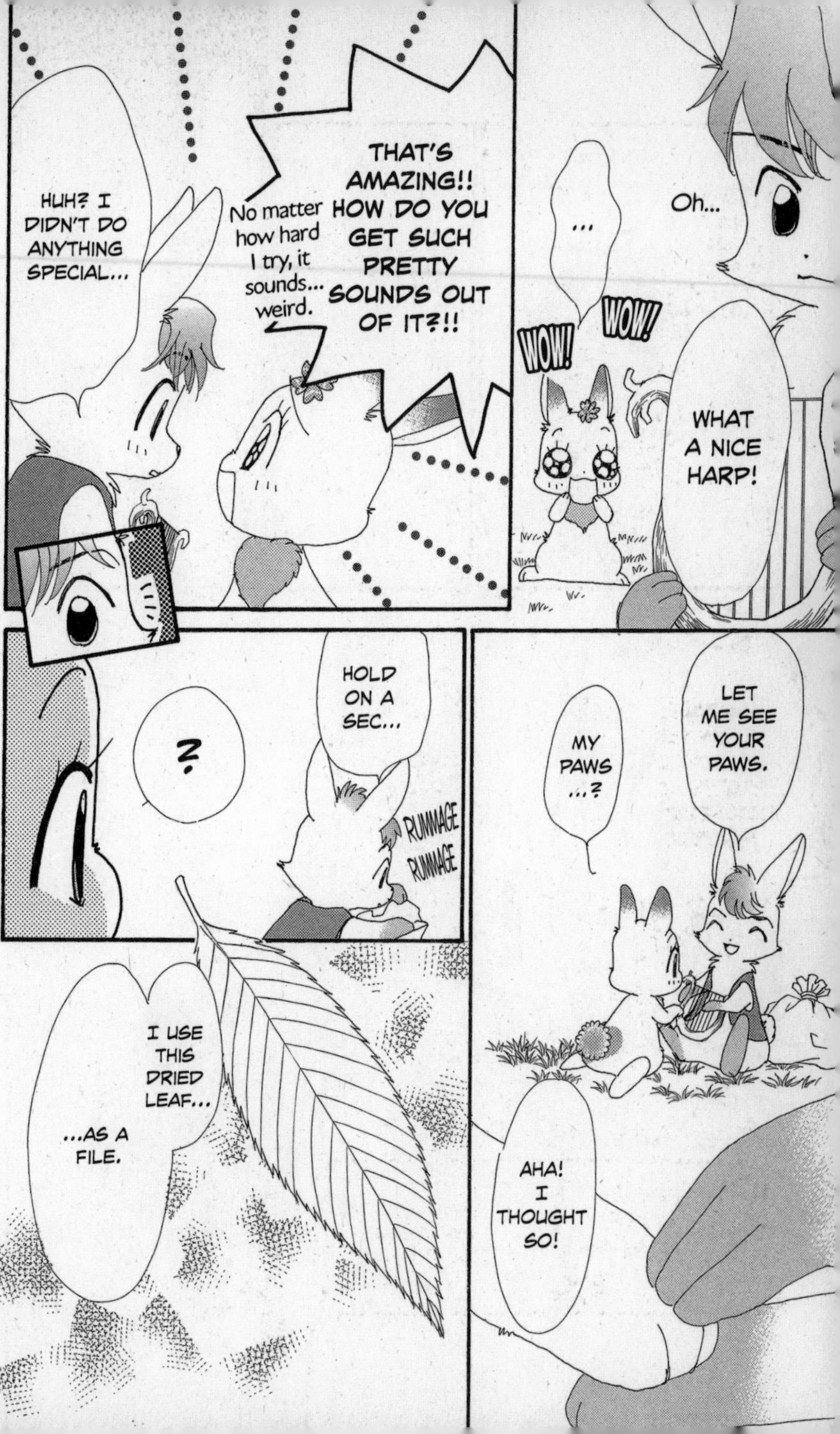
Oh...
...
WHAT A NICE HARP!
WOW! WOW!
THAT'S AMAZING!! HOW DO YOU GET SUCH PRETTY SOUNDS OUT OF IT?!!
No matter how hard I try, it sounds... weird.
HUH? I DIDN'T DO ANYTHING SPECIAL...
LET ME SEE YOUR PAWS.
MY PAWS ...?
AHA! I THOUGHT SO!
HOLD ON A SEC...
?
RUMMAGE RUMMAGE
I USE THIS DRIED LEAF...
...AS A FILE.

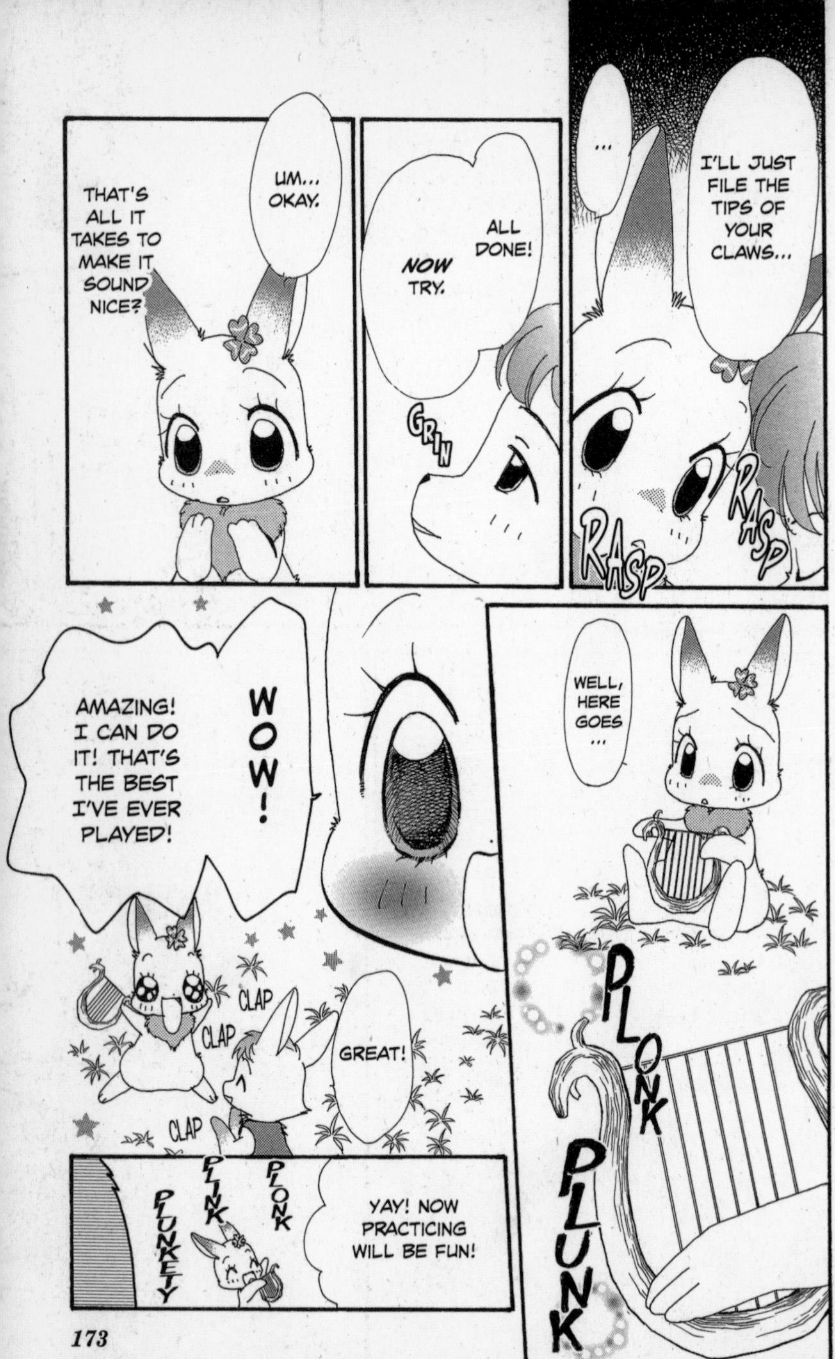

I'LL JUST FILE THE TIPS OF YOUR CLAWS...
...
RASP
RASP
ALL DONE!
NOW TRY.
GRIN
UM... OKAY.
THAT'S ALL IT TAKES TO MAKE IT SOUND NICE?
WELL, HERE GOES ...
PLONK
PLUNK
WOW!
AMAZING! I CAN DO IT! THAT'S THE BEST I'VE EVER PLAYED!
CLAP
CLAP
GREAT!
CLAP
YAY! NOW PRACTICING WILL BE FUN!
PLONK
PLINK
PLUNKETY

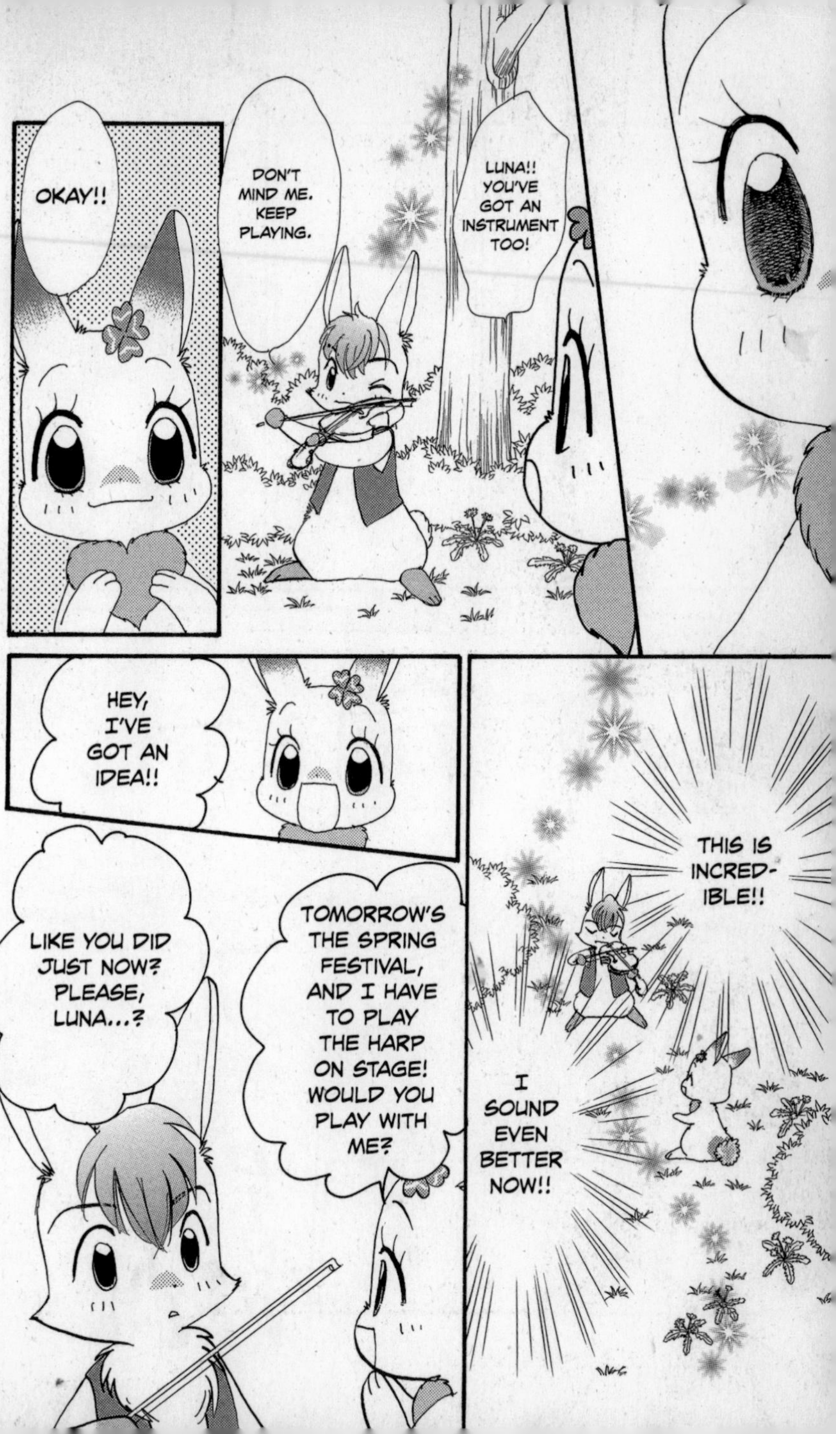
LUNA!! YOU'VE GOT AN INSTRUMENT TOO!
DON'T MIND ME. KEEP PLAYING.
OKAY!!
THIS IS INCRED-IBLE!!
I SOUND EVEN BETTER NOW!!
HEY, I'VE GOT AN IDEA!!
TOMORROW'S THE SPRING FESTIVAL, AND I HAVE TO PLAY THE HARP ON STAGE! WOULD YOU PLAY WITH ME?
LIKE YOU DID JUST NOW? PLEASE, LUNA...?

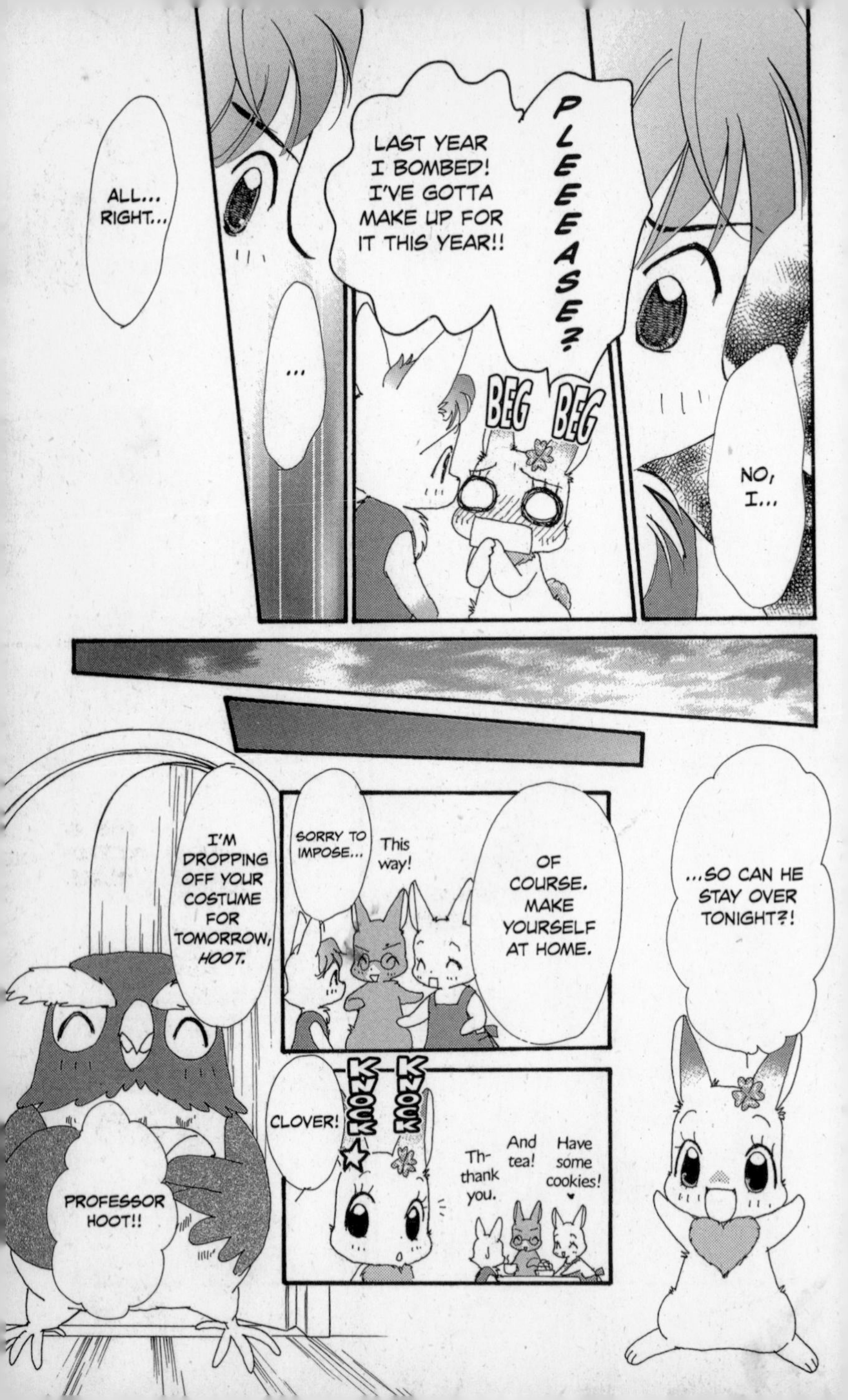
NO, I...
PLEEEASE?
LAST YEAR I BOMBED! I'VE GOTTA MAKE UP FOR IT THIS YEAR!!
BEG BEG
...
ALL... RIGHT...
...SO CAN HE STAY OVER TONIGHT?!
OF COURSE. MAKE YOURSELF AT HOME.
This way!
SORRY TO IMPOSE...
Have some cookies!
And tea!
Th- thank you.
KNOCK KNOCK
CLOVER!
I'M DROPPING OFF YOUR COSTUME FOR TOMORROW, *HOOT.*
PROFESSOR HOOT!!

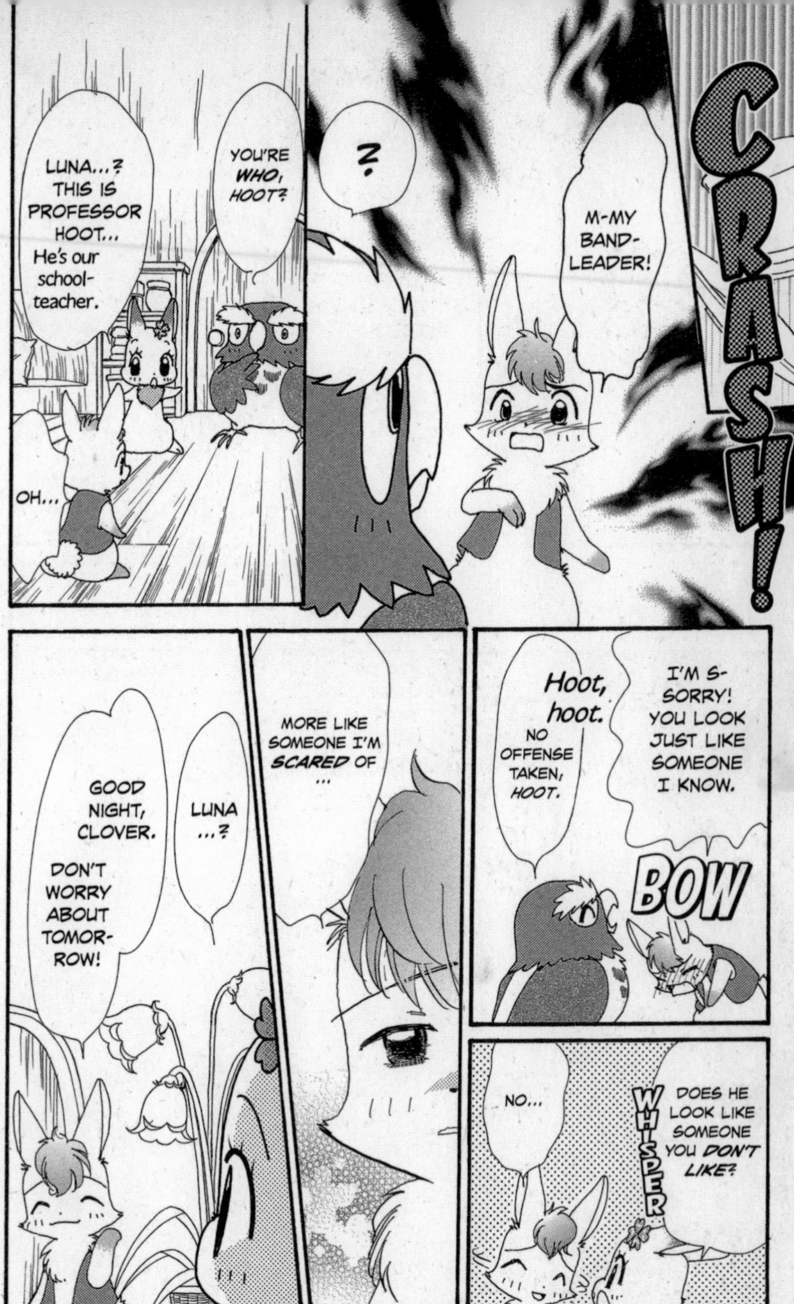
CRASH!
M-MY BAND-LEADER!
?
YOU'RE *WHO*, HOOT?
LUNA...? THIS IS PROFESSOR HOOT... He's our school-teacher.
OH...
I'M S-SORRY! YOU LOOK JUST LIKE SOMEONE I KNOW.
BOW
Hoot, hoot.
NO OFFENSE TAKEN, *HOOT*.
DOES HE LOOK LIKE SOMEONE YOU *DON'T LIKE*?
WHISPER
NO...
MORE LIKE SOMEONE I'M *SCARED* OF...
LUNA...?
GOOD NIGHT, CLOVER.
DON'T WORRY ABOUT TOMOR-ROW!

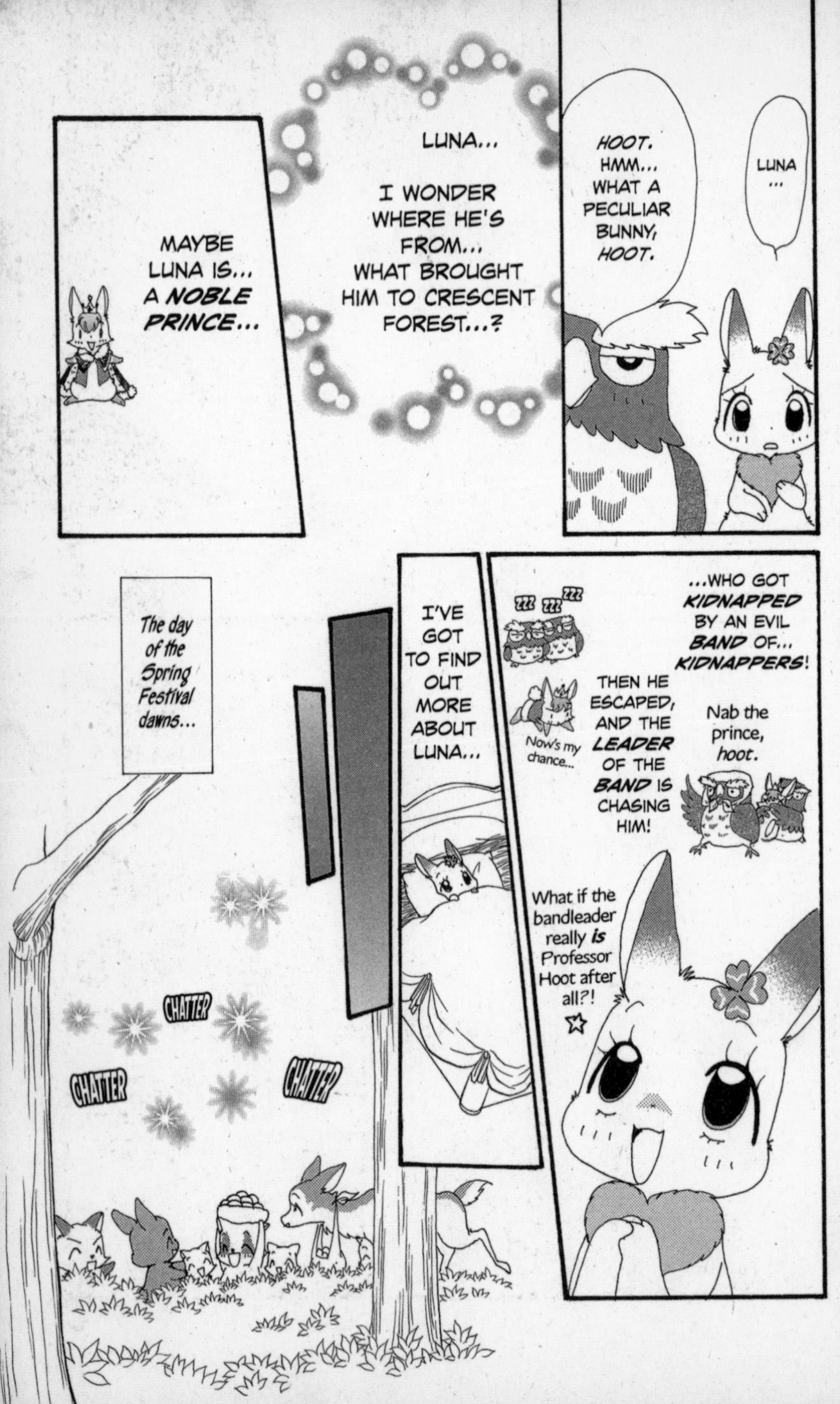
LUNA ...
HOOT. HMM... WHAT A PECULIAR BUNNY, HOOT.
LUNA...
I WONDER WHERE HE'S FROM... WHAT BROUGHT HIM TO CRESCENT FOREST...?
MAYBE LUNA IS... A NOBLE PRINCE...
...WHO GOT KIDNAPPED BY AN EVIL BAND OF... KIDNAPPERS!
Nab the prince, hoot.
THEN HE ESCAPED, AND THE LEADER OF THE BAND IS CHASING HIM!
ZZZ ZZZ ZZZ
Now's my chance...
What if the bandleader really is Professor Hoot after all?!
I'VE GOT TO FIND OUT MORE ABOUT LUNA...
The day of the Spring Festival dawns...
CHATTER
CHATTER
CHATTER

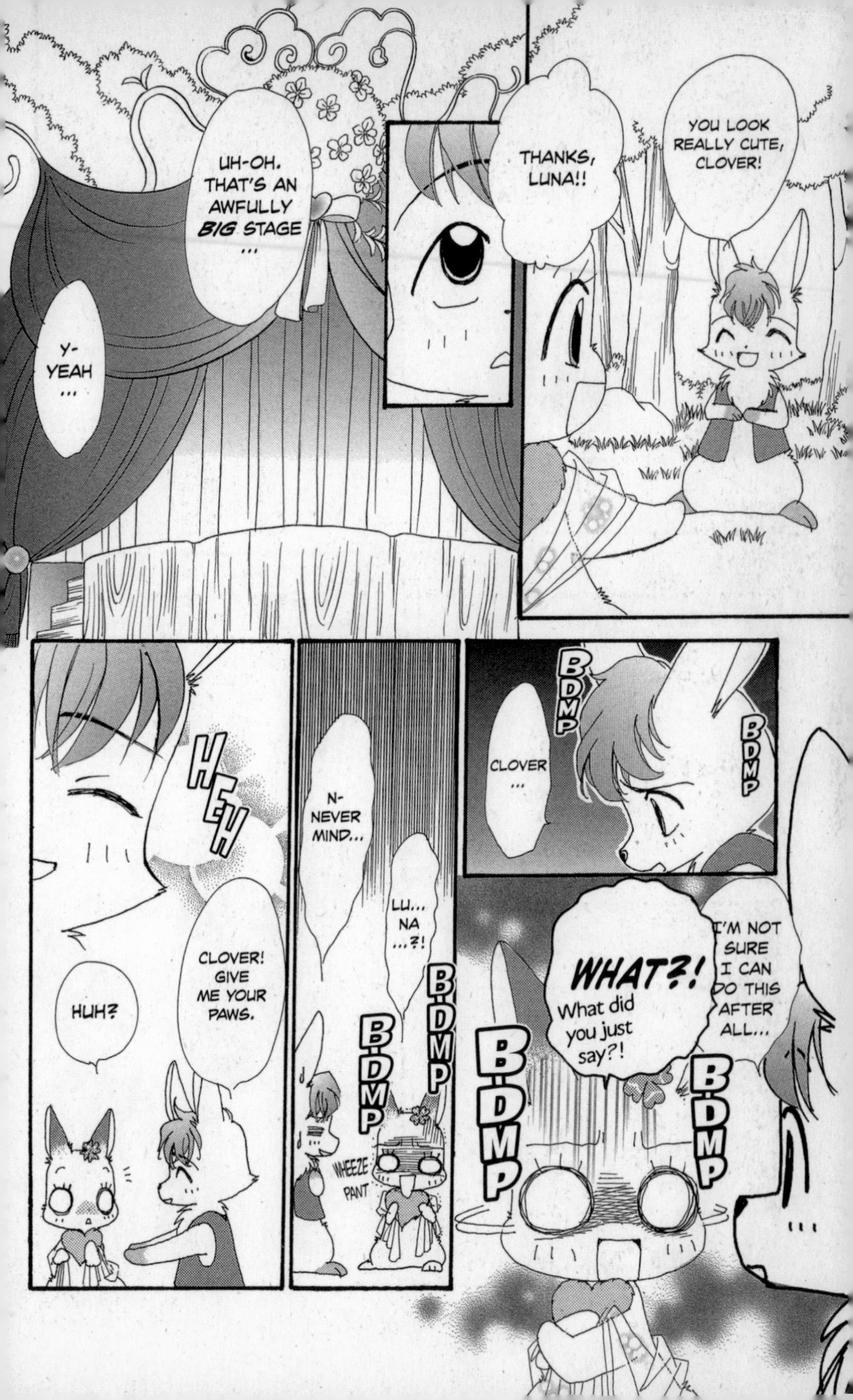
YOU LOOK REALLY CUTE, CLOVER!
THANKS, LUNA!!
UH-OH. THAT'S AN AWFULLY *BIG* STAGE ...
Y-YEAH ...
BDMP
BDMP
CLOVER ...
I'M NOT SURE I CAN DO THIS AFTER ALL...
WHAT?! What did you just say?!
BDMP
BDMP
...
N-NEVER MIND...
LU... NA ...?!
BDMP
BDMP
WHEEZE PANT
HEH
CLOVER! GIVE ME YOUR PAWS.
HUH?

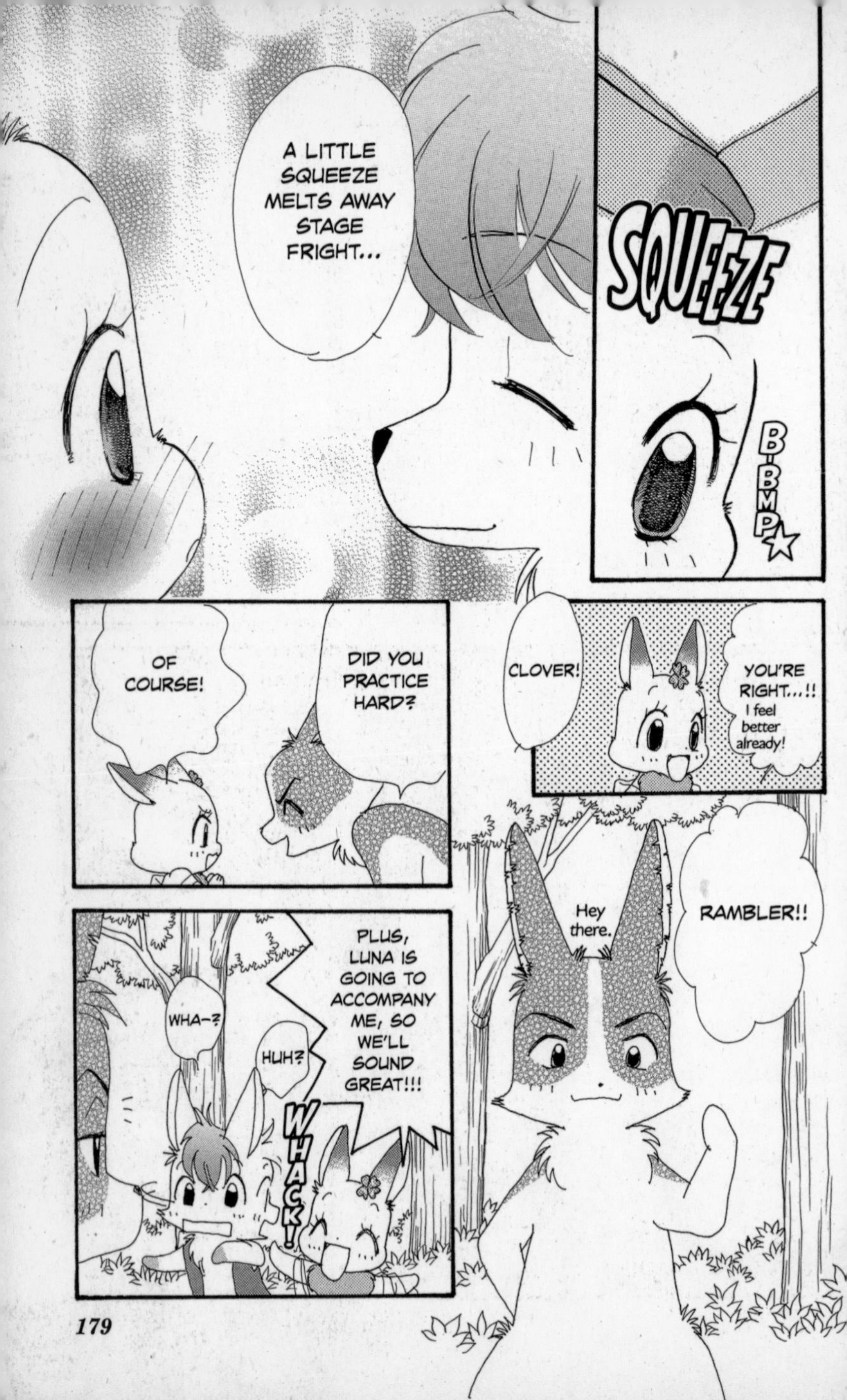
SQUEEZE
B-B-BMP☆
A LITTLE SQUEEZE MELTS AWAY STAGE FRIGHT...
YOU'RE RIGHT...!! I feel better already!
CLOVER!
RAMBLER!!
Hey there.
DID YOU PRACTICE HARD?
OF COURSE!
PLUS, LUNA IS GOING TO ACCOMPANY ME, SO WE'LL SOUND GREAT!!!
WHACK!
HUH?
WHA-?

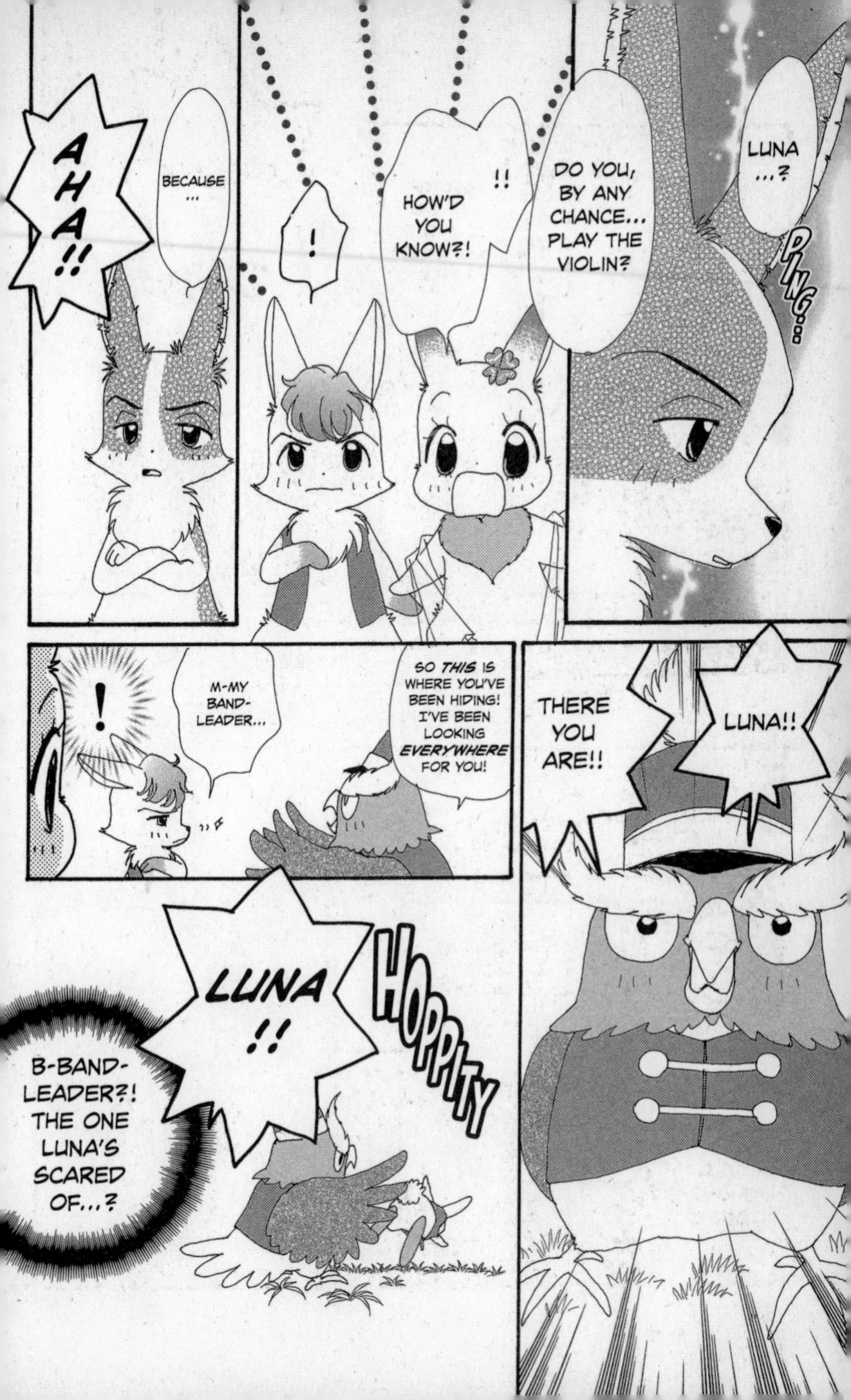
LUNA ...?
PING...
DO YOU, BY ANY CHANCE... PLAY THE VIOLIN?
!!
HOW'D YOU KNOW?!
!
BECAUSE ...
AHA!!
THERE YOU ARE!!
LUNA!!
SO THIS IS WHERE YOU'VE BEEN HIDING! I'VE BEEN LOOKING EVERYWHERE FOR YOU!
M-MY BAND-LEADER...
!
LUNA !!
HOPPITY
B-BAND-LEADER?! THE ONE LUNA'S SCARED OF...?

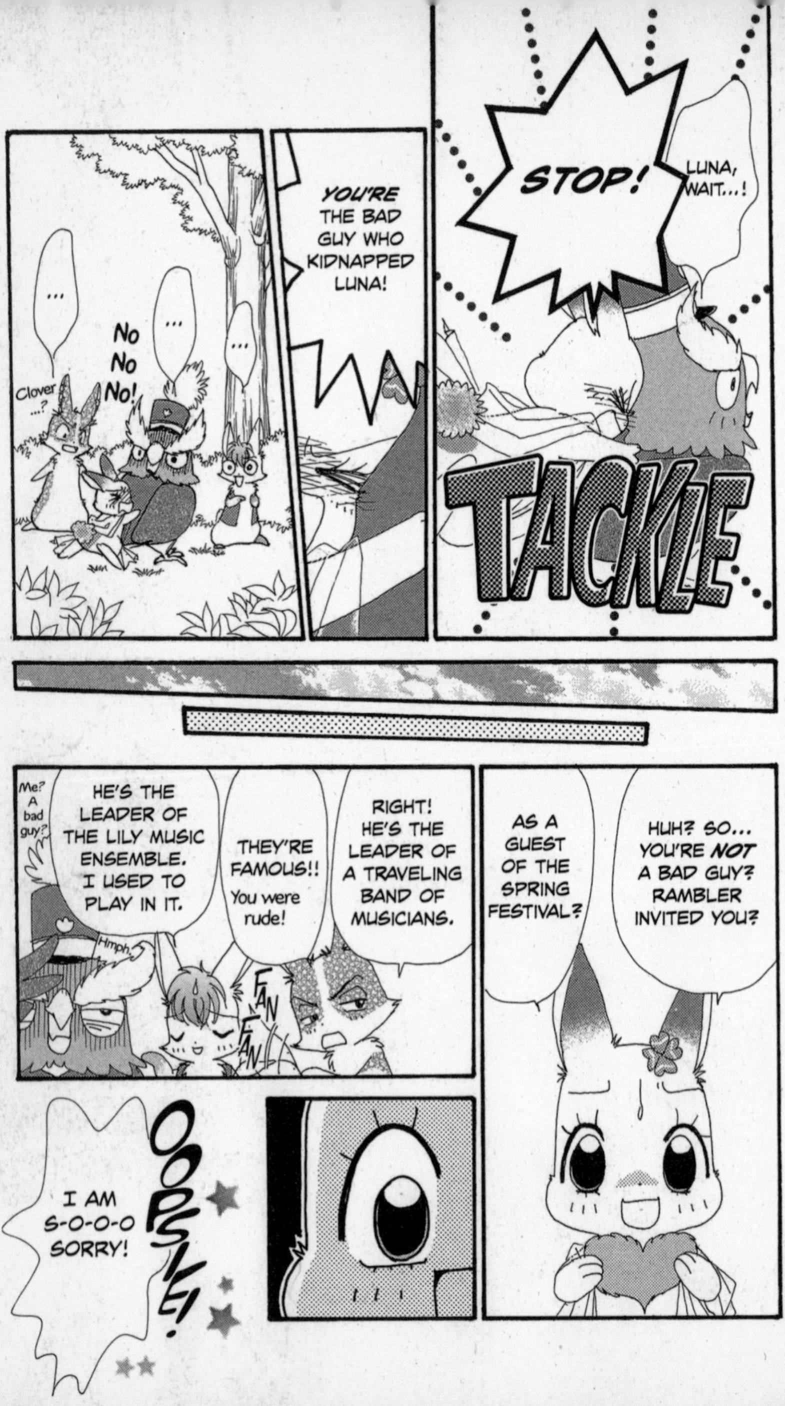
STOP!
LUNA, WAIT...!
TACKLE
YOU'RE THE BAD GUY WHO KIDNAPPED LUNA!
...
No No No!
...
...
Clover ...?
HUH? SO... YOU'RE *NOT* A BAD GUY? RAMBLER INVITED YOU?
AS A GUEST OF THE SPRING FESTIVAL?
RIGHT! HE'S THE LEADER OF A TRAVELING BAND OF MUSICIANS.
THEY'RE FAMOUS!! You were rude!
HE'S THE LEADER OF THE LILY MUSIC ENSEMBLE. I USED TO PLAY IN IT.
Me? A bad guy?
Hmph.
FAN FAN
OOPSIE!
I AM S-O-O-O SORRY!

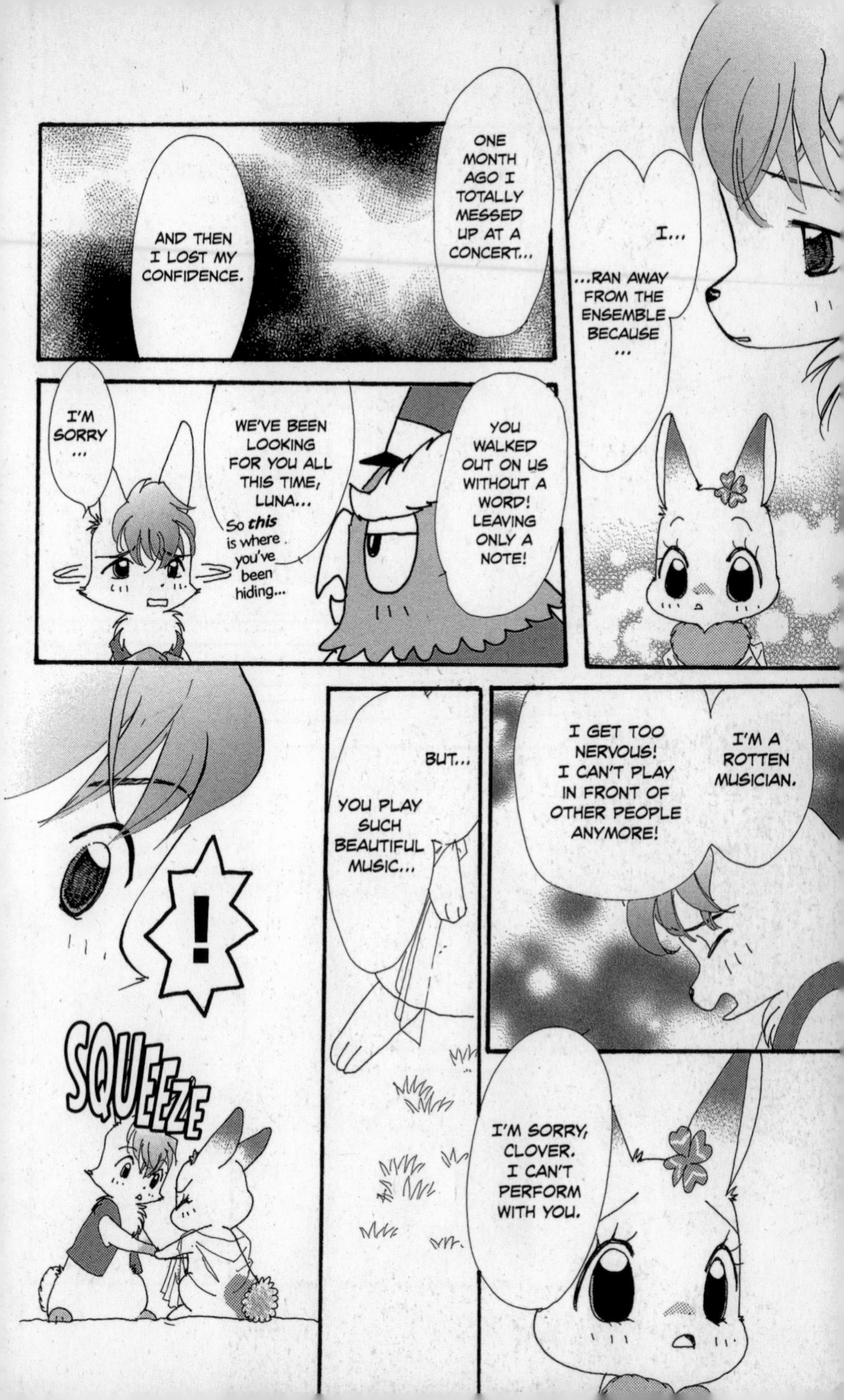

I...
...RAN AWAY FROM THE ENSEMBLE BECAUSE ...
ONE MONTH AGO I TOTALLY MESSED UP AT A CONCERT...
AND THEN I LOST MY CONFIDENCE.
YOU WALKED OUT ON US WITHOUT A WORD! LEAVING ONLY A NOTE!
WE'VE BEEN LOOKING FOR YOU ALL THIS TIME, LUNA...
So *this* is where you've been hiding...
I'M SORRY ...
I'M A ROTTEN MUSICIAN.
I GET TOO NERVOUS! I CAN'T PLAY IN FRONT OF OTHER PEOPLE ANYMORE!
I'M SORRY, CLOVER. I CAN'T PERFORM WITH YOU.
BUT...
YOU PLAY SUCH BEAUTIFUL MUSIC...
!
SQUEEZE

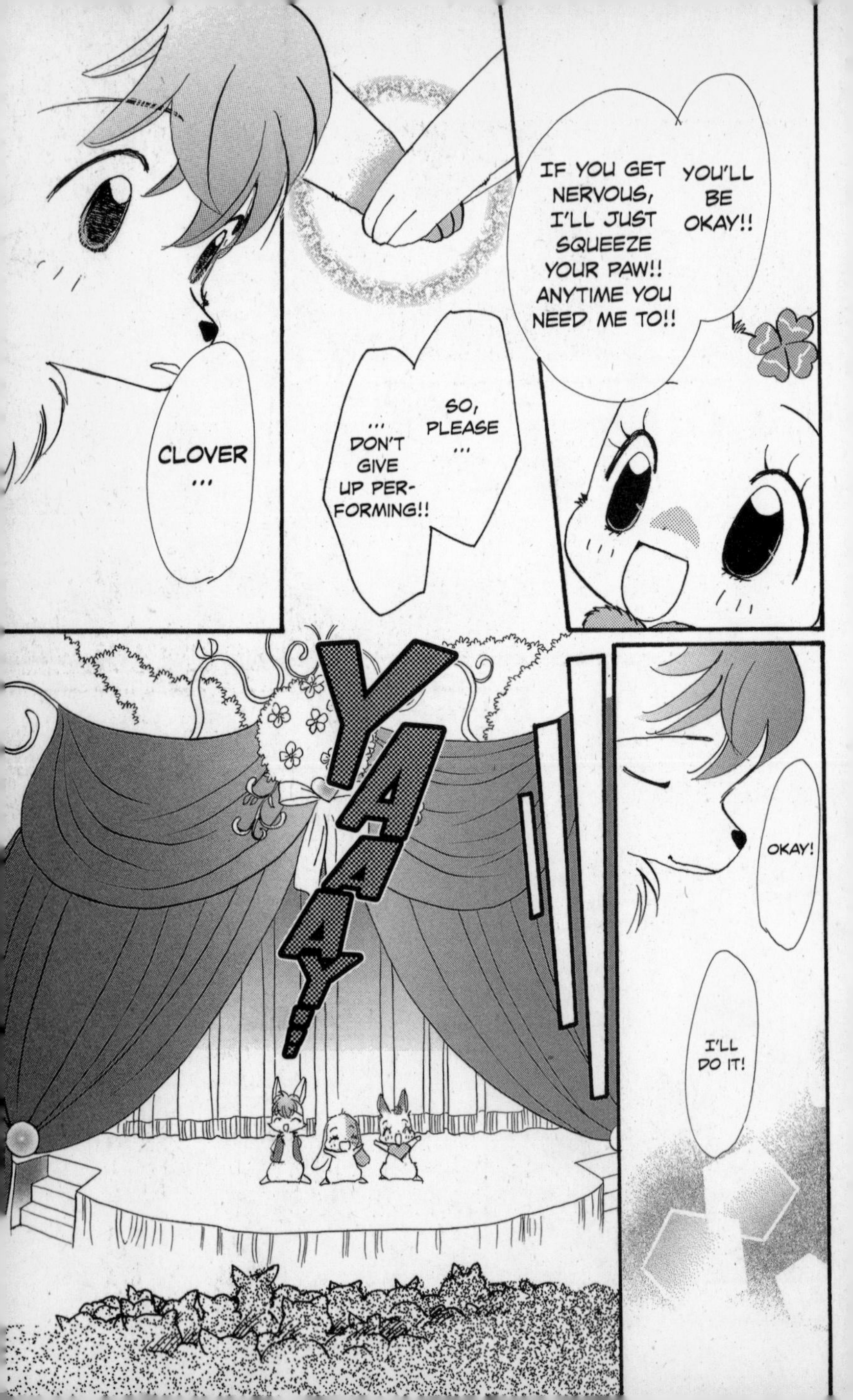
YOU'LL BE OKAY!!
IF YOU GET NERVOUS, I'LL JUST SQUEEZE YOUR PAW!! ANYTIME YOU NEED ME TO!!
SO, PLEASE ...
... DON'T GIVE UP PER-FORMING!!
CLOVER ...
OKAY!
I'LL DO IT!
YAAAY...

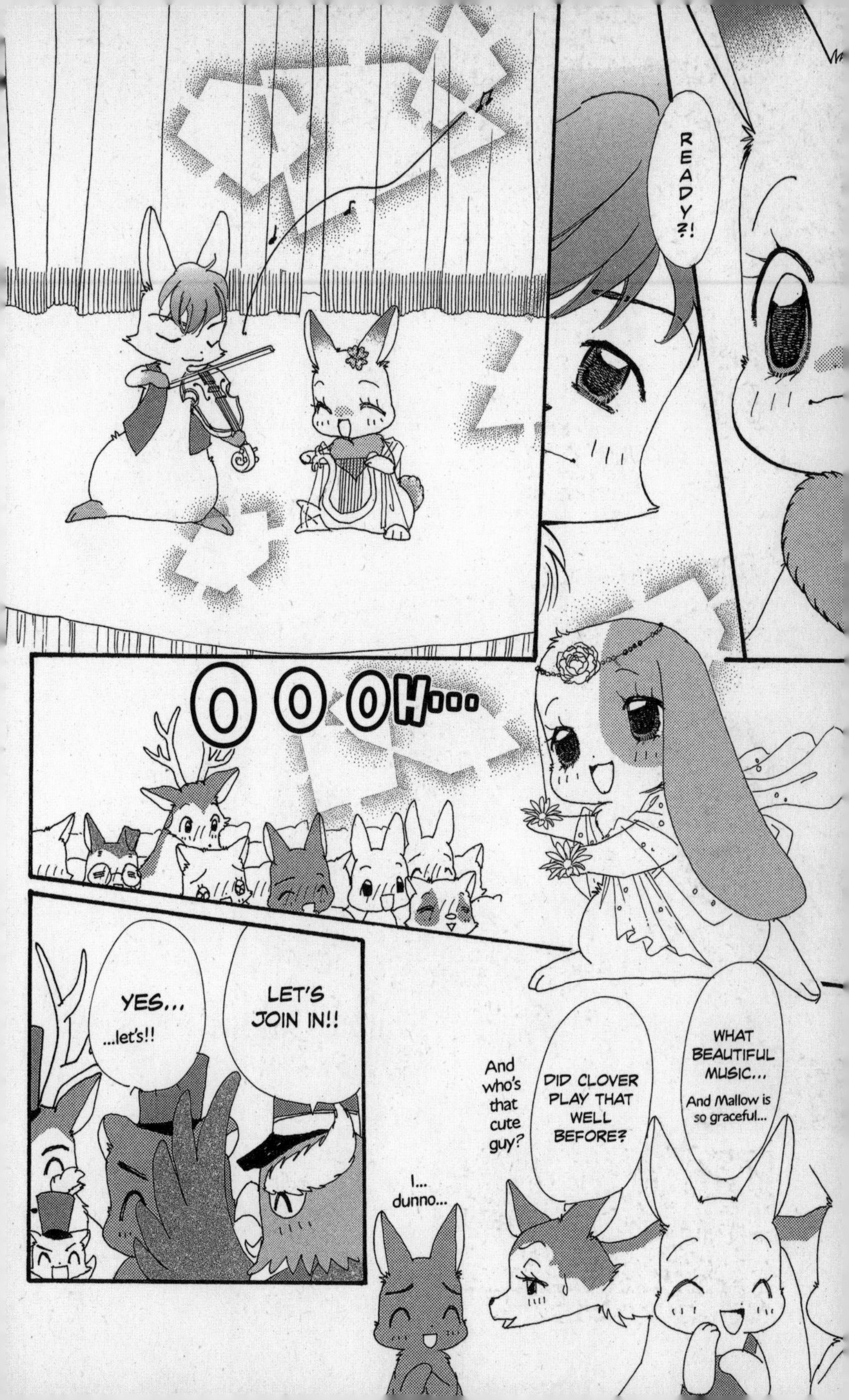
READY?!
OOOH...
WHAT BEAUTIFUL MUSIC...
And Mallow is so graceful...
DID CLOVER PLAY THAT WELL BEFORE?
And who's that cute guy?
I... dunno...
LET'S JOIN IN!!
YES...
...let's!!

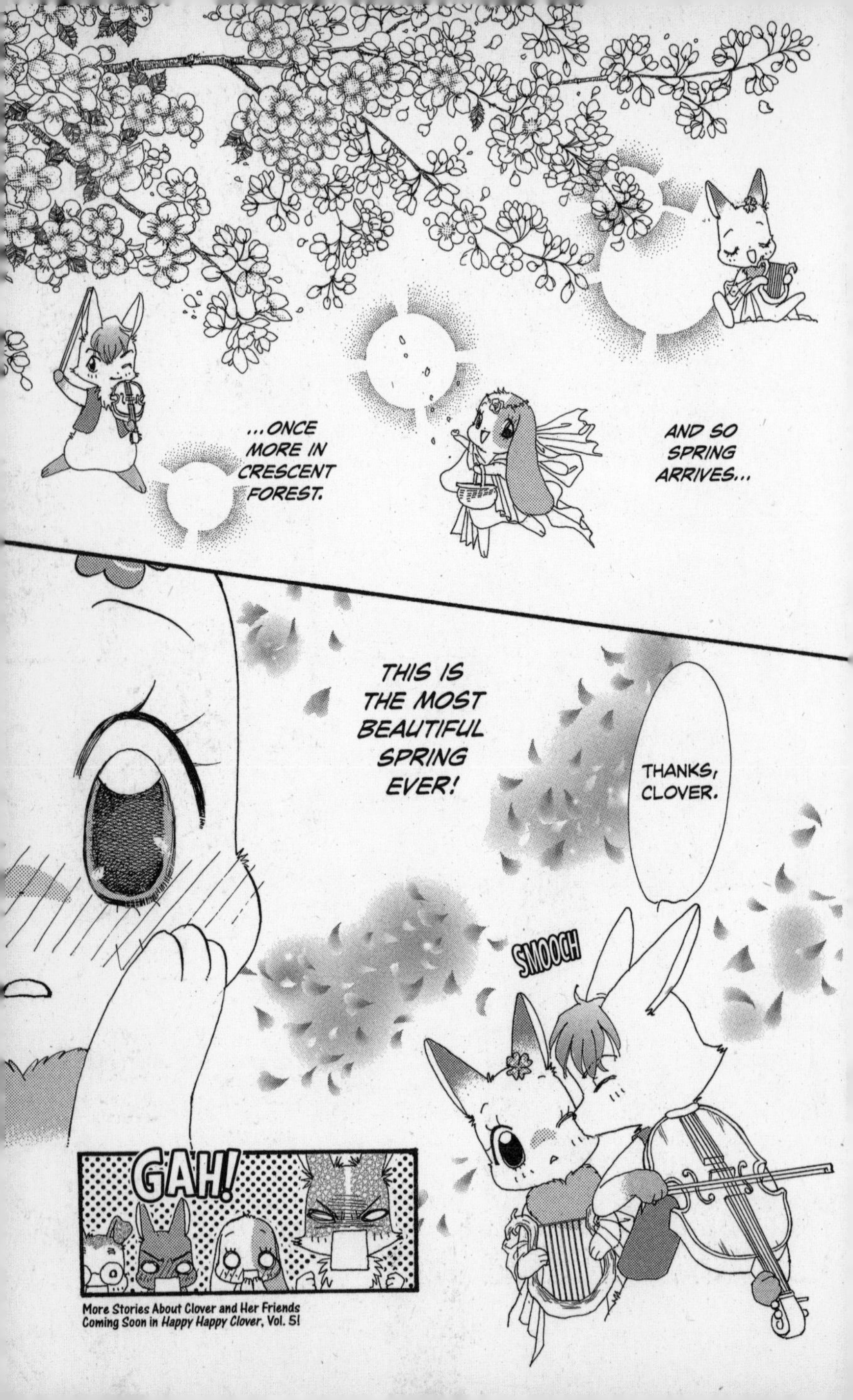
AND SO SPRING ARRIVES...
...ONCE MORE IN CRESCENT FOREST.
THANKS, CLOVER.
THIS IS THE MOST BEAUTIFUL SPRING EVER!
SMOOCH
GAH!

More Stories About Clover and Her Friends Coming Soon in *Happy Happy Clover*, Vol. 5!

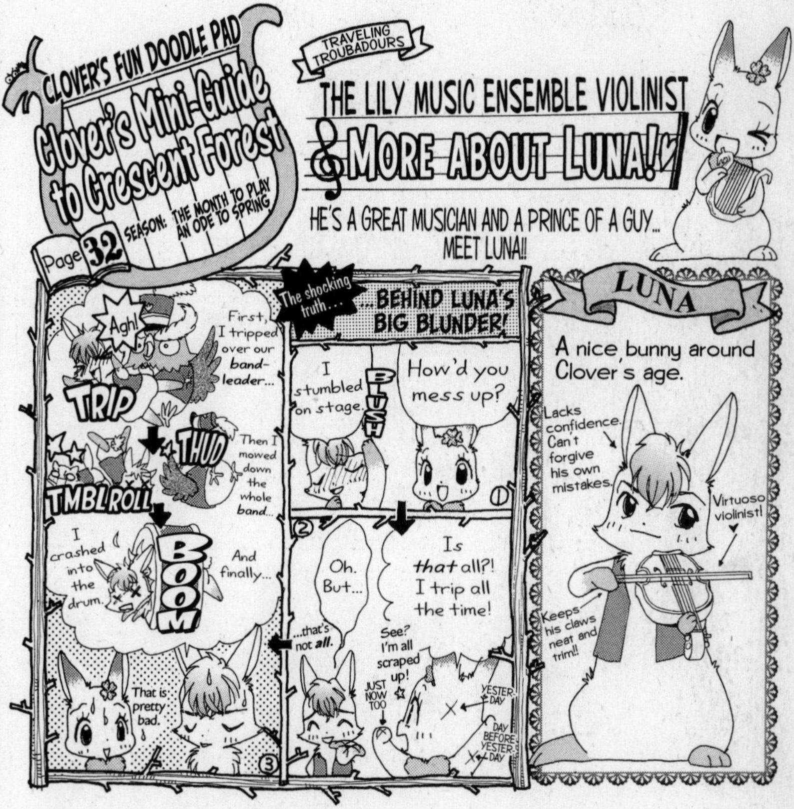

CLOVER'S FUN DOODLE PAD
Clover's Mini-Guide to Crescent Forest
SEASON: THE MONTH TO PLAY AN ODE TO SPRING
Page 32
TRAVELING TROUBADOURS
THE LILY MUSIC ENSEMBLE VIOLINIST
More about Luna!
HE'S A GREAT MUSICIAN AND A PRINCE OF A GUY... MEET LUNA!!
LUNA
A nice bunny around Clover's age.
Lacks confidence. Can't forgive his own mistakes.
Virtuoso violinist!
Keeps his claws neat and trim!!
The shocking truth...
...BEHIND LUNA'S BIG BLUNDER!
How'd you mess up?
I stumbled on stage.
BLUSH
Is that all?! I trip all the time!
See? I'm all scraped up!
YESTERDAY
DAY BEFORE YESTERDAY
JUST NOW TOO
Oh. But...
...that's not all.
First, I tripped over our band-leader...
Agh!
TRIP
Then I mowed down the whole band...
THUD
TMBLROLL
And finally...
BOOM
I crashed into the drum.
That is pretty bad.

BEHIND THE WOODLAND SCENES

THE MAKING OF HAPPY HAPPY CLOVER

SPECIAL BONUS!

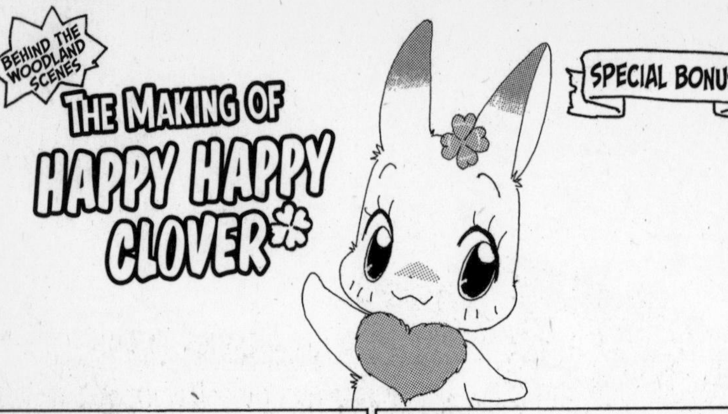

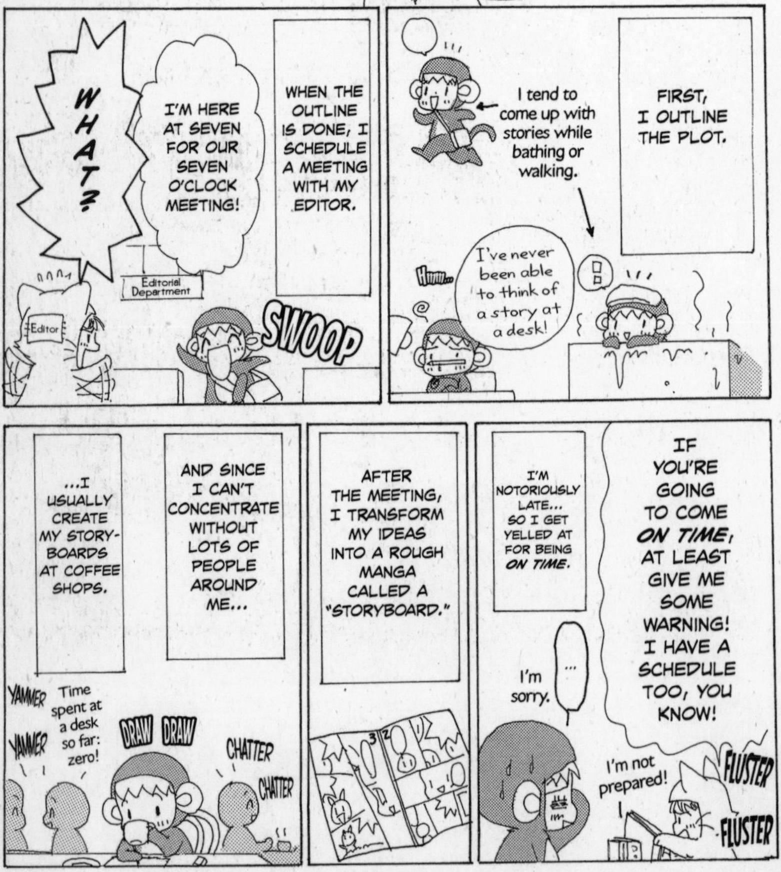
FIRST, I OUTLINE THE PLOT.
I tend to come up with stories while bathing or walking.
I've never been able to think of a story at a desk!
Hmm...
WHEN THE OUTLINE IS DONE, I SCHEDULE A MEETING WITH MY EDITOR.
I'M HERE AT SEVEN FOR OUR SEVEN O'CLOCK MEETING!
SWOOP
WHAT?
Editorial Department
Editor
IF YOU'RE GOING TO COME *ON TIME*, AT LEAST GIVE ME SOME WARNING! I HAVE A SCHEDULE TOO, YOU KNOW!
I'M NOTORIOUSLY LATE... SO I GET YELLED AT FOR BEING *ON TIME*.
...
I'm sorry.
I'm not prepared!
FLUSTER
FLUSTER
AFTER THE MEETING, I TRANSFORM MY IDEAS INTO A ROUGH MANGA CALLED A "STORYBOARD."
AND SINCE I CAN'T CONCENTRATE WITHOUT LOTS OF PEOPLE AROUND ME...
...I USUALLY CREATE MY STORY-BOARDS AT COFFEE SHOPS.
DRAW DRAW
CHATTER
CHATTER
YAMMER
YAMMER
Time spent at a desk so far: zero!

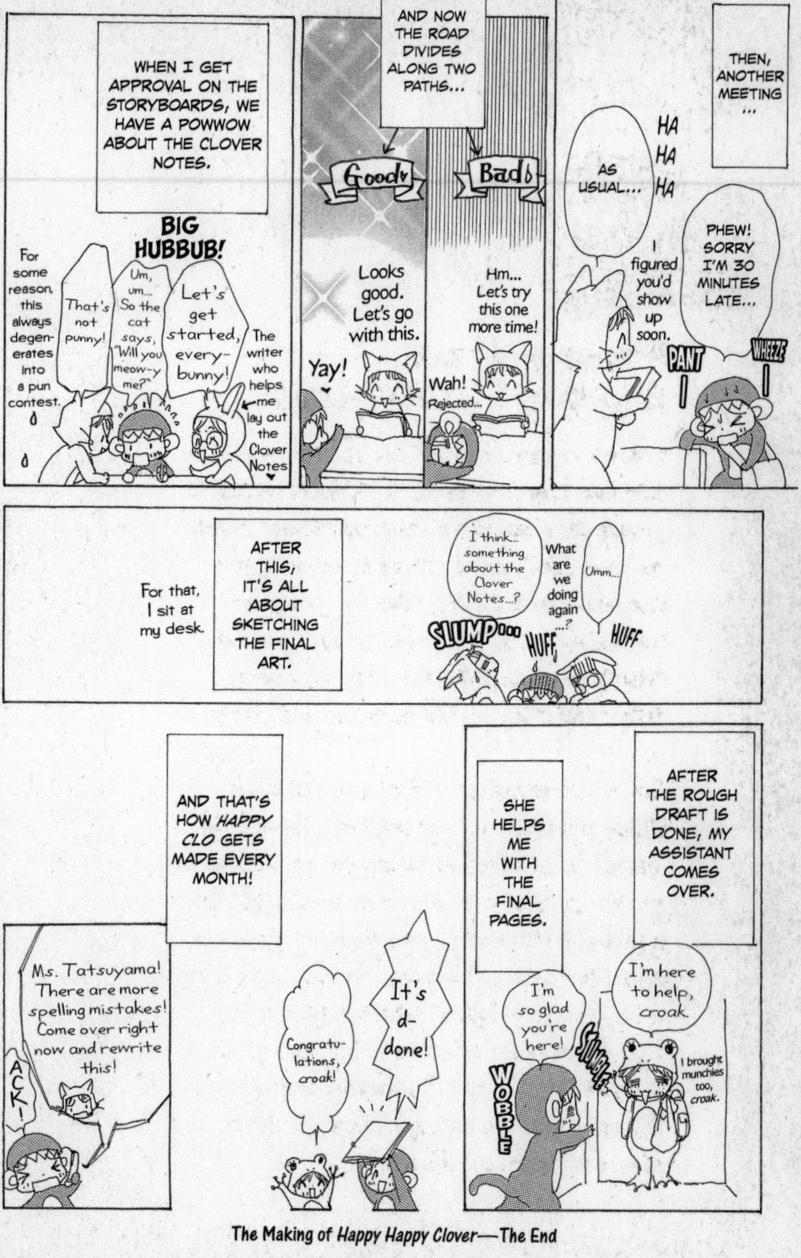
THEN, ANOTHER MEETING...
HA HA HA
AS USUAL...
I figured you'd show up soon.
PHEW! SORRY I'M 30 MINUTES LATE...
PANT
WHEEZE
AND NOW THE ROAD DIVIDES ALONG TWO PATHS...
Good
Bad
Hm... Let's try this one more time!
Wah! Rejected...
Looks good. Let's go with this.
Yay!
WHEN I GET APPROVAL ON THE STORYBOARDS, WE HAVE A POWWOW ABOUT THE CLOVER NOTES.
BIG HUBBUB!
The writer who helps me lay out the Clover Notes
Let's get started, every-bunny!
Um, um... So the cat says, "Will you meow-y me?"
That's not punny!
For some reason, this always degenerates into a pun contest.
Umm...
What are we doing again...?
I think... something about the Clover Notes...?
HUFF
HUFF
SLUMP...
AFTER THIS, IT'S ALL ABOUT SKETCHING THE FINAL ART.
For that, I sit at my desk.
AFTER THE ROUGH DRAFT IS DONE, MY ASSISTANT COMES OVER.
SHE HELPS ME WITH THE FINAL PAGES.
I'm here to help, croak.
I brought munchies too, croak.
STUMBLE
I'm so glad you're here!
WOBBLE
It's d-done!
Congratu-lations, croak!
AND THAT'S HOW HAPPY CLO GETS MADE EVERY MONTH!
Ms. Tatsuyama! There are more spelling mistakes! Come over right now and rewrite this!
ACK!

The Making of *Happy Happy Clover*—The End

Message From
Sayuri Tatsuyama

I have two parrots now. They're so cute and adorable I can't stand it! ★ When I'm about to go out, they call to me chirping, "Tweet tweet!" so I can hardly bring myself to leave. ♥ ♥ ♥ But sometimes if I say, "Bye, I'm going out!" when they're really focused on eating something yummy, they act like they're thinking, "Whatever..." Then I feel very sad and lonely!

Sayuri Tatsuyama loves furry animals! Before *Happy Happy Clover*, she created a ten-volume manga series called *Pukupuku Tennen Kairanban* starring puppies and other cute pets. In 2001, it was the 47th winner of the annual "Shogakukan Award for Children's Manga." *Happy Happy Clover* is so popular in Japan that it has been made into an anime and a Nintendo DS video game. But they haven't been translated into English yet. Tatsuyama lives in the city of Osaka in Japan. Her dream is to have a huge dog.

Happy Happy Clover

Available June 2010

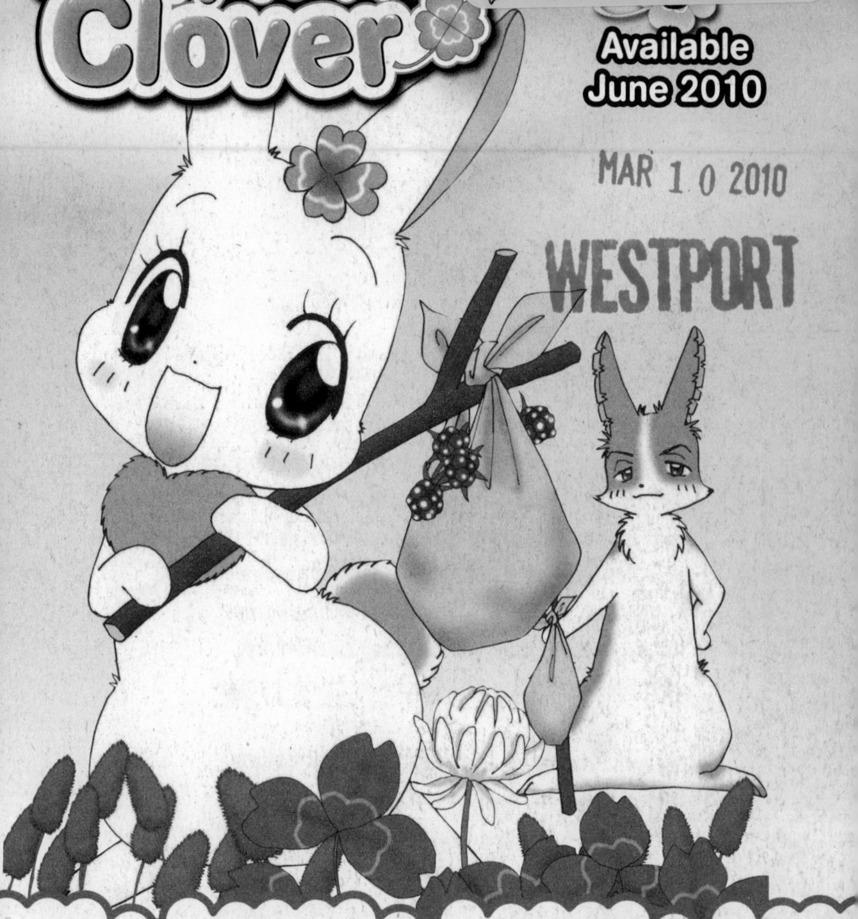

Clover and Hickory magically transform into each other, Mallow figures out what she wants to be when she grows up, and a forest fire threatens to destroy Clover's dream of traveling with Rambler. *Hop, Clover, hop!*